To Betty,

with many thanks for
your interest and support,

Regards,

Jan Fittenley

GW00691214

SEPARATE LIVES

Also by Jan Henley

Other Summers

SEPARATE LIVES

Jan Henley

Hodder & Stoughton

First published in Great Britain in 1995
by Hodder and Stoughton
A division of Hodder Headline PLC

10 9 8 7 6 5 4 3 2 1

British Library Cataloguing in Publication Data

Henley, Jan
Separate Lives
I. Title
823 [F]

ISBN 0-340-62466-3

Typeset by Avon Dataset Ltd, Bidford-on-Avon, B50 4JH

Printed and bound in Great Britain by
Mackays of Chatham Plc, Chatham, Kent

Hodder and Stoughton
A division of Hodder Headline PLC
338 Euston Road
London NW1 3BH

For my cousin, Linda

My thanks to family and friends who have given their time and support – especially my husband, Keith Henley; my parents, Daphne and Bert Squires; and Wendy Tomlins.

"I find myself again. I am no shadow
Though there is a shadow starting from my feet. I am a wife.
The city waits and aches. The little grasses
Crack through stone, and they are green with life."

Sylvia Plath (Three Women: A Poem for Three Voices.)
from Winter Trees *reprinted with kind permission of the Author and*
Faber and Faber Ltd

Prologue

1960

His big hands closed around her throat, and yet Kate's first feelings were of confusion rather than fear. His anger was hot and wild, but his sunken eyes were smiling.

Is that how you get your pleasure? She didn't speak out loud.

The words were grown-up words. Kate had heard them once – bitter on adult lips. But she shouldn't have been listening, and so it was better to slink away down the narrow stairs than find out more.

Now she thought of those words again. *Is that how you get your pleasure?* Adult pleasures were alien to a five year-old child.

She stared at the vein on his temple – it was the throbbing pulse of his head, the heart of his head, and it seemed to hold the key to whatever was happening to her. He flew into rages. She didn't know why. It was part of her life.

'I'll bloody throttle you, I will,' he muttered through clenched teeth.

The vein was mesmerising her, so she tracked a path down, down, to thick lips and a snail-trail of saliva dribbling through the stubble forest of his jaw.

He squeezed tighter. She squealed – high, not human at all.

This fear took her by surprise – clutching at the pit of her stomach – drawing, squeezing, like he was squeezing.

Her eyelids fluttered like black fans only half-hiding those dizzle-dazzle pictures of light, and then the darkness was total. She was gone. Tripping and tumbling and gone.

'Let go of her.' The unlikely softness of the determined female voice stroked Kate back into consciousness.

'Let go of her, I say.' Desperation rising. Hands tugging at tight fingers that had a kind of animal grip after all. 'She's only a child, for God's sake . . . Kate? Kate?'

1

Claw your way back. Somehow, anyhow, claw your way back. That's what it's all about.

'She's young. She'll get over it. It was a lucky escape. But you should think on it. You'll have to watch her. And you'll have to watch *him*.' The doctor paused. Touched the fat, finger-tip bruises.

'I'll look after her.' There was a new stranger-something in her mother's voice that almost scared Kate, even while she trusted her.

'There's no need for anyone to know,' her mother continued. 'She's only a child. She might even forget, God willing.'

That was the answer, then. Block it out. Push it away. Close the curtains. Forget.

1

It was a perfect late afternoon slowly dimming into dusk, as Kate Dunstan sat sipping Calvados on the terrace. It was the summer of 1975. And this was a different world.

The tiny chateau in Normandy that they were renting from Stephanie's Aunt Rae threw its eccentric shadow onto the lawn.

'It's small and it's damp, but you won't care about that. You're young. When you're young you don't notice the damp . . .' Aunt Rae's eyes misted over – with an exciting memory of youth and wet grass perhaps.

The ancient chateau wasn't only damp, it was also choosy about how often it would provide hot water. The wiring was dodgy too; a black curtain could descend at any time. And the doors and windows spoke a creaking language of their own. There were unexpected cubby holes, wooden beams and low ceilings that could crack your head open. And Hannah had convinced herself that it was haunted. But all three of them loved it.

'It's like a miniature Gothic castle.' Hannah's brown eyes were wide as the three of them began to explore.

And Kate could only nod in reply. It was hard to believe that this would be her home for the next two months. It was a long way from her parents' terraced house in Ridley. Too far perhaps . . .

And now, at the end of their stay, the terrace was heady with the fragrance of trailing white summer jasmine. Fifty yards away was their own private pool – complete with pond weed and leaves from the beech tree, standing like a sentinel on guard.

Opposite Kate, Stephanie lounged on the wooden bench, her paisley sarong tied loosely around her waist, revealing long, brown legs that went on forever. And next to her was Hannah, blonde head bent in concentration as she scribbled furiously.

Kate sighed. 'It feels like we just got here. How can it be our last night already?'

She raised the glass of sharp, apple liqueur to her mouth, savouring the smoothness as it kissed her lips and coated her tongue. They had feasted on a supper of warm camembert on toast accompanied by a green salad drenched in walnut oil. The Calvados had been saved for this, their last night together. An appropriate finale. And there was certainly a sense of finality in the air.

Kate felt a slightly bloated contentment. But it was a contentment she still couldn't quite believe in. A contentment that didn't make that crucial leap into happiness.

'In a few days time we'll be back in Dorset, dreading the next teaching practice, writing essays and moaning about the weather. Not terribly inspiring, is it?' Stephanie's mobile features twisted into an expression of mock horror.

Kate shook her head.

It was true. Teachers' training college and England seemed a million miles away. Another time, another life.

'I can't bear the thought of leaving this place.' Hannah spoke for them all.

She was still writing, pushing back the fine blonde hair bleached almost white in the sunniest summer Normandy had experienced for ten years – so Aunt Rae had informed them.

'But we'd get bored out of our tiny minds if we lived here all the time.' Still, Stephanie's husky voice didn't sound certain. She stretched long, brown limbs. 'And how could we earn any money? Tourists don't come here in the winter. This place dies. Even Aunt Rae practically closes down.'

She tapped a pack of Gauloises on the table top and lit one. The strong sweet smoke settled over them and then rose, mingling with the fragrance of the flowers and the cider apples from the orchard over the way.

Money? Since when have you had to worry about earning money? The silent question came from some black side of Kate's mind, and for a moment she panicked, afraid she'd spoken aloud. Was it Stephanie's fault that her parents were loaded up to the eyeballs, and wanted their daughter to have everything money could buy? Stephanie Lewis-Smythe lived in

4

another dimension. As Kate kept telling herself, money wasn't everything. But it could sure make life a damn sight easier.

She glanced at Stephanie's tanned face – high cheekbones, wide mouth, perfect teeth, framed by raven-black hair. And the kind of dark blue eyes any man would be eager to drown in. Yes, it did seem that Stephanie had everything.

'Every paradise has to have boundaries.' Hannah chewed the end of her pencil thoughtfully.

'And Hannah's going to write a poem about it,' Kate teased.

She ducked the playful swipe of the notebook. The other two took this easy relaxation for granted. But Kate felt as if she were fidgeting on a tightrope. It was an elusive kind of balance.

Hannah could spend hours toasting her golden body in the sun, writing poetry and communicating with the waves. But the waves didn't even whisper to Kate. And sometimes the faraway expression in Hannah's wide brown eyes made Kate want to shake her into some sort of reality. Someone had to tell Hannah Thompson that she couldn't spend her entire life lost in a dream.

And yet Hannah's poetry had a kind of magic. One night they'd persuaded her to read to them.

'No. You don't want to hear this stuff.' Hannah sat back, half-laughing.

'Oh, yes, we do!' Stephanie insisted.

'And we promise not to laugh!'

Hannah, self-conscious at first, soon got into her stride, letting the words lead her into a new confidence. And it seemed to Kate, prepared to be cynical, that Hannah's poems captured the very spirit of this place, a spirit that she'd hardly allowed herself to notice. The sense of history and heroism, the easy and natural balance of wood, farm, orchard and stream. An equilibrium that Kate had often searched for, and never discovered. It was all there.

'*Arrogant cliff standing proud . . .*
stroked by the begging of sensual sea . . .' Hannah murmured.

Kate forgot to criticise. She was touched in a way she'd rarely allowed herself to be touched before. She'd always been so down to earth – too rooted in realism to appreciate poetry. But this place was special. It was as if Hannah had taken a film of blindness from her eyes, and shown her how to see.

Hannah had changed. Maybe it was getting away from that tight-lipped

5

mother of hers. Or maybe it was something in the Normandy air. Hannah's creativity had been unleashed this summer. It was running wild. And Kate was so jealous she could scream.

Instead, she sighed. 'Steph? Fancy a swim?' Kate needed action.

'I've packed my costume.' Stephanie smiled sleepily. Everything she did was a lazy drawl.

While Hannah wrote, Stephanie painted. Only Kate had no outlets for her frustrations and dreams. Even her vague ambition to teach was born more of circumstances and her mother's dreams than her own desires.

She leaned forward, a new urgency in her voice. 'Hannah?'

'I've packed mine too.' Hannah was wary. 'And it's getting a bit cold.'

Suddenly Kate was irritated by these two. Her best friends. But they had no sense of adventure. They were strangers to risks. Strangers to Kate Dunstan's world, where nothing came easy.

Her green eyes burned dangerously. 'Who needs costumes?'

Grabbing her glass, she drank more Calvados, her restlessness fired by the alcohol.

'Huh?' Stephanie's eyes widened.

'Let's swim in the nude.' Kate's eyes glittered. It seemed daring – the tiny private pool was overlooked by the farmhouse over the way. Anyone could turn up. There was no lock on the wooden gate.

But there was a greater risk. To be naked was to be vulnerable. To shed self-consciousness like the clothes you wore was never easy – even after three glasses of Calvados.

Kate had their full attention. She felt the excitement shoot along her veins like a drug. It would be a perfect end to a near-perfect summer.

'Are you crazy?' Hannah shivered.

Kate tossed back her streaky auburn hair. 'What's crazy about going for a swim? This is our last chance.'

'I don't know, Kate . . .'

Hannah the prude would always hang back. Hannah the virgin, who left the room whenever Kate and Stephanie started talking about sex. She needed some unbending. And maybe Kate was the girl to do it.

She sprang to her feet. 'Come on, Hannah,' she wheedled, standing behind her, slowly massaging her slim shoulders with sure rhythmic strokes. 'It'll be fun. Let yourself go, for once. It's our last night.'

She felt Hannah relaxing against her. 'Just think of that cool water washing over your bare skin.' She knew just how to appeal to Hannah.

'Hmm.' Hannah still sounded unconvinced. Southern middle-class inhibitions. She had a long way to go.

Smiling her feline smile, Kate glanced across at Stephanie, who she knew would already be with her. Stephanie liked to shock. She grabbed at the bizarre, as if without it she might have life sucked away from her completely.

'Mmm. Sounds like heaven to me.' Stephanie pulled off her shirt in one dramatic gesture, to reveal smooth brown skin and full breasts. 'So what are we waiting for?'

Laughing like a child let out early from school, she ran lightly down to the pool, long-limbed and graceful, pulling off her sarong on the way. When she got to the edge, she looked back at them, removed the last piece of skimpy white lace she wore, chucked it in the air, and plunged into the blue, leafy pool.

Kate giggled, pulling off her shorts and T-shirt to follow Stephanie. At the poolside she too turned around, auburn hair resting lightly on the pale, creamy shoulders that she didn't dare expose to the sun.

'Come on, Hannah,' she urged for the last time.

Hannah said nothing. There might have been a kind of longing in her eyes, but Kate was too far away to tell.

She shrugged. She'd done what she could.

Turning, she executed a perfect swallow dive into the shimmering blue. She suppressed a gasp of shock. The water was like an icy hand on her heated skin.

Taking a deep breath, she swam effortlessly underwater, leaves catching in the hair that fanned behind, transforming her into a kind of rustic mermaid.

She blinked as she emerged to face Stephanie. 'Hello, stranger. God, it's cold in here.'

But there was a strange hunted expression in the dark blue eyes that surveyed and silenced her. For a moment she was still, and they stared at each other without speaking.

'Invigorating, you mean.' Stephanie grinned her lazy grin and the moment was gone.

Kate blinked it out of her mind as she swam off. It was nothing. She'd imagined it. Girls like Stephanie didn't know what it was like to have problems. They had it all.

She just wished she could say the same about herself.

Lying on her back, floating into a new kind of sensuous satisfaction, as the cool water washed over her tired limbs, Kate stared at the darkening sky. How many storms ahead? How many black moments?

A slender form slipped into the water beside her, with hardly a splash or a ripple.

'Kate?' It was Hannah, with her scared eyes and uncertain smile.

'Isn't this wonderful? Aren't you glad you took the plunge?' Kate whispered. It seemed a heresy to speak too loudly.

Hannah nodded, closed her eyes, and moved off into the liquid depths, her slim body snaking into an even crawl.

The night air cloaked the water with a sense of peace, touching the naked skins of the three girls as they swam silently through the rippling blue.

A night bird shrieked in the darkness. Kate looked back towards the Chateau des Marettes, to the rustic wooden table and the three glasses of Calvados. A notebook of Hannah's, a sketch pad of Stephanie's. What did Kate have to call her own?

She shivered as she felt the exclusion creeping up on her once again. Even here, in the water that caressed her like an unselfish and patient lover, it was never far away.

She didn't belong in this place. It had been easy for the others to come, but not easy for Kate. Her mother had scrimped her fare from the housekeeping. Kate had earned more than enough to pay her back – it wasn't as if she'd been swanning around having one long holiday. In fact Stephanie's Aunt Rae, who ran a tourist company in Rouen, had worked them pretty hard all summer.

But that wasn't the point. The point was that she was different from Stephanie and Hannah. They lived in another world. They might pretend that class and money didn't matter, but Kate knew better. Because she was northern working-class through and through. Useless to pretend otherwise: She was the kind who got things done instead of sitting around talking about it. It was different for Kate. She didn't belong.

Then a long, late shadow fell over her naked body, and she felt a new kind of warmth seeping past the bitterness. Hannah and Stephanie were on either side of her, treading water. Wet hair hung in seaweed tails and framed their glistening childlike faces as they blinked the water from their eyelashes.

As Kate stood up, Hannah reached out a slender hand to touch her face.

'I think we should make ourselves a promise.' Her brown eyes were solemn.

'What sort of promise?' Kate stared from one to the other.

'A pledge of support.' Stephanie stretched out her arms over the shoulders of the other two girls. Wet skin clung to wet skin.

In that moment, Kate imagined that each recognised the others' vulnerability. Welcomed it and cherished it. Pretences were dropped, faces were unmasked. It was the closest she'd ever felt to anyone. Even Jason. Even the child.

'A promise that this summer in Normandy is just a beginning,' Hannah said. 'That we'll stick together – the three of us. Always be there if we need . . . well, you know . . . a friend.'

She seemed embarrassed at the show of sentimentality.

Kate smiled. In that moment she loved them both.

'Hang on a sec.' Stephanie pulled herself out of the pool and ran over towards the table, long, brown limbs gleaming, heavy breasts swinging.

Kate watched, fascinated, as she grabbed the three liqueur glasses, and ran back without spilling a drop.

She leaned forwards, handing a glass to each of them, before sliding back into the pool with her own.

'To friendship.' She raised her glass. 'May it go on forever.' Her eyes narrowed. 'And may nothing – and no one – stand in its way.'

'To friendship,' the other two echoed.

There was a moment of silence as they drank, looking into each other's faces.

Stephanie broke it by chucking her empty glass into the bushes and doing a backward flip in the water. 'Who needs men?' She laughed. 'It's women who give you what you need.'

'Oh yeah?' Kate grinned. 'I hadn't noticed. What was that bloke doing in your room the night before we left, if he wasn't giving you what you needed?'

They exchanged a glance of wicked delight as Hannah began to climb out of the pool.

'He was just helping me pack, darling.' Stephanie's eyes widened into beautiful innocence.

'Oh, I get it. So *that* was why it took you so long . . .' Kate followed the silent Hannah out of the water, watching as she ran towards the chateau, arms folded tightly around her breasts. Shy little Hannah.

9

Naked and erect, Kate stood looking down into the pool, water dripping from the white body outlined against the gathering dusk.

Stephanie stretched out her arms in a gesture of submission. Her dark skin gleamed, shiny as a seal's in the dim light.

She stared up at Kate. 'Men give you what they think you need. That's the difference.'

'D'you think so?' Kate couldn't take her eyes off her. She'd never had Stephanie down as a feminist. The opposite, with the easy, sensual lifestyle she led.

'Of course.' Stephanie's eyes glittered in the darkness. 'I thought you felt the same.'

Kate thought of Jason. She began to shiver.

There was a movement behind her, and Hannah reappeared across the grass, laden with towels.

Smiling her thanks, Kate wrapped one around her and turned back to Stephanie. But Stephanie was swimming away – quickly, as if she'd said too much.

They stayed on the terrace until the pool was only a shadowy circle of silver under the spotlight of the moon, and the rest of the garden was clothed with darkness. Only then, when the last drop of Calvados had been dredged from the bottle, did they reluctantly accept that their last night here was over.

Kate stayed awake long after the other two were breathing heavily in their beds.

She could still feel the touch of their naked wet bodies on hers. Vulnerability. The bond of togetherness. It hardly seemed possible that it could be so easy to belong.

2

A month later, back at college in Dorset, it seemed to Kate that Normandy's magic had lent a fresh loyalty to their friendship. With the new sense of togetherness between them, her instinctive feelings of exclusion faded, until they could almost have been forgotten.

Almost but not quite. The memory of Normandy lay side by side with that other memory – of the Kate Dunstan who had fallen in love with Jason at seventeen. Who had been careless and carefree, until she was ripped in two.

They had parted over a year ago now, and yet it had not ended for Kate. Still it haunted her. Still it returned sometimes in hunted dreams. Still she wanted to scream: Oh Jason, how could you have become someone quite different from the boy I thought I knew?

It wasn't until October that Kate took any notice of the tall fair lad with the cool eyes who kept hanging around Hannah. Why should she? Student friendships and student life had a casual flow, from breakfast into lecture into coffee into tutorial. And so it went on. A few conversations over coffee didn't mean a thing.

But one Friday afternoon she came across the two of them playing table football in the Common Room.

'What a band! You should see them live, Hannah.' He let out a whoop of victory as the little ball shot past Hannah's defence. ' "My Generation" . . . Whew!'

'Oh, Tom.' Hannah was giggling in a way that was unfamiliar to Kate. Her face was flushed. She shook her head in mock self-disparagement and pushed a strand of blonde hair behind her ear.

Oh Tom, indeed . . .

'Here, let me.' Kate took over her two lines of defence. 'You go into

11

attack.' Her eyes briefly met his. She caught the flicker of amusement.

'Oh, Kate. It's you.' Hannah seemed nervous as she moved over to make room. 'This is Tom McNeil.'

'Hello, Tom McNeil.' She glanced at him again. He was over six feet tall with soft, floppy fair hair and pale blue eyes.

She'd seen him around – on campus you saw everyone around. She knew he was in third year, studying drama, and spent a lot of time with a dark-haired girl called Dian something or other. Interesting . . . Kate kept her eyes open and she probably saw more than most.

'Kate?' He was laughing at her, his hands resting lightly on the handles that controlled his table football team.

'Kate Dunstan.'

He was attractive all right. And didn't he just know it. So did she. Kate knew the sort only too well.

'And I thought I knew all the girls.'

'Then you thought wrong.' Kate didn't allow her eyes to soften. You couldn't afford to with blokes like this. Give him an inch and he'd take a hundred yard dash.

Kate opened the catch to release the last ball on to the table. It rolled backwards. She grinned as she spun the handles. 'Goal!'

'Hey, I wasn't ready.' His eyes clouded as if he didn't like to lose. 'And spinning's not allowed.'

'I can't see any rules written down anywhere.' Kate glanced nonchalantly around.

'Hmm.' He still wore a reluctant smile as he looked at Hannah. 'So this wildcat is a friend of yours? Does she purr as much as she hisses and spits?'

Kate shivered. There was something about the way he was gazing at Hannah. She could feel the exclusion creeping up on her once more, so much a part of her that she could almost taste it. She tried to shake it off, but it clung to her until she was staring at Tom McNeil with open animosity. These two seemed to share something beyond her experience. Yet how could they? Hannah hardly knew him. Hannah avoided men.

'Oh, stop it Tom.' Hannah was actually blushing, a soft red flush stealing on to her lightly tanned cheeks. It made her look even prettier than usual. 'Leave her alone.'

'I'll try.' The three of them moved away towards the window as someone else came to claim the machine.

'Green cat's eyes.' Tom murmured softly. He touched Kate's auburn hair casually with the back of one hand.

Instinctively she flinched. But she doubted if Hannah even noticed.

'An angry tabby perhaps?' His smile returned, but Kate knew it wasn't for her.

Hannah giggled.

'Very amusing.' Kate glared past the lean outlines of his face. She didn't like Tom McNeil. He was a threat. His hands took too many liberties, and his voice was too insidious. He'd snake his way into your senses and stay there – if you let him.

She glanced at Hannah, who was looking at him with an expression suspiciously akin to hero-worship. Jesus, no. Surely he hadn't done that to poor Hannah? Already?

She flung a protective arm round Hannah's shoulders. 'Ready to come back to Ford?'

'I suppose so.' Hannah nodded.

In Royal Ford, their hall of residence, the three girls all had rooms on the fourth floor. It was how they'd met – as isolated students far from home. For Stephanie and Hannah it was their first time. Flung into a desperate acquaintance, because it was that or stay alone in your room all weekend. Sharing tea bags had been only the beginning.

But now there was a shade of regret in Hannah's dark eyes. 'See you later, Tom.'

They moved towards the door. Kate turned.

Tom was staring after them thoughtfully. 'You certainly will.'

It may have been a promise, but to Kate it sounded more like a presentiment of doom.

'Don't you like him, Kate?' Hannah was subdued, as they strolled through the leafy grounds of Royal Ford. She'd been nervous about introducing Tom to her two friends, and with good reason it seemed.

She felt rather than saw Kate stiffen beside her. 'More to the point – do *you* like him?'

Hannah nodded. 'Yes. Yes, I do.' She sounded surprised at herself.

'Enough to go out with him?'

Hannah's steps slowed as she considered the question. 'It's not that simple,' she said.

Ever since she could remember, Hannah Thompson had been scared of men. And according to Mother, it had started even earlier than that . . .

13

* * *

'You were still in your pram. You almost went blue, you screamed so loud,' Mother had said. 'Even your father started you off.' A grim smile on thin lips.

The fear had become a part of Hannah. Fear of men – uncles, teachers, doctors. Particularly Dr Hefton with his tobacco-smell, craggy eyebrows and forbidding frown.

'You have to see him. Don't be silly,' Mother said.

Terror. And above the fear, another layer of memory. The pleasure on Mother's face. It was all so confusing. Could Mother possibly be glad that Hannah was terrified of men?

Later, her fear became more controlled, but it never quite went away. It stayed with her during high school – growing narrowly focused in a single-sexed environment.

'You'll be happier with girls,' Mother said.

Safer, she meant.

Protected from the real world, so that when it caught up with her Hannah suffered panic at a boy's smile, dumbstruck confusion at his first words. And blind terror if he tried to chat her up.

'I've never been out with anyone before,' she admitted to Kate.

Several had asked over the years, and Hannah never got used to it. But she was bright. She cultivated just the right kind of indifference to put them off, so they thought she was choosy rather than scared. So they'd call her a snooty bitch and leave her alone. That was best. It was the only way.

Kate stared at her. 'Never? You're kidding! Why on earth not?'

Hannah looked down. How could she explain? An awful embarrassment flooded over her, as it did when Kate and Stephanie talked about sex. Sex. That one little word sent a hot pink stain to bruise her neck – spears of confusion piercing her cheeks and ears.

'It's different for you, Kate,' she said at last. 'You haven't been sheltered like I have. You spent a year travelling around Europe before you came here. I don't know the first thing about boys. I'm scared.'

Kate was silent for a moment. 'But didn't anyone talk to you at school?' she persisted. 'About boys and sex and stuff? Not even your mother?'

Hannah shook her head. Mother had contributed nothing but an impersonal white leaflet explaining periods. And Hannah was far too embarrassed to listen to the talk at school. She didn't have the courage to get books out of the library, and consequently, at nineteen, not only was she still a virgin, but what she knew of men and sexuality would be no secret to an eight-year-old child.

'So how come everything's changed for Tom McNeil?' Kate asked.

Hannah dismissed the note of sarcasm as she smiled her vague, dreamy smile. 'There's something different about Tom. He's not like most men. He's gentle. He's funny . . .' Her voice tailed off. How could she explain? 'Come to think of it, he's not like anyone I've ever met before.'

Oh God. It was serious then. Kate squeezed Hannah's arm tighter, as if she could keep her down to earth. She was worried. Hannah seemed to be flying off to the moon.

'But Tom's already got a girlfriend – hasn't he?' She kept her voice cautious and casual.

'You mean Dian?' Hannah's voice changed. It became harder – not like Hannah's voice at all. 'She's not his girlfriend. She never has been. It's more of a platonic relationship. You see, she was upset over some chap and Tom tried to help her get over it, that's all.'

'Yeah?' It had never looked much like that to Kate.

'Oh, she tried to keep him to herself. She took advantage of his good nature, got really possessive.' Hannah was confiding, her brown eyes darting from left to right through the trees and undergrowth. 'She drove him crazy.'

'Uh huh.' Kate let out a silent groan. It was a good script. But how could anyone live in this world and be so innocent?

'She didn't understand him,' Hannah concluded, her voice soft and gentle once more.

'And you do?' Kate couldn't help it. She turned to face Hannah – her green eyes burning with the doubts she ached to communicate to her.

But Hannah looked right through them. Kate saw her look, way beyond the doubts, to a distance peopled only by Tom McNeil.

'Not yet,' Hannah admitted, walking on, swinging her bag of books on one arm with teenage carelessness. 'But I will.'

Her voice rang with conviction. Kate let out a deep sigh. She would just have to pray that Tom McNeil got bored with Hannah before he took her heart and hurt her. But she wouldn't count on it. Hannah might not be much of a challenge to a bloke like him. But wasn't it true that every man wanted a virgin?

* * *

Tom was whistling as he let himself into his flat. There was a lot to look forward to, and he couldn't wait to have some of it. Starting from tonight at the college dance, if possible.

'I'll be there,' Hannah Thompson had said, a gentle promise in those dreamy, brown eyes of hers.

And something had stirred inside him – something that he'd denied to himself for longer than he cared to remember. Something he still half-wanted to deny. He had no use for love. Not now and not any time in the future. Love might make a man whistle, but it also had the nasty habit of making a man helpless. And Tom didn't intend to be helpless ever again.

'Hi, Tommo.'

Tom blinked with surprise. 'Dian . . .' This was getting to be a habit. Once he'd invited her because he couldn't get enough of her. It wasn't only her sexy body, but also the fact that she made him laugh – a rare commodity in a woman. But these days she turned up unannounced. And it wasn't quite the same . . .

'I thought you'd never get here.' She pouted prettily. Dian was stunning, but she had too many white teeth. Sometimes Tom wondered if she was devouring him.

'I had a late drama practice. What's up?' Tom threw down his bag and went next door to the bedroom. Why had he ever given her a key? It was a small flat, cheap to rent, but his own – he'd resisted all offers to share. One year in hall had been enough for Tom – he needed more space. And he certainly needed space from this woman.

Dian. And yet in bed she was like a dream come true.

From their first day at college they had literally seen each other across the crowded lecture theatre, and gravitated together. Both were overwhelmingly attractive to the opposite sex, and both possessed a kind of amoral cynicism. The truth was that they'd both been hurt and they'd both imagined it was the kind of hurt that happened to others, not to people like them.

'He was a bastard,' Dian confided that first evening. 'His idea of a good time was football, the pub and a bit of a beating to follow.'

Tom pulled a face. He wasn't the sporty kind, and roughing up a woman was not his way. 'Was that why you left?' He gazed into her hazel eyes. They were liquid with longing, and he'd had enough to drink to dissolve in them.

16

'No.' She shook back the dark hair that hung almost halfway down her back. Farrah Fawcett layers – but Dian was no angel. 'I took every beating. Some of the time I didn't even mind.'

He stared at her with incomprehension.

'A bit of rough stuff isn't the end of the world.' She sucked the words between her full, sensual lips, and he felt himself getting a hard on.

'Then why did you leave?' He fidgeted uncomfortably and poured out more wine. Tom needed to know more about this strange and tantalising girl.

'I found him in bed with some guy.' She began rolling a cigarette.

Tom had never seen a woman roll a joint before and had never rolled one himself, only joined in smoking it at parties. She offered it to him and he took it.

'Some guy?' Tom felt out of his depth. He drew on the thin tube of card and felt the hit immediately. 'Was he gay?'

Her hand was on his arm, her fingers playing with his sleeve in a vague kind of way that excited him. He found himself wondering what those fingers could do to various parts of his anatomy.

'Oh, he was both ways, you know? But I wasn't interested. He was getting pretty heavily into speed and stuff, and well, when it's over . . . why drag the thing out?'

Tom put the spliff in the ashtray and took both her hands in his. He knew this wasn't the half of it. Dian had stayed with the guy through drugs and beatings. But it must have torn her apart when she discovered he wasn't even hers in bed. He stared at her breasts, rising and falling under the tight black T-shirt, and wished he could undo one of the buttons. But maybe he should wait until she cheered up. Or maybe he should wait for even longer. Much longer. He sighed.

'How about you, Tom?' she asked. 'What's your story? How did you get hurt?'

No. He stiffened. That was strictly out of bounds. 'I'll tell you one day,' he said. 'When you've got a box of Kleenex handy.'

Dian smiled. 'Poor Tom.' She reached out to him. Slowly funnelling her fingers through his fair hair, her eyes half-closed.

He watched her.

'Be warned. If ever I go to bed with you, Tom . . .' Dian paused, lending the idea a delicious taste of mystery. 'I won't ever fall in love with you.'

17

Her mouth was close and she smelt too nice to resist. He kissed her.

It was easy, so easy to become friends, survivors, and part-time lovers.

'No strings,' she said, as he undid the first button of her T-shirt. Her eyes burned into him.

'No strings,' he agreed.

She meant it all right. But Dian liked to live, and she was in love with passion.

'It won't work. It never does.' Tom was a realist. He undid another button.

'It will if we decide on the rules and stick to them.' She was determined and she was beautiful. Hot and sultry and beautiful. 'I don't want to get involved, Tom. Believe me. I've had enough of all that commitment stuff. I can't go through that kind of pain again.'

It was easy to ignore the still, small voice. Tom undid the last button. 'All right by me. So long as we know where we stand.'

When it came to it, they didn't stand too often. But sex was just a way of satisfying an appetite. It had never meant much more.

And it had gone on like that between Tom McNeil and Dian Jones for the best part of two years. Friendship and part-time sex. He'd enjoyed it so much, that when it went on for longer than he'd intended, it was easy to convince himself that he'd been wrong about Dian. That she would never be a problem. That she wouldn't make demands. That no one would be hurt.

But this summer the scenario had changed irrevocably.

'I don't wanna go home, Tommo.' Dian had complained. 'The parents are so straight, they drive me crazy. Can I doss over with you for a few weeks?'

The first sense of foreboding nudged at his mind.

'Please, Tommo?' She moved closer, her body swaying ever so slightly in all the right places. The best places.

'I operate alone, Dian.' Everything was telling him, no.

'I won't cramp your style, darling. You know me.'

Almost of its own volition, Tom's hand reached out to fondle her buttocks. 'I certainly do,' he said.

'Well?' She arched away from him, her breasts so close . . .

'Okay.' The thought of having Dian available, whenever he should want her, won through.

So she stayed at the flat. And without the busy campus life, something had changed. Dian had changed.

She began to make those demands – demands on his time, demands on his affections, and demands on his bed. And over the past months she'd got worse. She'd stopped seeing other men, other men that she'd always flaunted in his face before. Other men whose sexual proclivities she'd discussed with him until they were both screaming with laughter and desire. She'd become like all the rest.

And here she was again.

'What are you doing here, Dian?' His voice was sharp, unwelcoming.

'Not a lot.' She didn't seem to notice his tone. Instead, she ran her fingers through her long, loose hair.

Tom sighed. She was wearing a dress of blue jersey that clung to every curve of her body. He shook his head with despair. He really shouldn't have given her a key.

'It's been a crappy day. And I wanted to see you.' She eyed him speculatively. 'I thought we could stay in and order a takeaway.'

'I can't afford it.' He glared at her. He was a free agent and she was making him feel tied. She was making him feel that he owed her something for all those nights of passion and hot, hot sex. He didn't want her here, not like this, not now. Her fault, and the fault of the jersey dress of course.

She pouted. Beautiful sulky mouth.

'I've spent too much of this term's grant already.' And most of that had been on Dian, come to think of it. She had expensive tastes. What she was doing here at college he couldn't imagine. Dian would make a lousy teacher. Of drama and of anything else.

'My treat.' Her voice slid, soft and sensual, all over him.

'Sorry, Dian. I'm going out.' He tore off his sweater. A cold shower was what he needed right now.

She pulled a face. 'Not yet, Tommo. Don't go yet.'

He peered into her eyes. 'You've been smoking grass again.' Dilated pupils. He could always tell.

'It's brilliant for getting rid of inhibitions. I'd say it's exactly what you need.' She fumbled in her bag.

'Not now, Dian.' He frowned.

'You're right.' She threw down the bag. 'More important things on the agenda than inhibitions.' In one fluid, graceful movement, she pulled off the jersey dress and slipped her feet out of her platform shoes. Underneath, she wore nothing but a band of black lace that held up her

19

stockings. Her dark and luscious hair fell silkily past her shoulders. She tossed back her head and smiled the slow, sexy smile that never failed to turn him on.

'You just want to get me into trouble.' His voice slurred with desire. When he saw her naked he wanted her. But he made no move towards her.

She reached for him, pressing her palms on his shoulders, pushing him down to a kneeling position on the floor in front of her.

'No, Tommo, I don't want to get you into trouble. I want to give you a little present.' She bent until her breasts were swinging lightly in front of his face.

He groaned. The hardening nipples were inches from his mouth. She was a witch.

'And I want you,' she whispered. 'That's all I want.'

Her words weren't entirely accurate. Dian wanted much more than that. She always did. She wanted to occupy him all evening, drive him crazy with those swaying, sensuous curves, and then keep him at it for hours.

By the time he got her out of the shower, Tom was exhausted. He washed the scent of her musky perfume off his skin, cleaned the taste of her from his mouth, his hands, his mind.

By that time it was past eleven. And what Dian wanted next was to snuggle up close to him in his bed, not be reminded that he was going out to the college disco.

'I suppose you're going to meet *her*?' Her voice slashed through his rapid preparations.

'*Her?*' he mocked, poking out his tongue.

She ignored him, perfect pert nose stuck in the air with disdain.

He laughed. It had been so good between them before she'd started to care.

Tom realised that she knew about Hannah. She'd seen them together, and must have recognised what was going on. No one knew him better than Dian. But even Dian didn't know exactly what Tom had in mind for Hannah Thompson. No one did. Tom hadn't even finished planning it himself.

'You're a bastard, Tommo.' Her voice was matter of fact. But that didn't mean Dian accepted the situation. A bastard was a challenge, and Dian would do what she could to rise to that challenge. To change him.

'No strings – remember?' He picked up the crumpled jersey dress and threw it back at her.

She caught it and frowned. 'Yeah . . . Still, it's a bit much to jump from my bed straight into hers.' But to Tom's relief, she yanked the dress over her head.

Her dark eyes appeared above the collar, scrutinising him. 'Even for you, Tommo.'

He pulled on a clean white shirt and jeans. 'First, it was my bed. Second, I'm not sleeping with her. And third, what the hell do you expect me to do when a beautiful lady comes into my bedroom and takes all her clothes off?'

'Any beautiful lady?' She had her coat on. She was rearranging the layers of her hair in front of the mirror, adjusting the ragged fringe that hung in her eyes.

He came up behind her and smiled. 'Whaddya think?'

'I don't know.' She turned to face him, her expression begging for something he couldn't give.

He kissed her nose. 'Only ladies called Dian who happen to have delicious tits.'

'Shut up, Tommo.' She was smiling, but it was a reluctant smile.

And he knew then that it was over between them. It was time to move on. Dian was the sexiest woman he'd ever had, but he had to wave her goodbye. She was getting too involved. He had no choice. Because love wasn't in the game plan, and even if it was, he could never love a woman like Dian. They were too alike. He knew her too well. He didn't trust her. How could he?

Tom pulled on the denim jacket. 'See ya, kid.'

Besides, there was Hannah. She was the immediate future. He wanted Hannah Thompson. And no one was getting in the way.

3

The Friday night college dance was nothing like the discos Kate had ever come across before – tame affairs where girls danced round handbags and boys stood on the sidelines waiting for a slow smooch and a possible promise. There weren't any punks or skinheads either. Students came to the Friday night discos to drink beer and dance.

As always, Stephanie, Kate and Hannah had arrived together, but Stephanie was already deep in a clinch with one of her admirers. Sometimes it seemed to Kate that it was more out of boredom than desire.

'She's unbelievable.' Kate was torn between envy of Stephanie's effortless sensuality, and the morals of her own upbringing. Morals pelted at you in childhood had this way of sticking like burrs, even when you spent half your life pulling them off. And where she came from, even a one-man girl didn't like to be seen to be going too far.

'How can she behave like that?' Hannah frowned.

'Everyone to their own.' Kate shrugged. She would never judge as she herself had been judged. But over and above the pounding bass line of the latest glam rock she was aware of Hannah's disapproval. Something was bugging Hannah.

'How many has she gone through since term started?' Hannah leaned forward. A strobe light flickered her way, giving her delicate features an eerie quality.

Kate raised her eyebrows. 'How the hell should I know?' This wasn't like Hannah. Never before had she criticised Steph. From nowhere, the image of Stephanie's pained expression in the pool at Les Marettes returned to her.

'Where I come from she'd be called a slut.'

'Hannah!' She was shocked.

At least Hannah had the grace to look ashamed. Her slender fingers twisted nervously around the glass of cider she held. 'Well, she would.'

She looked up with defiance. 'And she's being called worse than that here, as well.'

'Who by?' Kate's voice was dangerously low.

'Does it matter?' Hannah looked away, towards the sea of writhing bodies, the mass of student faces. 'By everyone . . .' Her voice tailed off.

'Hannah?' Kate peered into the shadows, realising that Hannah was close to tears. She put a hand on her bare arm, her eyes softening. 'Isn't it up to Steph how she lives her life? People will always talk – you can't stop them.'

Bloody tittle-tattle. Hadn't she had enough of that in Ridley? People with nothing better to do than twitch the net curtains and live other people's lives.

But Hannah wasn't listening. Hannah was staring at Stephanie as she returned to their table. And Kate didn't trust the expression on the face that was normally so gentle. This wasn't worth a row. And yet a row was brewing – she could feel it in the air, hear it in the tempo of the music. And she could see it in the restlessness of Hannah's eyes as she craned her neck from side to side.

Suddenly Kate knew what was wrong with Hannah. She was looking for Tom McNeil. And he hadn't turned up – yet.

'Another new partner?' Hannah's voice cut into the unfamiliar tension between them.

Stephanie grinned, stretching her long, lazy body out in the chair. 'Variety is the spice of life, darling. Why should sex be any different?' She lit a cigarette.

Kate smiled, but she couldn't imagine it for herself. Didn't sex and love go hand in hand? She'd always thought they had with Jason. But Jason had let the decisions of other people take away her future. That wasn't love either.

She watched the tall, greasy-haired lad Stephanie had been dancing with. He looked their way, hesitated, then swaggered to the bar as if rejection was part of the game. Maybe it was. Maybe that's where Kate had gone wrong. Because she'd never rejected Jason, only ever welcomed him with open arms and defenceless heart.

Stephanie followed her gaze. 'Rick Allen. One of the PE guys,' she supplied. 'You should try it, Kate. Pounds and pounds of pure hunk and muscle.' She laughed, her eyes narrowing slightly as she looked at Hannah.

'Don't you ever want to have a proper relationship with any of them?' Hannah was sitting stiff and upright in her chair.

Stephanie's eyes darkened into an expression Kate had never seen before. Behind them, over and above their voices, the music rose to a crescendo.

'What do you mean by a proper relationship?' Stephanie mocked. 'Chaste kisses and holding hands? Getting married in white before you know if you like his touch? Letting a man walk all over you? Wanting what you know you'll never have?' She was breathing heavily. Beads of sweat began to collect on her brow. 'Is that a proper relationship, *darling*?'

'There are other things apart from sex.' Hannah's voice dropped to a whisper. There was a break in the music, but still they both had to lean forwards to hear her.

'Such as?' Stephanie's eyes were glistening with unshed tears.

She and Hannah both. She and Hannah both. What the hell was wrong with the two of them?

'Such as friendship.' Hannah wouldn't look at either of them. 'Commitment. Loyalty.'

'You can get those from a woman. Or at least that's the theory.' Stephanie's words were barbed with meaning.

Hannah was becoming flustered. She flicked a strand of blonde hair out of her eyes. 'And from a man,' she said. 'You can get them from a man too.'

'Grow up, Hannah.' Stephanie was swaying slightly as she got to her feet. 'Take a look at the real world for a change. All men want from women is sex and slavery. It's pathetic. But things are changing, and women are learning a few lessons at last. The sexes are separate. That's why there has to be a battle of the sexes. We lead separate lives. And so we have to fight. Sex and slavery. That's what it's all about.'

She flung back her dark hair and strode away from their table, through the mass of damp, writhing bodies. Damp with sweat, sex and energy. Her tall figure graceful even in baggy jeans and a T-shirt. Class. It clung to Stephanie like morning mist and Kate was envious as hell.

She turned on Hannah. 'What's got into you?'

Hannah was trembling violently. 'Well, it's not fair. People think we're . . . you know, easy. Just because we're her friends.' Her brown eyes were huge and vulnerable in the dim lights of the dance hall.

The music resumed its tireless beat. Hannah leaned closer. 'You know what I'm talking about.'

Yes, Kate knew. But she didn't want to. 'It's just spite. Jealousy.' She chose the words with care. 'We should stick up for Steph. That's what being supportive is all about.'

Hannah was silent.

'Why can't you ignore them?' Kate became irritated. What was the matter with Hannah? Weren't they on the same side?

'I just can't.' Hannah stared at her. There was a kind of desperate, lost look about her tonight. So Tom McNeil was screwing her up already, was he?

'Why not? We're not living in the Dark Ages any more.' Kate took a long swig of her beer, as if this proved it. 'Men think they're Mr Macho Wonderful when they do it. So why shouldn't women sleep around?'

She blinked as Hannah drew her chair nearer. Their faces were a few feet apart.

'*You* don't.' Hannah's gaze held hers. 'You don't get involved with anyone, do you, Kate? Why not?'

They were very close. Around them the music pulsated, beating into Kate's eardrums. Suddenly she felt very tired. What was she doing here anyway? The respectable route of teaching was her mother's dream, not hers at all. She sighed. If they'd been in a different place, even a different time, maybe she would have told Hannah about Jason.

She wanted to. It was eating at her, needing to be heard, desperate to be told, as if only then could she begin to heal. But not now. Not here. Maybe on the way home, in the quiet, leafy darkness. Maybe then Kate might tell Hannah about Jason.

But in the meantime, Hannah needed an answer.

'I got burned,' she whispered. 'It teaches you not to play with fire.'

Stephanie wandered back to their table, but the evening was spoiled. All Kate wanted to do was return to her tiny study bedroom at Royal Ford, where she could listen to the music she liked on her tatty record player, without getting beaten down by the volume of someone else's bass line. Where she could give her memories of Jason the window test to see if they could stand up to the harsh realities of daylight – where all the stains would show. But these were slender securities.

She needed to go home. She must visit Ridley this weekend. Now that people had forgotten to talk about her, now that Jason had found himself a new girl, it was time to face what had driven her away. So that she could take more steps into an uncertain future and a world where it was never easy to belong.

She thought of Normandy – their last night in the pool at the Chateau des Marettes, nestling on the banks of the river Risle. It all seemed so far away. And maybe it was her fault. Because she was a sham. That story of travelling around Europe – lies, all of it. Made up on the spur of the moment to explain away a lost year. Because Kate couldn't bear for them to know the truth – to look at her the way her old schoolfriends in Ridley had looked at her, the neighbours, the head teacher. It seemed everyone knew. Small town morals . . .

If their friendship was built on lies, then wasn't it bound to crumble?

As the last note of a rock and roll number died away, she glanced up. Striding across the dance floor was the tall figure of Tom McNeil. His fair hair was slicked back from his face. He was wearing tight blue jeans, a denim jacket, and desert boots, and most of the girls were looking his way, even Stephanie. She caught her breath.

'How's the merry threesome?' His eyes sought out Hannah's. But he was aware of Stephanie. Kate could see it in his hooded expression, the way he carefully didn't look in her direction.

'Rehearsing for Macbeth.' Stephanie's voice was dry, but she was examining Tom with some interest.

Tom was grinning at Hannah, holding out his hand to her, and Kate saw her face actually light into happiness. Oh God. She was beginning to feel distinctly queasy.

'Dance with me, Hannah?' It wasn't even a question. Not when the answer was already in Hannah's eyes, and his fingers were already touching her hair.

Hannah smiled and nodded. She rose, and they drifted off into the slow bluesy music that signalled the beginning of the end of the evening. Kate watched Tom as he glanced back over Hannah's shoulder. Not towards her – she was sitting in the shadows, but towards Stephanie. Open admiration mingled with resentment. And at the same time, his hand crept round Hannah's waist like a serpent.

Kate shivered. He was drawing Hannah closer. He was smiling as he looked away, his attention re-focusing on the girl whose slim body was moulding into his own. The strobe flickered over him, illuminating his white shirt into violet. Echoing his smile.

And in that moment, with that smile, Kate knew who had been saying those things about Stephanie. She was one hundred per cent sure.

It hadn't been a conversation overheard by Hannah at all. That would never have upset her so much. And, more to the point, she wouldn't have overheard it in the first place – Hannah wandered around lost in a dream, didn't she? Kate was the one who overheard conversations. It was Kate who knew which way the wind was blowing. If people were talking, she would have heard them.

Only Tom McNeil could have said those things. Those coffee breaks in the common room hadn't been so innocent after all. He'd been poisoning her mind. Planting the first seeds of separation.

Her eyes narrowed. She'd been right to distrust him. She'd wanted to save Hannah from being hurt, that was all. But this was worse than she'd feared.

Kate didn't want this world – her new world – to alter. She didn't want to have endings floating in the air like lost kite strings. She wanted everything to stay the same. It was too soon. And she was scared of change.

Tom McNeil was building barriers to separate the three of them. He had declared war. Tom wanted Hannah to himself, and he wasn't prepared to share her. He was going to fight dirty.

Kate sat up straighter in her seat. When it came to fighting dirty, she knew it all. She had the experience. And she would fight him until she dropped. They would see who would win in the end. Sex and slavery eh? He wouldn't know what had hit him.

Dancing with Hannah, drifting into and beyond the song, Tom felt an urge to protect the small figure in his arms, a need to possess her.

'You were so late, Tom,' she breathed. 'I thought you weren't coming.' She laughed at herself as if to deprecate the words.

But Tom was conscious of a surge of triumph. 'Did you now?' He held her closer still, pressing her in towards him, until their bodies were following the exact pattern, his rhythm becoming her own. 'That's nice.'

She relaxed against him at last.

That was how it would be. She merely had to be coaxed into the right directions. He smiled. She was his, and she didn't know how to hide it. 'I told you I'd be here, Hannah. You don't have to worry.' His hand crept from her shoulder to her hair, tangling it lightly away from her serious face. 'I never make promises I don't intend to keep.'

'Don't you, Tom?' She seemed to be teasing – but he wasn't sure. And then her blonde head nestled further into his shoulder and he bent to drink in the scent of her. She was a breath of fresh air. Unlike Dian, she smelt of flowers. She could have been innocence personified, this girl. That's what he liked about her the most.

'I feel like I've known you forever.' He murmured the words into the soft fragrance of her hair. Men had no idea how powerful romance could be. Other men. But Tom knew.

She glanced up at him, surprise in the dark almond eyes.

But before she could speak, the dance ended, and he took her hand, leading her towards the door. 'I lost track of time. It was this essay I was trying to finish. Oh, I know I shouldn't have let it take over like that.' He paused, his eyes scorching into hers. 'You will let me take you home though, won't you? I need to talk to you.'

She shot him a long appraising look. 'What about?' She was scared, he could see it etched into her face.

'Anything. Everything. Nothing in particular. I just want to talk.' Tom tilted her chin, bending closer. 'Don't worry, Hannah,' he whispered. 'I'll look after you.' He wasn't a fool. He knew he had to go slow or he'd lose her. And he liked that. It was part of her charm.

'Okay, then.' She nodded, looking up at him, trusting him.

People were drifting off into the night. Hannah signalled to the fiery girl called Kate and grabbed her duffel-coat. Tom tucked her small hand under his arm. They walked out of the door, and he turned to see Kate's frown as the lights went up in the hall. He grasped Hannah's arm more tightly as the winter night hit their hot faces.

She rested against him like a small animal needing warmth.

'Why did you say that?' Her voice was soft. 'That you feel like you've known me forever?'

His step quickened. He wanted to get ahead of the stragglers. 'Because that's how it seems.'

There was a pause. 'It seems like that to me too,' she confided at last.

He smiled. Victory was in sight.

As they walked through the wrought iron gates, into the grounds of Royal Ford, he abruptly steered her off the tarmac drive towards the trees.

'Hey . . .' But she laughed, not seeming scared any more.

Their feet squelched into the wet grass. The undergrowth was dripping and dark, the branches of an ancient oak towering over them. They stopped by the tree trunk, and he leaned a denim-clad arm on the damp bark.

'The truth is . . .' Facing her, he traced a pattern across her chin with his fingertips. 'I don't know a thing about you. You're a bit of a mystery, Hannah Thompson.' He laughed. 'And I don't even care. You see . . .' He paused. 'I know everything that matters.'

'And what does matter?' Her voice was light.

Hannah couldn't believe that this was actually her – wanting to flirt with Tom, longing to hear all these sweetest of sweet nothings that she'd always scorned before.

'I think you know what matters,' he said.

She eyed him curiously. The night was dark, but his eyes flared with some deeper meaning when they looked into hers. Could this be real? He was painting a circle of magnetism around their two bodies. And she might never be able to pull herself out of it again.

'Do I, Tom?' She couldn't quite give in to him. They were very close. She stared at the faint rising of his chest under the crisp, white cotton shirt he wore. If she were to reach out her hand, she'd be able to touch it. Her gaze was clamped on to his chest. Beyond that, into his face, she didn't dare look.

'Be honest with me, Hannah,' he urged. 'Let yourself go. Give in to the moment.' His voice was compelling. His hand crept to her face, fingers brushing her cheek with a dash of static.

Hannah blinked, dazed by his careless touch – a hand on her face, a glance into her soul. Too dazed to remember the male dangers lurking so close. She couldn't reply. And yet she knew she'd said yes to Tom McNeil without considering the question. What hope was there now? Her shoulders sagged.

'That's better,' he soothed. 'Relax. There's nothing to be afraid of.' She could hardly register the words. Only smell the scent of him – faint cedar and patchouli oil, mingling with whatever it was that didn't come out of a bottle or a bar of soap, and was turning her legs into the legs of some wobbling matchstick girl.

'So where have you been hiding, Hannah Thompson?' he teased, taking her hands in his. 'Tell me everything about yourself.'

'There's nothing much to tell.' Despite her fear, Hannah's gaze rose to his lean face, to his mouth. Mesmerised by his lips. Her throat was dry.

30

'I'm pretty ordinary.' God, that sounded feeble. If Kate were here she'd be screaming with laughter by now. Or dragging her away from the enemy. She looked around his tall figure, but the drive was deserted.

'Ordinary? Not to me, you're not.' He pulled her closer, cradling her face between his hands, smoothing her hair from her cheeks and brow.

Hannah closed her eyes in submission. His touch filled her with liquid warmth. It flooded her senses, overpowering even the raw easterly wind.

Now his hands were on her shoulders with fresh urgency, as he drew her closer still. She felt as if she were a character in a dream somewhere. Only she wasn't sure if it was even her own dream. She only knew she was being dragged to a place she'd never intended to visit. And yet she wanted to be that character. She wanted to go to that place. She had to.

He was caressing her shoulders and arms, his hands slipping to her waist as he released the toggles of the tawny duffel-coat she wore. His arms twined around her, as he lifted her nearer. She thought she saw Kate's hooded figure walking alone down the driveway that led to Ford. And then she was gone.

Hannah's hands were on his shoulders, and she couldn't breathe. Touch was something she had never lived with.

'Oh God,' she murmured. Her parents had never touched, never kissed, never held, like Tom was holding her now.

Tom was nibbling her neck and Hannah was enjoying it.

What would Mother say?

'I only want to keep you safe.'

She groaned as Mother's voice sliced into his touch. No. She didn't want to hear that voice now. It didn't belong here with the tenderness. She was leading her own life now. A life entirely separate from what she'd left behind.

Go away, Mother. Hannah opened her eyes as Tom's butterfly kisses swept a path towards her face. Tom's fair head drew back. Then he bent. Closer he came. She couldn't move.

Safe and secure. Safe and secure.

Hannah's lips slowly parted in response.

This then was what Mother had been protecting her from all these years.

His mouth closed on hers.

Her head swam. This was what it was all about . . .

She wrapped her arms around his neck.

This wonderful and absolute delight.

'I could do with some of that.' Rick Allen smirked.

Stephanie glanced over to the trees, and did a double-take as she recognised Hannah's slim, taut body, cleaving to Tom McNeil's, in a kiss that looked like it was one hell of a kiss.

'Christ . . .' She blinked.

'That's one of your little friends, isn't it?'

Stephanie hated that grin of his. He might be all hunk and muscle as she'd told Kate, but right now he was slobbering like a hyena.

'So?' She walked on. She still hadn't forgiven Hannah. But that didn't mean she wouldn't defend her to the ends of the earth if necessary.

'So – she's tasty . . .' He hung back, still watching.

'Leave her alone, for Christ's sake.' Stephanie grabbed his sleeve. Why was Rick such an animal?

'Oh, it's not her I'm after.' He laughed thickly as he slung his heavy arm back over her shoulder. 'You've got no worries, baby.'

She winced. He was a brute. Rick Allen would be big and heavy in bed. Big enough to hide under, maybe. She laughed without humour. 'You're coming up, then?'

His eyes travelled insidiously from the mass of thick dark hair, past her mocking beautiful face, and over the entire length of her body. 'Just try and stop me.'

Stephanie didn't flinch. 'I wouldn't dream of it.'

As they reached the steps to the entrance, she slipped easily from his hold. 'You go first then. It's the fourth floor. I'll meet you by the lift.'

It hadn't taken Stephanie long to realise that the only way of guaranteeing an entrance into hall for a partner of your choice, was for him to go in alone. No one questioned those going in alone, and no security man could know all the faces. That's how she got her lovers into Ford.

She watched him swagger through the doors, all self-confidence and balls. And she felt the urge to run. So strong, her muscles were twitching. Anywhere would do.

Then her expression hardened, and she followed him inside, up to the fourth floor, quickly, before she could change her mind.

'C'mon baby.' He was all over her before she could even get her key in the lock.

'Get off.' She giggled. It was all part of the game. She could smell the tobacco on his clothes and the beer on his breath, although she'd been drinking herself. Stephanie Lewis-Smythe drank a lot these days. She'd come a long way from her exclusive girls' school in Kent. She could down five pints of Newcastle Brown as fast as any man.

'You shouldn't smoke if you're in PE.' She wound long fingers through his hair as he followed her inside.

He kicked the door behind him.

'Who the fuck cares?' Rick grabbed her, his mouth nuzzling her neck and she felt herself bend a little.

Stephanie waited for the passion to take over. It was like a tidal wave. It came and it went – a meaningless flow, a rhythm of sexuality that was totally unimportant to anything that mattered.

And yet she needed it. And when it came, as it always came, as his hands moved expertly underneath her T-shirt, she breathed a hot sigh of relief.

Already his breath was coming fast and thick, as sweat gathered on his brow. She closed her eyes. It mattered to men so much. It always amazed her how much it mattered to men. Now that he was here, wanting her, it seemed almost unimportant to Stephanie. Part of her could look down at them both and laugh.

He was massaging her breasts and pulling her on to the bed. He was fast, but Stephanie needed him to be fast, so fast that she couldn't think. So that she could drown in it – this brief meaningless passion – and so that it would be over almost before it had begun.

The instant he finished, he was climbing off her. A mountain scaled. A battle won. A woman enslaved. Never just orgasm.

'That was great, baby.' His arrogant face was brick-red.

'Yeah?' This was the part she hated. Stephanie looked away in disgust, pulling the sheet over her half-naked body in belated prudishness.

'But it was too quick. It'll be better in the morning.' He sighed his thick sigh of male satisfaction.

She shuddered, despising him. Hating the look of heaving shoulders and damp chest, and hating the imbalance of his male body – some parts too big, others pathetically small and spent. And she loathed the look in his eyes – not the hunter of half an hour ago, that had been bad enough. But the master regarding his slave.

'You won't be here in the morning.' She crawled out of bed, still holding the sheet around her, grabbed the kettle, and put it under the cold tap at the wash-basin.

'What?' He stared at her. The masterly mask slipped just a fraction.

'You heard.' She smiled politely. 'I'd like you to leave now, Rick. If you don't mind.'

She wanted to drink some sobering black coffee alone. To look out into the night and think her own thoughts undisturbed. She didn't need him any more.

'What if I do mind?' His pale eyes challenged her.

She shrugged. 'It's my room.'

He sat up, naked on the bed, sinking the solidity of his hairy legs into the quilt, as if suddenly self-conscious about his own body. 'What did I do?' Rejection disguised under a thin coating of humour. Rick was skating lightly over the ice. 'Didn't you get off?' He grinned. 'Want to try again?'

The thought made her ill. 'No thanks.'

'So what did I do then?' His lack of understanding was pitiful.

'Nothing.' That was the point. He'd done nothing for her – but then, she'd never expected him to. Never even wanted him to. Why was it so hard to explain?

She sighed. 'Let's be honest. You got what you came for, didn't you?'

His eyes narrowed. 'You're bloody weird, you are.'

Stephanie shook back her dark hair. What was the point of trying to communicate with a man like this? 'Look, I'm not being funny, but I need some space right now.'

His face was animal-blank.

'Christ . . .' One hand rested on her hip. The other firmly grasped the white sheet around her shoulders. 'You wanted to have sex with me, right?'

'Yeah . . .' He nodded warily as if this was incriminating evidence.

'And I wanted to have sex with you.' More debatable, that one; but that was Stephanie's problem, not his.

His eyes widened as if he hadn't been aware of that part of the equation. His shoulders twitched. 'No need to put it like that . . .' he began.

'Well, how should I put it?' She was beginning to lose patience. Did he need it to be a surrender or what? Couldn't it be a joint enterprise?

He laughed with faint desperation. 'I dunno. Do you have to put it at all? I'm not into talking. Doing's more my style.'

The kettle boiled.

'Well, we've done it, haven't we?' She turned to face him. 'What's the point of prolonging it? We're never going to be college romance of the year, are we?' She tried to hide the disdain, but it was stamped indelibly on her upper-crust features. On the high cheekbones, the downward tilt of her wide mouth, and the slant of her deep blue eyes.

'What's the big hurry?' There was a curious kind of wheedling violence in his voice. He got to his feet, still naked, and came closer, his eyes fixed on the sheet she clutched around her.

'No hurry.' Stephanie recognised the danger immediately. He was a strong man. She'd threatened him. She didn't want him now and yet she could see the desire still burning in his eyes. It fascinated, and yet repelled her.

'That's better.' He nodded, reaching out his big clumsy hands towards her.

Stephanie closed her eyes as the rough fingertips grazed the soft skin of her shoulder. She could smell his male sweat. Sucked into her nostrils, making her sick.

He laughed, master of the situation once more. 'I'll have two sugars. And it's a bit late for all this modesty, isn't it?' He plucked at the white sheet, and it slipped, past the voluptuous curve of her breasts.

Stephanie turned away from him, her breath coming in short gasps. She needed her inhaler, but she was damned if she was going to do it now, with this animal in the room.

She spooned coffee into two mugs. Calm. She must stay calm. 'Stay for coffee then. But two of us couldn't squeeze into this bed for the whole night. Look at it.'

But she could feel him behind her, his breath on her bare back. Brute force won every time. The bastard only wanted her again because she'd tried to get away from him.

'It's not so small. It'll be nice and cosy.' His rough hands tore off the remainder of the sheet, and cupped her breasts possessively, holding her captive.

No. She was not having any more of Rick Allen. The taste of him was like acid in her throat. Her skin was on fire, and her eyes – only half an hour ago heavy-lidded with desire – were clear and unafraid. She was not having that brutish body pounding away on top of her. No more. She'd anaesthetized herself back to reality now, and she wanted him gone.

'Don't touch me.' She elbowed him deftly in the ribs and escaped from his hold, backing away, a warning in the intensity of her blue eyes.

He laughed. 'That's not what you were saying earlier on.'

'It's what I'm saying now.' She spoke slowly, trying to take deep breaths, her chest wheezing in distress. She needed Ventolin. 'I want you to leave. And if you don't leave, I'll scream. Loudly.'

She waited. She hadn't meant it to go this far. She'd badly mishandled the situation. Misjudged the strength of his male ego.

It was touch and go. He stared at her, through her, past her, as if not knowing whether or not to bluff her out. There was a moment of indecision, so tangible it seemed to rest in the air between them.

And then he turned, grabbing his shirt.

'Stupid, fucking bitch,' he muttered. 'What is it with you? You're not just a whore. You're bloody weird, you are.' He pulled on his tight-fitting black cords.

Stephanie closed her eyes. Soon he would be gone. Soon she would start shaking. In a moment she could grab her Ventolin, and in a moment she would be alone.

'I'm out of here.' He picked up his jacket, and flung open the door. 'But you just wait, you stuck-up bitch. We're not finished yet. You just wait . . .'

She slammed the door behind him and turned the key. Scrabbled in her bag for her inhaler, and took deep grateful breaths. A near escape. Maybe he was right. Maybe she was crazy. Maybe Daddy's little darling should leave these boys alone.

There was the letter – still crumpled in a discarded ball by the mirror. Why hadn't she chucked it in the bin? Did she need to read it one last time?

She smoothed the sheet until it was legible. '*Darling*', it began. All Daddy's letters began with a darling. Darling, here's a cheque. Darling, why don't you ever come home for the weekend? Why do you see your brother Miles and not see me? Darling, just tell me what you need and it can be yours. Come back to me, darling. If it's just a question of money . . .

Why bother to read it? All his letters were the same. They all stank of poor little rich girl. They all belonged to a past that she wanted to get away from.

Without reading further, she screwed it up once more, and threw it in the bin. Then she picked up her coffee and walked, naked, over to the window.

Opening the curtain, she stared out into the grounds of Royal Ford. The moon was a narrow arc high above the trees, and below was the dense dark mystery of undergrowth and grass.

Stephanie wanted to be like the rest of them. She didn't want to be a privileged person who never had to work for anything. If you never worked for anything, you achieved nothing worthwhile. She wanted to be appreciated for who she was – not where she'd come from. Not appreciated because of Daddy's money, or Mother's family. Mother was dead and long-gone, all she had ever been to the young Stephanie was a trail of expensive perfume from the nursery to a room that was out of bounds, never someone to love.

But now Stephanie wanted to find her own niche – to shake off the shackles of privilege, and live in the real world for a change.

She leaned on the sill, her dark hair waving around her shoulders. Somewhere out there were schools full of kids who'd never have half of what was hers for the taking. There were kids with talent, who would be squeezed by the school curriculum into a quite different shape from the one that nature intended.

And those were the kids that Stephanie wanted to teach. Those were the ones that she wanted to show what art was all about. Learning to look below the surface. She wanted to show them that art was about emotion, not just about seeing. And that what you saw could be something quite different from what everyone else saw. That art wasn't about rules and regulations, or even directions. It was about the innocent eye. The mind, the hand and the eye in harmony.

Stephanie saw Hannah and Tom walk from the hidden, secret shelter of the trees, to the doors of Royal Ford, totally absorbed, each in the other. There was a last lingering kiss, and then Tom touched her face goodbye, and Hannah's suddenly solitary figure walked inside alone.

She clutched the window sill so tightly that her fingers hurt.

At last Rick emerged from the building, loping off without a backward glance.

Tom stood motionless for a few minutes, then he walked away, down the drive. Halfway to the gate he turned to look back at the building.

Stephanie had the lights low, but she saw that he had seen her naked half-figure, framed in the window. And she saw that he couldn't look away.

She smiled slowly. Hannah might be lucky – because Hannah was in love. But that kind of love wasn't for Stephanie. That kind of love would never be hers.

It seemed like an eternity as she and Tom McNeil stared at each other in the shadows of the night.

Rising to her feet, Stephanie ran her hands lightly over her body, moving from her shoulders across her breasts and down over her hips. And only then did she turn away.

She sighed and shook her head. Tom McNeil wanted more. Maybe Hannah wasn't so lucky after all . . .

4

The following weekend, Kate was sitting on the number 98 bus, travelling from the station to Ridley. Making the transition from college life back to childhood and school days. Pushing thoughts of Stephanie and Hannah and the unfamiliar tensions between them to the back of her mind. Allowing the past to creep into the new world. It had to be faced.

But already the weather seemed more wintry and bleak than the weather she'd left behind in Dorset. The houses were small, cramped rows of terraces like the house her mother wanted to escape from. And the people were too interested in your business. She used to think it was worth it for a smile on a friendly face, but now she wasn't so sure. When you wanted to be left alone, it was a hefty price to pay.

The conductor grinned as he collected her money. 'All right, lass? Back for the weekend, then?'

'Yep.' She forced a smile of reply on to her pale face, but her lips felt tight and unyielding. She didn't know him from Adam, but she had a weekend case squatting at her feet. In Ridley that was more than enough for a conversation starter.

The window was steamed, and Kate rubbed it impatiently with her sleeve to get her bearings, as if she didn't know the entire landscape by heart. It was written on a placard behind her eyes and probably always would be.

The old red bus was rumbling into the village now. And on the left, just past the next stop would be Jason's parents house. She held her breath.

The bell rang and the driver braked. An old woman creaked off the gangway, as Kate peered into the murky distance. It was only early afternoon but Ridley was cloaked in one of the mists that seemed to come from the moor and hang suspended, dank and unforgiving, over the village.

She could just make out the white-painted house – she and Jason had helped his dad with that, three summers ago. And the bent apple tree in the front garden with its crippled branches that brought back those distant voices . . .

'It'll have to go,' Jason's dad used to say.

'But the blossom's so pretty in the spring.' His mum's protests always won through, because they came from the heart. She used to cut sprigs of the fluttering pink and white, and put them in vases on the landing. Every time Kate went up those stairs, there were petals on the carpet. And the scent of apple blossom hit her full in the face like an unexpected spring day.

And as for Jason . . . He used to kiss his sweetheart under the branches of the apple tree. Any opportunity he got.

Treacherous tears momentarily blurred her vision, and Kate almost missed the battered Citroën parked outside.

Her heart flipped. Oh my God.

As the bus groaned onwards up the hill, past the house, she sat back, bolt upright, as if someone from that house might be watching from behind a window.

'*What's she doing here?*'

'*What's she looking at?*'

'*Can't she keep away?*'

Jason's Citroën. It must be. While Kate had been in France last summer, Jason had been working on the pumps in the petrol station down the hill. He'd been saving to buy the car. She knew that, because in Ridley everyone knew what everyone else was doing. And maybe even why.

So Jason was here too, here for the weekend.

Kate began to stumble to her feet, almost falling over the navy case.

'Hey, lass. This isn't the stop you were after.' The conductor with the kind eyes helped her back to her seat. 'I'll give you a shout,' he promised.

Kate sensed hysterical laughter mounting inside her, and she pressed her lips more tightly together. What did it matter that Jason was in Ridley for the weekend? Maybe it was better this way. She'd come back to face the past, and that meant facing Jason.

She'd seen him in the distance many times, but in the last two years it had proved easy to avoid Jason, even in Ridley. There had been two summers away – one in Normandy and one helping out at her Aunt's farm. There had been Easters when she heard that Jason was on canal holidays with friends from university. And lonely family Christmases. Oh yes, it seemed to Kate that since she'd broken up with Jason, fate had conspired to keep them apart.

'Your stop, lass.'

Funny, she knew it all so well, and yet when it came to it, she'd almost missed it. The stop she'd got off at for years. Taking another deep breath, Kate launched herself and the navy case on to the pavement. There it was, over the road – the house she'd grown up in, the house that had heard more than its fair share of rows and tears. And the garden that had seen so many secret kisses. She blinked. How many net curtains had twitched when Kate was saying goodnight to the boy she loved?

'See yer then.' The conductor waved a cheery hand as the engine heaved into life, and Kate found herself waving back, her heart inexplicably lighter. She'd been wrong. It was friendliness, not just idle curiosity. And it did have this way of making you feel good after some of those cold Southern stares.

Inside the small, cosy kitchen of her childhood, her mother was buttering bread. She always buttered before she cut, and Kate was inexplicably annoyed on the many occasions she found herself doing the same.

'Kate!' Eileen Dunstan wiped her hands on the floral apron, and took a step towards her. She was dark and neat as ever, but she looked tired.

'Hi, Mum.' Kate looked away, not wanting to see that weariness, not wanting to care or wonder about it. She offered her cheek for the kiss that was now convention rather than affection, but couldn't accept the arms that were stretched out in welcome.

Soon she was back in her usual place on the wooden chair by the boiler, listening to small talk, but not joining in.

Having tried work and tutors, Eileen's eyes were becoming tinged with desperation. 'And how are those friends of yours? The ones you went away with?'

Kate groaned silently. Oh yeah. Mum had liked the sound of them from the start. They had the right backgrounds, the right class.

'They're okay.' She didn't want to think about Stephanie and Hannah just now. She had to think about the job in hand. Facing the past. Finding a way of coping with the grief of parting. And the grief of loss.

Eileen turned away. 'And have you found yourself a boyfriend yet?'

Kate wasn't deceived by the lightness of her tone or the straightness of the back presented to her. She was aware of what her mother wanted to know. And they were standing on dangerous ground.

'I haven't been looking.' She took the tea offered to her, but refused to meet the questioning green eyes so like her own. 'I've been working too hard.' Her tone grew defensive. 'Well, you wanted me to go there to work, didn't you?'

Eileen sat down heavily beside her. 'Of course I did, love, but . . .'

'Jason's home this weekend. I saw his car.' Why had she blurted it out like that? Just because she couldn't stomach one of Mum's homilies about all work and no play? Kate gulped at her tea and winced as it scalded the roof of her mouth.

Eileen drew back, her expression changing. 'I heard he would be.' Her eyes were scrutinising her daughter carefully, although when she spoke again her voice was pure indifference. 'But what's that to you, Kate?'

'How can you ask that?' All the betrayal surged to the surface. Wasn't a mother supposed to be there for you? Wasn't a mother supposed to understand? 'You, of all people!' Kate's eyes blazed.

She half-rose to her feet. There was Mum, sitting so innocently, as if she'd played no part in breaking Jason and Kate in two. Not much she hadn't. She'd virtually torn them apart with her bare hands.

Eileen looked down into her cup. Slowly she stirred the liquid around. 'That's in the past, Kate.' Her voice was kind but firm. She seemed untouched by her daughter's anger. 'I can't believe you're still holding a torch for him. Isn't it about time you put it all behind you?'

'How can I?' Kate clenched her fists to stop herself striking out. If she couldn't cry about it then she had to hurt.

She shouldn't have come here.

She scraped back her chair and went to the window. The mist had lifted already. That was the character of the mists of Ridley. They came upon you when you were unaware, and were gone before you even realised that you couldn't see so clearly.

Outside, beyond the tiny back yard, the shadow of Raddlestone Moor loomed over the village.

'You have to.' Eileen's voice was urgent. She had risen to her feet and was standing behind Kate.

Kate could feel her presence and smell the faint lavender perfume, even before her mother gripped her arms.

'It was a long time ago. You were barely more than children.' She paused. 'And you know Jason's found himself someone else . . .'

'Of course I know.' Kate pulled away. She couldn't bear her mother to even touch her. She'd taken something too precious. 'You wrote and told me yourself. Have you forgotten already? You didn't leave out a thing.'

Eileen sighed. 'I didn't want you to keep on with this . . . this . . .'

'Infatuation?' Kate spun round to face her. 'That's what you thought it was, didn't you? That's what you've always thought it was.'

Eileen shook her head. She leaned heavily on the work-top. She was looking old.

Determinedly, Kate turned away.

'I didn't want you to get hurt.' Eileen's voice was a faint whisper.

'But I did get hurt, didn't I?' Kate gripped the sink. 'Thanks to you.' And what had hurt her the most – apart from the expression in Jason's hazel eyes just before he turned to leave – was the overwhelming lack of control in her own destiny. Mum took over and she took everything. And Kate had no power to stop her.

'I did it for the best.' Her mother's mind seemed to have drifted away from this conversation, out of the kitchen, into a private past perhaps.

'In your opinion.' Kate hated the sneer in her own voice. But she wanted to hurt. She needed to twist the knife a little.

Eileen stared at her. 'Was that the future you wanted for yourself, Kate? Saddled at eighteen with a boy like Jason, not two pennies to rub together, and . . .'

'Did you ever give me the chance to decide?' Kate's words were wrung from her heart.

Eileen was silent for a moment. She was trembling with emotion. 'I'm sorry if you felt that way,' she said at last. As if she hadn't known. As if Kate hadn't told her exactly how she felt.

She shrugged. What use were apologies now?

Eileen made another move towards her. 'The two of you have got different lives now, Kate. You should stay away from Jason. There's no reason to even see him.' Her eyes were pleading, but Kate couldn't respond.

'It's a bit difficult to do that in a place like Ridley, isn't it?' A harsh, strained laugh followed her words. Hiding the rising panic. The pain that wouldn't go away.

43

'But you'll be qualified soon.' Eileen's soft voice seemed to fill the room. Once, that voice had sung her lullabies, chanted nursery rhymes, comforted and crooned. 'When you're teaching you won't want to live round here. Neither will Jason, come to that. You'll be wanting to get your own place, in a better area, near a nice school . . .'

'What's wrong with the school round here?' Kate shot the words out at her. Weren't mothers supposed to want their daughters to stay close to them? Weren't they supposed to be sad when their daughters wanted to fly from the nest?

Eileen sighed once more. Her green eyes were tinged with a pain that Kate couldn't understand. She was the one with the pain, not her mother.

'Why would you want to live in Ridley?' Her mother looked around the small cluttered kitchen as if it encapsulated her life. 'This place is a backwater. You know what they're like around here.' She seemed to be rehearsing some speech glued into her mind with bitterness. 'What is there here for a girl like you?'

A girl like you. A girl like you. Echoes of the voices of Ridley.

Was that what Mum thought of her?

'What is there in Dorset?' Kate's voice broke. 'Will I be respectable in Dorset? Will I be safe in Dorset?' She was shouting. She knew she was shouting but she didn't care.

'Quiet.' Eileen moved towards her. 'These walls are too thin. People will hear.'

'People already know.' Kate stared at her. Their eyes locked in some sort of primeval battle. 'Everybody knows. Everybody knows all about our family.' Her voice rose once more. 'They know what you think of this place and they know what you think of Dad. They know what I've done and they know what sort of a girl I am. So why bloody bother to hide it?'

She strode to the back door and yanked it open.

'Kate. You don't understand. Wait . . .' But Eileen's words were lost in the north-easterly breeze as Kate grabbed her anorak from the porch, and stormed outside.

She needed to be alone and she needed to think. And on the other side of the alleyway, down the passage and then up the hill, Raddlestone Moor was waiting – just as it had always been waiting.

Eileen shut the door, moved to the window and watched Kate cross the back yard into the alleyway. Her eyes darkened with the ache that had settled inside her. How could she stand by and watch her daughter moving so far away? And yet how could she let her stay here?

It was impossible. And useless trying to talk to her. There was too much she couldn't say. Besides, Kate wouldn't listen. She was wild. She'd always been wild. Yet Eileen had forgotten that indisputable fact, when she tried to sort out the mess those two had got themselves into in their last year at school.

Was it possible that she could have been wrong about Kate and Jason? She thought of her husband Joe, and she frowned. No. She hadn't been wrong.

She'd only wanted to prevent Kate going through what she herself had gone through. All she'd ever wanted for Kate was for her to have a different life.

Picking up the tea things, she moved wearily to the sink and rolled up her sleeves to do the dishes. It hurt a bit. The plum-coloured bruises on her upper arm seemed to stare at her with reproach. Where had she gone wrong with Kate?

Eileen glanced at her watch. Joe would be home soon. Home from the pub, hot and heavy with the beer and the smoke. He'd been there since twelve, drinking and playing dominoes. He took the afternoon off every Friday, and it was always the same. She shuddered. She knew what was coming all right when he lurched home from the pub on a Friday afternoon. And he wouldn't be best pleased if Kate was around to disturb him.

Without realising what she was doing, she gripped one of the best rose teacups so fiercely that the delicate china broke in her hands. Eileen stared at the jagged pieces. At the blood on her fingers as it dripped slowly into the soapy bubbles of the washing-up water.

All she wanted was for Kate to get on, so that she could achieve something in life. So that she could have some freedom. Find the chance to be happy.

She herself was trapped in this world, but Kate didn't have to be. Eileen had saved her from all that. She'd given her the opportunity to make a different sort of future for herself. A future that Eileen had only ever dreamed of.

Kate trudged slowly up the heathered slope of Raddlestone Moor. She should have stopped for long enough to grab her walking boots or even her wellies, but as usual she'd acted first. Too impetuous, that's what Mum always said. Too impetuous for her own good.

She smiled. Already her hot temper was cooling in the quiet stillness of the moor.

Jason had called her his little savage. He'd pushed her mane of unruly, russet hair from her face, and looked into her fierce, green eyes.

'Don't ever let anyone tame you,' he'd said.

'I never will.'

And she'd believed it, because with Jason by her side she'd felt invincible. He was the school hero. Captain of the football team as well as the best fast bowler the school had ever had. And so much more besides . . .

Kate walked on. She had always come here to think. To be alone, and of course to be with Jason. They were only thirteen the first time they kissed. So many of their discoveries had been made together. And Raddlestone Moor was one of the few places in Ridley where you were free from those twitching net curtains and spying eyes.

She got to the top at last, only a little out of breath, and looked down on the village below, in the valley, sitting in the cleft of the heathered buttocks of the moor.

Ridley became even smaller when you were up here. The people more insignificant and even easier to laugh at, as they went about their business and everyone else's business besides. Not knowing they were being looked down on. Not knowing how tiny they were compared to all this. This was the real world – the world that mattered. Ridley was nothing. Its people were nothing. What did she care for any of them? Even her mother. Even her father – he was hardly aware of her existence – or so it seemed to Kate.

The breeze was whipping strands of auburn hair into her face, and then as she turned, streaming it out behind her. Kate hugged her arms against her windswept body, and looked around. The sky was darkening and the clouds drawing in. And in the distance she could see a figure climbing the hill towards her.

'Damn.' She spoke aloud. Wasn't Raddlestone Moor the one place around here you could count on being alone? Especially on a chilly December afternoon.

She was about to leave by a different path, when something stopped her. Some memory of a certain stride. So she waited. She stared at the figure. Tall and broad-shouldered. Blond hair, arms swinging. He was coming into focus.

'Jason,' she breathed. Was it possible?

She could run. There was time to run.

The thought was only a fleeting one. It was gone before she'd even considered it. Wasn't she supposed to be facing the past? And anyway, she was rooted to the spot, a silly smile fixed on her face, her heart thumping with terror and a crazy, wild exhilaration.

'Hi, Katy.' Only Jason had ever called her that. He stood in front of her, his cheeks flushed from the walk, but otherwise looking exactly like the Jason of two years ago.

'Hello, Jason.' She was surprised she could speak. Her mouth felt too dry to function. All this time of thinking about him, and here they were on Raddlestone Moor together once again.

'So how've you been?' He looked down, scuffing his boot on grass closely cropped by grazing sheep.

Did he care? She wanted to ask him, but he might run away again. 'Okay,' she said.

'How's college?' He still wouldn't look up at her.

'It's fine.' She stared at him, drinking every detail in, now that she had the chance. The photograph in her drawer at Ford had never done justice to the sexy droop in his smile, or the depth of his hazel eyes. He was still a lovely lad, was Jason. Almost a man now.

She looked away, a faint flush stealing on to her pale cheeks. Time seemed to have stopped, and here they were being buffeted by the wind on Raddlestone Moor, twittering away to each other like casual acquaintances with nothing else to say.

She couldn't bear it. There was so much to say. There had always been so much. She took a deep breath.

'What are you doing up here?' Had he been drawn here, as she had been drawn here, in contemplation of the past? Her eyes drifted to the small clearing behind the bushes where they had often made love.

For the first time, he looked up, following her gaze. A moment of understanding dawned. 'I thought I might find you.'

'Oh?' Her treacherous heart jumped.

'I heard you were back this weekend.'

They shared a swift smile. What you heard in Ridley had always been a mutual amusement. Until two years ago.

'And *I* heard about your girlfriend.' It just slipped from between her dry lips – this piece of bitterness.

His face and neck flushed red, and he pulled at the collar of his anorak as if it were choking him. Kate smiled a secret smile. She enjoyed making Jason feel uncomfortable. And it had always been so easy.

'Natasha? Yeah, well . . .' He fidgeted. 'It's been a long time.'

Yes, a long time. And now he had Natasha. Who was she? Was she blonde, cool and beautiful? And did he love her? Probably. Why had the gorgeous Jason Parker ever loved Kate Dunstan?

'What did you want to talk about?' It seemed to Kate that this was a conversation she'd played over in her head too many times for it to be actually happening.

'About why you're avoiding me.' The hazel eyes were earnest.

'I see.' What the hell did he expect?

Kate half-turned away from him, looking into the distance of Ridley and civilisation. She was irritated. She saw that she was making him nervous. And she suddenly remembered why the gorgeous Jason Parker had fallen in love with Kate Dunstan.

It was because she was the only one who had seen the vulnerability behind the hero. The one who had recognised the cracks in the mask. That's what Kate had found in him that the rest of them couldn't see. And that's what had ultimately let her down. His vulnerability. His weakness.

'I wanted to put things right between us. If I can.' He was so unsure.

Suddenly Kate felt strong enough to be honest. She'd always been strong with Jason. He had needed her strength to fall back on time and time again. She'd always been the leader.

She twisted round to face him, her eyes raw and open. 'It's too late to put anything right,' she told him. 'You can't change the past. I was crucified, Jason. It hurt. All of it hurt.' It still did, of course. But she couldn't quite tell him that much.

'Oh, Katy.' He reached out for her hands.

She waited for the shock of electricity that had always run constant between their fingertips, but it never came. She stared at him in disbelief. Jason had become some nervous stranger.

'It was terrible,' she admitted. She hadn't been strong then. She'd been weak and vulnerable and he'd never know how much she'd needed him. But he hadn't been there for her, had he? 'No one seemed to be on my side.' Not Jason. Especially not Jason.

She saw again the expression in his eyes just before he turned away from her two years ago. The one she had held in her mind ever since. His fear. His doubt. His betrayal.

'You'd better do what your mother thinks right, Katy,' he'd said. 'It's probably for the best.'

One word from him and she would have run with him to the end of the world so that she could have their child. So that they could stay together instead of being torn apart.

'But Jason . . . It's our baby.'

That's when he'd turned away. 'I'm sorry, Katy,' he said.

She walked from him then, too proud to plead, too proud to beg. And she did what he wanted. For the last time.

The wind on Raddlestone Moor was getting colder. Kate shivered.

'I'm so sorry, Katy.' Jason hung his fair head. 'About the baby.'

'Our baby.' Her eyes were hurting. She willed him to feel it too.

He nodded. 'They told me it was a girl.'

'I called her Justine.' Kate's voice softened. It had seemed important to give her a name – even for the few hours that she belonged to her.

'Justine . . .' he echoed.

She turned away. Hearing the name was hard. For too long it had existed only in her mind. 'They probably changed it. The people who adopted her.'

'Katy . . . We were so young, Katy.'

The tears were like acid on her cheeks. She couldn't reply.

They'd been up on the Moor when they first made love and up on the Moor when she first tried to tell him she was pregnant.

He had brushed it away like he tried to brush anything away that he didn't want to see.

'Don't be silly, Katy. You can't be. Just wait another week or two.'

Another week or two stretched into another month, and by the time she plucked up the courage to tell her mother, she was five months gone. Too late for an abortion. She knew even then that Jason wouldn't help her. She could see it in his eyes.

Perhaps Jason had only ever wanted a pretty face to make him feel good. Was Jason like that? The girl you dated in high school wasn't supposed to create complications. She was supposed to be worn on the arm like a middle-aged battle-axe might wear her handbag. This is attractive. This is useful. This is mine. Was that how it had been for Jason?

She couldn't cope alone so she had to tell her mother. And once Eileen knew, it was out of their hands. She swept Kate away to her brother's place in Scotland. Hid her from the world and from Jason too.

'I miss you, Katy.' Jason's comforting hands were on her shoulders. He was pulling her round into his arms. And she felt nothing. 'I miss you,' he repeated. 'You were always so strong.'

'I only seemed to be.' Her voice was a whisper. 'I wasn't really strong at all.' Not strong enough to cope with the voices of Ridley . . .

'She let him go too far.'

'She's up the spout, you know.'

'Nothing but a little tramp.'

And then Jason's mum. 'He doesn't want to see you.'

Jason, oh Jason. How could you have done this to me – let me go to a strange place to have our baby alone?

And now he was indulging in regrets. Now that it was much too late. Two years too late.

'I'm sorry, Katy. They said it was best to leave you alone. That it was the only way . . .' He dropped to his knees in front of her. His voice faltered. He looked up. There were tears on his face. He hadn't cried two years ago.

Kate stroked his golden hair, cradling his head and comforting him. Perhaps that was the way it should have been. She had always been his comfort-giver. She should never have expected anything in return.

At last he drew away, his eyes half-closed. He got to his feet, still holding her arms, drawing her closer as if he wanted to kiss her.

'But now you have Natasha.' She spoke gently. It was a shock to discover that she wanted to pass the responsibility of comfort on.

His face changed. He frowned. 'Yes. We get along okay, but . . .'

'Go back to her, Jason.' Now Kate was being strong.

'But it's not how it was with you and me, Katy.' He looked like a child deprived of an old and favourite toy.

Kate fought the urge to smile. She hadn't come here to smile. But that's what Jason had always been – a child. She just hadn't noticed before. Maybe he might grow up one day but she wouldn't be around to see it happen.

'Go back to her.' It had always been Kate telling him what to do. She should never have been surprised at Jason letting her down when she needed his strength and support. Why shouldn't he? Theirs had never been an equal partnership.

Still he hesitated. He stared at her, his hazel eyes unblinking. 'But we can still be friends?'

The father of her child. The child she gave away. The child she was forced to give away because all other choices had been taken from her. She had been handed another future – but did she want it?

'Yes, we can still be friends.' Now, they could. Now that their past was done with. But they never would be. They had shared too much.

He nodded, satisfied, squeezed her hand for one last time, and trotted off down the hill as if he knew she needed this time alone. Jason didn't really want her back. It would all be too complicated for Jason.

Kate watched him go. She was free of him. She always had been free of him, but only now did she realise it. Only now did she see that the loss she'd been mourning was the loss of the child, not the loss of Jason.

Mum was right – damn her. She would never have been happy with Jason. She would have looked after him at first, then she would have resented his weakness, and then she might even have kicked him. He'd have been like a dog worrying at her heels until she was mad with the irritation of it. Not the dog's fault. Not Jason's fault. Sooner or later she would have struggled to be free of him. And what of the child, then?

Kate closed her eyes and let a sad, sweet memory of Justine's face approach. Framed in her white crocheted shawl, Justine's sad, wrinkled old-lady baby face. Blue unseeing eyes grazing her heart with their innocence. Soft tiny fingers groping for touch. Grasping for life. Justine.

Kate's pale face was set and determined. She glared down at Ridley as if it were the enemy.

And in that moment in a peculiar kind of triumph, she put them into her past. Jason and Ridley. She divorced them from her new life – cut herself loose. She was free to look to the future. That future would never hold Justine. But there would be other pleasures. There was college. There were Stephanie and Hannah and a new world to belong to. She could take the first steps, but she was conscious of a sense of foreboding. Was she moving into a new future, or was it only the start of a new kind of pain?

5

'Hannah's late.' Stephanie Lewis-Smythe studied the expensive moon phase watch that her father had given her last birthday. She must stay calm.

Over the past three weeks she'd become used to Hannah being late, Hannah using lame excuses to break arrangements, Hannah spending every minute of her spare time in the company of Tom McNeil. And it was bugging her far more than she'd ever admit. So much for female friendship. When something in tight jeans and designer stubble came along, then that was the end of it.

'So what's new?' Kate hardly glanced up from the script she was studying.

'She promised to be here on time, that's what.' It was almost a wail. Stephanie flung back her dark mass of hair with irritation. 'It's my last chance to make any changes to this.' She shook her copy of the script in the air. 'My only bloody hope of getting it right. Honestly . . .'

Jumping to her feet, she began pacing the hall – long-limbed, with a hunted expression and pursed, angry mouth. 'I haven't even finished the set design. And as for the lighting plan . . .' She turned to face Kate, her eyes washed with fury. 'What's got into her? Doesn't she think we've got anything better to do than hang around here all day?'

Kate's green eyes widened in surprise. 'No point getting wound up about it.'

'I want to get wound up.' Stephanie pouted and lit another cigarette. She wasn't supposed to smoke in here but what the hell . . . She didn't care. When she felt this tense, it was smoke or explode.

'It's about time someone told Hannah that there are other people in the world besides Tom McNeil.' Damn Hannah. She knew how important this was for her.

Everyone working on the drama unit had to choose a scene from a play and direct a small production, with a month to cast it, rehearse, prepare stage directions and do a simple plan of the lighting, props and set details.

Stephanie's last essay had been shaky – she needed a decent assessment here, to pass the unit, and she'd explained all that to Hannah. But what chance did she have if her leading lady wouldn't even turn up for rehearsals? Face it, she didn't have a hope in hell. And she had something to prove. Because in their different ways, back home in Kent, they expected her to fail . . .

'You don't have to do this, my darling.' Daddy's voice, low and reassuring. The night before she first came to college. Even then he was trying to pull her back. Back into a security that had become sickly and destructive.

'I need to.' She couldn't look at him. He had so much power, so much money, so many people at his disposal, that he was hard to stand up to.

'But why, Stephanie?' Smooth and persuasive.

She closed her eyes. 'You wouldn't understand.'

'Try me.' His hands on her shoulders. The perfect father routine. Gentle discipline mingled with a whisper of freedom. Promises of enough money to live a good life, to never have to work for a living. Never make her own way, achieve anything that meant something. Really meant something, not handed on a plate.

'I need to do it for me. To . . . I don't know, prove something to myself.' Slowly she raised her dark head. Slowly her blue eyes met his blue eyes. She watched them cloud over. He didn't want to hear this.

'You don't need to prove anything,' he said. 'Look at you.' He turned her by the shoulders. Turned her so that she was facing the mirrored wardrobe. So many bloody mirrors in her room that she couldn't avoid seeing herself even if she wanted to.

She closed her eyes once more because it was the only way.

'You won't fit in there. They won't be your kind of people. Our kind.'

'No?' But what was their kind? Did this man, her father, know the slightest thing about what she felt inside?

'And let's face it, darling . . .' Tender. Tender loving care. Daddy's shelter. 'You're not used to that kind of regime. Halls of residence,' he scoffed. 'Writing essays, examinations. It was difficult enough for you at school. You don't need all that. You deserve more. You're an artist.'

'Am I?' She felt herself weakening.

'You need to have the freedom to dabble. And I can give it to you.'

She frowned. Dabble. That's all it was to him. Darling Stephanie and her little frivolities. Humour her and she's all yours. 'Can you?' Conversations with Daddy had this way of becoming one-sided. As if she couldn't even equal him with words.

'Look at yourself.' The voice was more insistent now. She couldn't refuse.

Slowly she opened her eyes. He was standing behind her, his hands pressing her down, making her his possession, owning her like he'd always owned her, like he wanted to go on owning her.

'You're beautiful.' His voice was husky now.

She trembled under those hands. What did he want from her?

'You don't need to prove anything to anyone,' he said. 'You're beautiful and you're my daughter. You can do whatever you like with the world. It's yours for the taking.' A smile of satisfaction spread over his handsome face.

'Mine for the taking,' she echoed. But bestowed by him. Always bestowed by him.

'That's right.' He removed his hands. A shaft of late evening sun highlighted the dark shadow of his jawline. The lines around his mouth were the marks of aggression, not laughter.

And just before he turned away, she saw it. The glimmer of triumph in his eyes.

'So I'm beautiful, am I?' She spoke each word with care.

He was at the door, his hand resting on the door knob. 'Remarkably so,' he said. Already he might as well have been out of the room in body, as he was in mind. Dealing with the next challenge, the next item on his busy agenda.

She sprang to her feet, took two paces forwards, until she was inches from her own reflection, her breath steaming the glass. Then she slammed her fist into the mirror, into the beautiful face he wanted her to see. It didn't even crack. The face that she hated. 'So bloody what?' She screamed into thin air. 'I'm beautiful and you've given me the world. So bloody what?'

Behind her reflection she saw only an empty space. She spun around, but he was gone. Tears filled her eyes, but she wouldn't cry. Not today. She flung more clothes in the suitcase on the bed. She had to break free from a past that was stifling her. Where her life was so intertwined with other lives that there was nothing left for herself.

She needed to branch out alone. Find her own way. 'I'm going,' she muttered. 'And you can't bloody stop me.'

The next day she took the train from Kent to Dorset, although she knew he'd ordered a Bentley to take her. What an operator he was. Sticking to the appearances of triumph, even in defeat. How could she turn up at teachers' training college, go to her new life, and the new world she'd chosen, in a white Bentley, for Christ's sake? He'd begged and begged her to at least take the MGB for her own use in Dorset, but he just didn't understand. She didn't want to be marked out as different from the rest.

Miles took her to the station. 'You're lucky to be out of here.' His eyes were hooded with misery.

She took his dark face in her hands. 'I'll be back.' Because of him she'd be back. Not for the dim distant memory of a mother who had never breathed love, only indifference. And not for Daddy who would suck the life out of her. But for her seventeen-year-old brother, she would come back. 'And you come to see me, d'you hear?'

His face lit up. 'You want me to?'

She kissed his cheek. 'Of course I do, dummy.' Her lips lingered on the warmth of his skin.

'I'll miss you,' she whispered, drinking in the scent of him. Little boy lost, was Miles.

'You wanted to go, Steffi.' The sulkiness returned, spoiling his young male beauty.

She sighed. She worried about Miles. 'It'll be your turn soon,' she said.

'Maybe.' His eyes were evasive.

He was still at school, doing A levels, still firmly under the parental thumb. But his future too, was in jeopardy. Daddy didn't want him to go to university. Daddy was scornful about further education of any kind. He already had his son's future mapped out – Miles should enter the family business and to hell with what Miles might want.

So Miles too must escape, before he was sucked into the undercurrent. And she didn't know whether Miles possessed the strength to make that vital leap. 'Take care.' She grabbed her bags and jumped gracefully on to the train.

'And you.' He looked up at her as she wound down the window and leaned out. The train hissed into life.

'Bye, Miles.' She blew him another kiss, and saw his reluctant smile. But the last sight of him was the look in his blue eyes. A look of deep and silent reproach.

What would happen to Miles now that she wasn't around to protect him from the full force of parental possession? It seemed to Stephanie that wherever she went, she was pulled into caring where it would be easier not to. And those that she cared for the most were the vulnerable, the ones that bruised so easily. Like Hannah.

Kate watched Stephanie, wondering what she was thinking. Her eyes were shuttered and distant, but there were signs of tension – her fingers fiddling nervously with the fringe of her suede bag and her pack of cigarettes.

'We could always start without her,' she suggested.

'There's no point,' Stephanie snapped. 'But where the hell is she?' She ground out the words, took one last drag and stubbed the cigarette end under a black leather boot.

'No prizes for guessing the answer to that one.' Putting down her script, Kate wandered to the window. The bleakness of the grey outside promised snow. She shivered. No sign of Hannah.

'She spends every minute with that creep.' Stephanie's words were laced with a scorn that made Kate wince. 'Every bloody minute of the day.'

'But not the night.' Kate turned, and they exchanged a glance of mutual understanding.

'Well, she wouldn't, would she?' Stephanie leaned forwards, tapping long fingernails on the wooden table in front of her. Her eyes narrowed as she looked into the distance. 'Isn't our Hannah pure as the driven snow?'

So it still rankled – what Hannah had said to Steph at the college dance. Her barely veiled accusations of easy morals. Kate wasn't surprised. Since her weekend in Ridley, the tension between the two of them had stretched towards breaking point. And Kate didn't even want to consider what that meant to their friendship.

'She won't stay that way for long.' Kate sighed. 'Not with a bloke like Tom McNeil.' At college, virgins were a virtually extinct species. If you were going with someone then you had sex. It was as simple as that.

Kate stared through the window, the glass steaming under her hot breath. Outside, students wandered across the stiff winter grass, rucksacks and bags slung over their shoulders. Heading to tutorial or lecture or back to one of the halls. Chatting, aimless, laughing at each other's jokes. College made you institutionalised, locked inside your own little world. It was scary.

'It'll soon be Christmas.' She spoke aloud, the words sounding like a pronouncement of doom.

Back to Ridley for three weeks of playing happy families. Of pretending that Christmases now were anything like they should be. Only the breath but not the touch of kisses on the cheek. While Dad got drunk down the pub, becoming more brutish and remote with every pint he swallowed, and Mum tried too hard not to complain.

'I don't want to think about it.' Stephanie sounded wistful.

'Why not?' Kate turned to face her.

'Because I feel like I'm drowning.' Stephanie's voice was low, and Kate would swear there was a streak of fear running through it. Her eyes were helpless as a child's as she looked up at her.

'Drowning?' Kate was confused. She wouldn't mind drowning in all that money. She wanted to offer comfort, but the resentment was eating at her sympathy, denying it any value.

'You wouldn't understand.' Stephanie's long body was curled foetus-like on the chair.

No, Kate didn't understand. She wasn't sure she wanted to understand.

'Living with my father is like eating too much candy floss,' Stephanie laughed, lightening the atmosphere.

'Oh yeah?' Kate was relieved to be back on familiar ground. All her intense conversations had been with Hannah, not Stephanie. Without Hannah there seemed to be some kind of balance lacking. As if Hannah were the bridge between them.

'Still, candy floss is better than a cold house and a frozen family,' she said.

'Is it?' The jewelled blue eyes bored into her.

'And you've got Miles. You're always saying how much you miss him.' She'd seen a black-and-white photo, and from what she could tell, Stephanie's younger brother was a beautiful male version of her. Another one who had it all.

Stephanie's expression changed once more. Not fear this time, but something Kate couldn't immediately catalogue.

'Yes, I've got Miles.' She lit another cigarette. 'But Miles is locked into it too. Families, guilt . . .' She eased herself off the chair, with a languorous movement and joined Kate by the window.

Families and guilt. Kate sighed. She knew all about that.

'Maybe we should spend Christmas together,' Stephanie murmured. 'It's just you and me now, Kate. We can kiss goodbye to Hannah.'

Kate frowned. She hated the thought of losing Hannah. And she didn't want change. She wanted their friendship to blossom, not just fall to pieces when the first man came along. 'Just 'cos she's seeing some bloke, doesn't mean we can't still be friends.'

'He's not just some bloke, darling,' Stephanie warned in a dark voice. 'Tom McNeil is a manipulating bastard.'

Kate wasn't arguing. But that wasn't the point. 'We can't give up on Hannah,' she said. 'It won't last.' Hannah wasn't lost to them – she would still remember the pledge of support they'd drunk to in Normandy. She had to.

'It doesn't look that way to me.' Stephanie gazed out of the window. Her expression was calm but Kate sensed the underbelly of anger resurfacing.

'He'll get bored with her.' How could it end any other way?

'Maybe not.' Stephanie's brow creased. 'Maybe Tom McNeil will end up falling madly in love with Hannah.'

'And maybe pigs can fly.' Kate's green eyes were scornful. 'You said yourself he's a manipulating bastard. You know that type as well as I do. Love them, leave them, and guess who picks up the pieces.'

Stephanie shrugged. 'Perhaps.' There was a look in her eyes as if she could see into the future. As if she knew what would happen to Hannah and Tom. To them all perhaps. And as if it saddened her.

An unknown fear snatched at Kate's heart.

Stephanie turned to face her. 'Why don't you come to us for New Year? We have quite a bash.'

'Oh, I don't know . . .' Kate hesitated. She wasn't sure that she was ready to be thrown into the bosom of Stephanie's upper-class family.

'It'll be wild.' Stephanie grabbed her hands, her face suddenly childlike with excitement. 'My lot will be bearable over Christmas if I know you'll be there soon. C'mon, Kate. Please?'

Her enthusiasm was utterly contagious. Kate grinned. 'Okay. I'd love to.' She experienced a moment of horror. 'But what should I wear?'

Stephanie giggled. 'You don't have to impress anyone, stupid. It doesn't matter. Anything. Whatever you like.' She tossed back her dark hair. 'And New Year's Eve will be fancy dress, it's traditional. But you don't have to worry – I'll fix you up. It'll be fun.' Stephanie was bubbling like champagne, and she was irresistible when she was in this mood.

Kate felt the buzz of adrenaline. A glimpse of another world. Stephanie's world. A world of glamour – well, it would be glamorous for a girl from Ridley. Music and dancing and lot of gorgeous rich men . . .

'Sorry I'm late.' Hannah's blonde head and repentant face appeared in the doorway.

The other two exchanged a look of understanding. It was impossible to be angry with Hannah.

'Forget it. Come on, now you're here.'

But Stephanie's wide smile faded, as the tall, lean figure of Tom McNeil followed Hannah into the studio.

Hannah hesitated. 'You don't mind . . . if Tom waits for me?' Her face was flushed and her dark eyes excited, but still her hand reached instinctively for his.

Insecurity. Kate glanced at Stephanie's set expression. How would she take this intrusion?

'And what if I do mind?' Stephanie's face was flushed too, but it wasn't with love. Her eyes were wild and angry as she strode to the table and began sorting out scripts.

'I won't interfere.' Winking at Hannah, Tom positioned himself by the door.

'Dead right you won't.' Stephanie moved towards him. Her blue eyes were cool, giving nothing away.

'Does it bother you?' He eyed her with lazy confidence. 'Me being here?'

Kate caught her breath.

For a moment the tension in the air was taut between them. Then Stephanie spun round on her heel.

'Oh, who bloody cares? Let's just get on with it.' Her voice became brisk and professional as Kate and Hannah took their places. 'From the start of the scene. Action please.'

But it didn't go well. The dialogue was more stilted than Pinter could ever have intended, Hannah kept fluffing her lines although she was reading from the script, and her wide brown eyes strayed far too often towards the figure in the doorway. Even Kate was finding it hard to concentrate with this particular audience of one. And instead of encouraging and easing them into the atmosphere of the play, Stephanie was shouting out directions like a demented sergeant major.

'Move downstage on that line, Hannah. I told you that before.'

'No, you didn't. The other day I was meant to walk across to the table . . .'

'What's the point of me directing if you won't listen to a word I say?' Stephanie's voice rose.

'Well, it's only a production for end of term assessment.' Hannah was peeved. She pushed a strand of fine, blonde hair behind her ear and frowned. 'It's hardly the West End.' She looked across at Tom and giggled nervously.

'For Christ's sake, Hannah!' Stephanie took a threatening step towards her.

'How about a coffee break?' Kate intervened swiftly. She jumped up, putting a wary hand on Stephanie's shoulder. She could feel her trembling.

With a sullen nod, Stephanie broke away from her and stormed into the store-room.

'I'll get it.' Hannah sashayed to the door, apparently oblivious to the tension in the studio. 'Give me a hand, Tom?'

But Tom was staring after Stephanie. 'I want a word with her.' He brushed Hannah's hand aside, and moved away.

'I'll help you.' Kate led Hannah outside. This was going from bad to worse.

'He'll calm her down,' Hannah said reassuringly, as they walked towards the coffee machine. She pulled some change from her bag. 'He's good at that.'

And I bet that's not all he's good at. But Kate didn't say it aloud. In the face of such blind devotion, she wouldn't dare.

In the store-room, which doubled as a dressing-room for performers, amidst the assorted props and wardrobe, with the smell of greasepaint clinging to her nostrils, Stephanie leaned against the wall and took deep, calming breaths. She could do with a puff of Ventolin. But this was crazy. She mustn't let him get to her like this. It was Hannah's life. She didn't need protecting. Let her make the mistakes and screw it all up. Why not?

Now where had she put her lighting plan? She'd left it in here earlier when she was working out which spotlights to use in her production, but it seemed to have disappeared. She put a hand to her brow. It seemed everything was against her today.

'Stephanie.' His voice was low.

Her eyes hardly flickered. She couldn't even say that she was surprised. 'What do you want?' She wouldn't turn and face him.

He chuckled. The sound had a malicious ring to it, and she shivered involuntarily.

'I might have some suggestions for you.' He moved closer as he spoke, until he was near enough for her to smell him. Patchouli oil. It didn't suit him one bit. He should be wearing oil of skunk or something.

She still wouldn't look round. 'I don't need your suggestions. I thought you said you wouldn't interfere.' She caught sight of the lighting plan, and picked it up gratefully with shaking fingers. What was he after? And if he was in here, then where the hell was Hannah?

Tom reached out to touch a costume hanging on the rail beside her. 'When are you having a dress rehearsal?'

'Tomorrow.' At last it seemed safe to turn and face him. 'Do me a favour and get Hannah here on time.'

He laughed, his gaze travelling the length of her tall, slim body, lingering on the curve of her breasts under the sweater.

Her eyes half-closed. She knew he was thinking of the night in hall when she'd stood naked at the window. Jesus, why had she done that? She didn't know what got into her sometimes.

'A favour? I'd do you a favour any time.' His meaning was unmistakable. 'Sweet Stephanie.'

'Very amusing, Tom.' As always she took refuge in scorn. Scorn was defiant, but it would be a hell of a lot easier to be defiant if she weren't trapped in a store-room with him. He had some nerve. But she must stay calm. She wouldn't so much as blush. She mustn't give Tom McNeil the satisfaction.

He laughed again, softly this time. 'You shouldn't be so proud. Hannah says you've been having problems with your lighting for this little production of yours. Is this the plan?' He moved closer, his body almost touching hers, as he leaned to peer at the drawing. Too close.

She nodded, her fingers numb, clamped on the piece of card.

'Do you want me to take a look at it? I remember my first attempt was a right cock-up.' His voice was low and caressing. His hand brushed ever so gently against hers.

62

'I told you. I don't need your help.' She was still shaking and she hoped to God he couldn't feel it. Because it was here again – this treacherous animal of arousal, snaking its way around her groin. What the hell was the matter with her? Would she never escape it?

He put a hand on her arm. It felt hot, even through the thick Aran she was wearing. 'Are you sure?'

Stephanie stared at his hand, her entire body rigid. She forced her eyes to meet his – the heels of her black leather boots had given her the extra inches she needed, to be exactly the same height as Tom McNeil. 'I'm sure,' she said. She looked down at his hand again. Waiting.

'Have it your own way.' His hand dropped impotent to his side. He grinned, as if he'd been playing a game with her. Teasing and torturing. Then he turned, and in a moment he was gone.

But Stephanie knew how much he wanted her. And all she could think about was Hannah. Poor, poor, foolish Hannah.

It took her a good five minutes to recover her composure and go back into the studio. By the window, in profile, she saw Kate – her pale face set as she stared towards the doorway. Her green eyes were narrowed, and her mouth turned down with distaste.

Stephanie followed the direction of her gaze. In the doorway, Hannah and Tom were kissing as if they were alone in the world.

'For Christ's sake.' She flung the lighting plan on the table. The man had no morals. Her eyes glittered as Hannah and Tom broke apart to stare at her.

His expression was questioning and innocent. So was Hannah's.

'Steph? What's up?' Hannah had no idea. She just had no idea.

Stephanie could feel it rising – anger and frustration, hot and crazy inside her, like some forgotten passion. 'Let's leave it till tomorrow.' She bundled her stuff haphazardly into her bag, slung it over her shoulder, and strode to the door, practically pushing them out of the way. She glared at Hannah. 'And this time, for pity's sake, make sure you leave him behind.'

Hannah watched helplessly as Stephanie stalked down the corridor, the heels of her leather boots click-clacking a path away from her. And she felt she was losing something, although she wasn't sure what it could be. She knew Stephanie was angry with her – but she didn't know why.

Moments later, Kate too was gone, her expression noncommittal and her eyes downcast.

Hannah turned to Tom. 'I ought to go after Steph. She's upset.' She wavered, torn between claims of a friendship that had become rickety since the college dance, and the mocking light in his eyes.

'What's she got to be upset about?' Tom demanded. 'She's only jealous.'

'Jealous? Stephanie?' It was hard to imagine. When someone had as much going for them as Stephanie, what on earth was left to be jealous about?

'Innocent little Hannah Thompson.' His hand brushed casually against the softness of her hair, his thumb stroking her cheek. 'Isn't your friend looking for love?'

Hannah was doubtful. 'Maybe, but . . .'

'And you've gone and found it without even trying.' His voice rang with confidence. His smile made her melt. 'We've found it.'

It was a confidence Hannah needed more than anything. But there were still other claims on her loyalty. She shouldn't have brought him here today. But Tom had this way of making all her doubts seem silly.

'Why on earth should she mind me being there?' he had demanded. 'Isn't a play supposed to have an audience? And besides, I might be able to lend a hand. I went through it last year, don't forget.'

'But I don't know whether Stephanie . . .'

'Don't be silly, Hannah.' His voice rebuked her. 'You're being childish. You're not ashamed of me, are you?'

What choice did she have? Hannah allowed him to persuade her against her better judgement, and now she was paying the price. The pain in Stephanie's eyes – that was the price. No matter what she'd done, no matter what they were all saying about her, she was still her friend. And like Kate had said – you should stick up for your friends. That's what mutual support was all about.

Hannah pulled away from him, her eyes already distant. 'I'm going to find her.'

'Hang on a minute.' This time his hands were rough as he tugged her back.

She frowned.

'That's exactly what she wants, isn't it?' His face was very close to hers, his fair skin smooth as a child's until it reached the angular jawline.

'What do you mean?' She stared at him, knowing she should go.

Tom clicked his tongue impatiently as if she were being particularly dense. 'She wants to dictate your life, Hannah. Can't you see that? She wants to have you running after her every minute of the day.' He sighed. 'Don't let her get away with it.'

'Get away with it?' She was mesmerised.

'With thinking she can behave like a spoilt little rich kid whenever she feels like it.' He spread his hands. 'C'mon, Hannah. I didn't say anything to upset her. I offered to help her. What more could I do?'

She hesitated. 'Well, nothing I suppose. But . . .'

'You've got to let her see that I mean something to you, Hannah.' Tom was making it a test. His voice was urgent, a hot whisper in her ear. 'It's the only way she'll ever accept me.'

Was he right? He'd seen so much more of the world than she had, and he seemed wise in a way that eluded Hannah. She rarely attributed dark motives to anyone.

She wavered, her skin rapidly turning to goose-flesh. He was so close, and the air was layered with the unspilt passion between them.

'And I do mean something to you, Hannah. Don't I?' A sudden shy note in his voice. She wanted to cradle his fair head against her breast. Watch her tears stain his skin until he could feel her fear.

She sank into his arms. 'Of course you do, Tom. You know you do.'

As she raised her face towards him, open and submitting, he bent his head to kiss her lips. Gently at first and then with an abrupt and rising longing, that shot past him and entered Hannah like a flame. Licking her with a breathless kind of passion that shocked her.

Meanwhile, she was off-guard, and his hand was creeping under her sweater.

'Tom . . .' She put her hand over his, stopping its passage towards her aching breasts. 'Not here.' Her words hung in the sudden distance between them.

'Where then?' His voice was thick.

She pulled away, the fear slithering through her veins, chasing away desire. 'Nowhere.' She hung her head. 'Not now. Not yet.'

The lines of his lean face became harder, his eyes cold. He turned from her, as if she were a stranger. 'You don't love me then.' Almost spitting the words.

Before she could reply, Tom was striding down the corridor, in the opposite direction to the one Stephanie had taken. He called out to her over his shoulder. 'So go after her, why don't you? What the hell do I care? It's pretty obvious how unimportant my feelings are.'

She ran after him, her heart thumping so hard that it seemed to be punching through her rib-cage. She'd never seen him like this before. 'I do love you, Tom.' She clung to his arm.

'I don't think I want your kind of love, Hannah.' He shook her off, his pale eyes indifferent to her distress. 'You're cold as ice, you are. You don't give a shit about pleasing me. About my needs.'

Why was he doing this? Why was Tom trampling on what had been so special? She couldn't reply. She could only look at him with utter misery in her brown eyes.

He seemed to soften. 'Can I help it if I want to touch you?'

She shook her head. This was out of her control.

'You're enough to make anyone go a bit crazy.' At least he'd stopped walking. And there was no one in sight.

She stood on tip-toe, threading her fingers through his hair. 'You just have to be patient with me, Tom,' she pleaded. She wouldn't be pushed into this. Not even for Tom. She couldn't be.

'But for how long?' His expression changed as if he were thinking of someone else, his eyes glazing with the memory of some past passion.

Hannah shuddered at the spear of jealousy that darted through her. Tom was her first love, but of course there had been many others before her, for Tom. So many others like Dian Jones with their sultry sexiness and easy sensuality. She could never be like those girls.

And even if she could bring herself to go to bed with him, to give in to this serpent-like desire that tempted her in his kiss, wouldn't she only disappoint him? How could she live up to those that had gone before her? And how long would it be before Tom left her? Left her for one of those girls whose eyes followed him unrelentingly around the campus. How could she compete with what they were offering him?

'I can't tell you, Tom. But if you won't wait for me . . .'

He was silent.

'I should be getting back to Ford.' Hannah felt drained and lost. She'd been a fool to imagine that there could be love between herself and Tom McNeil. They were too different, worlds apart.

He put out a hand to stop her. 'I'm renowned for my patience. I'll wait for you, Hannah. As long as it's not for ever.' His eyes were suddenly smiling again. 'Friends?'

Hannah blinked, trying to take it in. 'Friends.' She nodded. But the relief didn't seem quite real. She sensed that it was only a superficial dusting. The dread still lay heavy on her heart.

'That's my girl.' He slung an arm around her shoulders, and they walked on side by side. His warmth seemed to soak deep into her flesh. She loved the feel of it – his arm possessing her.

'Do you forgive me?' he murmured, teasing her.

'Oh yes, Tom.' Hannah knew it was her fault. She was frigid, wasn't she? She didn't know how to open up. She needed to trust, she was aching to trust. But trust was elusive – it hid around corners and refused to come out and be counted.

He grinned. 'Then prove it by spending Christmas here with me.'

Hannah's stomach dipped into panic. 'Oh, I couldn't do that, Tom.' Mother and Dad would go crazy. She couldn't think of it. Midnight Mass was the highlight of their year. They were lip-service Christians – only bothering with church at Christmas and Easter. There would be carols around the glitzy silver of the artificial tree. Mother couldn't stand pine needles on the carpet. No presents until after the Queen's speech. A small sherry before lunch and a small port to finish.

'Why not?' Tom's voice was casual, but she knew she'd let him down. Again. How could she explain about her life, her parents with their narrow conventions and obsession with the done thing?

'It's Mother and Dad.' She sighed. 'You don't know them. It would be the end of the world if I didn't make it home for Christmas.' She tried to laugh it off, but it was there between them. Another barrier to happiness.

He shrugged. 'You'll be missing a ball.'

'How do you mean?' The fear sliced through her. She hated that tone in his voice.

'We have a good time here at Christmas. Not to mention New Year.' He laughed. 'There's a whole heap of us who can't face the folks at Christmas – all that turkey and crackers and pretending to have a good time.'

Hannah nodded miserably.

'So we stay here instead, get drunk and have parties. It's cool.'

Her eyes narrowed. 'And is Dian one of the girls who don't go back home?' This jealousy was threatening to take her over. She loathed it, looming obscene and ugly above her, but she couldn't stop it. It went hand in hand with her feelings for Tom.

'Dian?' His expression was all innocence. 'I dunno. Maybe. Does it bother you?'

She wanted to scream. Yes, it bothers me. Of course it bothers me. I've seen the way she looks at you as though she wants to rip all your clothes off. But she couldn't say it. She couldn't say any of it. What right did she have? She wasn't sleeping with him herself, now was she? 'Of course it doesn't bother me.' Who was she trying to kid?

He laughed again, and this time she hated the sound, almost hated him as if that were possible.

And at that moment they came to the main gates. Royal Ford was one way, his flat the other. Different directions for Tom and Hannah.

He held her for only a moment, his lips brushing against her hair. 'See you tomorrow, Hannah.'

Nothing about tonight. She was supposed to be working but she would have put it off for Tom. It would give her a chance to spend some time with Stephanie and Kate, but she would have put that off for him too. More fool her. She hardly remembered the pain in Stephanie's eyes that she'd wanted to understand, to heal. Already it was out of her mind. Her mind was full of Tom McNeil.

'Okay.' Her sad eyes met his. Why did it feel like he was punishing her? Punishing her for not giving him what he wanted. Did that mean she had lost him?

When he was out of sight Hannah took to her heels and raced across the car park, towards the road that led to Ford. Tears were clinging to her face as she ran into the wind, but most of all there was anger in her heart. Anger with herself and anger with Mother and Dad. The people who had asked too much of her. The people who had cast her into the role they had created for her. Who had made her what she was.

6

'You've been very quiet all week.' It was a definite criticism. Jean Thompson paused mid-row over the fawn pullover she was knitting, in order to survey her daughter.

Hannah fidgeted under the scrutiny. 'I've been thinking.' What an understatement that was . . . Since the end of term, since leaving college and West Dorset – the place that held the man she loved, she'd barely stopped thinking. Terrifying thoughts and fears scuttling through her head at every opportunity. Mad elation followed by desolate foreboding. My God, Hannah had written ten poems in a week and thrown every one of them in the bin. This was making her crazy.

On Christmas Eve, when people everywhere were celebrating, Hannah had cried alone in her narrow single bed. Past midnight – and what was Tom doing? Was he at one of those parties he'd taunted her with? Dancing with Dian perhaps? Holding her body close to his, as he had held Hannah's? Whispering the same kind of promises?

And on Christmas Day, as she pulled crackers with Mother and Dad – who read out jokes with poker-straight faces – she remembered his words and moaned silently. If only she'd been brave enough to accept his offer. He'd wanted her. She could be there with him now, instead of sitting here being cross-questioned by Mother.

Her frown drilled into Hannah. Could she read her mind? She flushed at the thought. Her mother had always been good at making her feel transparent.

'Are you eating properly?'

'Of course I am.' Half the time she didn't even notice what she was eating. There were more important things to think of. Like Tom. She smiled.

Jean's sniff was delicate and yet conveyed a wealth of meaning. 'And are you keeping up with your work? College isn't supposed to be some sort of playground, you know.'

'Yes, Mother.' Hannah's reply was automatic. Words ingrained since childhood. That's what her life here consisted of. A life of 'Yes Mother, no Mother,' with nothing in between.

Jean resumed her knitting. But there was a new suspicion in the tightness of her hold over the knitting wool. 'How can I keep an eye on you when you're so far away? How can I make sure you're . . .' She glanced round, as if to check that Dad hadn't slipped back into the room without her noticing.

No chance. Hannah guessed that he would be having a crafty smoke down by the garden shed. Once he'd got away from the firing line he wouldn't be hurrying back for the next round.

She was impatient. 'Make sure I'm what?'

Jean pursed her thin lips. 'Behaving yourself, of course.'

Hannah stared at her angular face, at the eyes that had become invisible of emotion under the thick lenses of her glasses, and at the fair greying hair scraped into an uncompromising permanent wave that was dry and scratchy as sandpaper. To her annoyance, she could feel herself colouring once more.

'What on earth are you on about, Mother?' Her tone was haughty, but the words were too late in coming.

'Hannah Thompson!' Jean swooped like an eagle. The knitting was discarded. She stood up. She was a tall woman, who towered over Hannah like she towered over most people. Especially poor Dad.

Hannah became flustered. She bit her lip. 'What? What did I say?'

'What have you been up to, would be more to the point, my girl.' Her mother's grip was pincer-persistent as she pulled Hannah to her feet. 'Out with it now. You can't fool me. Never have and never will.'

Hannah tore herself from the hands that held her. The only time that Mother ever touched her now. Where had all the kisses gone? Where were those sweet hugs of childhood that she thought she could remember? Had they never existed after all? She drew herself up to her full five feet three. 'I haven't done anything,' she said with defiance.

Jean peered at her, disbelieving. 'The truth now?'

'I haven't done anything to be ashamed of,' Hannah elaborated, not meeting her gaze.

Her mother's eyes narrowed. 'Perhaps I should be the judge of that.'

It was all too much. Hannah knew that she'd had enough of her. Resentment overcame even fear and domination when the tower was built high enough. 'For heaven's sake, Mother,' she snapped. 'Just leave me alone.'

She hardly noticed the jaw dropping with amazement. Hardly thought of the bully's reaction when a victim stands his ground. She brushed past her and flung open the door.

'Where are you going?' Jean's voice was strangely thin and unsure.

'Into the garden.' Hannah couldn't even look at her. Her head was pounding. 'I need some fresh air.'

Gordon Thompson was leaning on the shed, staring into the night. He jumped guiltily at the sound of approaching footsteps, and then relaxed. 'Oh, it's you, love.'

'Honestly!' Hannah was seething. 'She drives me bonkers.'

'What's she been saying?' Her father sucked on his pipe with obvious pleasure. The fragrant scent of the tobacco filled the air, before drifting off into the night. It was mostly quiet in this part of Sussex, although it wouldn't be quiet for long if they built the by-pass that was being talked about. But in the meantime it was a peaceful landscape, the outskirts of a village backed by the South Downs on one side and yet barely two miles from the sea.

'She thinks I've been up to no good,' Hannah laughed nervously. What would Tom say if he could hear that? Would he appreciate the irony? Probably not, at this moment in time. Things had cooled between the two of them during the last week of term. He had seemed abstracted, otherwise involved. And Hannah knew only too well that there was only one way she could really get through to him.

'And have you, lass?' Dad's kind brown eyes were very like her own. She took his hand.

'No, I haven't.' She paused, wary even with this man who wouldn't hurt a fly. 'It's true that I've met someone, though.'

Gordon patted her hand. 'Someone special, love?'

Hannah nodded. How could she tell him? So special that she couldn't say Tom's name without an intake of breath. So special that to feel his touch was to take a first tentative step into paradise. So special that to be apart from him like this – with their last argument still standing between them – was a physical pain hard to bear.

71

'Have you told her?' Gordon nodded towards the brightly-lit house. The outside of it was as neat a facade as its immaculate interior. Not a broken plant pot or a stained brick spoiled the perfection. And inside the house of her childhood not a crumb would mar the carpet. Dust was given no settling time there.

Hannah shook her head. 'Not yet.' She gazed around the shadows of the small garden. Grass like a bowling green and earth freshly dug. Mother wouldn't have it any other way. 'How do you think she'll take it?' she ventured.

'She won't be too happy.' Gordon frowned. 'You know your mother as well as I do. But she might come round in time.' He shot his daughter a searching glance. 'If it lasts that long.'

She sensed that he was warning her to be cautious – at least it was as close as Dad would ever come to a warning. Why rock the boat? Does she really need to know?

'If it lasts that long . . .' Hannah's stomach dropped with the weight of the fear. No. She couldn't imagine it over. It had hardly begun. And yet Tom had been so unloving, so cool. Something had to change . . .

Gordon carefully tapped the ashes from his pipe into the metal bin by the shed. The sound reverberated around the dark, moonlit garden. 'She's all right, your mother,' he said. 'She just worries too much.' There was a kind of desolate protection in his gentle eyes. A kind of need to be guardian over the wife who bullied him. Hannah could hardly believe it.

She stared at him. His face was in the shadows once more, telling her nothing. How could he speak up for his wife after the way she treated him? Hannah had been watching for years, watching a kind, ineffectual man have the life drained out of him by a dominating woman. She'd seen many a humiliation that had made her squirm – but there must have been many she'd missed.

He caught her eye. 'I know what you're thinking, love,' he said. 'But take my advice. Don't assume everything's the way it seems.'

Hannah smiled. He loved Mother. Dad really loved her after all she'd put him through. And somehow, despite everything, that thought cheered her. His loyalty against all odds gave her a warm feeling as she stood there shivering in the night. Tomorrow was the last day of the year. Soon it would be time for a new beginning. Would 1976 herald a beginning for Tom and Hannah? Or had their story come to an end so soon?

They linked arms as they wandered back to the house, and Hannah felt

close to him in a way she rarely had before. That was Mother too –
keeping them apart, getting in the way of any father-daughter friendship
that might have a chance of developing. What was Mother so afraid of?
Couldn't she get any answers from this man who loved her?

'Why does she worry about me so much?' Hannah asked. 'She's not
just trying to protect me, is she?'

She felt him stiffen. Felt some barrier separate their new-found
friendship. 'I can't tell you that. You'll have to ask her.' He blinked as if
even these small words represented some betrayal.

They reached the back door and trudged into the kitchen with bright,
cold faces.

Jean was making coffee. 'Wipe your feet, you two,' she snapped.

Father and daughter exchanged a quick smile.

'Has she told you?' Jean spun around and moved towards them. There
was a wildness in her eyes, but her voice was perfectly calm.

'Told me what?' Gordon looked up, and Hannah registered the guilt on
his mild face.

Poor Dad. He'd never be able to stand up to her. He didn't have the
guts, or maybe he was too afraid of losing her. When it came to the crunch
he'd always hide his head in the sand. That's why Dad was still only
deputy manager in the small branch of the bank, despite Mother's
ambition and thinly-disguised contact-making. That's why the poor man
had to go outside to get a smoke, so that he wouldn't taint the pristine
cleanliness of the house they existed in. That's why he'd been dragged
from his Northern working-class background into a world where he didn't
know his way around.

'Told you what she's been up to, of course.' Jean glanced from one to
the other as if it were a conspiracy. 'I know there's something. I can read
you like a book, young lady.'

Hannah stepped forwards, a challenge in her dark eyes. 'Yes, I've told
him.'

'Have you now?' Jean glared at her, hostile, her hand lifting as if she
wanted to strike out, before twitching, and falling to her side. 'Out with it,
then.'

'I've told Dad because he makes an effort to understand.' She stayed
still, straight and brave. Perhaps it was becoming easier to stand up to her
mother at last. 'He doesn't condemn me. He doesn't make me feel that
I've committed some sin.'

'What sin?' Jean's voice was low. She still seemed in total control.

'There is no sin, Mother.' Hannah tugged off her duffel-coat and threw it on the back of a chair. Her voice was cold. 'That's exactly what I mean. You're jumping to conclusions. You always do. All I've done is go out with a boy from college a few times. That's all.'

There, it was said. Part of it at least. Hannah breathed deeply, thankfully, as some burden slipped from her shoulders. And yet it hardly summed up the relationship between Hannah and Tom.

'That's all?' The words echoed around the white antiseptic tones of the kitchen walls. Jean sat down in the chair, her mouth crumpling. 'That's just the beginning, my girl.' Instinctively, she smoothed the creases from Hannah's coat. She shook her head. 'You little fool.'

Suddenly scared, Hannah looked around for her father, but he'd disappeared. They might be friends, but his friendship obviously had well-defined boundaries. She was alone, so she had to fight alone. And she knew she had to fight. There was no backing down now. She had to be strong.

She folded her arms in front of her. 'Why am I a fool? What's wrong with going out with boys? I'm not a child. Don't you want me to find a man to love? To get married some day? Don't you want me to be happy?'

Jean's harsh, hysterical laughter filled the air between them. 'Happy? Do you think men make you happy?' She rose from the chair and came closer, until her face was inches from Hannah's own.

Hannah didn't flinch, although she longed to run. Although her mother's freesia perfume was filling her nostrils, almost making her retch. Her gaze was fixed on the powdered nose, the delicately rouged cheek. The doll-like perfection of a face that was old enough to know better.

'A man might make a woman happy. Why shouldn't he?' The right man. A man like Tom. Hannah stood her ground. But something told her that her mother was close to saying too much. And Hannah was scared of hearing too much. Even if it was something she should have heard a long time ago.

'They don't.' Jean's voice was a hiss of misery and bitterness. 'Take it from one who knows. Then perhaps you won't be disappointed.'

Hannah thought of Stephanie, and her heart started beating faster. What was it that had created such bitterness in these women? Where had they gone wrong? Why did they seem to hate men? She'd always been scared

74

of men. But never had she experienced this hatred. 'It's my life, Mother,' she said staunchly. 'I have a separate life to lead. I can't be tied to you for ever.'

'All right, my girl.' Jean grabbed her by the shoulders with sudden violence. 'If it's your life – then you go and make a mess of it.'

Shocked, Hannah drew back from the distorted mask that was nothing like her mother's face.

For a moment Jean stood motionless. Then she swung away from Hannah, her steps slowing as she moved robot-like to the drainer, picked up a cloth and started wiping down surfaces.

Hannah stared at her. 'Mother?'

Jean smiled. 'You go and get yourself whatever reputation you choose,' she said. She rinsed the cloth carefully under the tap. 'Only just remember that I brought you up to be a nice girl.' She draped the cloth out to dry, and twisted round to face Hannah once more. 'So unless you behave yourself, you'll be no daughter of mine.'

'Mother,' she pleaded. Why was she doing this?

'It's dirty, Hannah.' Jean Thompson moved closer, gripping the back of the chair. Her knuckles were blue-white with tension. 'It's dirty. And it's dangerous.'

'Shut up.' Hannah put her hands over her ears. She wouldn't listen. 'Shut up,' she screamed.

'Just remember that, Hannah.' Jean had regained control. Her mouth had reformed into its perpetual thin line, and her colour returned to pale powder-pink. 'There's only one reason to put up with . . . with *that* kind of thing . . .' Her lip curled.

She couldn't even say the word, Hannah realised.

'And that's if you want a child. If you've got anything else in that dirty little mind of yours, you might as well forget it right now. Because you'll hate it. You were meant to hate it. Nice girls always do.'

Stephanie came to meet Kate at the station. She was driving an open-topped navy blue MGB, her raven-black hair streaming in the wind.

Kate's eyes opened wider. 'I didn't know you had a car.'

Stephanie jumped out gracefully, kissed her, took her case, and threw it into the back. 'I haven't, darling.' She pulled a face and climbed back in. 'It's one of Daddy's little toys. Great fun to drive though.'

Kate got into the passenger seat. She didn't want to admit that she'd never ridden in a low slung sports car like this before. Stephanie would laugh, and Kate couldn't bear that. She was nervous enough about coming here as it was. Usually, self-confidence came easy. But Stephanie's world was too alien, too tempting. She changed the subject. 'How was your Christmas?'

Stephanie frowned. 'Grim. The price Daddy put on love was even higher than usual this year.' She laughed to soften the harsh words, but Kate could see the pain flickering once more in her deep blue eyes, and for a moment curiosity overcame trepidation.

'You don't get on with your father at all, do you?' What was it that Stephanie had said – that living with her father was like eating too much candy floss? It sounded far too sticky and sugary for comfort.

Stephanie took a left hand bend too fast. She glanced across at Kate. 'It's that obvious, is it?'

Kate grinned. 'Why don't you like him?'

'I love him.' She braked hard. 'But he's not easy to like. Or to get on with if you fancy keeping any life of your own. Daddy's into control.' She shivered.

Kate knew about people like that. 'What does he do for a living?' She leaned back in the seat.

She was enjoying this drive through the Weald of Kent. There was a kind of bordered formality to it, befitting its reputation as the Garden of England. They had left the main road and were covering the shaded leafy lanes dotted with the occasional squat tiled oast house and white windmill, at a rapid pace. Stephanie drove fast but with easy confidence, and although it should have been cold in an open topped car, even on a mild December day, it was glorious to feel the breeze buffeting through her auburn hair and stinging her skin. Excitement mingled with apprehension, making her forget the cold.

'He's a financial consultant.' Stephanie's tones were clipped. 'Top dog stuff. Excellent brain and even better connections.'

'Connections?' Kate couldn't understand her obvious bitterness. If Stephanie had been brought up in a council house in Ridley with a father who spent most of his time down the pub, and a mother eaten up with dissatisfaction, then maybe she might realize how lucky she was.

Stephanie swung the MG past wrought-iron gates into a driveway lined by ornamental yews and a mass of red-berried golden and green holly. 'Mother's family,' she explained. 'Old money and all that.' She laughed without humour. 'I expect Daddy had to have his name hyphenated just to get into one of their garden parties.'

Kate blinked. Not so much at her words, although they were mind-boggling enough, but at the sight of the house that had just come into view at the top of the drive. Atherington Hall was more like a mansion – all white facade and Georgian windows. 'Jesus wept!'

The tyres of the MGB screeched loudly on the gravel as they pulled up outside the front door.

'What's up?' Stephanie followed the direction of her gaze, squinting, as though trying to see it through Kate's eyes. 'It's not as bad as it looks.' She leapt out, all long legs and jeans, pulling Kate's case out of the car behind her.

'Not as bad . . .' Kate fiddled with the door release catch, and stumbled as she got out. She was unable to tear her eyes from the house in front of her. What was she doing here? She didn't belong in a place like this. This was another planet – not just another world. If she'd had any idea it would be like this, she never would have come.

'For heaven's sake, Kate.' Stephanie grabbed her arm. 'Stop mooning around. It's only a house.'

Only a house . . . Kate looked across the grounds. They stretched as far as the eye could see.

'It was Mother's, of course.' There was a strange sadness on Stephanie's beautiful face. 'In her family for generations.'

'Oh?' Kate knew that Stephanie's father was a widower but now her mind was reeling.

'It's well and truly Daddy's now.' Stephanie's voice was harsh. 'He got what he wanted, didn't he?'

'I'm sorry about your mother, Steph.' Kate put a hand on her arm.

But Stephanie shrugged. 'I hardly knew her.' She ran up the steps to the front door. 'Daddy's the only parent we ever knew.'

Kate followed her. It was true, then. Money wasn't everything. What use was a cold shell – even a beautiful and perfect shell – if there was nothing inside it?

They walked through the door, into an elegant mosaic-floored entrance hall. The white walls were adorned with Renaissance art, and a huge chandelier hung from the domed ceiling. 'This is unreal . . .' Kate's eyes followed the path of the winding staircase, up to the gallery on the first floor, where a tall and imposing figure looked down on them.

'Hello there.' The man ran lightly down the stairs with an athletic grace that reminded Kate of the girl by her side. He was so completely in place here, that she had no doubts regarding his identity.

'Julian Lewis-Smythe. And you must be . . . ?' He stretched out a hand, took hers and clasped it warmly. Kate got the impression that he knew only too well.

But he was very appealing. She blinked. 'Kate Dunstan.'

'Yes, or course. Welcome to Atherington Hall, Kate.' It was obvious where Stephanie got her looks from. Not only was he tall, with a muscular frame as well-proportioned as it was well cared for, but this attractive man had possibly the bluest eyes Kate had ever seen, a wide smiling mouth, and a shock of thick, black hair, with streaks of silver and grey.

'Thanks for asking me.' She smiled, trying to overcome her uncharacteristic shyness. It would be so easy to feel overpowered. This was all too much – this place, the people who lived here. She simply didn't belong. How on earth could she stay here for even an hour, let alone the three days she'd promised Stephanie?

'To tell you the truth,' his voice became deliciously intimate, 'it's a rare pleasure to meet one of Stephanie's friends from college.' Taking her arm, he guided her towards the stairs. His aftershave was understated and suited him perfectly. A man like this could hypnotise without even trying.

Kate attempted a smile, but her lips were clammy and stuck together.

'Sometimes I wonder what stories she tells you all about us.' His tone was warm and captivating. Charm oozed from every pore.

He didn't require a reply. Kate laughed as she glanced at Stephanie who was still carrying her battered case. Oh my God. Kate wanted to crumple with embarrassment as she noticed it. And as for the scruffy anorak and muddy plimsolls she was wearing . . . The warmth of his greeting had made her forget her appearance but now the shame flooded through her. She'd briefly considered making more of an effort – but Stephanie would have laughed herself silly.

Stephanie raised mocking eyebrows. 'They wouldn't believe the truth, Daddy,' she said.

The smooth firm hand stiffened on Kate's arm, and she glanced up at him in surprise. The tension between these two was undeniable. But he laughed, and the moment was gone. 'Such a sense of humour, my little girl,' he murmured.

His choice of words was not lost on Kate. And clearly not lost on Stephanie – whose face clouded with irritation.

Kate took a deep breath. She must say something or he'd think her an idiot. And for some reason she didn't want him to think that. She wanted to make a good impression, she realised. 'This is a beautiful house, Mr Lewis-Smythe,' she began, belatedly aware that she'd submerged her fast-fading Cheshire accent.

'Julian, please,' he beamed. 'The rest is such a mouthful, don't you agree?' But he looked as if he relished that particular mouthful. 'I'm glad you like the place. It's my absolute pride and joy.' He glanced at Stephanie. 'You must get my daughter to show you around. And you must have a drink. Stephanie will take you to your room.'

You must, you must . . . Control, Stephanie had said. Kate had the strangest feeling – as if his attention had wandered – or maybe it had never been there? As if he was so expert at making the right noises that he could play the perfect host without deliberate intent or thought. His last words gave this away. They indicated dismissal, and sure enough, he moved from her side, leaving her standing alone at the bottom of the stairs.

'C'mon, Kate.' Suddenly Stephanie was beside her, and she flipped back to reality. 'You can unpack your stuff, and then I'll treat you to a grand tour.'

It seemed to Kate as they wandered from room to room, that each one was more stunning than the last. And yet she'd be scared to sit down in any of the antique chairs, or touch any of the rich brocades. They moved from the well-stocked library beside Julian's study that was out of bounds, across to the dining-room on the other side of the hall.

Kate gazed out over the landscaped lawn. In the distance she could see two tennis courts, and an area enclosed by glass.

'The pool,' Stephanie supplied. 'Whatever the weather, Daddy does ten lengths every day before breakfast.'

Kate shivered. 'He's very brave.'

'Self-disciplined, more like it,' Stephanie corrected. 'That's why he's successful.' Her voice tailed off as if there was more she wanted to say. But she remained silent.

Kate watched her. She was quieter here, less self-confident in her own territory, as if her personality was actually eroded by this place. Or by her father, perhaps.

Kate followed Stephanie into the bright and airy lemon-painted sitting-room. 'You could live with someone here and never see them,' she commented.

'It does have that advantage.' Stephanie brightened. 'Come and see my studio.'

The studio was the only room that reflected Stephanie's personality. The only room that reflected any personality when Kate came to think about it. It was small, but well-lit by a French window leading to the garden. In one corner was a sofa-bed with a sleeping bag thrown across it, and in another was a rocking chair. A small record player surrounded by albums was on the floor. But the rest of the room belonged to the artist – it was cluttered with easels, high stools, tubes and trays of paints, pastels, chalks and dyes. And stacked with canvases everywhere.

Canvases daubed with bold bright colour – abstract art, cubism, stark geometry. Layers of collage, and naturalistic portraits too – of men working by the roadside, and people with weathered faces and oh-so-blue eyes playing boules in a French orchard. There was a rich vibrancy in the work that moved Kate, demanding total attention.

'Stephanie!' She wandered around, peering into corners, marvelling at the variety of medium and subject. 'I've never seen any of this stuff before.' She had only seen the pencil sketches Stephanie did at college, and last summer's prolific sketching in Normandy.

Stephanie bent to select a Bowie album, placing it carelessly on the player. 'It was France that really got me going,' she said. 'Especially Giverny and Honfleur. Since then I've hardly stopped.'

Kate smiled, remembering last summer.

'If it's good enough for Monet, then it's perfect for me,' Stephanie had said, the first time she saw the village of Vernon nestling on the bank of the River Seine. They'd had their first sight of it from the train, just like Monet himself had done. 'No wonder he wanted to live here.'

They braved the tourists to wander around the house and garden at Giverny, the riotous, seething colour that the artist had surrounded himself with, the tranquillity of his water garden, the elusive harmonies of light, colour, air and water. It was all here.

Stephanie's paintings acquired an impressionist slant – a way of looking at the world that still remained her own. And she painted the countryside, the sea and the people of the land she quickly grew to love.

'You never draw any of the tourists we show round,' Kate commented as she peered over Stephanie's shoulder once more, into the grizzled face of the bad-tempered Frenchman who owned the cafe in Les Marettes.

'Trappings,' Stephanie muttered. That remained her sole explanation, as her pencil skipped over the paper once more. This time it was the old lady who bought her baguettes from the baker down the street. She wore a scarf around her head, whatever the weather, and her small brown eyes peeped out of a face as wrinkled and brown as a walnut.

Kate knew that Stephanie and Hannah both saw something special in the people of Normandy and their countryside. Something that came to life in Hannah's poetry and in Stephanie's art. Something that reached out to Kate too, although she couldn't put it into the right words. It was in the simple earthiness of the Normans themselves, a pulse of life perhaps. A kind of crustiness that hid an inner strength, loyalty and warmth.

It was only now, looking at her work in this studio, that Kate began to fully appreciate what Stephanie might have seen in Normandy, and how different it was from what she lived with.

'I'm surprised you're bothering with college at all.' Kate's voice was husky and admiring. 'This stuff is good.'

'Not good enough to sell. Not yet. Not good enough to make my name. Or to make any money.' Stephanie tore her fingers through her dark hair. 'I've got a long way to go.'

Kate stared at her. What was she on about? 'Well, you wouldn't exactly be a struggling artist, would you, Steph?' Her outspread arms embraced their surroundings.

Stephanie coloured, either with anger or embarrassment, Kate wasn't sure which. 'But I'd be dependent.' Her voice was low. 'On him.'

Kate stared at her, uncomprehending.

'I'd be swallowed up by him.' Stephanie shivered. 'Don't you see? I'd never know if I could have made it on my own.'

Kate thought of Julian's mesmerising charm. She was beginning to understand Stephanie's problem. 'But does that really matter?' Her voice was gentle. After all, the man was her father. Wasn't he entitled to want the best for his child?

'It matters.' A strange intensity shone from Stephanie's blue eyes. 'I've got to do it alone.' She stroked one of the canvases thoughtfully. 'And anyway, I want to teach art. I want to give something back.' She hesitated. 'It's hard to explain, Kate.'

'I think I know what you mean.' Kate put an arm around her. At least she was trying to explain, for the first time since she'd known her, Stephanie was opening up, revealing a side to her that Kate had never guessed the existence of.

'I feel that I can do more for art this way.' There was a determination in Stephanie's expression, that Kate could only respect.

'I expect you're right.' She grinned. 'But all this money . . . It seems one hell of a shame to let it go to waste.' Her working-class roots were really coming to the fore now. It was obvious that she'd grown up where penny-pinching was a way of life.

'Money.' Stephanie's voice was loaded with scorn. 'It doesn't get you anything that matters, Kate.' Her eyes fired with intensity. 'I want to live in the real world, not in some wealthy insularity.' She flung back her head in a passionate gesture. 'I hate them, you know, the money people. It's different if you've worked for it. But those that just sit back and inherit – they're so flimsy and thoughtless. Little pieces of net you can see right through. They wouldn't recognise a real feeling if it hit them between the eyes. They're insipid. They don't care about anything that matters.'

Kate stared at her. In the background, David Bowie, alias a starman, alias Aladdin Sane, was singing about escape into fantasy.

Stephanie shrugged. They exchanged a glance of understanding, linked arms and together walked out of the studio which Stephanie carefully locked behind her. They stepped through an archway, and Stephanie opened a glass door that led into a green, leafy conservatory. It was resplendent with tropical colour, blooming cacti, and the sweet, heady scent of gardenias and stephanotis.

Lounging on a wooden bench was the most beautiful male specimen Kate had ever seen, and she saw Stephanie's expression change. That's when she knew. This was what she cared about. This was what mattered.

'Miles!' There was a breathlessness in Stephanie's voice, a new lightness in her step. 'This is Kate.'

He looked up from the book he was reading, a lazy scowl spoiling the perfect beauty. And Kate revised her opinion. He was attractive, yes, but there was a fragility about him that made him too frail to be masculine. While Stephanie's beauty had an earthy vitality about it, his face was white and drawn, the hand holding the book too thin and sensitive. 'Hello.' He smiled, but it played around his mouth and didn't touch his eyes.

'Be nice to her,' Stephanie warned. 'I'm going to make some coffee.'

She left them, and Kate was immediately desolate. Stephanie was her one link with reality in this place. She sat down cautiously.

'You're one of Steffi's friends from college, I suppose?' His voice was a not particularly pleasant lazy drawl.

Kate was irritated, her hackles rising at his tone. 'Sounds like you don't approve?'

He shrugged. 'She always goes her own way. It doesn't matter to her whether I approve or not. Whether any of us do.' His lip drooped sulkily.

Kate frowned. 'You miss her, I suppose.'

The eyes that gazed intently into hers for just a split second, were filmed with a raw intensity. 'What the hell do you mean?'

She drew back, shocked. 'Brothers and sisters aren't always close, are they? Sometimes they fight like cat and dog.'

He relaxed. 'It depends on whether or not they have to join forces against a common enemy.' His laugh was high, effeminate. Kate sensed the strain he was under, so close to the surface that he was almost crackling with nervous tension.

'Don't listen to him.' Stephanie came back with the coffee pot and three mugs on a tray.

The fragrance of fresh coffee filled the air, reminding Kate that after all, it was winter. Somehow in this luscious conservatory, it felt as if there was a summer's day waiting outside. 'Why not?' She grinned.

'He over-reacts.' Stephanie sat down, placing a hand firmly on his trembling arm.

Kate looked away, feeling superfluous.

'He'll be leaving here soon, won't you, Miles?' Stephanie's voice was gentle yet persuasive. 'A few failed A levels don't mean a thing. There's plenty of things you could do.' She pulled a pack of cigarettes and a lighter from her pocket, and lit one, inhaling deeply.

'You're not working, then?' Kate couldn't imagine it.

He barely glanced at her. 'I only left school last summer. I'm what you might call in limbo.'

'You need to get away from this place,' Stephanie muttered.

He glared at her. 'Maybe I can't.'

She sighed, blowing out the smoke. 'Maybe you won't even try.'

Kate looked from one to the other of them in confusion.

'I've got a slot being prepared for me,' Miles supplied, his voice sardonic and cold. 'It's not as easy as she thinks to get out of it. I've cried off until next April. But after that, I don't have any choice.'

'Prepared by . . . ?' Kate sipped her coffee, guessing the answer.

'By Daddy.' Stephanie's voice was bleak. 'I told you. He wants a finger in every pie. He calls the shots around here.'

'And we run.' Miles jumped to his feet. Every muscle in his slender body seemed to be straining at the leash. And there was a desperation in his eyes that touched her, although she didn't even know him.

She stared at the tropical greenery surrounding them. Glass on three sides. It seemed like a garden of Eden – and yet that was far from being the full story. These two made it sound more like a prison. As Ridley had been Kate's prison. Stephanie had made her escape, but she sensed that it was different for Miles. Already Miles had hopeless acceptance written on his face. Only time would tell. And Kate guessed that the answer lay in the not too distant future. But maybe for Miles, it was already too late for escape.

7

It was an hour till midnight. Another bloody New Year's Eve, and Tom was getting steadily drunk. Why had he let Dian drag him to this party?

'You can't stay here alone.' She had arrived at his flat at eight o'clock, handed him a bottle of white wine, and slipped off her coat. Underneath she was wearing a black halter neck dress reaching her ankles but slit to the thigh. The backless dress revealed the sheen of soft skin, the sensual curves of hip and breast. Her thick hair hung loose past her bare shoulders and she reeked of musky perfume and sexy promises.

'I wasn't intending to.' So what was he intending? Up to the last moment he'd kind of hoped that Hannah would walk in the door, but that was just living in cloud cuckoo land. Hannah had dealt with his coolness at the end of term in the same way she dealt with most things – with a sweet resignation that only made Tom more dissatisfied than ever.

'So what were you going to do? It's New Year's Eve, Tommo.' She laid a hand on his arm.

Get drunk. That's what he always did on New Year's Eve. Get drunk and remember that other New Year when the bubble had burst. When love had taken a dive into the nearest cesspit. 'I dunno.' He shrugged. 'Who bloody cares?'

Dian's hazel eyes darkened with passion. 'Come on, Tommo. I care. We were friends. Why can't it be like it used to be?'

'Because we became a hell of a lot more than just friends.' He twisted away from her.

'So what will you do tonight?' Her gaze was scornful, raking over him. 'Go down the pub and drown yourself in self-pity? Get pissed, pick up some little tramp and have such a sordid time that you'll regret it before you draw your first breath of the New Year?'

He laughed. She had this way of nudging too close to the truth. And a way of reminding him how alike they were. 'It's over for us, Dian,' he told her.

She found a corkscrew and opened the wine, pouring herself a glass and handing him the bottle. 'Don't flatter yourself, Tommo. I've got other fish to fry.'

'Oh, yeah?' His interest quickened. 'And who would that be?'

'Come to the party tonight and you'll find out,' she teased. Her laughter bubbled like the wine. 'It's not a college do. There'll be new people for you, Tommo.' She moved closer, her fingers on the collar of his shirt, her sharp nails grazing the skin every so lightly.

She was turning him on. He looked away. 'What makes you think I want new people?'

She smiled. 'Because you get bored so easily. We both do. I know you, Tommo. You might think you want little Hannah Thompson. But if she came across for you, you'd be running in the opposite direction within a month, bored out of your tiny skull.'

He watched her, hot and silky with her clever tongue and her witch's eyes. Slowly, deliberately, he dipped his finger in her wine, and traced a pattern of wild baptism on her brow. 'Whose party is it?'

She smiled in triumph. 'His name's Steve.'

'Steve?' he mocked. 'Where did you find him?'

Dian reached out to tuck his fair hair away from his eyes. 'A pub in Dorchester.' She paused. 'Not jealous, are you, Tommo?'

She was so close that he wanted to grab her by those beautiful bare shoulders and crush her against him. 'Who, me? Jealous? What do you think?'

'I think if you're not jealous then you don't have a reason not to come along,' she purred.

He took her face in his hands, bending towards her. 'Okay, Dian,' he murmured. 'I'll take you to the party. But if I end up asking you back here, say no.' He paused, wanting to kiss her. 'Do we have a deal?'

Slowly, she licked her lips. 'Of course I'll say no, Tommo. Like you said, it's over.'

But with a belly full of beer, watching Dian squirming gently in the arms of the gorilla called Steve, it was hard for Tom to accept that she was not his any more. That he couldn't take her or leave her, as it suited him. There wasn't a girl at the party who had half of what came to Dian so naturally. And the more he watched her supple, dark body being pawed by the gorilla, the more he wanted her.

A Roxy Music number was on the stereo. Bryan Ferry's delivery was stylish and sexy. The gorilla called Steve had tried for Ferry's GI look and failed miserably.

Tom laughed into his beer. The fragrance of grass was in the room. Grass and sweat, tobacco and beer.

Eventually Tom lurched over to them. It was eleven-thirty. 'For old times' sake, baby?'

The gorilla frowned, but Dian smiled, turned towards him and sank into his arms. 'You're drunk.'

'And you're stoned.' He could see it in her face, the vague smile and dilated pupils.

'It's New Year's Eve. If you can't get stoned on New Year's Eve, then when can you?' She nestled in closer. He could smell her perfume. The musky scent sank into his senses, mingling with the intoxication of beer and wine.

His fingers drifted lightly over her bare back. She was hot to the touch. She looked up, her hazel eyes ringed with black, her lips full and pouting. He pressed his fingers against those lips, and she bit them playfully. God, he wanted her.

'You should try it yourself more often, Tommo.' Dian swept back her hair to reveal an arching neck. Arching and stretching like an animal arches and stretches. 'It's relaxing. And sex is more fun when you're stoned.' She smiled dreamily. 'Every sensation intensified.' She glanced at him from under dark lashes, and then looked over towards the door.

Tom followed the direction of her gaze. The gorilla was standing, arms folded, watching them. 'Sex with that,' he muttered. 'Jesus Christ.'

She laughed lightly. 'He's not that bad.'

'You're wasted on him.' Tom held her more tightly. The music was slow and smoochy, and tobacco smoke fogged the air. Voices and bodies seemed to be pressing into him, making him stumble. 'You're beautiful.' His fingers tangled through her hair. He wanted to kiss her. He wanted to take her out of that backless dress.

'And you're out of your head, Tommo.' Her hands slipped down from his waist, pressing against the hard fabric of his jeans.

He groaned. 'Dian . . .' What was she doing to him? How could she torture him like this?

'Yes, Tommo?' She bent, easing her tongue between the buttons of his shirt, flicking it across her chest, then laughing up at him.

'I need to get out of here.' He had to find some fresh air. He was sinking fast.

'Are you all right, Tommo?' Suddenly she was all concern.

He nodded, but the room was swaying drunkenly in front of his eyes.

'I'll take you home.' She was supporting most of his weight.

'What about Steve whasisname?' But he allowed her to lead him into the hall, find his leather jacket and even half-pull it on. There was no sign of the gorilla.

'Oh, bugger him,' she giggled. 'You and me go back a long way, Tommo. I'll look after you.'

The fresh air hit Tom full in the face like an unfriendly fist.

For the first ten minutes they sang love songs to passing cars, until Tom fell into the gutter by the village square. And then as Dian pulled him to his feet, the church clock struck twelve, and simultaneously there was an eruption of cheers and shouts from another party nearby.

'Happy New Year, darling.' Dian wrapped herself around him, and for the next ten minutes, all he was conscious of was her hair, eyes and heady perfume.

'Ah, Dian,' he murmured. 'Another bloody year.'

He was swamped by a drunken misery that wouldn't evaporate – even with this sexy body to comfort him. Because this was when Janice had betrayed him. New Year's Eve 1973. Etched on his brain with blood and tears. 'Janice, Janice,' he moaned.

'Who the bloody hell's Janice?' Dian was pulling him along the narrow street. His feet were numb and his body felt weightless.

She paused. 'I suppose that's your lost love, is it, Tommo?'

'I gave it all to that woman.' Tom was aware of darkness. Darkness and sparking street lights, wet pavements and distant memory. 'I loved her. I really loved her.' First love – hot and sweet. But then he'd gone and poured it all over her.

'Of course you loved her.' Dian held him closer, squeezing his arm as they walked unsteadily along. 'What happened?'

And suddenly, he needed to tell her. Some feeling was returning to his feet, to his head, and he needed to tell her. Not Dian particularly, but Dian was better than most. He needed to unload it. All this bitterness and pain. All the love that Janice had drained out of him until there was nothing left.

Only a dry kind of desert. A plateau of emptiness. He had to unload it, because it was weighing him down. Another bloody New Year.

'We lived together for eighteen months.' His voice slurred. 'Me and Janice and the kid.'

'You had a child?' Dian's voice was a whisper. It drifted away from him before he could catch it.

'Not my kid. Her kid. She'd been married.' She was the older woman, he was the toy boy. The fresh-faced boy straight out of school. Discovering sex, finding experience and falling in love.

'Ah.' A soft, sweet sigh.

'But I was like a father to that kid.' Self-righteous anger. 'I would have given him anything.'

'Yes, Tommo. Of course you would.' Dian's voice soothed away some of the pain.

All right then. She understood. 'And I gave Janice everything – everything I had to give.'

'Love . . .' she prompted.

'Love, support, hope . . .' His voice tailed off. His life. He'd given her his life. Loving Janice had been the only time he didn't have to pretend. Since then he didn't know who he was any more.

'And what did Janice do to you, Tommo?' Dian's hand around his waist was a white bandage to catch the blood.

'She went to bed with my best mate.' Tom had never uttered those words to another living soul. He'd never even uttered them to himself, and yet he could see the two of them in Janice's double bed as clear as if it had been yesterday. The image danced in front of him, mocking and true.

'Oh, my God.' Dian's grip softened and slipped.

'We had a party. It was New Year. I couldn't find her. I looked everywhere.' Now as then, his pale eyes darted from left to right into the shadows around them. As if in this New Year, he could find her once again.

'You were worried about her . . .' she prompted.

'I was worried. Everyone was drunk. Falling over and giggling. People were kissing in the bathroom. I was worried. And I thought, what about the kid, maybe the kid's woken up with all this racket, and she's trying to calm him down. Maybe she needs me.' He faltered. He'd always wanted her to need him. And yet Janice wasn't like that. She was self-sufficient. She needed no one.

'So you went upstairs.' Dian's voice was gentle. She was massaging his pain.

'I went upstairs and the kid was sleeping.' He tensed. 'I heard noises from the bedroom. And I thought, Jesus, someone's got a nerve, they're only bloody doing it in our bed.' He fell silent.

'So you opened the door . . .'

'I opened the door and I saw them. Janice and Brian. She was on top of him. She was giggling.'

'He saw you?'

'Oh, yeah. His eyes kind of bulged. He looked scared. He stopped her. He said – bloody hell – and looked straight at me.'

'What did Janice do?' Dian's voice was a whisper. She didn't seem like Dian, she was so close to all the shadows.

'She laughed.' Even now he could hear it. Her drunken laughter. Her loud drunken laughter tightening like a vice around his head. 'She laughed and I wanted to hit her. I wanted to hit them both, but I didn't have the guts. So I turned round and stormed out. I left the party. I walked the streets, and when I came back, the bloody party was still going on.' He shook his head in wonder. 'It was still going on.'

They passed some drunk lying in the gutter. Passed him right by, sparing him barely a glance.

Tom touched his face. It was wet. Tears on his face.

He sighed. Why was he telling her all this? Wasn't she the wrong person to tell? But there was no one else. There was no one else to tell on this New Year's Eve night.

'And so it was over,' Dian said at last. She had done something for the pain, but it was still there – a lost ache inside him.

'That was the worst part. It wasn't over.' That was when the worst of it really began. The humiliation of knowing that Janice cared so little. That he really was a toy-boy for her. That he'd never meant more and she didn't care who knew it.

'It went on,' he told Dian. 'I made it go on. I needed to forgive her – because I didn't think I could go on without her.' He hung his fair head in shame. 'But I had a huge bloody hole in my heart and it was getting bigger. Getting so big that there was no hope in hell of patching it up.'

'What happened to her? What happened to Janice?' Dian pulled her coat in closer, against the cold breeze.

'She met some rich guy at work and buggered off and married him. Just like that. Yet she'd always told me she'd never dream of getting married again.' He laughed. 'I never saw that it was only a question of money.'

'Poor Tommo.' They stopped walking. She reached up to stroke his hair.

He felt like a child again. He searched for her breasts under her coat.

She caught her breath. 'Tommo?'

'Come back to the flat with me.' He was stone cold sober now. His heart was grating against his rib cage and he needed some relief. Christ, he needed some relief. And only Dian could give it to him.

'You told me not to.' Her hazel eyes were huge in her face. Liquid hazel.

'I need you.' His fingers found the halter tie of her dress and undid the loose knot.

The black material snaked to her waist. His fingers found her bare breasts. 'Come back with me, Dian?' Her nipples were hot to the touch. Hot and aching. He felt them harden between his fingers, and between the fingers of the cold new-January night. Christ, how he needed her.

'Okay.' Her voice was a whisper of passion. 'I'll come back with you. I'll look after you, Tommo. I won't let anything hurt you again.'

Kate, dressed as Queen Elizabeth the first, at Stephanie's instigation – 'She was a redhead, darling, and it's such a lovely costume . . .' – was having a whale of a time. At least a hundred people had filled the cold imposing spaces of Atherington Hall, endowing it with an atmosphere of gaiety from dancing, laughter and seemingly never-ending champagne.

From nowhere, Stephanie produced a string of young men until Kate wasn't sure who to dance with next. Some of them were bores, and others only stared with unmasked longing at Stephanie.

But Kate forgot her resentment. It didn't belong here. And it was amusing to watch Steph, flitting from room to room, appropriately dressed as Titania, Queen of the Fairies, with a dress like rainbow gossamer, and a silver crown perched on her dark head. Her raven hair was entwined with flowers – and her blue eyes were strikingly beautiful against the white make-up of her face.

'I think Miles should be wearing your costume,' Kate observed to Leon. This tall, sandy-haired individual dressed as Peter Pan was by far the best of the bunch she'd met tonight. 'He's doing his sulky little boy routine.' From what she'd seen of him, the notion of perpetual childhood suited Miles rather well. A deep frown was drawn on his beautiful face.

Leon laughed, turning to follow the direction of her gaze. 'Our Miles is fed up because he feels trapped. Only he's not trapped in Never-Never Land.'

'He's trapped into conforming.' Kate gathered up the bulk of her skirt and sat awkwardly on a high-backed chair.

Leon shrugged. 'No more than the rest of us.' He smiled.

Was he laughing at her? She didn't know for sure.

'How about you? Are you trapped, Kate?'

She looked at him over the rim of her glass. 'Not any more, I'm not.'

He laughed. 'I bet no one would dare.'

'Don't you believe it.' She'd been trapped all right. Maybe she still was. Maybe Leon had a point – everyone was trapped by the expectations of others. Everyone had dreams to fulfil and conventions to keep. It was hard always to go your own way.

'And you?' Her eyes narrowed as she watched him. He was one of the rich kids, no mistaking that. But he lacked the smooth carelessness that she hated in some of them. She liked people who were still jagged around the edges. Who hadn't forgotten how to hurt and cry. Leon wasn't one of the cardboard cutouts. He was real all right.

'I'm like Miles.' He looked away from her, towards the people in their bizarre costumes.

Moving to the music, but not living the music, she realized. Not allowing it to seep into their bodily rhythms – keeping themselves stiff and apart, not letting themselves feel. This was a tight generation, stiff with tension, and it would need a lot more champagne before it could really let go.

'In what way?' she asked. Of course he was wrong. He wasn't like Miles at all. He was calm and funny, even attractive.

But she hoped he wouldn't make a pass at her even though there was something about this lanky individual that drew her. Told her he could be a friend.

'In giving in to family pressures. Working nine to five instead of dropping out and heading for Europe with a rucksack on my back.' He laughed at himself. 'That's what I'd really like to do.'

'That's what Kate did.' Stephanie was beside them. 'Didn't you, darling?' She lit a cigarette.

Kate felt the blood rushing to her pale face. Why had she let this stupid lie continue? Leon was looking admiring, and Stephanie was smiling proudly, hand on hip. The Queen of the Fairies with a fag in her mouth. What would they say if they knew the truth? And how could she tell them now – now that she'd basked in some kind of unwanted glory? 'It was nothing much,' she said quickly. 'Hardly worth a postcard.'

'But at least you did it,' Leon sighed.

Stephanie was on the edge of the dance floor. She'd seen Miles and was already moving towards him, concern in her eyes. Kate watched his frown fade as Stephanie approached. Her hand was on his arm. They stood side by side, the same height, Titania and her clown – deep in conversation. Despite their costumes they looked alike, seeming to belong together.

'Do you know Miles very well?' Kate was determined to keep the subject away from Europe.

'We went to the same school. I was a few years above him.'

'Steph's age, then. Are you a friend of hers?' She wondered if he was another admirer. Would she care if he was? Well, maybe a little.

'More of a distant cousin. I work in the company under the old man.' He nodded towards Julian, who was dressed as Napoleon, playing the perfect host once more.

'Isn't that the company Miles is supposed to be joining?' Kate was curious about this strange family. And the more she discovered, the more she felt there was to know. She'd barely touched the edge.

Leon's face darkened. 'Yes, it is. Miles is holding out, but Julian's determined to get him in as soon as he can. He thinks Miles is getting too involved with . . .' He hesitated, as though reluctant to say too much, 'certain people who may not have his best interests at heart.'

'Who?' Kate leaned closer.

He nodded towards the other side of the room where Miles and Stephanie had been joined by a slender male acrobat. 'His young friend over there, for one.' Leon's meaning was unmistakeable. 'He only got through the door tonight because Julian didn't recognise him.'

She frowned. 'So Julian's worried that Miles is homosexual?' She couldn't bring herself to say queer. But it made sense to Kate. Miles had that kind of bruised sensitivity. He seemed gentle – and depressed.

Leon nodded.

'And is he?'

He eyed her curiously. 'Maybe.'

'Then perhaps that's part of his prison.' Kate felt more sympathy towards Miles already. She could imagine that Julian and a homosexual son would be an uneasy combination, to say the least.

'You may be right.' Leon watched her in frank admiration. 'Julian would certainly have something to say about it.'

Kate tensed. 'But what gives him the right to run his son's life?' Her eyes radiated anger. This was a subject close to her heart.

Leon shrugged. 'Julian would never accept a homosexual son.'

'He's living in the bloody Dark Ages then.' Kate shook her auburn head in amazement. Or was Stephanie right – was Julian simply obsessed with control?

'Come on.' Leon took her arm. 'We're due for a spot of the old exercise.' He put down their drinks and led her on to the parquet floor.

'It's almost time.' He drew her closer.

She held her breath. His eyes were brown with amber flecks.

'Ready everyone?' The clock began to strike. One, two, three . . . On number twelve there were shrieks and cheers, and hundreds of silvery balloons descended from the high ceiling. Julian certainly believed in doing things in style.

'Happy New Year, Kate.' Leon leaned towards her, touching her face with his fingertips.

His lips were too close. Kate was scared. She turned her head, and they brushed her cheek with the slightest of pressures. She was conscious of a swift shaft of disappointment.

'Happy New Year, Leon,' she whispered.

He seemed about to reply, and then Stephanie was beside them, her face flushed.

'Happy New Year, darling.' She took Kate in her arms and they hugged, their bodies so close and warm that for a precious second Kate was reminded of that night in the pool at Les Marettes. Of naked, vulnerable bodies, and of friendship.

And then Stephanie was gone.

'What are you thinking about?' Leon's voice was kind but curious.

Kate looked up to see Stephanie slipping out of the room. She was filled with inexplicable sadness, and all she could think of was Hannah. Hannah should be here. Surely they hadn't lost Hannah? Surely their friendship was still intact?

'I have to go to the bathroom. Excuse me, Leon.' He was a special kind of person, but suddenly Kate needed a moment of solitude. She had to get away from this superficial cheer, and welcome her New Year in alone, in silent reflection of what had been and what might be to come.

She pushed through the bright costumes that seemed more tangible than the people inside them, and made her way towards Stephanie's studio. There was something scary about fancy dress – about masks that hid the familiar safety of a human face. Like ventriloquists' dummies, they seemed harmless enough – but inhumanity sat awkwardly on a human form. And it smelt of evil.

The studio was locked – of course it would be, so Kate looked around for a different retreat. Then she remembered the conservatory. Perfect. A summer night was just what she needed to chase these winter shadows away. She passed through the archway door.

The lights were low in the hothouse, the cacti looming like a prickly forest above her. Vines of passion flowers crept up the glassy walls, and a fountain trickled remorselessly in the distance. The only other sound was the whisper of the palms as their slender green fingers brushed other green fingers in the night.

Any yet, as Kate's eyes adjusted to the dim humidity of the tropical atmosphere, she thought she heard a faint rustle that was more than the rustle of plant life. She held her breath, took a step forwards, and then she saw them. Stephanie and Miles. Titania and her red-headed clown, kneeling by the fountain, face to face. So close there was barely an inch between them, their eyes locked together, their hands on the other's shoulders. Twin souls. Kate stared, entranced, unable to move away and unable to disturb them.

And then as she watched, they moved closer still – until their lips were touching. Silently they kissed. Kate stared, her eyes unblinking. The kiss seemed to go on for ever. It was a kiss of lovers, and Kate couldn't leave until it was over.

At last they drew apart, Stephanie took his dark head in her hands, and Kate crept out of the conservatory. Brother and sister, Stephanie and Miles, Titania and her clown. The couples swam through her brain. She was lost in a maze of bewilderment. What the hell was going on?

She couldn't face going back to the party. Leon would wonder where she'd got to, but she couldn't help that. She didn't belong with these people. She was utterly confused. And this new year promised to be even more perplexing than the last.

*   *   *

Tom awoke on the first day of the new year, with a groan that acknow-ledged both his hangover, and the dim memory of what had happened the night before. He rolled over, and sure enough, there she was beside him – Dian, dark, sultry and sleeping. Friend, lover, and now confidante as well.

'Shit.' He pulled himself upright. He was naked – of course he would be. He couldn't actually remember sex with Dian, but it must have happened. He'd have to be comatose to resist her particular charms, especially if she were lying naked in bed next to him.

'Jesus Christ.' Tom buried his head in his hands. His mouth tasted like milk well past its sell-by date, and his brain was hammering wildly. He must be crazy. He'd told Dian about Janice. A story he'd vowed to keep locked in his head forever.

The doorbell rang.

'Who the bloody hell's that?' Tom peered at the bedside clock. Just past ten. Who'd be dumb enough to disturb him at ten o'clock on New Year's Day? He just wouldn't answer it. He couldn't face seeing anyone right now.

But it rang again. And again. And there was an insistence to the ring, that forced Tom to get up and pull on some jeans. He tore his fingers through his fair tangled hair and went to the front door.

Hannah was standing on the doorstep.

He blinked.

'Hello, Tom.' The breeze was blowing through her blonde hair. She looked fresh and innocent as a summer's day. She made him feel totally disgusting.

'Hannah.' He stared at her, lost for words.

'Aren't you going to invite me in?' Her dark eyes looked down, towards a small suitcase squatting at her feet.

'In?' Tom was confused. What was Hannah doing here? How had she got here from West Sussex so early on New Year's Day? What was going on? And . . . Jesus Christ. His addled brain performed a backward flip – Dian was in his bedroom.

'You're not going to leave me standing on the doorstep, are you, Tom?' She smiled, a tender but wary smile that hovered around her delicate mouth. 'Now that I've come all this way to see you.'

He moved aside to let her pass by. There was something different about Hannah – but he was damned if he could see what it was. All he could think of was how to get rid of Dian. 'I'm half asleep. I'm sorry.' He tore his hands through his hair once more. 'I must look terrible. I feel bloody terrible. I got disgustingly drunk last night. I was missing you . . .' He took her case. He was waffling. It was squelching out of him like a conveyor belt of blasted manure.

'I'll make us some coffee.' Coffee, that's what he needed. Something to wake up his brain.

She followed him into the kitchen. 'I came by last night. My train was delayed and the bus didn't get me here till nine.'

'Jesus, Hannah.' He filled the kettle. 'Why didn't you tell me you were coming?' It could have been so different. No party. No Dian. No drunken confidences.

Her eyes darkened. 'I wanted to surprise you, Tom.'

He felt angry with her, bitter and angry because of what he'd done to her. 'You did that all right,' he muttered. 'I thought you were chained to Sussex for the holidays. I thought I was your second best.'

Her eyes filled. 'You're not second best, Tom. You'll never be second best.' She moved forwards, winding her slender arms around his neck. 'Happy New Year, Tom,' she whispered.

'Very touching.' The voice came from the doorway. Dian stood, tousled and sexy, wrapped only in Tom's dressing gown and a smile of sensual satisfaction.

Hannah spun around, naked terror streaking over her face. 'You? What are you doing here?' She let go of Tom, backing away from him. 'Tom?'

He thought fast. 'Dian brought me home last night.' Tom's voice was pure innocence. 'I was too drunk to walk.'

'Too drunk to even stand up,' Dian added maliciously.

He ignored her. 'She slept on my bed. I slept on the sofa. Isn't that right, Dian?'

It was a battle of wills. He could see that it was touch and go. He stared into her hazel eyes – making sure she knew the score. If there was ever to be friendship between them again – friendship or sex or anything else – then there was only one choice for her. It was no good begging with a girl like Dian. You had to overpower her. Use her own weapons against her. And use sex.

She looked away at last. 'Of course. What the hell do you take me for? And besides, it's bloody impossible to get a taxi at that time of night.'

Hannah's brown eyes darted from one to the other. She didn't know. She wasn't sure. She wanted to believe him, God knows, she needed to believe him. But having spent the entire train journey dreading that he'd be with Dian when she found him, her worst fears appeared to be materialising in front of her.

'Come on, Hannah.' The explanation was plausible, his expression believable – there was not a smudge of guilt on his smooth yet weary face.

'Tom?' she whispered.

'Jesus, Hannah. What kind of a man do you think I am?'

She stared at him, seeing the anger in his pale eyes. 'I don't . . .'

'Are you saying that you don't believe me?' He seemed outraged.

No one could be that good a liar. It must be true. Thank God. She must believe him. After that row with her mother, Hannah had packed her bags and caught the train the very next day. Only that stupid derailment had stopped her from getting here earlier – forcing her to find a B & B in the village, when all she wanted was to be with Tom.

She had used all her energy fighting Mother. She was drained, she had to get away, and there was only one place she wanted to run to. Tom's arms.

Hannah's fingers twisted nervously as she watched Tom. She'd done a lot of thinking. There was a very special New Year's present she wanted to give him. 'Of course I believe you, Tom,' she said at last.

'Good girl.' He grinned. 'You know that Dian and I are just close friends.'

The atmosphere changed abruptly. Tom began whistling, and Dian left the kitchen.

Hannah stared at her departing back. She would conquer this jealousy by standing up to it – like she'd stood up to her mother for the very first time. She would take this jealousy and stamp it out of existence.

She took a deep breath. 'I want this to be a new beginning for us, Tom.'

He took her hands. 'That's my Hannah. A new year, a new beginning.'

She waited until Dian had left the flat, then very slowly she undressed, one garment at a time.

He stared at her. 'You don't have to do this, Hannah.' His voice was strangely gentle.

'I do.' Her words were muffled in an agony of embarrassment. He'd never know the cost, but she didn't have a choice. It was the only way forward.

'Then let me . . .'

'No.' She straightened. Looked him in the eye with a new determination.

'That's what's different about you,' he murmured, as if to himself. 'You're not . . .'

'I'm not scared any more.' She took off the last item of clothing. It wasn't true. In fact, she was terrified. But she was going to conquer that fear. Head to head.

'You're beautiful, Hannah.'

Only now would she let him approach, let him hold her as she wanted to be held. Held and protected and loved.

'You were right,' she murmured into his smooth skin. 'My kind of loving wasn't loving – not really. There has to be more.'

He buried his head in her hair, and very slowly, his fingers caressed her back, her shoulders, and then with increasing urgency, the tempo rising, moved down to her thighs, her hips, the tight cleft of her buttocks. 'Hannah . . .' He picked her up, kicked the door open and carried her into the bedroom, laid her on the bed still warm from Dian's body, like a sacrifice.

Hannah watched as he fumbled with the zip of his jeans, tearing them off in his hurry to get to her. And she tried to smile as he stood above her, his manhood rising like a weapon of war in front of him. Fear – the old and the new – spiked her with tension, and then pain took over, as he loomed closer, thrust himself inside her. Pain, loss, fear.

That's when she closed her eyes. It was over. Her virginity was gone, but strangely the fear remained. It was over and it had meant so little. Surely there had to be more?

8

'This essay is a pain. How come some people can do it in a couple of hours when I'm still struggling with the blasted thing?' Kate threw down her pen in disgust.

'Search me. But I can tell you something, darling. You and I shouldn't be stuck indoors on a day like this.' Stephanie got up from the chair and wandered lazily over to the Common Room window. Outside, an early spring day was beckoning with all the scents of freshly mown grass and apple blossom in the air. 'We should get out of this place.' She flung back her dark hair. 'Writing essays is too much like hard work. We should have some fun for a change.'

Kate grinned. 'Let's do it then. Let's take a bus to Barstock Cliff on Sunday. Have a walk by the sea. Take a picnic. Go to a country pub.' Her green eyes gleamed.

Stephanie hesitated. She'd half-promised Miles to go back to Atherington this weekend. He'd phoned twice. The first time there had been a whine in his voice that she hated, so the second time she'd pretended to be out when someone banged on her door to get her to the phone. She couldn't bring herself to speak to him. Stephanie sighed. Who'd have thought she'd do that to Miles? After everything they'd been through together?

It was the guilt. Swamping her with responsibilities she didn't want and couldn't handle. She loved Miles but she hated Atherington. That was the truth of it. And every time she went back there she had this awful feeling she'd never make it out again.

'Okay,' she said at last. 'You're on.' It would do them both good. And it would also do as an excuse to herself not to go back to Kent.

'And let's ask Hannah.' Kate smoothed auburn hair away from her face. 'We've got to ask Hannah.'

She was stubborn all right. Didn't she realize that there was no point? 'She won't come, Kate. You've got to face it. She's living a separate life from us. She's hardly been near us for weeks.' They stared at each other in grim silence. It was true – they were a twosome now.

To their astonishment, when they'd returned to college after the Christmas break, Hannah appeared to have moved in with Tom.

'I never had him listed as the settling down type,' Kate remarked to Stephanie.

'Nor me.'

And when they did see her – floating through campus to a lecture or tutorial – she seemed too faraway for words.

'Love . . .' Stephanie said now with disgust.

'We should still ask her.' Kate wrinkled her snub nose. 'You never know.'

'You never know . . .' Stephanie repeated as Kate collected her books together. She knew all right. She'd known the score a long time ago.

'I'm late for linguistics. See you later.'

'Uh huh,' Stephanie nodded. Already she was feeling bad about the half-broken promise to Miles. Why was it that the more Miles pleaded with her, the more he reached out, needing her, the more she turned her back on him? Was it merely a legacy of their past, or did she think that she would harm him still further?

A shadow fell over her books.

'You're Stephanie, aren't you?' It was a soft, husky voice.

She looked up. The girl called Dian Jones was staring down at her, with a wide smile and friendly eyes. Stephanie nodded, warily.

'I was wondering if you fancied coming to a party tonight?' Dian perched on the table beside her. 'I'm trying to get some extra people together. How about it?'

Stephanie blinked with surprise. 'Maybe . . .' She hesitated. She rarely turned down an invitation to a party. And it wasn't unheard of for college parties to be virtually open house. 'Whereabouts?'

Dian told her. 'It's only down the road.'

Stephanie lit a cigarette, pushing the pack towards the dark compelling girl beside her. 'Is it okay if I bring a friend?' She would ask Kate. She needed cheering up. And who knows? If Dian Jones was still friendly with Tom, then Tom and Hannah might be there too.

But Dian shook her head. There was an expression of mystery in her dark eyes. She leaned closer. 'No one too straight,' she whispered. 'It's not exactly going to be a gin and tonic affair.' She paused. 'I'll meet you if you like. We can go together.'

Stephanie was flattered. Dian was older, popular and attractive. So she wouldn't ask Kate – what did it matter? It was only a party and they weren't exactly inseparable.

'Sure.' She nodded. Most of all, she was intrigued. She sensed the promise of excitement, and that's what Stephanie lived on. That's what kept her going – thrills and spills when she was in danger of going under.

She couldn't wait. What would a party be like, where gin and tonic was too straight?

They met at the campus gates, and Dian passed her a small roll-up that she knew immediately wasn't just tobacco. 'To get you in the mood,' she said.

Stephanie hesitated for only a moment. Some of the kids at school had been into drugs, but she herself had never bothered with them. She'd been discovering sex when the others were smoking behind the bike sheds and experimenting with brightly coloured pills. And besides, it had always scared her – having the illusion but not the reality of control. Cannabis was different though. She'd always wondered what it was like, and now seemed as good a time as any to find out.

After a slight hesitation, she sucked, and felt the immediate hit. Her head reeled. Scary . . . Then she relaxed. Wow. It was something else . . . A warm and pleasant sensation of well-being flowed over her. She giggled.

'I knew you'd be cool.' Dian took her arm. 'You can tell just by looking at someone.' She took back the spliff. 'And I've got plenty more stuff in my bag,' she whispered.

The party was two streets away, just behind the village square, in the basement flat of a Victorian house full of bed-sits. Narrow steps led down to the large sitting-room, which had a low red-painted ceiling and black walls. It was crammed full of people Stephanie had never seen before. This wasn't a college thing. This was a million miles away from college.

'Drinks are in here,' Dian was shoving her way through to the bright kitchen. Stephanie took in the torn lino flooring, stained white walls and the huge table awash with beer, cider and wine.

The music, blaring from the stereo was from the sixties – old Beatles,

Stones and the Beach Boys. Stephanie blinked. She stood in the doorway and stared. There was something appealing about the very sleaziness – the bodies, mainly dressed in jeans or draped in kaftans, sitting cross-legged on the floor, or swaying drunkenly to the beat. The couples kissing in corners, a few even writhing around in the dark shadows on the worn red carpet. The lack of inhibition, the fug of cigarette smoke spiralling to the ceiling, the pounding bass of the stereo, it all seemed wonderful. New, and different, and most of all rather daring.

'Have a good time.' Dian drifted off.

Stephanie found herself a bottle of wine and a beer tankard, and sat in the corner, stretching out her long legs and closing her eyes as the music drove an intoxicating rhythm into her head. She could feel herself drifting. This was the way to escape. This was the way to forget about family pressures, Daddy's cheque book syndrome, and Miles's reproachful blue eyes.

'Hi.' A smooth, familiar voice interrupted her thoughts. 'I wasn't expecting to see you here.'

Stephanie opened her eyes to see Tom McNeil's handsome face hovering over her, swimming into her vision. She sat up straighter. 'Hi. Where's Hannah?'

He laughed. She didn't like the sound. 'Can you imagine Hannah in a place like this?'

No way, come to think of it. 'Where is she then?'

He shrugged. 'She wasn't feeling too good so she stayed at the flat.'

'But you came.' Her eyes were disapproving. Still, he was floating in and out of focus. She blinked harder.

Tom shrugged and slipped down beside her, his back against the wall. 'We're not Siamese twins. And she doesn't own me.' His hand rested lightly on her thigh.

'I bet she bloody doesn't.' Poor innocent Hannah would have no chance against this man.

Stephanie frowned. But why did someone like Tom McNeil want Hannah in the first place? Why had he let her move in when it must restrict his womanising? She would have asked him but she was unwilling to prolong the conversation.

'What are you doing here?' His eyes were undressing her.

Stephanie removed his hand. 'Dian brought me.'

'Dian?' Tom's expression changed. She saw the anger gleam momentarily in his pale eyes, and then it was gone.

But it made her curious. 'Any reason why I shouldn't be here?' She reached in her bag for cigarettes.

He lit one for her, leaning close, the faint, fair stubble on his jaw illuminated by the flame of the lighter. 'I just didn't realise you knew each other.' His voice was carefully casual.

He looked thoughtfully over to the other side of the room to where Dian was dancing with someone who looked vaguely familiar. Stephanie frowned, but she couldn't place him – he had his back to her, and anyway she was feeling kind of stoned.

'It's nice to see you.' Tom leaned closer. 'This is a sort of secret rendezvous. Not many people know about this place.'

'Really?' The cigarette was making her feel drunk again. She could smell the patchouli that appeared to be Tom's trademark. The top buttons of his denim shirt were undone, and she could see the smooth skin, lightly tanned and flecked with dark chest hair.

His hand was on her shoulder. 'And it's nice to touch you,' he said. His fingers slipped to her neck and darted down under her shirt, inching towards the curve of her breasts.

'Piss off, Tom.' She shoved him away.

He moved into a squatting position, eyeing her curiously as if she were an unknown specimen he hadn't come across before. 'Why are you holding out on me?'

She knew he was remembering the night she'd stood at the window. The night she'd run her hands over her naked body and known that he wanted her. He'd taken it as an invitation. Well, he would, wouldn't he? Yes, he was attractive, and yes, he turned her on. There was a charisma about Tom McNeil that any woman would respond to, and Stephanie certainly wasn't immune. But . . .

'Because of Hannah.' She poured herself more wine.

'Hannah wouldn't know . . .' His eyes were pleading. 'It wouldn't hurt Hannah.' He licked his lips. 'C'mon. It would be fun. You know you want to . . .'

Dian was behind him. She reached down to massage his neck, and he squirmed under her fingers. 'Come and dance, Tommo,' she said.

He laughed, and got to his feet. 'I'm all yours.'

Stephanie watched them, noting the way their bodies moved together in a natural, familiar rhythm. It was pretty obvious that Tom was sleeping around, if not with Dian then with others. But she wasn't going to be added to his list, no way.

The thoughts spun in intoxicating spirals in her head. Tom would mess Hannah around – he would screw her up, that was for sure. Hannah should know what was going on. Poor Hannah. But how could she tell her? How could she hurt her like that? Jesus, she missed Hannah. How had someone so lovely ended up with a bastard like Tom McNeil?

She was on her second bottle of wine by the time Dian came over, leading a slim woman with a shock of blonde hair towards her. 'This is Lois,' she said. 'She wants to meet you.'

The woman called Lois sat down, scrutinised Stephanie with cool assurance, and immediately started rolling a joint. 'I haven't seen you here before.' She had light green eyes, and a kind of translucence to her face that fascinated Stephanie. 'Who are you? You don't look much like a college student.'

Stephanie told her. Some quality in the woman invited confidences, and she heard herself relating details about her life that she wouldn't normally dream of divulging to a perfect stranger. She heard her own words as if she were acting in a play somewhere. As if this weren't real.

'It's my brother Miles who bothers me the most,' she said. 'I love him. And yet I'm standing by, watching him sink.' He was sinking, and trying to drag her down with him until she couldn't breathe.

While Stephanie talked, the woman called Lois, with her blonde shafted hair and glimmering eyes, unfolded papers, fiddled with matches, crumbled dope on to tobacco, tore a piece of cardboard from Stephanie's cigarette packet, and produced the largest joint Stephanie had ever seen.

'And who are you?' It was about time she found out something in return. This strange woman with her air of absolute confidence bothered her. If Stephanie had only half of her self-assurance, she'd have no problems. Or so it seemed.

'This is my flat.' Lois lit the twisted end, and a spark spun into the air. 'I share it with a couple of other girls.' She gazed at Stephanie speculatively. 'It's always open house as far as I'm concerned. Remember that. And we throw a party like this on the first Friday night of every month.'

'It's amazing.' Doubtfully Stephanie took the proffered joint, holding it carefully between her fingers.

'Moroccan black,' Lois whispered in her ear. 'Great stuff.'

The echoes and flows of Pink Floyd were on the stereo now. Dream drifting into dream. People had stopped dancing, and most were sitting on the floor adding more cigarette burns and lager stains to the worn red carpet. The music washed over Stephanie, caressing her senses like a sheet of pure silk. She felt a haze of well-being, a sweet lethargy, a gift of timelessness. Someone was playing with her fingers. People were giggling, swaying, sleeping, drifting.

On the far side of the room she saw Dian with Tom. They were deep in conversation with the half-familiar guy who Dian had been dancing with. Greasy fair hair, arrogant smile. Christ. She blinked. It was Rick Allen. What the hell was he doing here?

As she watched, it seemed to Stephanie that the three heads moved into a circle of exclusion. A wave of paranoia swept over her. They were looking across at her and laughing. Rick and Dian and Tom, all laughing at her.

Tom's hand was creeping up Dian's smooth thigh . . .

Stephanie shook her head in sudden terror. She was scared. Stoned and scared. 'I have to be going.'

She wasn't talking to anyone in particular, but Lois looked up at her with drowsy eyes of regret.

'Already? You've only just got here.'

It seemed to Stephanie that she'd been here for ever. 'I have to go.' Maybe she shouldn't have come. There was a danger here, she could smell it in the air. And she could sense temptation too, like a drug, pulling her closer. She was being suffocated by the black walls, the smoky heaviness of the airless room, and the heavy tortuous monotony of the music, pressing on her temples. This was a dream world. And she didn't want that kind of escape. Or did she?

'Come again, Stephanie. Promise me?' Lois reached out to touch her hands. Her eyes were a survivor's eyes. The eyes of someone who understood. 'Come and see me again.'

Sunday morning, Kate couldn't repress a secret smile of triumph when Stephanie finally came down to breakfast. Wouldn't she be surprised . . .

'Morning.' Stephanie's tray contained only orange juice and one solitary slice of toast. Her eyes were ringed with dark shadows, but Kate registered this only briefly. She had other things on her mind right now.

'Guess what?' She leaned forwards.

'I can't imagine,' Stephanie drawled. 'Put me out of my misery.'

Kate grinned. 'Hannah's in her room.' That was unusual enough for starters. These days, Hannah's visits to Royal Ford consisted mostly of a quick sprint to pick up something from her fast depleting wardrobe.

'Really?' A spark of interest touched Stephanie's sleepy blue eyes. 'Lover's quarrel, do you think?'

'Could be.' Kate wasn't so sure, although Hannah had certainly been quiet when she'd spoken to her earlier. As if she had something on her mind.

'Let's hope so.' Stephanie spoke with feeling. She took a bite of her toast before pushing the plate away.

'And she's coming to Barstock with us today.'

'You're kidding!' Surprise mingled with pleasure on Stephanie's expressive face. Kate realised how much she had missed her. How much they'd both missed her. They got on well enough, but it wasn't the same without Hannah.

'It's true.' Kate smiled. 'She's coming to Barstock, and we're going to have a wonderful day.'

But Hannah was strangely subdued on the bus, and Kate soon followed Stephanie's example of staring out of the window at the lush countryside, rather than trying to make conversation.

There had been a lot of rain in the past months, and the hills and valleys of West Dorset were a dense and vibrant shade of green that seemed almost unreal. The bus groaned with the effort every time it climbed another hill, but the stunning vistas of patchwork fields dotted with sheep and tasselled with trees were worth it every time. And as the bus approached the thatched village of Barstock, with its winding road, church of Portland stone, and tiny tumbledown post office, there was the tantalising glimpse of sea.

The girls jumped off and headed for the South West coastal path.

'This is what freedom is all about.' Kate stretched out her arms towards the great, grey cliffs. There were spring promises close by – the tastes and tang of the salt-sea air, and the sharp whip of the breeze that tangled hair into warm faces.

'Chesil Beach.' Hannah nodded towards the sea, walking forwards until she seemed dangerously close to the cliff edge, a small and vulnerable figure. 'I came here once on a field trip with the school.' Her thin voice drifted with the breeze.

Stephanie strode towards her and took her arm. 'We'll look for some fossils this afternoon.' She spoke gently, as if she were addressing a child. Making promises for later.

Below them was a stone, sandy ledge. They stopped, looking out over the shingle bay of Barstock with its smooth, flat, grey and pinky-brown pebbles.

Stephanie brushed her dark hair out of her eyes and mouth. 'This place is like going back in time.'

'Let's find the fossil forest.' There was a new enthusiasm about Hannah. 'It's on the Ordnance Survey map.' She giggled, as the wind almost snatched the map from her hand.

'Good old Hannah.' Stephanie peered over her shoulder. 'Always a sucker for the past.'

They laughed.

'But just think. It existed millions of years ago . . .' Hannah's voice was dreamy. 'And yet a piece of the past is still here with us.'

The past. It could never be entirely eroded. Kate thought of Normandy. The land given to the Vikings. The sense of history was as ingrained into the very rock there, as it was here in Dorset. Even as recently as the D-Day landings that they'd all talked about so glibly to the tourists they were showing around Normandy beaches.

Hannah was right. The past always left some legacy. Fighting for the freedom of the next generation. The thought brought a lump to Kate's throat. She felt insignificant. Such a small cog. Was that all they were – products of their past?

As the morning went on, it seemed to Kate that the three of them were gradually slipping back into their old ways, into the easy relationship she'd cherished. But the sense of warm security had a fleeting feel to it. Because there had been too many changes, still hanging, unspoken, in the atmosphere between them. There were still parts of their lives that had to be aired, but all three seemed equally determined to keep them temporarily at bay.

'There's something I want to tell you,' Hannah said at last, when the final crumb of lunch had disappeared, and they reluctantly got to their feet to head back towards Barstock.

Kate sensed rather than saw the dark clouds gathering above them. She walked quicker, not wanting to hear it, whatever it might be, knowing instinctively that it wasn't the news she and Stephanie wanted to hear.

'And there's something I should tell *you*.' Stephanie spoke abruptly. Her voice was strained and unnatural. They both stared at her.

'What?' Hannah's dark eyes were scared. She fiddled nervously with the straps of her small rucksack.

'First, I want to know something. Is it serious between you and Tom?' There was a strange determination in Stephanie's expression.

Kate paled. What the hell was she up to? Stephanie was unpredictable as the weather. But please God don't let her spoil this perfect day. She looked across at the brooding expression on the lovely face and knew immediately that her prayer didn't have a hope of being answered.

'Well?' Stephanie was waiting for her answer.

'Yes, of course it's serious. I love him.' Hannah's eyes resumed their dreamy expression. A vague smile touched her delicate lips. 'I love Tom more than anything. I thought you knew that.'

More than anything. Kate sighed. More than her two friends, certainly. More than her world perhaps?

'Then there's something you should know.' Stephanie's voice was brittle now. She was forcing herself not to listen to the soft kind of caring in Hannah's voice. And Kate realised that it had to be that way.

'Sounds ominous.' Hannah laughed, but it was a nervous laugh, and her eyes pleaded with Stephanie as if begging for mercy.

But Stephanie refused to look at her. Instead she strode out ahead, tall and dark and cruel, her voice strident, carried in the wind. 'Don't make the mistake of thinking you're the only woman in his life, darling. Tom's screwing around.'

Kate heard the sharp intake of breath that seemed to mingle with the breeze, and realised that it was her own. What was Stephanie playing at?

Hannah blinked heavily, as if a stroke of reality was darting through the dreams, and then the vagueness returned to her eyes. 'Don't be silly, Steph,' she said. 'Tom wouldn't do that.'

'What makes you so sure?' Now Stephanie turned to face them. She was walking backwards, and there was a fierceness about her that made Kate take Hannah's arm as if she had to be protected.

'I know him.' Hannah looked away, out towards the sea, as it crashed on to the smooth shingle. She stopped walking. 'I love him. He loves me. He's not like that.'

She wouldn't hear what Stephanie was saying. Kate knew it, yet she also knew that the words would eat away at her in quiet moments. She would wonder. Hannah would wonder and her trust in him would be gone. One day, if not today, she would hate Stephanie for doing that to her, not thank her for the truth.

'Maybe you don't know him as well as you think.' Stephanie's voice was cold.

'You're wrong.' Hannah walked on, faster this time. 'You've made a mistake.'

'I'm not wrong . . .'

'Leave it out, Steph,' Kate intervened at last. She had to. Stephanie was twisting a knife, and Kate couldn't stand by and watch.

Stephanie turned on her. 'D'you think I'd lay all this on Hannah if it wasn't true? Shouldn't she be told if the guy's messing her around? Well, shouldn't she?'

Kate was silent. She felt torn in two.

Stephanie was close to tears. 'We're supposed to be friends, aren't we? Aren't friends supposed to be honest? Being supportive is nothing but a farce if we're not even honest with each other.' Her face was drained and wasted. And Kate saw in her eyes how much it had cost her to tell Hannah. So. It must be true.

'Stop it.' Hannah was screaming, a thin wail that was lost in the wind. She shoved her hands over her ears. 'I won't listen to you. Stop it.'

Kate tried to put a comforting arm round her but Hannah shook her off, turning on Stephanie like a wildcat. 'Why are you so convinced of all this?' Her voice was dangerously low.

Stephanie took a deep breath. 'I went to a party with Dian Jones on Friday night.' She looked over Hannah's left shoulder.

'You did what?' Hannah moved closer. She grabbed Stephanie's arms. 'You went to a party with Dian?' Astonishment mingled with angry confusion. 'Why?'

'Why not?' Stephanie still wouldn't look at her. 'She invited me.'

'She invited you?' Hannah dropped her arms as if she could no longer bear to touch them. 'So if Hitler had ever invited you to a ball, then you would have gone, knowing what he'd done to the Jews, is that it?'

Kate hid her surprise. Stephanie had certainly kept quiet about knowing Dian.

'Dian's hardly in the same league as Hitler, darling.' Stephanie looked as if she were trying to smile, but instead her mouth twisted in pain.

'She is to me.' Hannah crumpled.

Kate leaped forwards to take her in her arms. Stephanie's muscles twitched, but she didn't move.

'She is to me,' Hannah repeated. Her eyes were lost and frighteningly vacant. 'And I'm surprised that you believed her.' She stared at Stephanie with reproach.

Stephanie kicked at the coarse grass of the cliff. 'It wasn't what she said . . .' She sighed. 'It was seeing her with Tom. At the party.'

'Friday night,' Hannah whispered. 'I was sick.' She clutched her stomach as if the pain was still there.

Kate held her more tightly. There was a fragile numbness about Hannah, as if her world was cracking into pieces. It was worse than her anger, worse than tears.

'Did you actually see them . . . ?'

'No.' Stephanie looked away.

'What were they doing?'

'Just messing around.'

'Just messing around?' Hannah brightened. 'That doesn't prove a thing. They're old friends. Old friends often mess around. You don't know for sure? That he's actually sleeping with her?'

Kate watched Stephanie, witnessing the fight going on inside her. She guessed that Stephanie knew more than she was saying. Much more. Stephanie couldn't bear Hannah to be duped by Tom McNeil. And yet – how hard it must be to hurt her, how hard to know that she might be losing her friendship for good.

'I don't know for sure.' Reluctantly, Stephanie's sad blue eyes met Hannah's searching gaze. Their eyes locked in some sort of wistful understanding.

And then Hannah moved in closer. As if she were moving in for the kill. 'Why are you determined to spoil things between me and Tom?' she hissed. 'You're jealous, aren't you? You're jealous because you're desperate to find a man to love you, and I've gone and done it. Tom's right. You're so eaten up with jealousy that I have someone like him to really love me – for who I am, not just what I'll give him in bed – that you'll say anything to break us up. Anything.' She was breathing deeply, her slender body heaving with emotion.

Stephanie stared at her in horror. Her body arched, drawing back from Hannah's venomous attack. 'That's not true, Hannah . . .' she began.

'I won't listen to you.' Hannah backed away. 'I believe Tom, not you.

112

He's right about you. I tried to defend you, but it's true what they say. You're just a slut. No one decent will want you after you've been with . . . with everyone in trousers who comes near you. And it serves you right. You think you've got everything – money, brains, looks. But you haven't got love.' Her voice rose to a hysterical screech. 'You haven't got love.' And she turned and ran, flying away from them into the wind, her small figure disappearing back down the cliff path.

Kate stared after her in amazement. 'Oh, Steph.' Kneeling at her side, she took a tissue, and gently wiped the huge tears sliding down the beautiful face. Kate didn't have to guess how much those words had hurt her. The pain was drawn on her face.

'She didn't mean it,' she whispered. 'You must see that. It was Tom talking, not Hannah. He's poisoned her mind.'

Stephanie shook her dark head. 'But it's Hannah who believes him.' Her voice was stark, devoid of emotion. She rose to her feet, brushing the grass from her jeans. 'Let's get back.'

'Are you okay?' Kate wanted to comfort her, but Stephanie never allowed comfort. She erected a barrier to shield herself from anyone else who tried to share her pain.

'I'll survive.' She laughed humourlessly. 'But I don't know about Hannah.'

Slowly, they trudged back along the cliff. The promises of the spring day had turned horribly sour. The three of them were further apart than they'd ever been. Suddenly, all Kate wanted was to get out of Barstock, to be alone to think.

They found Hannah, slumped by some rocks on the bay and, together, waited in silence for the bus to take them back to college. And Kate continued to wonder but didn't dare ask. What was the something that Hannah had intended to tell them that day? What had been on her mind, before Stephanie dropped her bombshell? She sensed that it was important, and she knew that whatever else happened, she simply had to find out.

9

Stephanie left Kate and Hannah in the village, and returned to Royal Ford alone. She didn't want to talk; she needed something to take away the sting of Hannah's words. Hannah and Tom McNeil . . . what little game was that bastard trying to play? And all the time, she could see his hand resting on her leg, that same hand creeping up the inside of Dian's thigh.

The day was overcast now – it seemed more than just hours since they'd left for Barstock – and her steps became still more heavy and slow. A deep depression was washing over her. She felt as if she were hanging on by her fingernails. Hanging on to the sides of some sort of salvation. Only those sides were slippery, and she couldn't keep hold. They were smooth curves and she needed rough edges she could cling to.

Then, outside the building, Stephanie saw the black Bentley – the one that Daddy drove. Was she dreaming? She rubbed her eyes, and as she did so, he strode out of the doors of Royal Ford, much too real for a mirage. He saw her immediately.

'Stephanie! Where the hell have you been?'

She flinched. 'We went for a walk. From Barstock. The bus has only just got back.' The defensiveness was automatically creeping into her voice. She heard it and she hated it. What business was it of his anyway? She straightened and glared at him.

'The bus?' He shook his dark head in despair. He probably hadn't been on a bus since childhood.

She was irritated. 'Surely you remember buses, Daddy? Big red things – or green or yellow depending on the area . . .'

'Shut up, Stephanie.' Suddenly she was aware of his drawn white face under the slick tan he'd acquired on last winter's holiday in the sun.

She took a cautious step closer. 'What is it? What are you doing here?'

He'd never ventured near the college before. It must be serious or he wouldn't be here now. Jesus Christ. What had happened.

His eyes clouded.

'Is it Miles?' It came out as a whisper. Somehow she knew.

He nodded.

This was her punishment then. Stephanie's shoulders sagged. She'd ducked out of a weekend back at Atherington when Miles needed her, and now something dreadful had happened to him.

'What is it? Is he all right? Is he hurt?' She was trembling and in a blur she felt her father descend the steps, and reach her side. He put an arm round her but, as always, his touch meant pressure, and she shied away from it.

'He's disappeared.'

Relief flooded over her. Only disappeared. He could be anywhere then. He wasn't hurt. Daddy and his bloody melodrama. She almost laughed. 'Is that all?'

His blue eyes were cold as slivers of steel. 'No, Stephanie. That isn't all. As if that's not enough. I'm seriously worried about him.'

'Why?' She frowned. Some students came down the driveway, pausing to admire the Bentley and watch Stephanie and Julian curiously.

'Because he hasn't taken anything with him,' he hissed. 'No clothes, no books, not even his toothbrush. And anyway, where would he go?'

'There must be lots of places.' Maybe it was enough for Miles to just get out of Atherington. Well, she'd wanted him to escape, hadn't she? 'He could be with . . .'

'I've tried there.' Her father wouldn't even allow Ken's name into the conversation.

Of course he wouldn't. Ken was homosexual. According to Daddy, Ken had dragged Miles into unspeakable habits. Ken was the unmentionable – so how worried must Daddy actually be if he'd contacted Ken? She stared at him.

'So you don't know where he could be? You have absolutely no idea?' His voice was accusing.

Stephanie hung her head. It was a barb straight to the heart, and it was true. Once Miles would have come to her. He would always have come to her in the days when she'd shown him how much she cared. Days long gone. Now he had to be content with words.

'He's not here.' This was hardly the place that Miles would run to, even if they had still been as close as they once were. This was Stephanie's territory, not joint territory.

'I expected you to at least have some suggestions.' He was exasperated now, smoothing his dark hair from his brow as he did when he wasn't quite in control.

'How long has he been missing?'

'Since Friday night.'

Since realising that she wasn't coming back for the weekend. But it wasn't very long. 'Miles isn't a child any more,' she murmured. 'He'll turn up.'

Some more students appeared and Stephanie saw her father's irritation increase. He probably thought they shouldn't allow students near halls of residence on the days when a black Bentley stood outside.

He grabbed her arm. 'Let's get out of here. We'll have some tea somewhere and talk.'

Talk? She hesitated. 'There's a café in hall. You could be my guest.' She half-wanted to show him where she spent her time. Half-wanted some kind of normality. It would be pleasant to be taken in proudly on his arm, even to show off her handsome father.

But he frowned. 'Don't be ridiculous. We can't talk surrounded by jabbering students. We'll find a hotel.'

Sulkily, Stephanie climbed into the passenger seat of the Bentley. He started the engine. Over the years she'd come to hate the soft, controlled purr that reminded her of Daddy himself.

'Did you say anything to Miles?' she asked, when they were seated in the tea-room of Dorchester's plushest hotel, amidst starched white linen and delicate porcelain. 'To make him run away?' Perhaps that was unfair – but Daddy was responsible too. She couldn't shoulder all the guilt alone.

'Nothing.' He wouldn't meet her gaze. 'Of course he was due to start with us tomorrow . . .' His voice tailed off as he stirred his Earl Grey thoughtfully.

Stephanie stared at the silver spoon spinning the liquid around. She wanted to be cruel. 'That's probably one reason he left,' she said. 'He's never wanted to work for you. You must realise that.'

Her father was silent.

Stephanie lost patience. 'Why do you think he took so long shilly-shallying around since he left school? He's got his own life to lead, but you won't let him. Miles has taken off because he didn't want to join up.' And it was like the army. There was the same degree of control, even if it was more subtle. You might not be yelled at in Daddy's company, but you'd sure as hell be got at.

'What else would he do?' There was a sneer in his voice that she hated.

Stephanie was aware that Miles was a disappointment to their father. He had probably been a disappointment since his first frequent tears had shown his feelings, and since his regular four-year-old bed wetting revealed his lack of control. And he'd never learned to cultivate that control. Miles lacked everything his father held dear – single-mindedness, determination, ambition and the ability to lead others. This latest disappointment was only one of many, but it might also be the last straw.

'He could have his own life for a start.' It was easy to stand up to Daddy when she was doing it for Miles. It was where she herself was concerned that Stephanie had a problem. Her father's hold over her was emotional and personal – based on a peculiar intimacy. It didn't affect her defence of Miles.

'Perhaps he's not even capable of running his own life.' Julian selected a fruit scone and buttered it carefully.

'Have you given him the chance to try?' Her eyes bored into him.

'I'm attempting to save him from self-destruction, Stephanie.' His eyes hardened against her. 'If he joins the company then he has a certain protection. He has a future. Something to work for, some goal to achieve.' His knife fell from his hands, smearing white linen with cream. 'For heaven's sake! What do you think I've done it all for if not for my children, if not for you and Miles?'

'But if Miles doesn't want that . . .' It was no good. She could feel herself being ground down. His domination was taking over. His tone, his words, his mannerisms, his eyes. They were winners. Winners of every argument. And his son couldn't be a loser. Oh no, his son must follow in the footsteps carved out for him by the great man himself.

She lit a cigarette as a small gesture of rebellion, ignoring his cough of distaste.

'Miles has got enough problems as it is.' Julian sipped his tea, wafting the smoke away with his free hand. 'He's surrounded by bad influences. If somebody doesn't pull him out of the quagmire soon, he'll go under.'

She felt the reproach digging into her. 'It's not my fault. I've got a life too, you know.' And yet sometimes it didn't feel like that. Sometimes it felt as if her life was back in Kent, back in the past, with these people who owned her. That all the rest was just pretence.

He finished his tea, crumpled his linen napkin and stood up. 'I want you to come back to Atherington with me.'

'But I've got work to do, lectures to go to . . .' She could feel him looming over her. She stubbed out the cigarette in the cut-glass ashtray and stumbled to her feet.

'What matters most?' He glared at her. 'Finding your brother or a few silly lectures?'

'They're not silly . . .' She was beginning to wheeze painfully. Damn this bloody asthma. It always hit her when she most needed to be composed.

'You cared about him once, Stephanie.'

'Too much.' She didn't want to remember . . .

Sweet, stolen kisses in the summerhouse.

'How will it be, Steffi? How will it be with girls?' Eyes that seemed to be her own eyes, staring at her with love.

'Like this, like this.'

'How will I make them love me?' Soft lips parted.

'Do this, and this, and this.'

Two slender boyish bodies in the first flush of adolescence. Enjoying, exploring, living a dangerous delight. Each day a dangerous delight. Not even knowing how it had first happened. Only that it had happened through love. Through closeness and curiosity, and knowing that they were different from all the others. That they were special. That there was no one else. And that they were alone – together and alone.

Julian was eyeing her curiously. 'Well, if you ever cared for him, you'd better come home with me now and help me find him. Because he's in trouble. I know it.'

She stared at him, not understanding. Why did he have to assume that Miles was in trouble? Why couldn't Miles just take off if he felt like it?

Stephanie sighed. 'But I can't help him now.'

So many times she had said that to him, when he'd begged her for love, begged her for more.

'I can't help you now, Miles,' she'd said.

Because she knew it was wrong, and she knew that it was destruction, not delight. So she had to be cruel. Always, it seemed, Stephanie had to be cruel to those she loved the most.

'You've got to help him. You've got to help me find him.' Daddy's hands were on her arms. He was shaking her. 'I don't know what's happened between you two. But I do know that since you came to this place, Miles has been going downhill fast.'

'No.' She couldn't stop staring at him. How could he do this to her, heap more blame on to the pile of guilt she already had? 'It isn't my fault . . .'

'Take the responsibility, girl.' His voice was rough. 'Stand up and take it.'

Suddenly she wondered what he'd sounded like before he met Mother, before he founded the company, and skipped into the money world. Had he been real? Had there been rough edges that a girl could cling to when her fingers were slipping on the soft smooth curves? When she was ever so slowly going under?

'I know where he might be,' she said at last. She had tried to deny the knowledge, and even now she hoped she was wrong.

His eyes met hers. 'Where?'

In the summerhouse, that's where he might be if he really was in trouble. If he hadn't managed to escape after all. He would be in their retreat. In the summerhouse that nestled half-hidden within the ancient apple orchard.

Oh yes, some crazy person had built a summerhouse that was shaded by all the trees. Only one part of it was ever sunny, just a small streak of sunlight, while the rest became dank and coated with lichen and moss, the inside damp and cold, the glass stained green.

But in that sunny spot, Miles and Stephanie had made love in the warm days, knowing they'd never be disturbed because no one ever came to the summerhouse. Sometimes Daddy threatened to have it knocked down, destroy the orchard, and make it as perfect as the rest of the grounds. But he never got around to it. And so it remained their summerhouse. Their summerhouse to lie naked in. His first woman, her first man. First love, only love. Sometimes it seemed to be the only love that would ever be possible.

But if she were right . . . Stephanie lay back in the leather seat of the Bentley, and closed her eyes. If Miles was hiding in the summerhouse – then it would be her fault. It would be her that he was looking for – still. And it would be her who had let him down.

* * *

Hannah jumped off the bus so fast that Kate almost lost sight of her. In a moment she was just a streak of blonde hair and tawny duffel-coat disappearing into the distance.

'Hannah!'

She didn't stop.

Kate caught up with her at last in the college library, where she had her head stuck in a book of metaphysical poetry. She was frowning.

'John Donne knew what it was like,' she told Kate moodily.

Kate hid her irritation with some difficulty. She couldn't blame her for being upset, but Hannah was behaving like a prima donna. 'Stephanie was only thinking of you,' she said. 'She cares about you.'

'Stephanie was thinking of herself.' Hannah shut the book with a decisive snap. 'And Stephanie was wrong.'

Kate shrugged. Hannah had clearly made up her mind what to believe and who to believe. It was Tom McNeil all the way.

'So there's no point in hounding me.' Hannah glared at her, as if preparing for further attack.

'I'm not.' Kate sat down, flipping nonchalantly through a newspaper propped on the heavy mahogany stand. Why was everyone so damned sensitive?

She looked around her. The library was part of the original Victorian building, once magnificent, but now the huge musty room was almost deserted, its books reaching to the ceiling dusty and untouched.

'I didn't come here to hound you,' she repeated. 'I came to find out what it was you wanted to tell us.'

Hannah flushed, and bit her lip nervously. 'Tell you?'

'Yeah. I know there's something. That's why you came over to Ford this morning.' She laughed. 'Don't tell me you got a distinction for that essay last week?'

Silence. Hannah shook her head.

'You've had a poem published?' Hannah rarely sent her work to magazines, but occasionally she plucked up the courage and then suffered from rejection for the next six weeks.

Hannah shook her head once more.

'What then?' Kate was beginning to lose patience.

'I'm pregnant.' The words dripped like tears into the heavy silence of the library.

121

Kate stared at her. 'Oh no! Jesus, Hannah, how awful.' She felt a rush of guilt. When Hannah had confessed her ignorance and total lack of sexual experience, Kate should have talked to her. You could never trust men to take the responsibility.

Men. The thought scurried through her head. Leon – tall, gangly and sandy-haired, stooping to kiss her last New Year's Eve. The kiss had never really been a kiss. He'd written twice – casual, chatty letters that Kate had no intention of answering. Men like Leon were too nice to get involved with. And the other kind . . . the other kind included Tom McNeil.

She should have offered Hannah advice. There was no excuse. And yet . . . one minute Hannah had been running like a scared rabbit at the very mention of the word sex. And the next she'd as good as moved in with Tom.

'I'm sorry, Hannah. I should have said something. It was my fault . . .' But Kate's repentant voice tailed off as she looked at Hannah once more. She was standing erect and proud, and the brown eyes were confident and clear.

'What are you on about, Kate? Why should you be sorry?'

Kate blinked. 'Well, you didn't want to get pregnant, did you? You didn't do it on purpose?' God, Hannah was so lost in her romantic dreams it was a wonder she ever got anything done.

'No, of course I didn't.' Hannah moved gracefully over to the window.

Kate's eyes narrowed calculatingly as she stared at her waist. How far gone could she be?

Hannah turned. 'But now that I am . . .'

'Oh, Hannah. I know how you're feeling.' Kate's voice broke with emotion. It was as if her own past was coming back to haunt her, just when she'd assumed that it had taken its proper place as distant memory, no longer close enough to hurt.

The memory of being in love. And the memory of finding out she was pregnant. Waiting for the monthly cramps that never came. Searching frantically each time she went to the loo, every morning, every night. The horror, the fear. And then . . . when she could deny it no longer, the hopelessness. That awful dip of the stomach that should be only morning sickness, but couldn't be, because it carried on through every hour of every day. A sickness that had become a constant part of her.

Questions. What shall I do? What shall I do? Kate Dunstan, all alone with no one's hand to hold. No one to say, 'It'll all work out.' Because it wouldn't. It couldn't. That awful certainty that the whole world knew. That everyone was staring, talking, like they always talked in Ridley.

'Do you, Kate?' Hannah's voice was mildly enquiring. 'Can you really imagine what it's like?'

Kate's pale skin was burning. She couldn't tell her. She still couldn't tell her about Justine and the lost year.

She nodded. 'We've got to be practical.'

That was the important thing. Hannah needed someone to look after her, to help her through this. She wasn't capable of making decisions in her vulnerable state of mind. She needed someone to do her thinking for her, and she needed someone's hand to hold. And it wasn't Tom's hand she needed either.

'Have we?' Hannah smoothed her blonde hair away from her face. 'I don't feel practical,' she admitted. 'I just feel kind of warm and good.'

Kate's eyebrows arched into exasperation. 'How far gone are you? Two months? Three months?' She couldn't be much further than that. Whatever had happened when Hannah jumped into the bed of Tom McNeil had happened sometime over the Christmas holidays. Until then, she'd been safe.

'I've just missed my third period.' There was a kind of reluctance in Hannah's voice. She was still staring out of the window, her mind lost in whatever it was she saw out there.

'Oh, that gives us plenty of time.' Kate felt only relief. Lucky Hannah. She might be a dreamer, but at least she'd had the brains to tell someone. Something could be done.

'Plenty of time for what?' Hannah's brown eyes were curious as she turned towards Kate once more.

'Well, for . . . for . . .' Kate faltered. 'You are going to have an abortion, aren't you, Hannah?'

She watched Hannah's expression change from bewilderment to a kind of slow anger. 'An abortion?' Her small, white hands fluttered protectively in front of her stomach. 'An abortion?' She almost spat the word. 'No, of course I'm not!' She glared at Kate as if she were a murderer at the very least. 'I couldn't kill my baby,' she whispered. *But you could,* her eyes seemed to say.

Kate's shoulders dropped. 'What *are* you going to do then?' Hannah must be crazy. Surely she wasn't planning to have it? Kate would have to tell her that the worst pain – the very *worst* pain – would be giving the baby away.

'What do you think? I'm going to have my baby, of course.' Hannah's eyes were cold.

'And then?' Kate couldn't believe she was hearing this.

'I'm going to keep it.' Hannah's mouth set in a stubborn line. 'I don't have a choice.'

I don't have a choice . . . The words echoed in Kate's head. No, Hannah was wrong. She did have a choice. It was Kate who hadn't been given a choice. It wasn't fair. She felt as if Hannah had been given her choice – the one that belonged to her. 'You do have a choice, Hannah,' she murmured, getting to her feet.

Hannah backed away. 'I don't.' Her eyes were scared.

'What about college?' Kate was on fire. How could Hannah throw so much away?

'I'll leave. It wouldn't be the end of the world. I'm not sure I'm cut out to be a teacher anyway.' She laughed nervously. 'I panicked my way through the last teaching practice, you know I did.'

'That's just lack of experience.' Kate brushed her words angrily into the distance. Hannah had a wonderful way with the infants she taught, warm, imaginative and kind. Like some replacement mother figure. Mother figure . . . She stiffened. 'So you'll leave? Just like that?' Her voice was incredulous. 'What about your parents?'

Hannah blinked.

'What are you going to tell them?'

'I don't know.' She looked away. 'I haven't decided yet.'

Kate moved in closer. 'And what about Tom?'

'Tom?' Hannah's eyes flickered nervously around the library, and came to rest at last on a vase of red tulips on the desk.

'Have you told him?' Kate watched, as Hannah moved towards the vase. She touched one of the blooms and drew back, her hands dusted with yellow pollen.

'No. Not yet.' Hannah smoothed the pollen between her fingers. It gave the skin a golden glow.

'I thought not.' Kate folded her arms, feeling a shaft of triumph. How could Hannah be so dumb? Did she really think that a bloke like Tom McNeil would want to take on the responsibility of a woman and child? Whatever else he might be, a martyr he was not.

'He might be pleased.' Even Hannah sounded uncertain.

Kate laughed. It wasn't a pleasant sound, and its echo reverberated around the dry, musty room. 'Grow up, Hannah!' Stephanie had said that too, not so long ago, and now it seemed to Kate that Stephanie was right. Hannah had filled her own head with some daft romantic notion about giving up her work for the man she loved. She was behaving like an irresponsible idiot.

And as Kate stared at her, it seemed that it wasn't just Hannah standing there, her eyes hurt, her hands coated with pollen, but Hannah and her child.

And the loss inside Kate made her ache. The loss that was Justine – still living somewhere, but with a different mother and a different father. Lost to her.

'I could never give my child away.' Hannah was gazing down at her hands. 'Whatever happened.'

'You don't know that.' Kate's throat was dry, her hands damp with sweat.

'I do.' Hannah's voice was soft and musical. 'I can't understand women who do that. I could never give away my baby, even if we were penniless, living on the streets, whatever. I just couldn't.'

In that moment, Kate hated Hannah Thompson. She looked down and her fists were clenched, her knuckles white. Justine . . . 'You're a fool, Hannah,' she muttered. 'A bloody fool.'

'And you're as bad as Stephanie.' Hannah's voice was barely a whisper. 'You like to pretend you're only thinking of me. But you're not. Not really.' She held her head high. Her eyes became cool and distant. 'If you were a real friend you'd give me some support, instead of trying to run my life. Instead of telling me what to do. Mutual support – wasn't that what we promised?'

Kate stared at her. Was that true? Could it be that Hannah's vulnerability had made them both want to take her over? Was Kate trying to take the decision away from Hannah, just as her own mother had once taken the decision from Kate herself.

She couldn't bear the thought. And she couldn't bear to look at Hannah's smug, self-righteous face any longer. She couldn't bear the pain. 'Oh, go jump in a bloody lake, Hannah!' she said.

Kate stalked out of the room. She'd tried her best to keep the three of them together, and it had been thrown back in her face. All Hannah really cared about was Tom McNeil and having his kid. She just wanted to play mothers and babies.

Hannah would have a child who would taunt Kate like Justine's memory still taunted her. Stephanie was right. They could forget Hannah. It was just the two of them now.

She stopped at the phones in the entrance lobby to make a call to her aunt's farm in Cheshire.

'Do I need some help with the lambing over Easter?' the kind voice crackled over the telephone wire. 'You're a gift from heaven, Kate. You come as soon as you can. And stay for as long as you like.'

Hannah stayed in the library until she was sure Kate had left the building. She'd expected Stephanie to think her crazy for contemplating giving up college, but not Kate. She had hoped that Kate, to whom she had entrusted so many secrets from the past, would understand. Sometimes Stephanie was too close for understanding. But that had changed too.

Hannah sighed. She was stunned at Kate's attitude, devastated that even she couldn't be pleased for her. And shocked to the core. Abortion and adoption were two options that she hadn't even considered, would never consider. Because already she loved this child.

Since moving in with Tom, Hannah's college life had become redundant. She felt as if the force of Tom's personality had swept everything from her world, everything except his own presence, so that Hannah could start afresh. And she had needed that clean sweep more than anything.

'It's not that I mind you having friends,' Tom had said to her, when she expressed a desire to see the other two girls. 'Although I do want you to myself. I want to be with you, every minute of the day.'

She'd laughed, unable to hide her pleasure, not wanting or needing to hide it. Confident in his love. 'What then?'

'They can't stand me.' Tom stroked her hair. 'They both hate me, I know they do. They want to run your life.'

'That's not true . . .' So many times she had said those words to him. So many times she had defended Kate and Stephanie. And yet every time she saw them, they seemed determined to prove him right.

And Kate had just done it again. Kate wanted her to kill their baby.

Hannah rested her hands gently on her stomach. It was true that pregnancy had made her feel warm and wonderful, better than she'd ever felt before.

She loved Tom. She wanted him to be her world. She too wanted to be with him every minute, drowning in the very scent of him, the touch of him, the sound of his voice murmuring her name. And now, more than anything, she wanted to have his child.

Perhaps it wasn't medically possible, but it seemed to Hannah that this child was already whispering to her, through the soft lining of her womb. And she was whispering back. Making promises of protection. This child, growing every day inside her, would need Hannah as no one had ever needed her before – even Tom. She would be everything to this child, created between the two of them, and that's why it was so special. That's why the child would be everything to her too.

She would be blissfully, bloomingly pregnant. She would live with her man, and bear his child, and forget about stuffy old books and stuffy old classrooms. And while she was becoming a mother of the earth, while her body was lost in instinctive communications with Nature, Hannah would be at her most creative.

She was already bursting with the poetry of the experience that lay ahead. Yearning to scribble it all down in long nights while her belly grew huge and while Tom lay sleeping beside her. Her man. It wasn't the end of anything for Hannah. It was only the beginning of the kind of writing she wanted to explore. She didn't want her poems only to be published in the college student magazine. She wanted more. Words meant so much to her, but they were worthless without experience. She would write, and she would have Tom and their baby.

Hannah walked slowly out of the library. That's what she wanted. It seemed to be all she'd ever wanted. But the voices of Kate and Stephanie were making her wonder. Bestowing doubts and fears that only Tom could sweep away. Why did they hate him so? Forget the past. He was her future.

There was only one thing left for Hannah to do before her life could fall into place, and she would do it tonight. She would tell Tom about the baby, and then she could relax in the joy of it. And at last forget the fears.

10

As soon as she entered the flat, Hannah heard Tom singing. She smiled. It was good to hear him happy.

'I'm back.' But it was hard for her to get used to living this way. She remained in limbo, crouched in some halfway house between her study room at Royal Ford, and her lover's flat. Tom had given her a key, and he wanted her there all the time. But it remained *his* flat. Still Hannah lacked the courage to make it her own.

'Where are you?' This wasn't the life she'd envisaged for herself. And if she ever had, in unguarded moments, allowed the possibility of life with a man to creep in, then it had been the conventions of her parents' marriage that she had pictured. Not this bohemian life that both thrilled and scared her at the same time.

'In the shower.' There was a pause. 'Come here. I've missed you. I want to see your pretty face.'

She smiled, throwing her bag and duffel-coat down on the sofa, loving the way he wanted her around him. 'I'm coming.'

In the tiny bathroom he half pulled back the shower curtain to reveal his long, loose-limbed body, wet and lathered. 'Where have you been all my life, sweetheart? You've been bloody ages – I was beginning to get worried.' Looking remarkably unperturbed, he bent to kiss her, spraying her with the water that was clinging to his wet hair and face.

'Tom!' She leapt back, laughter springing readily to her eyes, curving the corners of her delicate mouth.

'Why were you so long?' He slapped more soap on his belly, and Hannah had to look away. It was ridiculous, so ridiculous, that after everything that had happened between them, she found it impossible to look at his naked body without embarrassment.

'They were going to Barstock, and I tagged along. I thought you wouldn't mind . . .' She tailed off, feeling guilty, as if Tom could only be happy when she was by his side.

'And how was it?' His voice became curt, as it always did when Stephanie or Kate were close to the conversation.

'It was terrible.' At least she could be honest. 'I'm beginning to think you were right about those two trying to run my life.' Hannah determinedly ignored the stab of betrayal that these words brought to her heart. She didn't want to think about her two friends in that way. But hadn't they forced her into it? Stephanie's accusations and Kate's cruel words of advice had cut her more deeply than they'd ever know.

'Come in here.' Tom's voice changed again, becoming husky and warm. He drew the curtain back further, invitingly.

'There isn't room.' Her inhibitions were pulling her away, so real to her, so close. If it was hard to look at his naked body, then how much harder was it to contemplate squeezing into the narrow bath with him to share a shower?

'Come on. I'll soap your back.' His voice, smooth and compelling, and the hypnotic power of his eyes, dragged her closer.

Slowly, Hannah tugged at her cream sweatshirt, and she slipped out of her jeans. She couldn't resist him. And she knew she had to go where he wanted to take her. Because if she refused, there were plenty of others just waiting to grab her place. Ready and eager. Plenty of others who would jump naked into a shower with Tom. He would think her a fool if she didn't go where he led. She had to keep up with him, or he would no longer be hers.

'You're beautiful, Hannah.' He held out a hand to help her in. 'There's no need for you to be so shy.' His eyes swept across the neat curves of her small breasts and slim hips. He pulled her closer.

Hannah felt her colour rising as his skin touched her. 'Tom . . .' Her giggle held a note of desperation.

He was lathering soap into his hands. Reaching out, he gently massaged her breasts until the nipples hardened and rose like mountain peaks in the snow.

'Oh, Tom.' She grabbed his shoulders, wet and slippery, the skin tight to her touch.

'Mmm, Hannah. How could you leave me for so long? There wasn't a soul to talk to. I even had to write a blasted essay.' His hands cradled her small, tight buttocks.

What would Mother say? The thought came from nowhere, trying to spoil her illicit pleasure. If it was pleasure – this bitter-sweet sensation. She took a deep breath. No. She wouldn't admit these thoughts. They could stay outside.

She had broken from Mother and Dad. Not in so many words perhaps; there was no gaping rift to patch with the kind of darning that would never survive a storm. She would still see them, talk to them. They remained a part of her life. But they wouldn't run her life. She had broken from them where it mattered. In her mind. In her heart.

Hannah had made a lunge for freedom. At last, she'd untied the umbilical cord. The cord of possession that had stretched and twisted over the years until it was ugly, until Hannah had absorbed all her mother's fears and made them her own. Fears that had tangled into a perverted kind of terror. Now she had broken from those fears, and her new identity was waiting. Somewhere.

'Silent little Hannah.' His long slender fingers were drawing circles in the soapsuds around her nipples. 'Let's do it in the shower,' he whispered.

'Stop it, Tom.' She laughed and pushed him off. But it was a playful push, and in seconds his fingers were back for more, with a renewed urgency that made her snatch for breath. This was a new kind of living, and she must bend to it. This was romantic and daring, and would liberate her more thoroughly than any gesture she could make alone. So she closed her eyes as the warm water rained on to her head, soaking into her hair, her skin, her senses.

'Your breasts feel different.' There was an odd note in his smooth voice, a note that made her eyes blink open. 'Hannah?'

'What?' The film of sexuality was gone from the pale blue of his eyes. She felt a dart of fear.

'Your breasts – they feel fuller, more rounded.' His fingertips explored.

She held her breath. She had to tell him. She'd promised herself it would be tonight, and perhaps naked in the shower was as good a place as any. At least he wouldn't be able to walk out of the flat before she had a chance to talk to him.

'I'm pregnant.'

The brief pause lasted a lifetime. For a few seconds Hannah looked carefully over his left shoulder, into the shiny white plastic of the shower curtain. It seemed to her that in the peculiar stillness, the temperature of the water rose, the fine drizzle creating steam on their wet untouching bodies. Then she looked into his face.

'Hannah . . .' His voice was slippery as the soap still clinging to the crevices of her body. 'Is that true?' He reached once more for her breasts, this time with a kind of wonder.

She nodded, reassured by his touch. 'I was terrified of telling you. I didn't know how you'd take it.' Now she searched his eyes. How had he taken it?

'It's amazing.' He shook his head, his hands moving down to caress her belly. 'It's just incredible. So what shall we do? Shall we have this baby, Hannah?'

A huge burden that she hadn't even been aware of carrying, slipped from her shoulders, and Hannah let out the deep breath that she'd been holding for the lifetime of waiting for his response. 'I want to,' she said simply. Her eyes were pleading. She was all his, she wanted him to know that. 'It means so much to me, Tom.'

'Then we shall.' He lifted her from the bath, climbing out after her.

Her skin was burning, yet she was shivering, her teeth chattering together as if determined to prevent speech. 'Are we crazy?' She stared at him, this stranger – Tom. This man she loved. 'We don't even know each other yet. Not properly.' They'd only just begun, yet here they were talking babies.

'I told you before.' He wrapped a huge red towel gently around her. 'We know everything that matters.'

'I don't know a thing about your family.' She felt a sudden need to explore his roots. Maybe if she knew what had created Tom, where he'd grown, where he'd had all his dreams, she might get some clue about the man who was so hard to understand. So compulsive. So vital to her happiness.

'You don't *need* to know anything about my family.' His voice was stern. He put an arm round her shoulders and led her into the bedroom.

'Don't you see them?' Her eyes stared into his.

'My mother's dead.' He eased her on to the bed, and lay down beside her. 'She died which I was thirteen.'

'Oh, Tom.' Her hand was on his arm. 'I'm so sorry.' She should never have said anything. He must have been close to his mother. She could hear it in the finality of his voice, and see it in the pain stamped on to his fine features.

132

'It was a long time ago.' He started playing with her wet blonde hair, twining it between his thumb and forefinger.

'And your father?' she whispered.

His eyes darkened into anger. 'Now him, I sure as hell don't need to talk about.'

Hannah leaned on one elbow, tracing a line across his lips with her finger. 'You're even more of a mystery than me,' she teased. 'With your secret past.' Only sometimes was she brave enough to tease.

'Maybe I am. But I know exactly what we're going to do in the future. Our future.' He slipped the red towel from her shoulders. 'We'll get married. Be a regular family. You, me and the baby. How about that?' A triumphant smile flashed across his face.

She stared at him. 'You want to get married?' she echoed. Now that, she would never have guessed. It was a long way from the bohemian lifestyle she'd dreamed herself into. And yet . . . a warm glow suffused her, although she was naked once more, the goosebumps stiffening her fair skin. Shouldn't she be relieved that she wasn't facing this alone? Wasn't this what she wanted? To be the wife of Tom McNeil? Wasn't it the ultimate gift he could give her?

'We'll get married.' He pushed her shoulders gently down into the softness of the duvet. 'And you'll leave college.' He rolled on top of her, his face close to hers, the light stubble on his jaw grazing against her skin.

Belatedly she realised his intentions.

'You'll stay home and look after our baby.' He eased himself into her. 'I'll be qualified, and go out to work. We'll be poor and ridiculously happy.'

She felt him rising inside her. Felt it, but experienced no pleasure. All she could thing of was the baby, tucked inside her womb. And all she could feel was Tom pounding and arching over her in attack. It was an attack on the vulnerable child growing inside her. The baby she'd sworn to protect was under siege from the man she loved.

It became a battle. Hannah closed her eyes so it wouldn't be happening in front of her immediate vision. And she tensed against his onslaught. But he seemed not to notice. He went his own sweet, solo way, pressing into her, pushing further and further into her, until she wanted to scream. But no sound would come. Her throat was dry and parched. She was under attack.

At last he came with a shudder, and rolled off.

Hannah breathed a sigh of relief. Only then could she reach out for him without fear, to twist her fingers lightly through the damp fair hair, kiss the soft clean skin of his shoulders, let her hand trail cautiously over his taut chest. Only then was she no longer in danger. Only then was her baby safe once more.

Hannah watched Tom with adoring eyes. She loved him. But a man couldn't share in motherhood. His needs were alien, he wanted the same parts of her. For so long there had been no love for Hannah. And yet now, already, there seemed almost too much. The juggler was a woman looming on her horizon. She would have to make them share.

Afterwards, Tom was only half-satisfied, without knowing why. An image of Dian's sultry loveliness escaped from wherever it was closeted, to dance and taunt in front of his closed eyelids. He sighed. Dian knew what it was like to give herself in bed all right. But still, it was early days yet for Hannah.

He propped himself up on one elbow and stared at her as she lay beside him. Was she asleep? Sometimes he awoke at night and whispered her name. 'Hannah . . . Hannah . . .' Because she was so still, her breasts hardly rising, her breath silent as a baby's.

Then, as now, there was an aura of stillness about Hannah that touched Tom deeply. He tried to deny it, disliking the notion that he could be affected beyond his control, but it hung over her, this stillness that sometimes seemed more like an accusation. In those moments she reminded him of Mary, his mother, with her sad brown eyes and tender resignation.

It hadn't always been that way. His mother's eyes had been proud in the beginning.

'My lad,' she used to call him.

'My little Ma,' he would tease. She was tiny like Hannah, her bones seeming too fragile to be held tightly. Yet there was a strength under that apparent vulnerability that could keep a family together when everything else was falling apart.

She let him go his own way, always giving, never asking anything in return. She would have given him her world if she could, and he probably would have forgotten to thank her. And because she never asked for his attention, Tom hardly noticed when the eyes became tinged with sadness. When the pain crept around her bloodless lips, and the lines became furrows on her face.

So. Maybe it was because of Mary that he'd felt genuine pleasure at Hannah's announcement. A child. He'd been shocked, of course, but Tom was expert at hiding his emotions. And as her words sank in, as he looked into the face that belonged to him as surely as his own – Hannah's face – and the slender body that was now totally his, he felt a kind of gladness. His son. It gave Tom a sensation of warm contentment just thinking about it.

He had been wrong to fly from commitment. Hannah was virgin territory and it was this untouched innocence that made her so exclusively his. He was the master that he needed to be. It gave him the power to do as he pleased, and power brought freedom. With Hannah in the background of his life Tom was free to live in the spotlight, and no possessive female could make any claims on him. With Hannah he could have it all.

The early evening sun shafted through the window, highlighting Hannah's damp blonde hair as Tom smoothed it gently from her face. Darling Hannah and her family concerns, her need to do the right thing. What was left of his family could go screw themselves.

He turned from her, as the anger rose hot and thick inside him. Waiting, as it was always waiting, for his father to bring it bubbling to the surface. IIis father the accountant, whose pale watery eyes lurked behind horn-rimmed glasses. Whose tall skinny body was immaculate in pin-stripes, braces, white linen and silk tie. Vernon McNeil, forever polishing – shiny shoes or shiny Volvo. Proud to polish the car every week without fail, instead of remarking on his own tediousness.

Jesus, how Tom hated that man. His hypocrisy, the secret life he led while the face he showed to the world was that of a man of figures, a man of convention, sorrowing widower and upright Christian.

Tom had caught them at it on the day of his mother's funeral. Vernon McNeil and Rosa Bartlett. In his parents' bedroom. He couldn't believe it. He just stood there and gaped.

'You could bloody knock.' Vernon pulled up his braces.

Rosa's full face was flushed, her lipstick smeared. 'We were only larking around, love.' The fear in her blue eyes. Tom had seen them come to dinner in days gone by, she and her husband Jim. He'd seen his mother spend all day cleaning and cooking for them. All his father had ever done was buy the bloody wine.

'How could you?' He glared at Vernon, his eyes hot with hating. 'Jesus

Christ. On the day of her fucking funeral.'

'Watch your mouth.' Vernon McNeil recovered his composure. 'It's nothing to do with you.'

'She was my mother.' Tom knew he had it all on his side – pride, right, good, everything Mary had ever stood for. Everything he'd never paid attention to.

'Shut up. You're not so big that I can't still take a stick to you.' His father towered over him but Tom stood his ground. He wanted to spit in Vernon's ugly self-righteous face.

'You bloody do, and I'll tell that lot down there.' Tom gestured with a nod. Downstairs, guests were waiting and drinking and probably thinking the widowed man had sloped off for a few private tears.

Vernon took a step towards him. He shook his fist. His face was as tense and white as the knuckles so close to Tom's face. 'You sneaky little sod . . . you wouldn't bloody dare.'

'Just watch me.' Tom spoke softly, hoping his father couldn't see how he was trembling. It was the first time he'd tried a dangerous bluff, and it would prove to be the first of many.

Rosa put a hand on Vernon's arm. 'Let him be. The kid's upset, and he's got a point. We shouldn't have. Not today.' She sighed. 'Too much mother's ruin . . . I should have learned to stay off it by now.'

'He's got a lesson to learn. Life goes on.' But Vernon backed off, reaching for his black jacket.

Tom turned on his heels. 'Not for Mum, it bloody doesn't.'

He went downstairs but he couldn't go back into the lounge. Couldn't face any more meaningless drivel or sympathetic smiles. He walked out, and as he wandered the streets, Rosa's words came back to him.

'We shouldn't have. Not today . . .'

And his fists tightened inside the pockets of his jeans. So it hadn't been a one-off for his father and Rosa. It was a long-running affair.

He thought of his mother, and the sadness that had grown in her eyes over the past months. And he realised. She knew. That bastard.

As soon as Tom was old enough, he left home, vowing never to return. His mother had been everything to him, but Vernon was nothing. He was just the shit who happened to be his father.

Tom turned back to the girl lying beside him. She opened her wide brown eyes, staring at him, trusting him. Darling Hannah. He needed her, but she

136

could have been all the women in his world rolled into one – Dian, Janice and even Mary herself, and he wouldn't be able to give her all his love. It was too late for that. If it had been Hannah he'd met, instead of Janice . . . then maybe it might have been different. But Janice's careless betrayal had finished him.

And just in case he was likely to forget, just in case he was likely to fall in love again, Dian had turned the screws. Already he had betrayed Hannah, and the first time was the only time that mattered. After the first time it was meaningless. After the first time, Tom had been immune from loving Hannah. He could do what he liked. He was safe once more.

Stephanie and Julian were crossing the lawns of Atherington Hall, heading towards the orchard, and the summerhouse. It felt strange. Stephanie had never walked this way with her father before, in fact it struck her that she had never walked anywhere with him. Side by side in the Bentley was about as close as it got these days.

'I can go on my own,' she told him. It felt wrong. She should never have mentioned the summerhouse to him at all.

He shook his head. 'I'm coming too.'

She faltered. Why couldn't he understand? 'Really, Daddy. It's better that I go alone.'

He turned to look at her, his dark blue eyes intense and brooding, as she tried to communicate with this man who had once seemed able to read her mind. But now he'd stopped listening to minds as well as words.

'No, I want to see him. I've got some things I'd like to say to that young man.'

'He might not be there.' Stephanie sighed. She hoped he wasn't.

This expedition felt like a betrayal. The summerhouse was their retreat. It belonged to the two of them, Miles and Stephanie. It always had, since the time they'd first gone there together, one spring many years ago. It was the one place they'd been able to escape from the pressures of home. The one place where they'd been safe, knowing they'd never be disturbed.

Stephanie hung back. By walking with her father to the summerhouse, she was telling Miles that he no longer had anywhere left to hide.

But it was too late now.

'Let's get a move on.' His words were grim and his mouth uncom-promising. He strode ahead.

She had to run to keep up with him. 'Go easy on Miles,' she begged. 'He hasn't done anything wrong.'

Julian glared at her. 'Are you joking? Don't you realise the value of my time?'

Stephanie sighed. That was his problem. Somehow time had, like his children, lost its original meaning. Instead of having intrinsic value, time was now only representative of money. Money lost or money gained, that was all. And what of his children? What did they represent to him these days, now that they were children no longer? When had he stopped giving them his time?

If she thought back, Stephanie could dimly recall summer afternoons on the lawn when time had meant nothing. Running with Julian over the grass. Being spun around until she screamed, playing cricket and rounders, struggling with an adult tennis racquet. She could even remember the fierceness of his love as he held her close.

'Stephanie . . . my little Stephanie. My beautiful girl.'

She blinked back the tears. Perhaps his love had been too fierce, his demands too intense to hold on to.

'Here we are.' Julian tugged at the rusty orchard gate.

'Let me go first.' The trees were just starting to bloom, the blossom thickening around their branches like capes around bent shoulders. The first petals were scattered on the long grass.

'Don't be ridiculous, Stephanie.' He pushed her aside. 'What does it matter who goes first? You're not a child any more.'

Stephanie didn't know what that had to do with it, but she wasn't giving in on this one. She slipped past him, scissoring through the trees, every sense attuned to the green-stained summerhouse at the far end of the orchard. As she drew closer, her breath came faster. She was starting to wheeze painfully, her chest tight, her throat dry.

At the door of the summerhouse she stopped, filled with inexplicable dread. Ivy almost obscured the door. But the clinging tendrils of the ivy had been wrenched from their resting place. And there was an awful silence hanging in the air. It seemed to Stephanie that for a moment even the birds had stopped singing.

The early evening sun was still glinting through the leaves, and yet as usual the summerhouse was mostly in shade. She stepped inside.

He was lying in the streak of sunlight where they had first made illicit and dangerous love. The harsh yellow lit his slim body like a spear of destruction. He was in that very patch of sunlight, inert where he had once found life, cold where he had once found love.

'Miles . . .' Her voice broke. She knelt by his side. The blood had set, stiff and glued to the knife with which poor Miles had slit his wrists. His face was cold. 'Oh, my God . . .'

'I want a word with . . .' Julian stood in the doorway, his voice tailing into bleak nothingness, his skin growing chalk-white under his tan, as he stared with disbelieving eyes at the body of his son.

An awful moan seemed to pour from Stephanie's throat as she buried her head against the chest of her dead brother. It wouldn't stop. She couldn't stop. All that existed in the summerhouse that evening was Stephanie's dark and never-ending moan of pain.

11

'Why didn't you go home for Easter?'

They were trudging across the muddy field to check on the new lambs. Kate didn't want to meet her aunt's enquiring eyes, so instead she looked into the distance. There had been an unexpected frost that night, the kind of chilly blanket that often covers up a bright, spring day as if to remind the world that winter is by no means over.

'I couldn't face it,' she said at last. Couldn't face her mother was what she meant. Hannah's news had brought all the old resentments back to the surface. What with Stephanie disappearing from the face of the earth – rumour had it her father had taken her back to Kent – Kate's loneliness had sunk into dismal self-pity.

Aunt Barbara frowned. 'They are your parents . . .' she began.

'Worse luck.' Kate kicked sullenly at a clod of wet earth. Not that she ever thought of them as parents. It was just her mother. It had always been just her mother for as long as she could remember. Dad was never there; Mum always put herself between them. He meant less than nothing to Kate. She wasn't sure that he had ever meant anything. Was that Mum's fault too – that Dad was only a dark, faintly menacing shadow in the background of her life?

'Ungrateful girl.' Barbara seemed about to say more, but her expression changed as they got to the big field. 'Won't you look at this lot? They're not doing so bad.'

They both laughed. Unperturbed by their cold night, the lambs were frisky as ever, finding their feet and bleating their hunger to the Derbyshire countryside. But Kate knew they'd have to bring them under cover if the cold nights continued.

'Your mum was taken aback when I told her you were coming here,'

Barbara remarked. 'I thought she knew, mind.'

'I need the money,' Kate spoke glibly. She squared her shoulders in a gesture of defiance.

'I'm not exactly paying you a fortune.' Barbara grabbed a lamb, gently examining it while the mother bleated loudly in protest.

'Every little bit helps when you're on a grant.' Kate watched her. That sheep had more motherly feeling than Mum had shown in the past few years.

'That doesn't change the fact that you didn't think to let her know where you'd be.' Barbara released the lamb and looked Kate full in the face. 'Or were you trying to make a point?' Like Kate, and like Kate's grandmother before her, Aunt Barbara too had the family green eyes, the auburn hair and the smattering of freckles on pale skin.

Kate shook her head. 'No . . .' But she wasn't sure. Maybe she was trying to tell Mum something. And what was wrong with that?

'Don't you see how bad it made her feel? Not knowing where you were off to? Realising you'd rather come here than see your own mother?' She rubbed muddy hands on her jeans.

Kate shrugged. 'She's not bothered.'

'Oh no?' Her aunt's voice was cool as she moved away.

'Why should she be? She only ever wants me out of the way.' Out of the house during loveless holidays, out of Ridley.

Barbara's face seemed to close up against her. 'Don't make hasty assumptions,' she warned. 'Your mother loves you, and you're a fool to doubt it.'

'Then why does she want me to leave Ridley?' That was the big question. Why did she want her out of her life?

Kate stared at the countryside that surrounded them. They were only twenty miles away, but these peaceful green fields seemed to be at the other end of the earth from the heathered shadows of Raddlestone Moor.

'Leave Ridley?' Barbara's green eyes were confused.

'When I qualify.' Kate leaned against the gatepost. Why not tell her? It was true, wasn't it? 'She wants me to move right away from here. To go and teach somewhere respectable,' she sneered.

Her aunt's face was a blank mask with a strand of sadness glinting through. 'Maybe she's got her reasons.' Her voice was soft.

She finished what she was doing, and the two of them began to wander back.

'She's got her reasons all right.' The bitterness returned. 'Like being ashamed of me, for starters.' Kate almost spat the words. Her secret fears, her secret shame. But it didn't matter in front of her aunt, because Barbara already knew it all.

'She's not ashamed of you.' Barbara took her arm. 'Don't talk daft. She adores you.' Her mouth was working as though there was more. And a hint of anger made the placid features seem bold. 'She just wants you to have a better life, that's all.'

Now they were getting to it. Now they were reaching the nitty gritty. Snob values.

'And what's so awful about *her* life?' Kate spun round to face her. 'Tell me that.'

Barbara was silent, her eyes downcast.

'She might be a bit short of money, but at least she's got a husband and a house of her own. She could work. She's not so badly off. Not as bad as some.' Kate was shaking.

'You don't know the half of it, love. Things aren't always what they seem.' Was she dreaming, or were her aunt's eyes wet with unshed tears?

'What don't I know?' She grabbed her arms. 'Tell me!'

Barbara shook her head. 'It's not my place to say.' She hesitated. 'You must ask your mother.'

But Kate hardly heard her. She was lost now, wallowing in the resentment that Hannah's pregnancy had made more poignant, more hurtful. 'At least she chose her own life.' Her voice was passionate. 'At least she was allowed to choose for herself.'

'It's not that simple.' Barbara stopped walking. Still she was looking down at the long wet grass clinging to their wellingtons, steaming in the early morning sun. As if afraid to meet Kate's eyes. To meet her questions head on.

'Has it crossed your mind that she might need you?' she asked at last.

Kate shook her head. No, it hadn't. She didn't even want that kind of thought to cross her mind. She wanted to be hard and uncompromising, so she could find out the truth. So she could hurt a little.

'Phone her, at least.' Aunt Barbara's voice was urging her on. But Kate wasn't sure she wanted that. And would her mother want it? It was all very well for Aunt Barbara to say that Mum loved her, but didn't actions speak louder than words?

'Kate?' Aunt Barbara was waiting.

143

She got the feeling that she wouldn't take no for an answer. She might not have the family temper, but she certainly didn't lack their stubbornness.

Kate nodded. 'Okay, I'll phone her.'

'Good girl.' Barbara squeezed her arm. 'And if you want to duck out of working here to go home, then you go ahead.' She laughed. 'We'll struggle on without you.'

Kate managed to smiled back at her. It was unlikely. She would talk to her mother – but more than that? She wasn't making any promises.

She phoned her that evening.

'Kate?' Eileen's voice was thin and distant and Kate felt the plunge of longing for home.

'I'm sorry I haven't been in touch . . .' She paused. What could she talk about? What could she say to her when she couldn't even see her face?

'It doesn't matter. It's good to hear your voice.' No recriminations. She sounded too tired for recriminations. Kate tasted guilt. Maybe, just maybe Aunt Barbara was right.

'Are you okay?' she forced herself to ask.

'Not too bad now, love.' The voice refused to elaborate, trailing off into nothing.

Now? Kate stared at the phone. Why hadn't she said? Why hadn't Aunt Barbara said that there was something wrong? 'What's the matter with you?' Her voice sounded so cold. She couldn't believe how cold and unfeeling she sounded.

'I had to go into hospital for some tests.' Eileen spoke reluctantly – as if the words were being dragged out of her.

Tests? Kate felt a new kind of panic. 'What for?' she breathed, clutching the receiver more tightly.

'Nothing important.' Her mother's laugh was weak and unconvincing. 'Don't you worry now. I'm fine.'

Kate paled. A nasty thought scuttled cockroach-like into her mind. Was this her mother's new martyr routine? Was this yet another dissatisfaction? But she pushed the thought away. It was uncharitable, and she was ashamed.

'Why didn't Dad tell me you were going into hospital?' Kate demanded. 'Why didn't anyone tell me?' Her voice rose. 'Is he there? I want to talk to him.'

'No.' Her reply was too quick in coming. 'He's gone out, love.'

Of course he'd bloody gone out. Where he always went. Down the pub.

Kate sighed. Maybe Mum did have some reason to complain. It couldn't be easy being married to a man like him. Laughter was all very well, and Dad was laugh a minute when it suited him. But Kate knew there was a darker side to him too. A darker side that was kept well hidden. Somewhere in her subconscious, there was more. Pushed aside perhaps, but not forgotten. There was a secret knowledge planted – that Mum was the parent to run to. Mum made decisions; she fed, clothed and protected. And much more besides.

Kate felt a wave of longing pass over her for her mother's touch. She wanted to see the small face framed with neat dark hair, watch her as she dried her thin hands on her floral apron. She wanted to sit by the boiler and tell her about Stephanie, and even perhaps about Hannah. About the baby.

'I could come and see you . . .' Her voice was eager but still couched in wariness. 'Before I go back to Dorset. I could come . . .'

'I wouldn't hear of it, love.' Eileen's brisk voice cut into her longing for home. Was it Kate's imagination, or could she detect a note of panic? Was the thought of seeing her daughter such an alarming one?

'Why not?' She tried to keep the hurt out of the words. She still had some pride.

'Because I won't have you letting Aunt Barbara down.' She heard Eileen take a deep breath. 'And I won't have you traipsing all the way over here, worrying for no reason. I told you – I'm fine.'

The hardness had returned to her voice. Kate could feel herself crumpling inside. 'You don't want me to come, then?' she asked.

Silence. The pause seemed to go on for ever. It went on, and as it went on, it slowly wound itself around Kate's heart.

'No. I'll see you soon, love. For a weekend, maybe? No need to bother this time.'

No need to bother. Kate was crushed. 'Okay.' She tried to sound careless. 'See you, then.' She put down the phone. She didn't care. She wouldn't care.

Her mother didn't want her around. How much clearer could she be, without actually saying the words? And how much rejection could Kate take, before she finally gave up on her mother for good?

Stephanie returned to West Dorset on the Friday, a couple of days before the start of summer term. She had thought she would never come back, but anywhere was better than Atherington. Better than having to hear Daddy's ghastly crying in the small hours of the night. And being unable to comfort him. Unable to comfort herself – obsessed only with blame.

She hadn't known what to do with herself in Kent. Awful reminders of Miles and childhood lurked around every corner. But she soon realised that it didn't make any difference where she was, because the reminders of Miles were in her head.

All she could see were images of his reproachful eyes. The blue eyes of Miles locked into her dreams, rose in front of her when she awoke, filled her mind in those last semi-conscious moments before she fell asleep. When she managed to sleep. More often she lay in bed and wept, the raw tears bringing no relief from the pain that had taken her into its cave of despair.

Friday afternoon, she found herself wandering aimlessly through the village and past the square. She stopped outside a huge Victorian house than looked vaguely familiar. Familiar from the before-life. The 'before Miles had left her' life.

She stared, was drawn up the grey steps, and saw her fingers pressing the bell marked basement.

'Stephanie!' The woman called Lois answered the door. She was dressed in baggy blue jeans, and a halter top.

Stephanie registered this, and the translucence of her pale face, in silence.

'You look like shit.' Lois grabbed her hand. 'Come on in.'

It was a relief for Stephanie to enter the sweet darkness of the basement. Her eyes had been hurting in the bright light of the sunshine outside. But here she felt cool, as if some unknown shadowy presence was at last easing some of the pain from her heart.

'Sit down.' Lois's hands were on her slim hips, her luminous green eyes narrowed in speculation.

Not needing to be told twice, Stephanie sank gratefully into the worn leather armchair. Here, she could rest. She knew that instinctively.

'I'll make some coffee.' Lois disappeared.

She seemed to be gone for ages, and while she was gone, Stephanie stared blankly at the red ceiling and black walls. There was a single low spotlight on the wall facing her. Its light filtered down on to the worn, red carpet, casting shadows that mocked and mesmerised Stephanie, until she sank into the first dreamless Miles-free sleep that she'd had since he died.

When she awoke, Lois was standing over her with a tray. She was smiling.

'I couldn't eat a thing . . .' Stephanie spoke automatically – she'd barely eaten since finding his body in the summerhouse. How the hell could she? Wasn't it callous to want to go on living? Wasn't it unfeeling to eat, drink, talk of other days?

'Oh, yes, you could.' Lois put the tray down by her side, and the tempting fragrance of coffee and scrambled eggs wafted closer.

'I'll try.' After the first mouthful, she couldn't stop. Her body demanded it. It seemed that ordinary living did continue after death, however much you didn't want it to. However much guilt you chose to shoulder.

Lois fetched a cushion and an ashtray and squatted next to her. She asked no questions, and Stephanie appreciated that. Just being cared for was special. Nothing was required of her. It was exactly what she needed after Daddy's hunted grief.

At last she finished and sat back, fumbling for her cigarettes. 'Are you an angel of mercy?'

Lois grinned. 'Hardly. But any fool could see what you needed.' She grabbed a record sleeve from the pile beside her, and took a small tin down from a shelf. Inside were cigarette papers, pieces of card, small packages wrapped in foil.

Stephanie watched her. She wasn't sure that this was what she needed at all, but on the other hand, Lois seemed to know the recipe better than she herself.

'Who are you?' She realised that she wanted to know more about this strange self-assured young woman.

'Does it matter?' Lois twiddled a match into the tobacco. 'I can be whoever I want. Can't we all?'

Stephanie shook her head. There was only one person she could be, no matter how much she longed for something else. Longed to be someone else. 'What do you do?'

'Do?' The green eyes mocked her. 'You mean when I'm not throwing parties and feeding waifs from the streets?'

'For a living. Where do you work?' Stephanie felt boring for asking such a mundane question. But she needed to know. Maybe this woman had a secret she could pass on to her.

'An advertising agency in Dorchester.' Lois told her the name. 'We specialise in disguising the product so bloody brilliantly that it becomes the one you always wanted to buy.' She laughed. 'It stinks of corruption and it's loaded with stress, but I happen to be good at it.'

Stephanie's blue eyes widened with surprise. 'Really?' What had she expected? She didn't have the foggiest idea.

The sardonic laugh rang out again. 'Yes, really.' She made an adjustment and lit the joint. The sweet scent clouded the air. 'It's a case of schizophrenia.'

'Come again?' Stephanie was fascinated. This woman was totally outside her experience, and she liked that.

'When I go to work I'm Miss Lois Field.' Her slanting eyes watched Stephanie carefully. 'I wear red lipstick and dark suits. And I smoke Rothmans. I work hard on presentations until I'm the most convincing liar you could hope to meet. I have business lunches where I seduce clients into thinking I can get their greedy hands closer to the big money.'

'And when you come home . . . ?' Stephanie's mouth curved into a smile.

'Like I said, I'm good at disguises. When I come home I'm Lois, who wears jeans and smokes dope.'

'And who feeds the waifs from the streets,' Stephanie added. It was an appealing idea. But could anyone exist in the world of capitalism and not let it touch them? Wouldn't their private values and dreams become touched and tainted too?

'And who throws parties.' Lois leaned against the wall, stretching out her legs.

Parties. It was Friday night. Stephanie shuddered. 'I'd better be making tracks.' The last thing she needed right now was a party. And yet she was reluctant to lift herself out of the comfortable confines of the leather chair. Here, she had been able to sleep. Here, she had been able – at least briefly – to let Miles slip into the background of her mind. She had even smiled. The realisation was mind-boggling.

'Not yet.' Lois's hand lingered on her arm. 'Have some of this.' She offered her the joint. 'It'll make you feel better.'

Stephanie eyed it doubtfully. But when her eyes met Lois's, she knew that she had to believe her. She must trust her – right now, Lois was all that she had to cling on to. And besides, wasn't it always easier to stay?

After only a moment's hesitation, Stephanie's hand reached out, her fingers brushed against Lois's fingers, and she put the cardboard to her lips, drawing in, the familiar aroma rising in her nostrils, the sweet rush clearing her head.

Lois leaned closer, her arms on the arm of the worn leather chair. 'So. D'you want to talk about it?'

And suddenly she did. It tipped out of her as if the scales had overbalanced, and she told the entire tragic story to this stranger-woman who had already heard how much she loved Miles on the night of the party when Stephanie had come here with Dian. It seemed unbelievable that it was only weeks ago – it felt like years.

'Stay as long as you like. Don't race off.' Lois's voice was soft. Easing away more pain. 'If you don't fancy the party we can just stay in my room. Be quiet, whatever you want.'

'Why are you doing this?' Stephanie stared at her curiously. She wasn't used to people being nice to her for no reason. In the world that she came from, it was money and status that brought you friendship and caring from total strangers. Not loss and heartbreak.

Lois shrugged. 'I want to help. I don't want you to be alone tonight. Because you look like you could do with a friend right now. Will that do you?'

Stephanie nodded. She thought of Hannah. She had lost Hannah too. And Kate was far away. She hadn't called out to her for help when Miles died, so Kate knew nothing of what she was going through. She had wanted to contact her – God knows how many times she'd picked up the phone to call Ridley. Once she'd even dialled the number and a worn female voice had answered. A voice with problems of its own. Stephanie hadn't said a word. She'd put down the receiver. It could wait until the summer term.

But now she was drifting into painless euphoria. 'That'll do me,' she said.

Rather than joining the party, it was the party that joined Stephanie – flowing into her and all over her, as she sat still curled in the leather armchair, shifting in and out of sleep, watching the bodies swaying around her, drinking the beer that Lois provided. And when she did finally realise that the party was in full swing, she decided to stay. Her limbs were too heavy to be moved, and besides, unlikely though it seemed, there was some slow healing process going on, and she wasn't fool enough to stop it.

Then, amidst the haze of tobacco smoke and laughter, she caught sight of a familiar face from another life. Of greasy fair hair and an arrogant grin.

Oh, God. It was Rick Allen. And as she watched him, it seemed that the leer on his face spread wider and wider until it was all that there was of him. Stephanie was scared.

She lurched to her feet. She must get out of here. She must at least get to Lois's bedroom where she would be safe. But where the hell was it?

Stephanie put a hand to her head as she stumbled past the dancing bodies, almost tripping over a couple kissing and petting in a corner on the worn beer-stained carpet. She made it to the kitchen. Kitchen. The white lights almost blinded her. She blinked. All her senses were swimming away. Where the hell were they going? She fumbled in the darkness, but she couldn't hang on to them, they were lost to her.

She grabbed the door knob and lunged into the narrow hallway, which was stacked with more bodies drinking and laughing. She was hemmed in, frightened beyond belief. Her limbs were weak and her chest was heaving. Any moment the wheezing would start and her inhaler was in her bag by the worn leather chair – much more than miles away. Lois's bedroom. Now which was it?

She opened one door. Empty except for a couple making love on the carpet. Jesus Christ. She moaned.

She tried a different door. There was matting on bare polished floorboards, hessian on the green walls. A big brass bed. A song came into her mind. 'Lay Lady Lay'. Bob Dylan. *Lay across my big brass bed*. This had to be it. This must be Lois's room. She shut the door, leaning against it. The relief shuddered through her body. Thank God. She was scared of Rick. She'd beaten him once, but tonight she was vulnerable. Tonight she wouldn't have been able to fight him like she had before.

The bed looked gloriously inviting. Stephanie climbed up and sank into its feathery quilted duvet. Heaven. Paradise. Just for a moment . . . Her eyes closed.

'Well, well, well . . .'

The voice woke her from some delicious slumber.

'Now that's a nice sight to see.' Rick was standing by the door. He closed it and approached the bed, thick fingers on thick lips. 'If it isn't Stephanie Lewis-Smythe . . .' He sneered the words.

Stephanie wondered if she was dreaming. It seemed like a dream, because Rick's burly figure with its hunched shoulders, kept switching to the right and then left of her vision. And suddenly there were two of him, and she screamed.

With one leap he was on top of her. 'Ssh.' His hand clamped on to her mouth, damp and heavy. 'Don't make so much noise.' His lip curled. 'I like my women noisy in bed, but not that noisy. Not when there's company close by.' He laughed.

Stephanie's eyes widened in terror. She struggled, but now his big hands were on her throat, and suddenly she couldn't scream. She could barely breathe.

Some voice of sanity told her to be still. She stopped moving, and watched him, suddenly alert. Her brain was functioning but her lungs were wheezing. She was stone cold sober. There was only one Rick in this bedroom, but one was more than enough.

His left hand remained on her bruised throat. Rick thrust his other hand inside her shirt, tugging the fabric apart, the buttons flying. He tore off her bra, and with a thick groan of satisfaction, he grabbed at her breasts. 'You owe me one,' he muttered.

'Get off me.' She had to fight. She pulled up her knees and kicked out as hard as she could, catching him where it would hurt the most.

'Fucking bitch . . .' He backed away, bent double.

Like a cat, Stephanie crouched and sprang off the bed, making for the door. But he was behind her in an instant, his hands latching on to her waist, hauling her back, slapping her face – one, two, three – throwing her on the bed like a pile of rags.

He was tearing at the belt of his jeans, and Stephanie was sobbing, beaten and hurting, huddled in the far corner of the brass bed, waiting to take her punishment for the betrayal of Miles, when the door opened and Lois walked in.

12

Lois seemed to take in the situation at a glance. She shut the door and the party noise out with a bang, and stalked into the room.

Stephanie had never been so glad to see anyone in her life.

'Are you all right?' There was compassion in the light green eyes.

Stephanie nodded.

Lois's expression darkened as she turned to face Rick. 'What the hell's been going on here?' She took a step towards him.

'It's no big deal.' Rick's shrug was casual, but his eyes flickered.

'No big deal?' Her voice dripped sarcasm. 'Who are you trying to kid? And what the hell have you done to her?'

Stephanie recognised hatred carved on the narrow features. Lois's face was tight with compressed fury.

She stepped closer. 'Was it you who ripped her blouse?' Lois was almost touching him now, her mouth twisting in anger. 'Well, was it?'

'Some girls like it rough.' He leered.

'Bastard!' Her hand shot out to deliver him a glancing blow on the jaw.

'Hey . . .' Rick stumbled, regained his balance and rubbed his face, a rueful expression in the shifty eyes. 'It got out of hand.' He looked warily across at Stephanie. 'I'm sorry, baby.'

'Get him out of here.' Stephanie's voice was muffled. All she could think was that he had to be out of her sight, out of the flat, out of her life. And she needed him gone now.

Lois hesitated. 'Do you want to take this further?' She leaned across the bed towards Stephanie, took her hand, stroking it gently, her voice becoming a croon. 'I'll help you, if you decide to do something about it. He tried to rape you. It's assault.' She paused. The silence was heavy between them. 'If women like you don't speak up, then men like him will do it again. And again.'

'Hang on a minute.' Rick's eyes were glazed and scared. His feet were shuffling. 'She didn't say no, last time . . .'

'I just want him out of here.' Stephanie's voice became tinged with desperation. She couldn't even think about it. She'd had more than enough of him.

Lois straightened. 'Piss off then, Rick.' Her voice was dangerously calm.

Stephanie noted, even through her own distress, that Lois was in total control of the situation. Her first impressions of this strange lady were reinforced. Men like Rick clearly held no threats for her. She knew exactly how to reduce them to trembling wrecks.

Despite everything that had happened, Stephanie began to smile. Maybe it was hysteria . . . maybe it was just relief.

'Don't ever come near her again. And don't come round here again either. I don't want your bloody sort in my flat. Fucking chauvinist arsehole.'

Stephanie's eyebrows arched in surprise. And she wasn't easily shocked.

Rick backed out of the room, not looking at either of them.

'He won't bother you any more. You're safe now.' Lois touched her face with tender exploring fingers. 'Are you okay? Does it still hurt?'

Stephanie shook her head. 'It probably looks worse than it is.' But yes, it still hurt. She still hurt. She hesitated. There was something she had to say. 'It was partly my fault. I was a right cow to him the last time we met.'

She told Lois what had happened, sparing herself nothing. This woman had been kind to her, she'd been more than a friend, and she deserved the truth. She should know the kind of life Stephanie led. And something told her that Lois, unlike Hannah, wouldn't judge. Neither would she be shocked. In fact she had the feeling that Lois could cope with just about anything that was thrown at her.

'So you see, maybe I deserve it.' Stephanie lay down on the bed, staring up at the ceiling. It was a pale leaf green.

'What a load of crap.' As usual Lois summed the situation up succinctly. 'You didn't deserve a thing. You said no, and he couldn't take it. That's what this was all about. The rest is immaterial.'

There was some doubt in Stephanie's nod. 'Maybe . . .'

'Things are changing for women, Stephanie.' Lois grasped her hand. 'And it's just the beginning. I'm not talking about sexual freedom and all that sixties stuff.' She shook her head disparagingly. 'That was only the illusion of freedom. The pill only made it easier for men to get what they wanted and take no responsibility for the consequences. And harder for women to say no.'

'What's changing then? What will happen?' Stephanie felt like a child. Sex and slavery, she was thinking. This was what she'd been waiting to hear.

'True equality.' Lois smiled. 'It's got to happen eventually. The end of sexual stereotypes for women, the end of getting the short straw. And, like I said, the right to say no.'

Stephanie smiled. Already she was feeling better.

Lois glanced at her barely covered breasts. 'Here . . .' She rose abruptly, pulled open the wardrobe and grabbed a denim shirt. 'Wear this.'

Stephanie took it. 'I told you that you were an angel of mercy.'

Lois laughed. But Stephanie saw the pleasure in her eyes, and she was glad. She pulled on the shirt, leaning back on the pillows, feeling as if she'd been here all her life. Perhaps she'd belonged here all her life. She closed her eyes.

She awoke some hours later, wondering for a moment where she was, remembering almost instantly what had happened. Rick Allen had happened. She curled herself up into a tight ball.

Someone – Lois, no doubt – had thrown some blankets over her. When she eased herself on to one elbow, she saw Lois sleeping on the couch in the corner.

'I've even taken her bloody bed,' she muttered.

She got up gingerly, feeling rough and raw, her head pounding, and went to the dressing table. By the dawn light filtering through the wooden slatted blinds, she peered at her face. One luscious plum-coloured bruise under her left eye, swollen lips, and a line of viciousness streaking from her right temple almost to her jaw. 'Jesus Christ,' she breathed.

'You still look beautiful.'

She turned. Lois was staring at her, blonde hair tumbled and tousled with sleep, her eyes as alert as ever.

Stephanie laughed. 'You must have terrible eyesight.'

Lois shook her head. 'A stupid bastard like Rick Allen could never take it away from you,' she murmured. 'Beauty goes deeper than a few bruises.'

Stephanie waited for embarrassment, but it never came. Usually she hated compliments, a legacy of Daddy's extravagant praises maybe. But from Lois's lips they were different. Acceptable. She smoothed the dark tangled hair away from her face. She felt curiously at home here – as if it were perfectly natural for her to be sharing a room with this woman.

'You should have turfed me out of your bed,' she remarked.

'No . . .' Lois yawned. 'You needed to rest. You've been through an unbelievable amount of trauma. First Miles, and now this thing with Rick. I'm surprised you didn't sleep for a month.'

Miles. He hadn't been her first waking thought. In fact she hadn't thought of him at all until Lois mentioned his name.

Lois seemed to know what she was thinking. 'You can't mourn him for ever,' she said. 'And sleep is the best healer. You have to give yourself time. Time to appreciate that you're still in the land of the living. Time to grieve. Time to get used to life again. All of those things – bit by bit, not all at once.'

Stephanie nodded. There was so much wisdom in this woman. 'I could listen to you for ever.' She laughed. 'I feel like I could stay here for ever.'

Their eyes met.

'You can move in here if you like.' Lois's voice was deceptively casual. 'I'm all on my own at the moment, so there's two spare rooms.'

Stephanie remembered the empty room from last night. The couple making love on the floor. 'What happened to the other girls?' She stalled. There was something so instantly appealing about the idea of living in this flat, that she was scared. It was almost too easy.

'Tania's finally moved in with her boyfriend, lock stock and barrel. She was never here much anyway.' Lois paused. 'And Chantal . . .' Her expression changed. 'Chantal just got tired of living in a basement.' She turned away, her eyes glazing over, before she smiled wistfully and the moment passed.

'So there's stacks of room,' she concluded. 'You'd be doing me a favour.'

Stephanie considered. She thought of the freedom, the thrill of having her own flat after a life of dependence. But how could she? Was she dreaming? She was at college. And it wouldn't be her flat. How could she even pay the rent?

'I live in hall. At Royal Ford.' It was impossible. Yet already the hall of residence, with its rabbit warren of identical study bedrooms, and even the college institution itself, seemed distant. She had wanted it so much. But now, since the death of Miles, Stephanie wasn't even sure if she had the heart to return.

Lois pulled a face. 'I couldn't live in one of those places. Doesn't it drive you crazy?'

Stephanie nodded. Oh yes, it drove her crazy at times. But it was a route towards getting what she had thought she wanted – a teaching certificate. Until Miles's death had pushed her ambitions into insignificance.

'I want to teach art.' Maybe if she said it with enough conviction, it would come back to her.

'Doesn't mean you've got to live in a funny farm. You can live outside the institution, can't you?'

'Yes, of course . . .' Still Stephanie hesitated. Hannah had bombed out of the Royal Ford threesome. Wouldn't it be betraying Kate, for her to do the same?

'Come with me.' Lois threw off the blankets and jumped up. Her spare frame was clad in an outsize man's shirt. 'I want to show you something.'

Cautiously they opened the bedroom door as if expecting the party to still be in full flow outside the green haven of Lois's room, but only the remnants of the party – glasses, beer cans, empty cigarette packets – littered the hallway.

Lois approached a third door, one that Stephanie hadn't even noticed, took her by the hand and led her inside.

This room was empty too. It was small, but the early morning light flooded through the east-facing windows. Some narrow concrete steps bordered by forget-me-nots in full bloom led up to a tiny overgrown garden.

'What do you think?'

'It's lovely.' Stephanie didn't even want to imagine how nice this could be.

'Wouldn't it make a great studio?' Lois's eyes were eager. She took Stephanie's other hand. 'Can't you just see yourself working here?'

'Ye-es.' Stephanie was wary. She wasn't exactly sure what was happening.

'Well, didn't you say how much you missed your studio back home?' Lois demanded. 'How can you work in one of those silly little study bedrooms? You could barely swing a cat.'

Stephanie nodded. She looked around, wondering.

'This is empty. You can have it as your studio. Whether you decide to move in or not,' she added quickly.

'But Lois . . .' She had to tell her how it was. 'I don't have money of my own. My father's loaded, but I want to be free of him. I don't want to ask him for a thing. He pays board and tuition but after that I take as little as possible, and I don't want to ask him for more. It makes me feel beholden. So I couldn't afford to pay you much rent . . .'

'I don't want rent.' Lois let go of her hands. 'But if you don't like it . . .' She turned away towards the window.

Stephanie couldn't bear to hear the hurt in her voice, after everything she'd done for her. 'I love it.' She moved closer to the slender white-shirted figure. 'I absolutely love it.'

'Then you'll use it as a studio?' Lois turned. Her eyes seemed huge against the incandescent glow of her skin. The dawn light invested her with an eerie quality, as if she wasn't quite real, this angel of mercy who had come so unexpectedly into Stephanie's life.

Stephanie nodded. 'I'd love to.' That wouldn't be betraying Kate or leaving her in the lurch. It would simply mean that Stephanie could take off sometimes and come here to work. 'If you're sure?'

'I've never been surer of anything in my life.'

They walked back to Lois's bedroom. She had regained her complete self-assurance. 'I don't need the money,' she explained. 'I want company, but only the right company. I don't want to live with a bloody idiot. I'd rather have you here, even if it is only part-time.'

Stephanie smiled. She could well imagine that this woman did not suffer fools gladly. And she felt flattered – as if she'd been chosen for a special rôle.

'I'll give you a key, and you can come here to work as often as you like.' Lois flopped on to the bed, stretching in contentment. 'Just think of all the masterpieces you could create here.'

They laughed. Stephanie perched on the brass bed next to her.

'We'll get you a studio couch or put-me-up or something, and then you can doss here whenever you like.' Lois narrowed her eyes. 'Whenever you can't face going back to the grey corridors.' She smiled. 'We could have fun.'

Stephanie smiled back. With this untapped well of pain inside her, the only thing that she could be sure of doing any more was painting. Because it was part of her. The way she made sense of everything. Already her fingers were itching to get started. It was like a dream come true.

Lois reached out, almost carelessly, trailing her hand along the length of Stephanie's arm. 'Quite, quite beautiful,' she murmured, as if to herself.

Fascinated, Stephanie watched the rapt expression on her face, as Lois's gentle hands moved to Stephanie's shoulder and neck, before drifting to her mouth. Tenderly, touching Stephanie's swollen lips.

Maybe she should have been surprised, but she was only curious and waiting as Lois twisted strands of Stephanie's raven hair between her fingers. 'Are you scared?'

She shook her head. No, not scared. This seemed the most natural thing in the world, and there was no threat in it. All she could feel was pleasure.

She lay down on the brass bed, and felt Lois's lips grazing her neck. Her fingers undoing her buttons until she was kissing Stephanie's breasts with a tenderness that Stephanie had never felt since Miles. A gentle touch that had been lacking in every man she had ever taken to her bed.

She looked up, and Lois's translucent green eyes were right above her, already half-lost in passion. 'Only if you want to, darling,' she said softly.

Stephanie smiled, although her lips hurt. It was what she wanted more than anything, she realised – to make love with this ethereal, strong-minded woman. This was what she had been hiding from for so long. This was a haven for art and for love. She could use some of Lois's strength. And this way she had some hope of healing.

Hannah was repainting their bedroom a sunny shade of yellow. It wasn't exclusively their bedroom any longer. Soon it would be the baby's room too, until Tom was working and they could afford a bigger place. She balanced herself on the top of the stepladder and surveyed her efforts. It looked happy and hopeful. She smiled. Yellow was so much more suitable for a baby than the murky shade of brown that Tom had been contented with.

She heard him come in. A key in the lock. A distant humming.

'Jesus wept.' He stood still, staring at the wall she'd just completed.

'Don't you like it?' Hannah's lip trembled. She'd known it would be a bit of a shock. Not that Tom hadn't agreed to her suggestion. But he'd laughed at her as she'd rifled through the colour charts, barely glancing at them himself. Tom might be interested in many things, but home improvements weren't top of the list.

'I'll need bloody sunglasses when I wake up in the morning.' But he approached the stepladder and hugged her legs.

'At least it'll give you a bright start to the day,' she giggled.

Tom groaned. 'So does breakfast cereal according to advertisements, but I can live without that as well.' He glanced up at her. 'Should you be doing this? What if you fall?'

'I won't fall.' She smiled, loving his concern.

'Supposing I make you fall?' He grabbed her, and she screamed playfully. He held her in his arms as if she were a baby herself before laying her gently on the bed.

'You shouldn't be painting in your condition,' he teased.

'Oh?' She was relieved that his mood had improved since last night. 'And what should I be doing?'

'Satisfying your future husband.' He slid a hand under the bib of her dungarees, taking Hannah by surprise. It shocked her, the frequency with which sex entered their conversations, their touching, their lives.

'Tom . . .' She struggled to sit up. 'Not now. The paint will go all streaky.'

Irritation clouded the gleam in his pale, blue eyes. 'That might be an improvement.'

'Don't be grumpy.' Hannah wound her arms around his neck. 'Why don't you help me get it finished?' This was something that she'd envisaged them doing together – painting, preparing and planning, everything from potential names to where to put the crib. Tom's apparent disinterest was hard to take.

He pulled a face. 'Because if I ever want to escape from the early morning nightmare of a bright yellow bedroom, I've got to do something about getting a job. And that means passing my exams.'

All he ever seemed to do these days was to revise. She'd never realised how much it meant to him. Hannah sighed. Of course she knew it was important. Tom was thinking of the future – especially the baby's future –

and she should be glad. But wasn't she important too?

Hannah was more dependent on his company now that she'd left college. Being alone in the flat all day had brought none of the peace and quiet she'd expected. She couldn't even write – sometimes she felt as if she were drying up inside from having too much time and nothing to do with it. Words had always been her salvation, and yet words weren't giving her any answers to loneliness and apathy. If it weren't for the decorating she'd spend half the day in bed.

'Why don't you do your revision here?' she asked. 'I won't disturb you.'

'Because I can't concentrate. I'd want to seduce you all the time. And I hate the smell of paint.' Tom got up, began packing more books into his briefcase. 'I'll go to the library.'

'Tom . . .' But already she knew she'd lost his attention. She'd had a chance of keeping him here in the flat, and she'd blown it. Now he was almost out of the door. 'About last night . . .'

He poked his fair head back round the bedroom door. 'Save it for later, Hannah.' And with a wave of his hand – not even a kiss – he was gone.

She heard the door slam. She wanted to cry, but she was damned if she was going to give in to it. It wasn't just pregnancy making her weepy, nor was it Tom's casual neglect. Yet again it was her mother who was trampling her emotions into the ground. Yet again, Mother was to blame.

Tom always said that Hannah was too fond of playing happy families, and maybe he was right. Happy families. Conforming to what was expected. That's why she'd invited her parents to the flat for a weekend. How could she drop her imminent marriage into the conversation during a long-distance phone call?

So Hannah prepared a grand dinner-party. She would tell them the news – about the wedding at least. And then, once Mother approved of Tom, she could choose her time to let the other news slip. Nothing was showing so far; Hannah was still wearing her jeans, even if she did have to undo the button at the waist sometimes.

Surely Mother would approve? When she met Tom – who could charm any living soul – and when she realised how happy they were?

Hannah ensured there was nothing on the menu for her mother to dislike or criticise. She splashed out on a lacy tablecloth and bought freesias from the flower-shop in the village square. She cleaned the entire flat, polished furniture that had probably never met with furniture polish in its life, and waited with trepidation for them to arrive, still half-surprised that they'd even agreed to make the journey.

And despite all her efforts, everything had gone wrong.

Jean Thompson was pushing the boeuf bourgignon disdainfully around her plate, when Hannah took a deep breath.

'Tom and I are getting married.'

Knives and forks clattered on to plates. Some red wine sauce splattered the lacy tablecloth. Hannah looked at Tom for reassurance.

He grasped her hand under the table and squeezed hard.

'Congratulations, my dear.' Her father kissed her warmly, his kind, brown eyes lighting with happiness.

'Thanks, Dad.' At last Hannah dared to look at her mother.

'It's a bit sudden, isn't it?'

Hannah couldn't see her mother's eyes. She was silent.

'Why wait when you're in love?' Gordon laughed nervously.

Hannah flashed him a grateful smile. 'We didn't want to wait,' she said pointedly.

Jean sniffed. Her disparaging sniffs had been the turning point of the evening. With every sniff, Tom had become less charming, less willing to please.

'Why should we wait?' he asked his future mother-in-law.

'Because a wedding involves so much preparation.' She scrutinised her daughter. 'When are you thinking of setting the date? After you've finished college?'

Hannah felt Tom staring at her and she shook her head quickly. No, she hadn't told them she'd already left college. One thing at a time.

'It'll be soon,' she said firmly. 'Very soon.'

Jean sniffed. 'What about the invitations that have to be printed? Hotels for the reception can be fully booked even a year in advance. And the church . . .'

'We're getting married in a Register Office.' Hannah's voice was quiet yet determined.

There was a staggered silence. 'Well.' Jean got to her feet. She leaned towards Tom. 'I didn't bring my daughter up to get married in a Register Office,' she breathed.

'You make it sound like a brothel.' Tom laughed, harsh and cruel.

Hannah's mouth twitched. 'Lots of people get married in a Register Office these days, Mother.' She sighed. 'It's perfectly respectable.'

Tom choked on his wine. 'And we must be respectable, mustn't we?' he mocked. 'Good heavens, yes. Or die in the attempt.'

'Tom . . .' Why was he being like this? He wasn't making any effort to please her mother, and yet he knew how important this was for Hannah. She still needed her approval.

Jean remained standing, a tall and powerful woman. But her mouth was working furiously, and she seemed to be losing control. 'And may I ask what's wrong with respectability, young man?'

Hannah wanted to crumple up in her chair and die a thousand deaths. This was far worse than her nastiest premonition. They hated each other.

'It's synonymous with hypocrisy, that's what's wrong with it.' Tom leaned back in his chair. His mouth twisted. He was laughing at her mother – enjoying himself, she realised.

The emotionless eyes behind the glasses were confused.

Hannah's stomach dipped with apprehension. Shut up, Tom, she prayed.

'Respectability is just a front you show to the world,' he jeered. 'It means bugger all.'

Jean flinched.

'It's not saying who you really are . . .' Tom's voice thickened as he watched her. 'It's not saying *what* you really are.' He downed the rest of his wine. 'So it's hypocritical.' He grinned at Hannah. She didn't like that grin. 'And we won't be hypocritical, will we, Hannah darling?'

She saw the anger still dark on his handsome face. Suddenly she knew what was coming. 'No, Tom . . .'

'So tell your parents the rest of our news,' he suggested sweetly.

Jean was shaking. Her eyes narrowed. 'Well, Hannah?'

There was no choice. 'I'm pregnant.' It should have been a moment of joy. But although there was joy in her heart, she was forced to keep it hidden.

Jean sat down abruptly, her face saying it all. 'I see.' But she looked as if she'd had the life drained out of her.

Hannah laid her hands on her stomach in protection. But as she looked at those hands, it seemed that all she could see were her mother's hands, cold and cruel, wrapping themselves around Hannah's piece of joy. It was stifled and submerged. No joy. No warmth. She looked tentatively

163

towards her father. Would he be disapproving too?

But Gordon's lined face was wreathed in smiles he clearly couldn't contain. 'I'm going to be a grandad,' he chortled.

'Gordon!' Jean's face made a thunderous promise for later.

He shrugged an apology. 'It's not so bad, love.' Then he turned to Hannah. 'You do care for each other? It's not a case of having to get married these days, is it?' He needed reassurance.

Hannah shook her head. She looked once more to Tom. Tom had behaved so badly, yet still her very heart seemed to want to rush out and meet him.

He got up and put an arm around her shoulders. 'I love your daughter,' he said. His voice was solemn. 'She's the best thing that's ever happened to me. And I'm going to make damned sure I make her happy.'

Hannah smiled, dispelling the fleeting thought that Tom had practised those lines on a stage somewhere.

'That's all right then.' Gordon beamed.

'All right?' Jean screeched. She was looking from one to the other of them as if they'd all gone quite mad. 'What about college? What about your career?'

'I'm putting it on hold.' Hannah looked down. She'd put her life on hold. She couldn't tell them what had changed. She couldn't explain how she felt – that this baby was everything. That Tom was her world now.

'On hold?' Jean blinked heavily. 'Is that how much your career means to you? I suppose your head's filled with fancy notions about writing poetry?'

'What if it is?' Hannah straightened. Her mother had always despised her need to scribble out her emotions, always belittled it and laughed at her.

'I don't know where you get it from.' Her mouth tightened. 'And pregnant into the bargain! I suppose that's why this wedding of yours has to be such a hole in the corner affair.'

'Mother . . .' Hannah tried to be patient, not hurt. After everything her mother had taught and given her, she could hardly expect her to be pleased.

'Then you won't congratulate us, Mrs Thompson?' Tom stood straight, tall and challenging beside Hannah, claiming her as his own.

Jean shook her head. 'You don't deserve it. You're eaten up with selfishness, the pair of you.' Taking a deep breath, she glared at Tom. 'I don't know what you've done to my daughter, but she's not the girl she used to be.' She got to her feet as she transferred her gaze to Hannah. 'And like I told her once before, I wash my hands of her. She's no daughter of mine.'

Hannah buried her head in the warmth of Tom's shirt. His grip tightened on her shoulder. She felt as if she had been handed over to him tonight. It was a case of possession, after all. And the fear stroked into her belly, gentle as the first kicks from the baby inside her.

She heard her mother leave the room. It was hopeless. She should have known it would be hopeless.

'I'm sorry, Mr Thompson.' Tom's voice remained calm. 'I've upset your wife.' He paused. 'But I have Hannah to think about.'

To her surprise, Gordon clapped him on the back. 'You're more man than me, son. More man than me.' Then he stroked Hannah's hair from her face. 'Give me a moment with my daughter?'

Tom nodded, shooting Hannah one last look of remorse as he went into the bedroom.

'I can't give her what she wants.' Hannah was sobbing, the hot tears scalding her cheeks. 'I don't even know what she wants half the time.'

'Don't fret.' Her father's hand was warm on her shoulder. 'She'll come round.'

Hannah looked up at him, her eyes raw and hurting. 'Maybe I don't want her to come round.' Hadn't she broken from her mother in her heart and mind? Maybe it was time to do it in body too.

She felt him tense. 'It hasn't been easy for your mother, you know.'

Still he defended her. Hannah could hardly believe it. Always he defended her, however badly she behaved. 'Why the hell not?' she shot out at him. 'Why hasn't it been easy for her? She's got you, hasn't she?' Her face crumpled as she registered his look of surprise. 'And you're wonderful.'

His laugh held an uncharacteristic bitterness. 'I've never managed to give her what she wanted, Hannah love,' he said. 'I'm not sure that I know either.'

She stared at him, uncomprehending.

'I thought I'd get through to her in time, mind. We'd only been living down South for a year, me and the old man, when I first laid eyes on your mother.' His expression softened. 'And she seemed pretty wonderful to me right from the start. Cool and icy, and a bit hoity-toity, but I didn't half used to wonder what was underneath all that.'

'And did you ever find out?' Hannah would give anything to discover what had made her mother what she was.

He shook his head, looking suddenly so old and weary that she wanted to reach out for him, take him in her arms as if their roles were reversed. As if she were the parent, and he the child needing comfort.

'I've always been a handy shoulder to cry on, like. That's about the most I could ever give her, the most she'd let me give her.'

Hannah grabbed his hands. He mustn't think that way. 'Come on, Dad. You must have given her so much more than that over the years. I know you have.' But she wasn't sure. All she could remember was her mother's domination. She couldn't recall Dad's contribution at all – Jean had stamped on it until it was misshapen and worse than useless. Why had she done that to the man who loved her? Was love such a frightening emotion that it had to be destroyed?

Rough fingers stroked her hand. 'We've had our moments.' His dark eyes were unfathomable. 'But it should have been a lot more than moments.'

'She loves you though.' Hannah couldn't bear her father's pain. It was tearing her in two. 'As much as she's able to . . .'

He shook his head. 'Not in the way you mean. She's stuck by me. But it's never been more than duty. And duty can be as dry as dust if there's nothing to liven it up, like.' He paused. 'Your mother – bless her – she's never been one for the physical side, you know?'

Hannah knew. She knew because her mother had passed that particular legacy on. Passed it on with irrational fears of men, and a little white leaflet that discussed periods from a purely biological point of view. She looked at her father sitting beside her, holding her hands in his. Sad and old with a wasted life. How did he feel about the woman he'd once loved? The woman who'd given him only moments?

He seemed to read her thoughts. 'I still love her,' he said. 'I know she looks down on me, but I still go on loving her.'

'Why?' How can you, was what she meant. How can you have so little pride? But she didn't want to humiliate him further. Hadn't he been belittled enough already?

'She gives me just enough to hang on to.' Gordon's voice finally broke, as the tears welled up in his eyes. 'That's why. Just enough to hang on to . . .'

* * *

Hannah climbed back up the stepladder to resume her painting. Her legs were aching, but she wanted to be finished. She wanted to have a bright room, not a little hole of darkness.

'I wash my hands of you,' her mother had said again as they left last night.

Cleanliness was next to godliness. It had always been that way.

'Wash your hands, child. Whatever have you been touching . . . ?' The voice belonged to Hannah's childhood, and now her mother belonged to that childhood too. She wanted no more of Hannah.

And although there should be so much ahead for Hannah, it was hard to accept, but indisputably true, that without the woman who had given her life, every step forward was too much like a step alone.

As he walked away from the flat, Tom McNeil too was brooding about the night before. Parents – they were the bloody end. But with a bit of luck he'd never have to lay eyes on Jean Thompson again. He would be looking after Hannah from now on. She belonged to him. Still, he hoped to God that Hannah hadn't inherited much from that snooty bitch of a mother of hers.

He went past the college, barely glancing at the library where he was supposed to be heading, and turned instead down a narrow street that led towards the village square. He looked up towards the attic window of a white house, grinned when he saw that the window was open, strolled up the pathway and rang the bell.

'Hello, stranger.' Dian, her hair dark and tousled, looked warily at him.

'Got a cup of coffee going spare?' Tom grinned his best grin, and watched her expression soften. Since the news of Hannah's pregnancy he had made a determined effort to resist the allure of Dian, and this had been made easier by a teaching practice and revision that had taken up his time. But Dian was like an ache that never quite went away. He had to admit that he'd missed her.

'Sure.' She opened the door wider. 'Come on up.'

Tom had to stop himself running up the narrow stairs after her. So instead, he watched her bum in tight denim jeans, as it swivelled slowly and tantalisingly in front of him. He was bloody fed up with Hannah wincing every time he came near her. He needed some light relief.

In her bed-sit he shut the door and took note of the books littering the small desk, spilling over on to the floor and even the bed. There were clothes strewn everywhere, blankets flung over chairs, and albums without covers stacked on the hi-fi. Dian was the untidiest person he knew.

Tom laughed delightedly. 'You're such a messy cow. Jesus, it's good to see you, Dian.'

'Black or white?' She turned to face him, the coffee jar in her hands, a slow sensual smile curving her mouth.

'Sod the bloody coffee.' He grabbed her, pulling her towards him, bending swiftly to taste her soft, full lips. The lips that would always part for him. 'I need you.'

'Tom . . .' But it wasn't a protest.

They collapsed on to the bed, giggling, sweeping books and papers out of their way, reaching for each other's bodies with delicious, grasping waves of pure lust.

'God, I've missed you.' He fell on her, his mouth swooping to her neck and her breasts as his eager fingers freed them from their lacy constraints.

'Oh yeah?' Her eyes closed.

'You don't know how much I want you.' He tugged at the zip of her jeans, easing them over the glorious curves of her hips.

She laughed, a throaty laugh that turned him on still more.

And she was more than ready for him. His fingers explored the liquid warmth that set him on fire. He couldn't wait another second. He plunged into her with a thick groan of satisfaction. 'Dian . . . Dian . . .'

It was over too soon. He knew it was over too soon, so he worked on her, giving her pleasure as always, thrilled at how easy it was to make her come. Dian. She was a hotbed of unbridled sexuality.

At last it was over. Their bodies were relaxed and saturated with the love that came so easily. Physically, they were a perfect match. Tom trailed his fingers across her beautiful flat belly. If only . . .

After a while Dian got up to make the coffee, her limbs graceful and free. He loved her proud nakedness. Dian didn't know the meaning of the word hang-up, and that in itself was an incredible relief.

'What's the latest?' She turned to watch him. 'Are you still seeing little Hannah Thompson?'

Her tone was disparaging to say the least. But what should he expect? In a sense, it was Hannah who had sent her away.

Tom stretched lazily, folding his arms behind his fair head, considering how best to break it to her. There was no easy way. He decided to go for it. 'We're getting married.'

'What?' She stared at him. Incomprehension sharpened into anger. She took a step closer. 'You bastard. What the hell are you doing here, then?' Grabbing his arm, she tried to pull him off the bed, her fingernails clawing at his skin, as if she wanted to tear him apart.

'Hey . . .' He shook her off, but sat up, reached for his clothes and began getting dressed. 'She's pregnant.'

Dian's hazel eyes widened. She sat on the edge of the bed. 'For Christ's sake, Tommo. How could you be so bloody stupid?'

He shrugged himself into his shirt. 'I thought she was on the pill.' To tell the truth he hadn't thought about it that much. As far as Tom was concerned, contraception was a female domain. All he knew was that no girl would get him in a bloody condom – no way. How would he feel where he was going?

'A girl like her?' Dian's lip curled. 'She probably hasn't even heard of the bloody pill.' Jumping to her feet, she grabbed a robe from the hook on the door and flung it on.

'Well, it's done now.' Tom watched her. She was shaking with anger. He'd expected her to be pissed off but he hadn't bargained on this venomous hatred. Still, he couldn't help smiling. Already he wanted her again.

She passed him a mug of coffee, and squatted at his feet as Tom sat on the edge of the bed. The robe parted, and he gazed at her breasts.

'That doesn't mean it's too late,' she whispered. 'You don't have to be saddled with a wife and kid just because the stupid cow wasn't taking precautions. You don't have to marry her.'

Tom put down his coffee, watching her all the while.

Dian slid her body between his knees. 'Hasn't she heard of abortion?'

Absent-mindedly, Tom's fingers reached out to massage one soft nipple. 'She wants to have the baby.'

'And you? What do you want, Tommo?' The nipple was erect and full. He turned his attention to the other one.

'It's kind of crept up on me.' Tom was evading the question. He knew, and Dian would know too, that such things as pregnant girlfriends didn't creep up on you. They pounced.

'Bollocks.' She grabbed his face in her hands. 'You want this kid, don't you, Tom McNeil?' Her eyes narrowed. 'You want Hannah Thompson to have your child. You actually want to marry her.'

Tom shrugged. It was hard to lie to her when those hazel eyes were only inches away, and she knew him so bloody well. 'She'll give me everything.' He looked away from her.

'I would have given you everything.' Her voice was a whisper of love.

She rose to her feet, the anger and the caring converging into one fast flowing river of bitterness. 'Will it make you feel important, Tommo?' she hissed. 'Will you be someone?'

Be someone, be someone . . . The words echoed in his brain. Maybe Dian would have given him everything. But she would have asked for too bloody much in return.

'Will it take away the hurt of what Janice did to you?' Her voice was scathing.

He rose to his feet, towering over her. That was the unmentionable. She'd promised never to remind him, and yet now she was using it against him. He'd known that would happen. Because that's what they were like – women like Dian, and Janice too. They could destroy a man. You couldn't trust them. No. The women you could trust with your secrets were women like his mother and Hannah.

Tom stared at Dian, half-naked, wild and fierce. He wanted to slap her face, but he wasn't a violent man. His head was throbbing. It seemed to Tom that his entire body was throbbing. You couldn't trust women like Janice and Dian. But they were the women you wanted. They were the women who made the blood rush to your head. Who you wanted to screw until you collapsed with the utter exhaustion of trying to make them yours.

Dian smiled, unafraid of the raw nerve she'd uncovered. 'And what about poor little Hannah?' she jeered. 'What will her future be? Will she be staying home, looking after your baby and cooking your meals, while you go out into the big wide world?' She laughed. 'To screw around?'

Tom grabbed his jacket. He should never have come here. 'It won't be like that.'

He opened the door.

She flung herself on to the bed. 'What do you think you're doing here now, Tommo? It already *is* like that.'

He slammed the door. He could hear the sound of her tears as he ran down the stairs. But it didn't stop. Even when he got to the college library, the sound of her tears was in his head, lurking under every bloody sentence he tried to read.

After a while Tom gave up. He didn't want to think about it, about what he was doing. It was women who analysed. Men got things done. So he'd just get on with it – and the women could do the worrying. About what the hell he was doing – and about where he and Hannah might be heading – together or alone.

13

Kate rang the bell for last orders, and began collecting glasses. She hadn't expected to spend the summer holidays working in a pub in Dorchester, but it had been a lot better than the prospect of Ridley. How could she meet her mother halfway when it seemed they had nothing to say to one another any more? Nothing shared. Neither had the summer been shared with Stephanie or Hannah. She hadn't even seen them. Last year in Normandy certainly seemed a long way away.

Kate had spotted the ad. on the college notice board in June – 'fourth girl wanted to share house for summer let in Dorchester'. She applied on impulse, soon finding this job which paid the rent and would add to the grant, to keep her nicely solvent next term.

The pub itself was small and well-furnished with mahogany tables and chairs, enhanced by tasteful amber and gold lighting and drapes. And it was in the right part of town so there was no fear of punks or lager louts. This was a haven for businessmen in smart suits, and for secretaries eating prawn salads and drinking white wine.

'Will you be in tomorrow, Kate?' Sitting on a bar stool in front of her, was one of those businessmen. Adam Horton – she knew his name, though little else about him.

He was drinking Scotch and flashing her self-confident smiles that said he was a man of status, an impression confirmed by every detail of his appearance from the immaculately sleek haircut, past the dark well-cut suit, down to the perfectly polished Italian black leather loafers. Adam Horton had money. He exuded the scent of money. And it was an intoxicating fragrance for a girl who had never had enough.

''Fraid not.' She tossed back her russet hair.

'A few days off?' He was watching her carefully. Adam Horton had probably got wherever he was now from watching people carefully.

Kate shook her head with some regret. Did he fancy her? With a man like this one, it was impossible to tell. He was rather an unknown quantity. She had told him her name but not much else.

He smiled. 'I'm sure you deserve a holiday.'

'Chance would be a fine thing.' She laughed. In the six weeks since they'd met in here they had played a kind of guessing game. All that existed between them was careful small talk and the many drinks he had bought her. But what now – should she tell him where she was going tomorrow, or was that against the rules?

'I'm a working girl. This is my holiday. I don't get to have any other kind.' She looked at him under her lashes. She was flirting with him. Did she find Adam Horton attractive? Or was that all it was – a game?

'Then you should make some changes in your life, my dear girl.' He licked his lips, as if tasting the last of his Scotch. 'Everyone needs a break.'

Yes. Kate smiled. There was something undeniably attractive about him. He must be forty if he was a day, but he was a big man, and she sensed power in him – this was a man who got things done. Who had others to do the running. Who was firmly in control. Adam Horton was the kind of man who would take a girl on wonderful holidays.

'Today's my last day.' She looked him full in the face, and noted his swift grimace of displeasure. It made her feel good. She had been so long without a man, so long keeping a distance from anyone who might dare to threaten her new-found freedom, that she'd become frustrated. And yet most men bored her. Their shallowness was irritating. She wouldn't think about Leon.

'You're leaving?' He leaned closer. 'Why? Don't they pay you enough here?' She could smell the whisky on his breath, but it wasn't unpleasant. It was part of his aura. Expensive spirits and expensive cigars. Expensive suits designed to disguise a midriff that might soon be bulging from too many five-course dinners.

'I'm going back to college tomorrow. Teacher training. This is just a summer job for me.' Her smile was intentionally challenging. She was staring at his mouth.

But did she really want to return? Kate wasn't sure. Sometimes it seemed that there was so much real life waiting round the corner, that college was just a waste of time. There were no guarantees that there would even be a job waiting at the end of it. Disillusion was sinking into her senses, making her want something more.

He nodded, as if some private theory had been confirmed. 'I never had you down as a barmaid. Bright girl like you.' His smile was approving, as his sunken eyes travelled down the length of the elegant black dress she wore.

Kate shivered. The manageress preferred her barmaids to wear black, and she had no objections. She was well aware that black set off the paleness of her skin, the green glitter of her eyes and the crown of auburn hair.

'Is that right?' she teased. 'I would've thought barmaids had to be brighter than most. It's not just a question of pulling pumps and mental arithmetic, you know.'

'Yes, but teaching?' He pulled a face. 'I wouldn't have thought there was much future in that.'

Much money, he meant. To a man like this, the future was only how much money you could earn in it.

'Maybe not.' Kate wiped down the shiny surface of the bar, and began stacking glasses to be washed. 'But what else is there?' It was a loaded question. But what harm was she doing by asking it? Even by flirting with him? Maybe Adam's aroma of masculine power was turning her on like a good body and a handsome face used to turn her on. The thought shocked her, and she looked away.

Adam was staring, responding to the challenge, his mouth relaxing into a smile. He hesitated, as if considering his next move . . .

She waited, hardly daring to breathe, the excitement battering against her ribcage.

'Time,' somebody called. It broke the spell.

'I must be going.' Adam rose to his feet, producing a small embossed business card from his breast pocket. 'If you ever change your mind about teaching . . . give me a call.'

Kate felt his eyes appraising her as she read it. 'Adam Horton. Independent estate and property agent. Personal services and valuation.'

So he was only an estate agent after all. She felt the rush of disappointment.

'Exclusive properties,' he murmured. 'You'd be surprised at the openings available in this business.'

Kate's eyes narrowed. It sounded interesting. He sounded interesting.

If he were to invite her out she would go, just for the hell of it, to discover more about him. But of course he wasn't going to. He was smoothing his jacket, about to leave, preparing to meet the world. Maybe she'd read him all wrong. Maybe he wasn't the type to go out with a barmaid. But still, he had a compelling charm – she hadn't read that wrong. It was in the bold lines of his nose, cheek and jaw. And it glinted like some mysterious secret in the deep-set grey eyes.

'I'll bear that in mind.' She tucked his card away in her bag.

He nodded. 'Goodbye, Kate. It's been a pleasure.'

A brief, much too brief touch of the fingers – the faintest promise of a thrill that might have been, and Adam Horton was strolling out of the bar.

Ah, well. Kate sighed. Perhaps it was a wasted chance. Maybe he was even married. A family man. She'd probably never know. Already his business card was burning a hole in her bag. But she had a life to get on with. A life back at college. That was the future she had to make herself look forward to.

After a week back at Royal Ford with no sign of Stephanie, Kate decided to visit the house in the village where Stephanie had often worked during the summer term. Where the intensity of her grief over Miles had kept her locked away from Kate, drawing back from her, as if gathering herself up into a tight ball of pain, that could only unravel through the emotion she poured into her art. Leaving no access for anyone.

Knowing of the closeness between brother and sister – knowing so much more than Stephanie realised – Kate had tried to share in her grief, to offer some shred of comfort. But Stephanie became withdrawn and secretive, spending more and more time at the house in the village – even nights – as if unable to drag herself away.

And although she felt rejected, Kate wasn't going to leave it there, no way. It seemed that Stephanie was treading a slippery path, and who else did she have to stop her from falling?

A small woman – in her mid-thirties perhaps – with curious, light green eyes and a shock of blonde-white hair, answered the doorbell.

'Hi?' Those eyes were questioning. Immediately confrontational.

'I'm Kate Dunstan.' She straightened her back. 'A friend of Stephanie's,' she elaborated, since the woman looked blank. Hadn't Stephanie even mentioned her?

'Are you indeed?' The woman's expression changed into one of hostility.

Kate became irritated. 'Is she around?' This must be the woman who owned the basement flat. But why was she acting like a jailer?

'She's working.' It sounded like a warning, but at least the woman backed off slightly and beckoned Kate inside. 'She always says she doesn't want to be disturbed, but . . .'

'And you're Lois, I suppose?' From the little Stephanie had told her, Kate had imagined some tall, immaculate businesswoman keen to support the arts. Not someone like this.

'That's right.' Lois shot her a strange look, and Kate thought she saw fear in her eyes. 'Come on down.'

It was like walking into the Black Hole. Kate shivered involuntarily. This wasn't the kind of place she'd relish living in. Apart from the darkness, lit only by the occasional naked bulb, the hallway was narrow and cramped, a sense of claustrophobia clinging to the very walls.

'She's in here.' Lois tapped lightly on a door.

'Yeah?'

Kate recognised Stephanie's husky drawl, and almost pushed past Lois into the room.

'Well, hi, stranger . . .' Kate blinked, her eyes re-focusing in the dim light. The room was a haze of sweet tobacco smoke – or at least she imagined it was tobacco smoke – and the curtains were drawn. A single spotlight draped in a black silk square provided the sole illumination for the small room, which was littered with canvases. Stephanie was standing with her back to the door, dressed only in a pair of paint-stained dungarees.

'Kate?' She swung around to face her.

Kate gasped. What the hell had happened to Stephanie? Her face, framed by a mass of tangled black hair, was gaunt and seemed drawn in pain, her body skinny where it had once been slender. Her beautiful eyes were ringed with dark shadows, her lips dry, and her skin pale. Had this happened in one summer?

'I know I look a mess.' Stephanie smiled ruefully, becoming, for just one second, the Stephanie who had stared at Kate in the pool at Les Marettes.

'Where have you been?' The question wasn't a sensible one, but Kate didn't feel sensible. She felt horrified.

'Nowhere. Only here.' Her expression was blank.

Kate moved forwards hesitantly, hugged Stephanie's thin body and felt the frailness, the bones of her ribcage, and the stiffness of her response. Stephanie hadn't wanted that hug. Kate's eyes narrowed.

'You look ill. And why is it so bloody dark in here?' Stalking to the window, she flung open the curtains.

Stephanie winced, shielding her eyes from the sudden brightness. 'Sunlight hurts . . .' she murmured.

'But it's so gloomy. It's unnatural.' Kate realised that she was talking too loudly. Perhaps she was trying to break the hushed, sombre mood of the room, as if the very atmosphere was responsible for Stephanie's decline.

'We prefer it that way.' Lois stepped closer, between the two of them, her eyes dense with controlled anger.

Kate blinked in surprise.

'It's better for working,' Stephanie said quickly.

'And what have you been working on?' Kate wandered over to a pile of canvases stacked in one corner. Her eyes widened. They were unlike all her previous work. They were scary. Stephanie had used a palette of only red and black, the strokes were unconsidered, dramatic and bold. There was a well of pain pouring like bloody tears from every one. Jesus Christ . . .

'Why are you doing this to yourself?' Stepping towards her, oblivious of the other woman in the room, Kate took Stephanie's hand to pull her on to the couch. 'Why are you torturing yourself like this? He's dead. But it wasn't your fault.'

'It was her loss.' Lois came closer. 'She needs time to grieve.'

Kate got up. 'Maybe she does. But she doesn't need this kind of shit to wallow in.' With a defiant gesture of her hand she encompassed the dark studio, the paintings that surrounded them, and even Lois herself.

'You've got a bloody nerve . . .'

Before Lois could say more, Stephanie too was on her feet, swaying slightly as if too insubstantial for balance. Kate found herself wondering when she'd last eaten.

'Can you give us a moment alone, Lois?' Her voice was gentle, almost caressing the anger from the other woman's eyes.

Kate watched in fascination. It was as if Stephanie had to defer to her. But why?

The older woman hesitated.

'Please?'

'Shout if you need me.' She turned on her heel and left the room, slamming the door behind her.

'What's her problem?' Kate frowned.

'She's only thinking of me.' Stephanie moved around the studio, tidying tubes and palettes away, screwing up scraps of paper. She seemed nervous and agitated.

'You look terrible,' Kate observed.

'I'm pretty hung up on this work I'm doing, that's all.' Stephanie frowned as she bent to light a cigarette.

'Hung up on it?' Kate stared at her and then at the easel where she'd been working. It was a scrawling, seething kaleidoscope of anger and agony. 'I wouldn't put it quite like that.'

'And how would you put it?' Stephanie's eyes seemed larger than usual, and there was a wild look about the huge dilated pupils.

'I'd call it obsession.' And obsession had a way of creating its own damage – it didn't need any help.

'I have to get it out of my system,' Stephanie murmured. 'Before . . .'

'Before you come back to Royal Ford?'

She hung her dark head.

'Or don't you plan on coming back at all?' Kate's voice was a bitter whisper. She missed her. Now that there was no Hannah and no Stephanie, it was one hell of a lonely life in hall.

'I don't know if I can.' Stephanie's voice was gentle, as if she really cared. And yet how could she, when she didn't seem to want Kate in her life?

'I'm scared.' The words escaped from Kate's lips. And as she spoke, she sensed that Stephanie felt the same. But what were they scared of? Their future? Of what was being snatched away from them?

'Don't be.' Stephanie gripped her arm. She sighed. 'I want you to understand. It's a different life here. Come to the party tonight. Please?'

'If it's a different life, it's not doing you much good.' She turned away. 'And I'm not wanted here.'

'Lois is being over-protective.' Stephanie's voice was persuasive. 'I'll talk to her. You might even like her. She's been a good friend to me, Kate.'

Kate didn't want to hear that. Why hadn't she been the one Stephanie turned to? She'd preferred to turn to some stranger, and that hurt.

'Will you come? For me?' Her expression was eager, pleading.

Stephanie had always been so hard to resist.

'I don't know.' Kate wasn't sure that she could face it.

'Please? It'll give us a chance to talk.' There was a strange desperation in the dim blue eyes, as if she were reaching out for help at last, as if she needed Kate.

'Okay.' The promises of Normandy were still closeted in her heart. How could she refuse?

Four hours later she was regretting her decision. The party was crammed full of bodies and more bodies. Squeezing, pawing, laughing, dancing. Flopped on cushions, sitting cross-legged in small circles, hardly talking some of them. Even Stephanie – stunning in a skintight black jump-suit in spite of her starved appearance – had little to say. If she was inviting Kate into her new world, she'd clearly decided not to hold her hand until she found her way around.

Wary of the sweet scent she recognised from Stephanie's studio this afternoon, which was fugging the air and making her woozy, Kate ended up drinking too much red wine instead.

She had nothing to say to these people. They irritated her. They were self-indulgent and ridiculous. All they wanted was to escape from their own little insignificant corners of reality. They were drifting their lives away. It wasn't a world Kate wanted to be part of. She wasn't hanging around here. If Stephanie wanted to reach out for help, she'd have to come and find her in the land of the living – where Kate was headed.

But first, she slipped into Stephanie's studio, to look once more at the strange paintings she'd been working on. As if they could provide some clue to her unbalanced frame of mind, the guilt and pain she was putting herself through.

She'd barely been there a minute, when the door opened, and she found herself looking into the classically handsome face of Tom McNeil.

'What are you doing here?' It was out of her mouth before she could stop it. And as usual when she was talking to him, she sounded childishly petulant.

But he only laughed. 'I might well ask you the same question. I haven't seen you here before.' In one hand he held a glass, in the other a half-empty bottle of red wine.

'So you're a regular visitor, are you?' She was only vaguely surprised. Any den of iniquity might well include Tom McNeil as far as she was concerned. A sudden thought occurred to her. 'Does Hannah ever come?' It seemed odd, asking this man about Hannah, almost as if their friendship had never existed.

He laughed, coming closer, to re-fill the glass she still held in her hand. 'Hardly.' His grin was wicked. 'Hannah would be shocked that people like this lot even exist.'

Kate couldn't repress a twitch of a smile. He was right, of course. Hannah might have moved in with Tom McNeil and even got herself pregnant before wedding bells could be heard on the breeze, but she would always remain infinitely shockable. 'How is she?' Her voice was hesitant.

'All right.' Tom clearly didn't intend to elaborate. Perhaps he had other things on his mind tonight.

Kate shivered, scrabbling for something to say. 'I hear that congratulations are in order.' A wave of self-consciousness swept over her – at being alone with Tom, drinking red wine in Stephanie's studio. Too much red wine.

He nodded, his pale eyes clouding. 'And why didn't you come to our wedding?' He leaned casually against the wall, watching her over the rim of his glass.

'Because I wasn't invited, why do you bloody think?' Her voice was sharp. She didn't want to remember all that. It had only been a small affair, so she'd been told, but Hannah had asked neither Kate nor Stephanie to witness the new pledge she was making, the pledge of loyalty to her husband that would effectively wipe out any pledge they'd made in the distant past. And by not inviting them to her wedding, Hannah had made it perfectly plain that she couldn't forgive either of her friends. So . . .

Tom clicked his tongue sympathetically. But there was a mocking laughter in his eyes that incensed her. He reckoned he'd won the battle for Hannah's affections, and she reckoned he was right. And good bloody luck to him.

'Perhaps you'll make up once the baby's born,' Tom grinned. 'All women like babies, don't they? They all start ooh-ing and aah-ing and knitting matinee jackets.'

'Hardly.' The baby. That was another thing she didn't want to talk about. Didn't even want to think about. She paced over to the window, opened the curtain and stared out into the night. There was an air of peace about the night-time silence that she longed to possess. But you couldn't possess it and still keep it the same. It wouldn't last. In the morning it would all look different.

'And I thought you were the one who had it all sussed.' He had drawn closer, and was standing right behind her, his smooth voice coating her senses. She could smell the fragrance of patchouli. It was making her dizzy.

'I always had you sussed.' She turned to face him, challenge in her green eyes.

'Kate . . .' His hand reached out to push some strands of auburn hair from her pale face. 'You're like an angry tabby – like I said once before.'

She flinched from the contact. 'Like you said once before.' A once before that seemed like lifetimes ago.

Kate twisted away from him, not trusting the silky promise of his voice and eyes, not liking the smiling mouth. The crease of a smile that she longed to press from his face with her fingertips. And especially not liking the swift rush of excitement that tunnelled through her body with the speed and velocity of a bloody express train.

Kate frowned. 'How long is it – before Hannah has the baby?' Her breath was coming faster. Her voice sounded weird. She had to bring Hannah into their conversation, to remind herself of who this man was. Who he belonged to.

Tom's expression changed as he put down his glass and tore his fingers through his fair hair. 'Christ knows. To tell you the truth, Kate, I'm already sick of this bloody baby.'

She stared at him. She and him both. It was almost the first time that Tom McNeil didn't seem to be acting a part, and it drew her to him. This shared disgust.

'Why?' she whispered, not really wanting to hear.

'Because Hannah can't talk about anything else. She can't think about anything else. It's taken her over. Taken us both over. I can't even recognise it any more – whatever there was between us.' He leaned on the back of the studio couch and buried his head in his hands.

'That bad, huh?' She felt sorry for him. He had most of her sympathy. But at the same time Kate was conscious of a sweet streak of revenge. She remembered how Tom had always been pulling them apart, wanting Hannah for himself alone. Didn't he deserve everything he got? Hadn't he been just too good at fighting dirty every step of the way?

'That's why I came here,' he confessed. 'I hate these druggie parties.

But I'm in desperate need of a friendly face right now.'

Kate absorbed the tension radiating from his lean body, suddenly knowing what had brought him here. Sex – the need for it – was a coiled spring inside him. And she recognised it so readily, because she felt like that too. How long had it been since Jason? For how long had sex been submerged in her past? Frustration had wormed its way around her senses, and the admiring smiles of Adam Horton had brought it to the surface. He had brought it to the surface but not released it. And now it was hurting her. Like it was hurting Tom McNeil. The tentacles of desire pulled her closer.

Whose friendly face did Tom need to see? 'Stephanie's friendly face?' She hazarded a guess.

'Stephanie?' Tom laughed. He grabbed his glass and downed the wine in one gulp. 'Who are you kidding? I might be desperate but I'm not desperate for a dyke.'

'What?' Kate stared at him. She could feel the blood draining from her face.

'You didn't know?' He came closer, his face almost touching her face. Whispering in her ear, his breath warm and drunken on her cheek. 'A clever girl like you, and you didn't even work out what was happening here?'

'Stephanie . . . ?' Her voice almost broke. And something inside Kate also broke. But all the confusing pieces were falling into place. Stephanie. Miles. Lois. No wonder Stephanie had been reluctant at first, to let Kate in on her new world.

'I must say, I was bloody surprised the first time I saw them together.' Tom's voice was insidious. Sliding snake-like over her. 'Of course, everyone knows Lois is as queer as they come. That's why she hides herself away in her own little underworld. So that no one in the real world knows what she's up to when she isn't working nine to five. But Stephanie . . .' He whistled. 'I always thought she was a bit of a goer. Although it explains why I never got anywhere with her.'

Kate was silent, doggedly assimilating it in her head. How could she have been so dumb? Was it just because she thought she knew Stephanie so well? That she hadn't recognised all the signs staring her in the face?

'Wasting all that on a dyke . . .' Tom was talking as if she weren't even there. 'Bloody shame.'

She glowered at him, but he wouldn't stop. The floodgates were open now.

He poured himself more wine, the red liquid spilling over the sides of the glass. 'But Dian saw which way the wind was blowing – she's a sharp one. I reckon she fixed them up, Lois and your little friend, so she could keep me to herself.' He laughed.

'Shut up.' Kate spoke softly, turning away from him. Outside, the full moon illuminated two lovers, each cradling the other's face. She pulled the curtain drawn with a snap of decision, as if closing an act of a play. Not the final act though, not yet.

'And now Lois has really got her where she wants her.' Tom's smile was a thin cruel line slashed into his face. 'Right there.' He indicated his thumb. 'You should tell Stephanie that it's not so easy to escape from Lois's clutches. It took Chantal over a year.'

'Shut up.' Louder. More insistent. 'Shut up.' This time it was a scream. The scream rang between them.

She turned back to face him. Tom grabbed her shoulders and pulled her closer, while the glass of red wine he'd been holding fell to the floor, splintering into pieces, staining the carpet between them with a slow spread of spilled blood.

Kate stared at him, his touch burning into her, feeling an insistent helplessness that wouldn't be denied. A hungry kind of helplessness. She remained silent.

'It's you I always wanted.' Tom pulled back her hair in a rough, possessive gesture. 'Bloody wildcat.'

And then his mouth was on hers, hot and demanding, and his hands were on her breasts, his fingers frantically undoing her shirt. His stolen kisses were a spark to the flame that had smouldered for too long. His hands were exploring, bringing her to the point of no return. His tongue was flicking across her parted lips, searching for response.

With a groan of bitter despair, Kate flung back her head, her hand reaching out as if in supplication and finding only Stephanie's easel, Stephanie's canvas. These fell to the floor as Tom's lips beat a pathway down her neck to her bare breasts. Her fingers dug into his shoulders. The heat of two frustrated years welled up inside her, and she knew that she was lost.

He struggled with the belt of his jeans, grabbed her legs and took her there and then against the wall.

And she knew, even as he thudded into her, that she should be ashamed. She knew it was the drink, and the words he'd used. They weren't even two people who had once loved Hannah. They were just two frustrated bodies, each consumed with need, forgetting all the conventions that should be holding them apart. Hannah. She had the baby. So why shouldn't Kate have Tom?

The baby, the baby, the baby. He seemed to take up the rhythm as he drove himself on. And then at last they came, simultaneously and powerfully, in the way that lust can sometimes overtake every other sensation.

Tom and Kate collapsed exhausted on the floor of Stephanie's studio. The smell of turpentine and oils was in the air between them. It had been crazy, and it was over.

14

Voices outside the studio made Kate's stomach lurch with panic. Oh God. She struggled to her feet. But it was too late. The door was pushed open.

For one awful, interminable second, Kate looked into Stephanie's face as she stood, tall and forbidding, in the doorway of the studio. Stephanie's studio. Kate paled. How could she have let it happen – and in Stephanie's studio of all places?

But there had been no time for thinking. Action had overtaken sanity with ease. If Kate had allowed herself to consider what she was doing – even for just a moment – then she would never have gone near Tom McNeil. Never have let his touch burn its way into her. But she hadn't paused – hadn't been able to pause – in that short, mad interlude of lust. It would be dishonest to call it anything else.

Stephanie stood absolutely still, watching the two of them.

Tom was struggling to his feet.

The sounds of the party were behind Stephanie, the music and laughter mocking what she had found. The horror etched on her face was hardening into a mask of hatred.

'Kate?' There was more than just a question in that husky voice. Stephanie sounded confused. As if the girl in front of her couldn't possibly be the Kate that she knew, trusted and loved. As if she must be someone else.

Kate couldn't bear that. Their eyes locked, and she recognised the shame of what she had done. Saw how low she had sunk in Stephanie's esteem.

'What the hell is going on?' But Stephanie didn't need an answer and no one seemed inclined to give her one. In the background, over her shoulder, distant party voices jostled for attention.

Kate was silent. There was nothing she could say. Then just behind Stephanie, almost hidden by her tall, accusing figure, she saw the woman called Lois. Could they be having an affair? It seemed ludicrous, unreal almost, and yet everything seemed unreal tonight.

'How can you ask what's going on?' Lois stepped out of the shadows, going for the kill with the cruel smile of a vulture. 'I would have said it was obvious.'

Kate shivered.

'Oh, lay off, for Christ's sake.' Tom was pulling his clothes into some semblance of order, and Kate rapidly began to do the same. It was one thing being almost caught in the act, but it was quite another having to endure the humiliation of standing around half naked and justifying it to everyone. Not that she could. She groaned. Not that she could.

'We've been looking for you, Tom.' Stephanie folded her arms in front of her, addressing him but not taking her eyes off Kate. 'You were wanted on the phone. The hospital have been trying to get hold of you for ages, and your mate Martin seemed to think you might be here . . .' Her lip curled. Still she stared at Kate. 'He said that if Dian Jones was here, then you wouldn't be far away. He seemed to think it was Dian you were looking for tonight.' There was a sardonic kind of pity in her eyes now, as she examined Kate's dishevelled appearance.

Dian Jones? Kate gave in to a silent sigh, her hands brushing ineffectually at her tangled auburn hair. So he had been looking for a friendly body as well as a friendly face – and it hadn't been either herself or Stephanie's he'd had in mind. Dian Jones. But anybody would do, it seemed.

Kate felt like a prostitute. Worse than a prostitute because she'd got nothing from him in return. If she'd been frustrated before, she felt ten times worse now. When Tom had driven himself into her, female satisfaction had clearly been the last thing on his mind.

'The hospital?' Tom's expression changed. He frowned. 'What's happened? It's not Hannah, is it?'

'She's having your baby, I believe.' At last Stephanie transferred the full force of her scathing gaze to Tom, as he tightened the belt of his jeans. 'Shame you were too busy and missed it.' Her voice was scornful.

The baby. Hannah was having the baby. My God. Kate felt ill. All she could see was Stephanie's accusing face, all she could feel was her own guilt. Why had she done it? But she knew the answer to that one. Her need

188

had carried her into his need like a tidal wave. Her inhibitions had been swept away by a bottle of red wine and a shot of sexual chemistry.

None of it had been real. She should have been stronger. She should have resisted him. Hannah was her friend, or she had been once. So why had Kate found it impossible to say no?

'But the baby's not due for another three weeks.' Tom pushed past them out of the studio, frantic fingers tearing through his hair, barely glancing at Kate.

That's how much she meant to him – less than nothing. A quick fuck on a Friday night. And she was glad. It was how she felt herself. She couldn't even look at his departing back. Why bother to pretend? And, what was even worse, he'd known when the baby was due all the time. So Tom McNeil was a brilliant actor. Should she be surprised?

'Try telling that to poor Hannah,' Stephanie yelled after him. 'Maybe you've got your timetables mixed up. A man with a pregnant wife shouldn't be screwing someone else at a party . . .'

Stephanie was breathing heavily, with some difficulty. She turned back to Kate. 'Why, Kate?' Her voice broke. She took a step forward, her hand raised as if she might strike her, a kind of manic wildness in her eyes that was horribly hypnotic.

It was all too much. Suddenly it seemed ridiculous. Kate moved away. 'Go sort out your own bloody life.' Her voice was cold and brittle as she nodded pointedly towards Lois, still standing there beside Stephanie, her thin lips smiling a gloating smile, and her pale green eyes luminous in the dim light. She was enjoying the show, anyone could see that. It made Kate sick. They all made her sick, the whole lot of them.

'I'm getting out of here.' And before they could say more, before Stephanie could justify or accuse or scream or cry, Kate was away. Through the straggling bodies in the hall, all too stoned even to be wondering what was happening in the studio. Up the narrow stairs two at a time, and out of the basement flat.

Fresh air. She shut the door thankfully behind her. Her head was pounding with the start of one hell of a hangover. And she could feel the heat of Tom McNeil still with her in the darkness, still burning between her legs.

Where could she go? For a moment Kate was lost. She couldn't stick around for recriminations from Stephanie and birth congratulations for Hannah. No way. She was finished with this place, and she was finished with them both. Hannah and Stephanie were too far away. Both slotted surprisingly neatly into their new worlds, happily playing the parts created for them. And what of Kate?

She walked back towards Royal Ford, the sobering breeze brushing her cheeks, her eyes huge in the paleness of her face. It was time for a new start. Time to open the curtain on a new Act. The curtain was old and musty. But Kate knew exactly where she was heading.

'Darling . . . I didn't know. Otherwise I'd have got here sooner.' Tom gathered Hannah into his arms as she lay, weak and exhausted in the narrow hospital bed.

She winced with pain. 'It was a bit of a shock for me too.'

'Sorry, my darling.' Tom was brimming with tenderness for her now that he'd had some release. But he was also still drooling over the unexpected sensation of victory over Kate Dunstan.

He licked his lips, slowly, tasting her again. She was a wild-cat and no mistake. And very nice too. He might have been looking for Dian, but he could have Dian almost any time. Variety was the best defence against getting involved. And guilt never featured at all. Guilt was for losers.

Hannah was still in the delivery room. There was a glimmer of triumph in the brown eyes that he hadn't seen before. 'It doesn't matter, Tom.' She grinned, looking so terribly young that his breath caught. His little Hannah. So precious.

'Look, there she is.' She pointed over to the small transparent cot. 'Your daughter.'

'My daughter . . .' he echoed.

For a moment he was surprised. Shouldn't he be having a son?

Slowly, almost reverently, he walked over, looked down at the small, wrinkled face above the pink cotton blankets. 'Is she okay?' he whispered. It seemed like sacrilege to talk too loudly. And the little prune face told him nothing.

'One hundred per cent, Mr McNeil.' A midwife bustled in. 'Congratulations.'

Her voice was disapproving and he swung round automatically to give her the full force of his blue-eyed stare. 'Were you the one looking after my wife for me?'

She hesitated. 'I was here.'

Eagerly, Tom clasped her hand. 'Thanks. Thanks for that.'

Abruptly the starched midwife became a girl like all the rest. 'That's okay. Your wife did all the work.' Lucky wife, her eyes were saying. Lucky wife.

'We appreciate it, I'd like you to know that.' He moved back to Hannah, his arm around her shoulders, his fingers playing with the lacy strap of her nightgown. They'd cleaned her up already. So quickly she'd become his Hannah once more.

The midwife's smile dimpled her cheeks. 'I'll give you half an hour before we take your wife up to the ward. I expect you'd like a bit of time together.' She laughed. 'And we don't want to disturb the other mothers, do we?'

Other mothers. Hannah and Tom exchanged a glance and a smile. The midwife left the room, seeming reluctant to go. Tom sat down on the bed and held Hannah's hand. Small and tiny and white. 'How did it go?' he asked her.

Not that he wanted to know too much about it. Birth was for women, not men, and Tom had little time for the kind of new-man approach that Hannah had been advocating in the last few months. Okay, so he'd gone along to ante-natal breathing exercises with her at the clinic, but he drew the line at having a go himself. What use was that to man or beast? When the time came, Hannah would know how to breathe. No worries there. Hadn't women been giving birth perfectly adequately for centuries? They hardly needed a man's help once conception was over with, did they?

'It wasn't too bad.' Luckily for Tom, Hannah didn't seem inclined to relive the experience. At least not yet. She was more concerned with the baby.

'Isn't she beautiful?' she whispered. 'Bring the cot over here.'

Tom got to his feet and did as she asked. Little prune face. Yes, she was beautiful. Perhaps after all a beautiful little girl might bring her own rewards.

'Pass her to me.'

Tom blinked. He wasn't sure that he could cope with that much responsibility. He flexed his hands uncertainly.

Hannah laughed. The status of motherhood had apparently endowed her with a new confidence. 'I'll do it.' She reached over, plucked her daughter out of the cot with an expert touch. 'You hold her, Tom.'

His eyes absorbed her calm expression. 'Of course I will.' He was scared, but at the same time, he longed to hold her – his child, his creation.

191

Little prune face. This tiny bundle with tiny fingers and just a scrap of fine black hair. The pride swelled through him. Gingerly he held out his arms.

Hannah handed the baby to him, and slowly he relaxed. Now that she was here, being held by him, dependent on the cradle of his arms for life itself, Tom looked down, and it seemed that the vacant eyes focused on him – for just a second. As if she knew. How could he have wanted a boy?

As he stared at her, the vulnerable blue nudged at his heart, and Tom felt the first protective stirrings of fatherhood. They were scary in their intensity.

'I'll look after you, my sweet,' he crooned. 'You'll have it all, you will. I'll make sure of that. And just let anyone try and take it away from you . . .'

'Tom?' Hannah was holding out her arms for the baby. So soon.

He turned from her. He didn't want to relinquish little prune face, not yet. He wanted to relish this early precious moment of fatherhood while he could. It was so special – so different from any emotion he'd ever felt before – that he could almost lose sight of all the parts he'd played in the past. This was what mattered. This was real. Fatherhood. While Tom was capable of such emotions, there was hope. He could change. He could love.

'Give me the baby, Tom.' Hannah's voice altered almost imperceptibly. She was demanding – it was in her eyes, her hands. She was saying, this baby is mine.

His shoulders sagged. 'What shall we call her?' They'd discussed names before. Or at least Hannah had discussed names, and he'd pulled the appropriate faces. But now she was real, she was here in his arms, and he didn't want to let go.

'Fleur.' Her voice hardened. 'We're calling her Fleur.' So. Already she seemed to be denying him something, this woman who had given birth to his child. But Tom wasn't sure what it was.

'Fleur.' The French connection. Hannah was dotty about the country. And what was wrong with that? After all, it suited little prune face.

'Tom?'

He couldn't hang on to her any longer. He handed the baby back to Hannah, feeling the loss, the sensation of the precious and rare being snatched away from him. He was the father, but this was Hannah's child. This was the price men paid for walking free of the pain. They were parent only in name. Women did the labour, women took the prize.

Tom stared at Hannah as she put the child close to her breast, and for a second he almost hated her. This was Hannah's child. And there wasn't a damn thing that Tom could do about it.

Eileen opened the cream-coloured envelope very slowly. Foreboding was nudging like a bad dream at her consciousness. Kate's handwriting, big and sloping and sure. How had her daughter travelled so far away from her? Eileen had wanted to shield her from what might hurt her. But not this . . . not this . . . She had never wanted Kate so far away.

On the other side of the table, Joe stuffed toast into his mouth. She couldn't look at him; he ate like a pig. He'd always eaten like a pig and it seemed strange that once it had amused her. Once she'd almost considered it endearing. Now it made the bile rise in her throat every time. She looked away.

'More tea.' He shoved the mug closer.

She put down the envelope, taking up the brown tea-pot with the worn cosy, watching the hot brown liquid steam into his mug. 'Here.'

'Ta, then.' His eyes were bleary. It had been another late one – she hadn't heard him come in, but the dial had been shining past midnight the last time she'd glanced in trepidation at the clock. Never sure if it was a relief that he stayed out so long, or if she should be worrying about his return. It had been a quiet night after all that, thank the Lord. Quiet, but for the rumbling of his bloated body as he snored the morning closer.

'What's that?' He nodded towards the letter. He might be bleary, but he had eyes like a hawk when it suited him. She should have opened it later.

'It's from our Kate.' Please don't take it from me, she prayed. I need to know. Whatever it is, I need to hear it.

'Don't know why she bloody bothers.' He scraped his chair back and stomped into the hallway for his coat.

Eileen breathed a sigh of relief. Once he would have snatched it from her. Once he cared. But now it was just the boozing and the cards. He could tell all the jokes he wanted down the pub of an evening. They'd all laugh themselves silly because they laughed at everything, that lot. Everything and anything, even before they were full of beer. She sighed. But laughter had to be paid for – didn't they know that much?

'Will you be having your dinner tonight?' She wanted to get the subject off Kate, in case he changed his mind. And how often had she seen his food blacken and shrivel in the oven? Shrivelling like she was shrivelling. A bit more spoiled with every day that passed. Shameful, all that waste. It broke your heart when there wasn't much to go round.

He stood over her, his face dark and brooding. There was a stench to that big body of his that never went away these days – a stench of stale beer, sweat and sleep. 'And where else would I be having it?' He lifted his hand towards her face.

She shrank instinctively, but his coarse fingers just rubbed at her withering cheek. He was laughing, always laughing, his big body shaking.

Lucky her, living with a bloke like that. That's what they all thought. They even said it to her face, while she tried to smile. They thought she was stuck up. A misery of a woman with aspirations above her station. But she had no aspirations left for herself, only for Kate. She herself was drying up with each week that passed. As if it was all being sucked out of her – anything that mattered. And so it was.

His laughter was thick and guttural. 'I'll be hungry tonight, lass. Just you wait and see.'

She shuddered. But she was used to his promises, and she knew only too well that a quick one round the corner after work was all it took for the evening rot to set in. It was killing him, and she didn't even care. Maybe she'd see him out after all.

Joe lumbered out of the back door. She heard his heavy footsteps cross the yard and heard the wood shudder as he slammed the back gate behind him.

In a frenzy now that he was gone, she opened the cream sheet of paper – only the one sheet – smoothing it out with love in worn, tender fingers.

'Dear Mum,' she read. 'I thought I should let you know that I'm leaving college.'

Her hands dropped to her lap, the disappointment curdling in her stomach. Kate at college, heading for a better life, was all she'd wanted. A chance for a career that would give her daughter some precious independence. A chance to escape . . . Well, they had no idea when they were young, how important it was.

Eileen looked around the tiny, cluttered kitchen. The worn lino and the tatty grey rug, the boiler that groaned and spluttered and needed replacing. The chipped enamel sink and the dripping tap. She rose wearily to her feet. Outside was no better – a back yard like every other back yard in the terrace. Nets at the windows, a best front room you hardly used. What was the point?

She leaned heavily on the sink and stared at the grey outside. Another mist on Raddlestone Moor. Dank and depressing and grey.

Kate. Why had she left? She had seemed happy enough – she had friends. Eileen had been so glad that she'd found friends. And she liked the work. After her first teaching practice she had returned to Ridley with a glowing face that had given Eileen so much heart after all that trouble with Jason. And surely she wasn't still brooding about that, about a boy who would have meant less than nothing to her after a year or two. About the child that would have tied her down like . . .

Eileen shook her head. She couldn't think about that now. She'd given Kate every opportunity. How could she throw it all away so carelessly? The anger strummed through her. An impotent anger with nowhere to go. The worst kind.

She glanced down once more at the cream paper. 'I want to taste a bit of real life. I'm going to live in Dorchester for a while. I'll let you know my address when I have one.'

When I have one . . . What did that mean? That Kate would be living on the streets until she found somewhere to stay? How would she manage with no money, no job? Yet even that was apparently better than returning to Ridley. Eileen sighed. Maybe she was right, at that.

But did Kate think that this real life of hers was around the corner just waiting to take her hand and help her along? Didn't she realise that it would pounce and it would crush? What would happen to her little girl when she found out what real life was really like?

There was nothing else written on the cream paper. No name. No best wishes or even love. Nothing. Just a vacant expanse of creamy white that knew how to hurt. And there was nothing that Eileen could do about it. All she could do was wait.

Kate entered his office, shown in by a blonde wearing too much make-up and an expression of curiosity.

'This is a surprise.' Adam Horton got to his feet. He didn't look in the least surprised. His face was bland and unruffled as ever, as if college students turned up every day of the week to remind him of promises he'd made in a bar somewhere. 'A pleasant one, of course.' The smile was certainly confident and seemed sincere.

'Did you mean what you said?' Her green eyes drilled into him, trying to discover how much was superficial gloss and how much of him was real.

'I always mean what I say, Kate.' He responded to the challenge without flinching. 'Do I take it that you're looking for a job?' He raised his dark eyebrows, and indicated a padded leather chair in front of the desk. Adam Horton seated on his managerial bum behind the desk and Kate Dunstan in front of it? No way. She wasn't stupid. She remained standing.

'I'm looking for work to tide me over. I'm not saying I'd stay at this stage.' She chose her words with care. Cards on the table. 'But I need to earn some money and I need to find somewhere to live.'

He laughed, looking her up and down, his grey, deep-set eyes approving and calculating. Calculating her worth maybe. 'You don't do things by half, do you, young lady?'

She winced. 'I won't be patronised.'

'Point taken.' He nodded.

So he was fair, that was one thing. Kate relaxed slightly. It had been all or nothing coming here. She had taken the chance of a few drinks in a bar and the intuition of what a man like Adam Horton might want, deep down, that he wasn't getting from his money and his women. And her instinctive knowledge of what he could do for her.

'If you can help me, I'll repay you.' Kate's voice was firm. A business arrangement, that's what she was proposing. But both of them knew it went deeper than that. There was already a bond of understanding between them. 'You wouldn't regret it.'

He rubbed at his smooth-shaven chin. She noted the dark hairs on plump fingers, and the gold signet ring.

'No, I don't think I would regret it.' Adam seemed to reach a sudden decision. 'Come with me.'

'Now?' She stared at him.

'Right now.' He plucked a sleek fawn raincoat from the mahogany coatstand, took her arm and led her out of the office. 'No calls,' he said to the blonde as they went through the shop front and on to the pavement. Smooth, so smooth.

A key-ring twirled between his fingers. 'In you get.'

Kate gaped at the gleaming BMW.

'Come on.' He was holding the door open for her. She liked that.

She slipped into the seat, breathing in the luxury. The scent of leather and opulence. His cigar smoke and expensive aftershave. The crisp newness of his white linen shirt and dark tailored suit. The fumes of a dry cleaner's polythene, carefully shrouding whatever was hanging in the back of the car. So a man like Adam Horton had to pick up his own laundry?

'Where are we going?' Her voice was faint.

'Wait and see.'

They drove out of town. Kate didn't know where they were heading, but she recognised the change as they got closer to the sea, smelt it in the fresh tang of the breeze through the open sun roof. He said little, but she was always aware of him, aware of the power that seemed to emanate from his broad figure, from the uncompromising contours of his face. There was an iron determination in the grey eyes that denied both comfort and complacency. He was a man who got whatever he wanted.

Adam swung the car through wooden gates, along a sweeping drive towards a big white house. There were late summer roses creeping up white walls, leaded light windows and a slate roof. It was picture-postcard beautiful.

'Nice house.' She was determined not to seem impressed.

'The view's better outside the car,' Adam drawled. Already he was holding the door open for her, moving fast for such a big man.

She climbed out and looked around. The garden was one huge rockery on several levels, sloping down towards the sea. The house was built on a cliff with sea views stretching out as far as the horizon. He was right. The place was stunning. 'Why have we come here?' She spun around to face him.

'Because this is the kind of house I sell.' Adam stood, one hand slung with casual possession over the perfectly polished maroon paintwork of the BMW, the other in the pocket of his trousers.

'I see.' She didn't, not really.

'So when I say I deal in up-market property, this is what I'm talking about.' His smile was slow and sure, softening the aggressive lines of his face.

Kate whistled. 'And who owns this place?' She knew the answer before he spoke.

'I do.' Pride gleamed in the sunken eyes. So he had a weak spot, after all. It was almost a relief.

'One of the perks of the job, I suppose.' She kept her voice light. But it was breathtaking. Because this man had it all. He was loaded, he had status, he was dripping with arrogant charm, and he didn't mind who knew it.

He threw back his head and laughed – a real belly laugh. Well, at least she could make him laugh, that was a start. 'If only it was as easy as that,' he said.

'I know . . .' she cut him short. She wasn't interested in some rags to riches story. 'It took a lot of hard work and more than a few deals to get you where you are today.' She had one hand on her hip, and she was laughing at him, goading him almost.

'Something like that.' His expression changed. He looked her up and down appraisingly, and Kate wondered if her skintight black trousers had been the right decision after all. And what had possessed her to come in this man's car to God knows where in the first place, when she hardly knew him? He wasn't safe. He was a predator, and she had no experience of predators.

'It's a big house.' She needed to say something, not wanting an awkward silence to spring up between them. 'Do you have a big family to live in it?'

He smiled, the tip of his tongue touching thick, sensual lips. 'I'm not married, Kate.'

Not married. She gulped, hoping that he was blind to the preposterous workings of her brain. All this, and he wasn't even taken. 'I see.'

'That's the way I like it.' He took her arm, leading her towards the garden, over to a small wooden bench thoughtfully positioned under an arbour of pale yellow roses. They sat down. The arbour provided shelter from the sea breeze and a heady fragrance to inhale as they gazed across at the magical West Dorset coastline. They were only about ten miles from Barstock, she guessed. These were the same grey cliffs that she'd walked along with Stephanie and Hannah. The cliffs that held so many secrets of the past.

'I'm going to offer you a job, Kate,' Adam said. 'I like your attitude. And I like you.'

'Because I'm bolshy?' She risked a sidelong glance towards the unyielding contours of his face. A touch overweight. Hair greying into silver at the temples. Forty if he was a day. Was he past his prime? Or did he have as much to offer as he seemed to be suggesting? Was this her mother's dream, or what?

'Because you say what you mean,' he corrected. 'You're honest, and I appreciate honesty. These days it's hard to find.' His eyes misted over.

'I loathe hypocrisy.' That was true enough. Her fists were clenched in her lap. But who was the hypocrite? How many of them could say that they were without pretence?

Adam smiled. 'Of course you do. I can see that. And there are a lot of hypocrites around. They're all the same – the creeps, the hangers-on, the money grabbers.' His voice was scathing. But the implication was that she was different. And she liked that. After all, she would never want this man for an enemy.

He drew back and stared at her. 'You remind me of what I was like when I started up. Deciding what you want, throwing caution to the wind. Just going for it.'

Kate smiled. It was a new start in a way, she'd already decided that. And she had been right to come here. Exactly on target. 'What kind of job?'

'Dealing with clients. Showing them around. You'll need some training first, of course.' He turned towards her, pushing back a few lost strands of auburn hair. 'And a bit of smartening up. A couple of suits, the right hair-do, a bit of make-up.'

She flinched at his touch. But his grey eyes were curiously objective. As if she wasn't quite her own person, after all.

'Not like your receptionist.' Kate pulled a face. She might not be immune to his brand of self-confident charm, but she wouldn't become a bimbo look-alike for any price.

His eyes glazed. 'That one's on her way out. She's a temp, and I've had enough of temps.' He smiled slowly. 'You're different. Knew it as soon as I laid eyes on you. You'll stay because you'll want to stay. I'll make it worth your while.'

'Yeah?' She felt the excitement, an excitement quite different from the thrill of sex, stuttering into life inside her. She wasn't even sure what she was taking on. But she wanted it, whatever it was, she wanted it.

'You'll be dealing with important clients.' His smooth voice was lining her world with chocolate-coloured icing. 'And if you play your cards right, the only way to go is up.'

She stared, mesmerised, as his hand slipped into his breast pocket.

He drew out a fat wad of notes, counting slowly. Twenties and fifties. More money than she'd ever seen in her life.

'A deposit for a flat to rent,' he murmured. 'A few nice things. Nice things never did anyone any harm.'

He took her hand, opened the curled fingers and pressed the money into her palm. Kate stared at him, confused. The challenge was in the steel shadows of his eyes. Was it really so easy? The money was hot and crisp. She felt her fingers curl back around it, her choices receding.

Adam smiled and patted her hand. 'Good girl. We'll be a fine partnership. I can feel it in my bones.'

Kate wasn't sure. She was only conscious of danger, and it wasn't far away.

He led the way back to the BMW which stood primed, poised and ready.

There was a moment of indecision. Don't patronise me – she wanted to say the words again. She felt they needed to be said again. But there was only silence, and a strange, tight tingling in her throat that made further speech impossible. She looked down at the money he'd given her. He had given. She had taken. And now he was waiting, his hand on the bonnet of the beast, powerful and possessing.

'Let's make tracks. Things to do. People to see.' He became brisk.

Everything had changed and yet nothing had changed.

Kate slipped back into the leather interior and smelt it all once more. Opulence, luxury, money, power. And she had just found herself a taste.

15

Hannah stared at the white sheet of paper in the typewriter and let out a groan of despair. Fleur had become a nine-month-old handful, but she was upstairs taking a nap at last. So this was Hannah's own time, the only time she ever had to herself since motherhood had entered her life. Even if it were only baby-sleeping time, when one ear remained always listening.

And that's how it seemed – not as if Hannah had become a mother with all the qualities it should entail, but as if this force, this dark *thing* called Motherhood had charged in uninvited, turning her life inside out and upside down until she didn't know where she was.

But Fleur *was* her life. She'd never be without her. And she had no regrets about the choice she'd made. Kate's suggestion on that awful day would never have been an option. Still, it was hard to have one's time sucked away. To have it devalued. Sometimes it was difficult to see much that was worthwhile in dirty nappies or building bricks. Difficult to have nothing of your own. To feel the very passivity and terrible sameness of motherhood chiselling away at your time, your personality, your dreams, your life.

She stared unseeing at the paper. Into the paper and through the paper. The house was a mess and she'd prepared nothing for dinner. But she'd promised herself an hour to get her thoughts down in print. This hour. She'd anticipated this hour into nothing. Because the words just wouldn't come.

Before Fleur, before pregnancy at least, she'd been almost too busy to find time to write. What with the demands of college, Stephanie, Kate, and then Tom, life had been hectic. She'd carried a notebook around with her everywhere she went, to preserve those snatched gems of conversations, those precious ideas that had flowed from her mind and through her pen like a never-ending stream of consciousness. But now the stream was as dry as desert. Those inspirations had scarpered. The empty paper mocked Hannah like a reflection of her own soul.

She pushed the typewriter away, tore her hair back from her face and felt the tears squeezing a treacherous pathway past her eyelids. These days she cried so often – too often. These days all she wanted to do was cry.

The doorbell snapped her out of self-pity, and quickly she wiped her eyes as she raced to open it, terrified that the quiet ring in an empty house would waken the baby. She was becoming paranoid. Motherhood was a time of wild paranoia that some never managed to shake themselves out of. Would she? Or was she too scared to let herself go under in the first place?

Who would it be? Hannah hesitated, hands on the latch. She never saw any college friends now that she lived in such a different world – it wasn't only the distance of ten measly miles that separated her new suburbia from college life. And if, close by, there were any women with young children as lonely as she, then she hadn't found them.

'Martin.'

He stood on the doorstep, tall, dark and shaggy like a well-meaning spaniel. 'Hello, Hannah.' His smile brought warmth to the day.

'Hi. Come in.'

Hannah was glad to see him. Maybe today she would have been glad to see anyone, but Tom's colleague Martin who taught Geography at the school was better than most. He was good company, kind, and always had time for her. Over the past months she'd learned to appreciate such things.

'Sorry to disturb you, Hannah.' He followed her into the kitchen. 'I just wanted a quick word with Tom, if he's around.'

She felt the stab of disappointment. Of course he'd want to see Tom. Tom was the one who had a life, wasn't he? 'You're not disturbing me,' she lied. 'You'll have to excuse the mess, though.' She suppressed the urge to babble – maybe conversation had been unheard inside her for too long. 'But Tom's not here. He's at the school. Drama rehearsals, I think he said.'

It might be the summer holidays, but it made little difference to the time Tom spent with her. She tried not to mind. But she wondered sometimes if he regretted marrying her and having Fleur. Having responsibilities to tie him down when at heart he was such a free spirit.

'Drama rehearsals?' Martin frowned, before a glimmer of understanding dawned in his hazel eyes. 'Ah yes. Drama rehearsals.'

'No peace for the wicked, is there?' She laughed. 'And people say teachers have it cushy.'

'Yeah.' He seemed embarrassed. She hoped he wouldn't leave.

'Have some coffee while you're here.' She smiled brightly, feeling it twitching in rebellion at her lips. Part of her simply didn't want to smile. Part of her didn't want to pretend.

He hesitated. 'Well, Hannah, I don't know if . . .'

'Please, Martin.' She put a hand on the sleeve of his olive corduroy jacket, and he looked down at it, seeming surprised.

'I'm a bit fed up today,' she confessed.

'Sure, I'd love some coffee.' Martin pointed to the typewriter. 'What are you working on?'

He was one of the few people she knew who had ever shown genuine interest in her writing. To most, including Tom, poetry only seemed to sum up her scattiness. A confirmation of personality type. It was humoured. Part of what made her the fluffy person she was.

Hannah sighed. 'Nothing at all, apparently. It won't come.' She pulled a face. Maybe she was becoming cynical. And some might say it was about time.

She put the kettle on, gazing out of the window into the tiny patch of garden at the back of the small terrace they had moved into in the spring. A new housing estate a couple of miles down the road from Purwood village school where Tom now worked.

'I'll dig some of it up,' Tom had said. 'We can grow a few vegetables. Fleur can even have her own little allotment when she's big enough.'

Hannah had responded to his enthusiasm. 'I'll plant lots of bulbs – bluebells and daffodils, crocuses and snowdrops. And maybe there'll be room for one of those little apple trees.'

'We'll be going to the garden centre every weekend,' Tom teased. 'Just like a regular old married couple.'

And she had leaned against him, in contentment. Her own home. Their own home.

Hannah sighed. They hadn't been to the garden centre once in the four months they'd lived here, and the garden was still bare. What had happened? Even the baby's room was still dark blue. When she thought of the sunshine yellow she'd painted the old bedroom at the flat, it made her want to weep. She may have been pregnant, but she'd had so much energy then. So much hope.

'What's the trouble, Hannah?' Martin was beside her. A sympathetic voice and a warm shoulder to cry on. And what else besides?

Hannah smiled at him. That was silly. She was safe with Martin – she knew it instinctively. He was the kind of man who rescued people and asked for nothing in return. He was sweet, generous and lovable. And not the type to be disloyal to his friends.

'Boredom, I suppose,' she said, keeping her voice light. 'You know all the stories about bored housewives. Well, maybe they're true. Fleur's adorable but she's not exactly good company just yet. And Tom . . .' she tailed off.

'And Tom?' he pressed, moving closer.

'In term-time Tom's at the school all hours.' Her voice hardened into bitterness. 'School's supposed to finish at four but I'm lucky if I see him before six. Sometimes later. He says he can't do marking and lesson planning here. That Fleur makes too much racket, and disturbs him.' She shrugged. Why was she telling this man all this?

'I see.'

Did he see? It wasn't much to complain about and that wasn't it, not really. 'It's her restless time,' she murmured. And when was her own restless time?

The thought unnerved her and she turned from him abruptly, thinking back as she busied herself with the coffee to the days when Tom had preferred to revise for college exams in the library. There had been no baby then. Only Hannah, pregnant and lonely, but still a distraction apparently.

'And here we are – school holidays, a wonderful day waiting outside, and where's Tom?' She sighed. 'In school. He can't keep away from the place. If it's not in-service training, it's some play he's producing with the amateur dramatic society and school.' She and Tom led separate lives now. The thought frightened her.

She turned back to him. 'You're not like that, are you, Martin?' Her brown eyes were wide.

He laughed awkwardly, taking the coffee she offered him. 'Geography doesn't entail so much extra-curricular stuff,' he said after a pause. 'Or maybe I'm not as dedicated as Tom is.'

'Tom? Dedicated?' She laughed. 'Dedicated to having a good time, more likely.'

Martin seemed to choke on his coffee. 'Perhaps you should think about yourself a bit more.' His eyes were serious. 'Perhaps you should live your own life – be independent.'

Hannah laughed humourlessly. 'What would you say if I told you I'd lost my independence? It gets pretty elusive when you have a husband, a baby and no job.'

He shrugged. 'I'm not just talking about financial independence, Hannah. There's a lot more to it than that.'

She laughed again. 'Says you.' Martin hadn't watched Tom swimming into the freedom of the big wide world, fully equipped with the water-wings of the breadwinner. Tom wasn't the one who would sink. And Hannah's dependence grew the further he swam out – it was harder and harder to keep up. Since her grant had stopped she had nothing to call her own. It ate away at her – the loss of choice that dependency brings.

'*Touché.*' Martin stared at her. 'But if you're that fed up, then shouldn't you be doing something about it?'

'What do you suggest?' Her tone lacked enthusiasm.

'See more of your own friends, for a start. Get your own life together. Make a few changes. Then it won't matter so much if Tom's not around.'

Your own friends . . . Hannah thought of Kate and Stephanie. But as always when she thought of them, the pain of loss was tinged with resentment. Of how Stephanie had tried to tear her away from Tom. And the things she had said about him – horrible, hateful things. And of how Kate had tried to take Fleur away from her. Selfish, both of them. After all their promises. But she missed them. Once more Hannah felt the tears threatening. She really missed them.

'Come on, love. It can't be that bad.' Before she knew what was happening, Martin's arms were around her and he was holding her. Not demanding anything. Only holding her. And she cried it out, just wept it out, the tears scalding her cheeks and soaking his shirt.

Martin stroked her hair and murmured soft words of comfort. 'There, Hannah. It's okay. Have a good cry. Let it out.'

After several minutes, she drew back, the tears smudged on her cheeks, embarrassment in her eyes. 'I'm sorry, Martin. I don't know what came over me.'

'You had the blues, that's all. I should have kept my big mouth shut.' His eyes were troubled, as he passed her the box of tissues from the top of the fridge. 'What you need is a break from . . .' The wave of his arm included the house, the garden, even more perhaps. ' . . . from routine,' he concluded. 'Tell Tom to take you on holiday.'

'He says we can't afford one.' As Hannah dried her eyes, she heard the faint wail from upstairs. 'Oh God, now Fleur's woken up and I haven't done a thing.' Already she was in the hallway. 'Don't go yet, Martin.'

Once upstairs she soothed the baby, and checked her own appearance before going back down to the kitchen. What had happened to her to make her cry all over poor Martin like that? Despair. Yes, but her despair wasn't his problem. She must apologise again.

Before she had the chance, Martin spoke.

'Look, Hannah,' he said. 'I hope you don't think it's a cheek. But how about coming out for a run in the car? Down to the coast. We could take a walk around, maybe have a picnic if you like.' He wouldn't look at her. 'Don't feel you have to say yes, but I'm at a loose end and, well, if you think Tom wouldn't mind . . .'

'Bugger what Tom thinks.' Hannah couldn't believe she'd said that. Her eyes widened in horror as she met Martin's surprised stare. They both laughed.

'That's the spirit.' Martin gulped his coffee. 'Shame to waste such a beautiful day.'

'What about the baby?' Hannah jiggled Fleur up and down, planting a kiss on the blonde fluff of her hair. She loved that clean, faintly milky, baby smell.

'Have baby, will travel. You've got a car seat, haven't you? I've noticed that Tom doesn't keep it in the car.'

'He doesn't, you're right.' She had teased him, but often wondered. Would a baby's car seat ruin Tom's image?

Tom had bought the car as soon as he landed his job, promising to teach Hannah to drive so that she could use it as much as he did. 'I don't want to be stuck on the estate all day,' she'd said, half-laughing. 'I'll need to get out and about.'

But, along with the vegetable patch, the driving lessons had never materialised. And the estate had become her prison. Hannah sighed. It was easy to find excuses for him – he was busy, there were already too many demands on his time. But sometimes the excuses seemed so stale and well-used. On a day like this one she felt the urge to blow his excuses to the wind like dandelion seeds.

'So will you come?' There was a boyish eagerness on Martin's kind face.

Was he kidding? 'I'd love to.'

Hannah passed Fleur over to him. 'You hold the baby, or put her in that cradle over there.' She pointed. 'And I'll get some food together.'

In the end it was almost an hour before they set off, after Fleur had been fed and changed, and Hannah had made up a picnic, thankful that she'd had both cold beer and cold chicken in the fridge for a change. Maybe it was her lucky day, after all.

'Is Barstock okay with you?' Martin asked.

A faint, wistful smile accompanied the nod she gave him. Barstock and the fossil forest. Stephanie's grave and beautiful face peering over her shoulder at the map. Kate chasing her down the cliff path. A year ago last spring, and she hadn't returned since.

Maybe they should be bad memories – it was after all the day she'd broken with both of them. But she wanted to return to Barstock, just as she wanted to see them both again. She was sure of that now. Stephanie and Kate. Where were they, and what were they doing?

She confided some of this to Martin two hours later, as they lounged on her tartan blanket after their picnic. Fleur, in her yellow sunhat decorated with red cherries, was happily playing with some long stalks of grass. And beyond them were the grey cliffs of Chesil Beach and the coastal path that the three girls had taken on that spring day just after Hannah had first discovered that she was pregnant with Tom's child. With Fleur . . .

She bent to kiss her, and when she lifted her face from the kiss she saw Martin watching her.

'You talk about them so much. So why don't you see those two friends of yours any more?' he asked.

'We drifted apart.' She couldn't say more than that, even to this man to whom it was so easy to say anything.

'Because of the baby?' He smiled at Fleur.

She shook her head. Not really.

'Or because of Tom?'

He was perceptive, she'd give him that. 'Perhaps,' she hedged. Of course it was much more complex than he could guess.

'Maybe you should get in touch with them again. Stephanie and . . . ?'

'Stephanie and Kate.' It was good to taste the names on her tongue after all this time. 'I don't even know where they are. I'd like to see them . . .'

She tailed off. Maybe one day. She wanted to believe that. Maybe one day.

She watched Martin playing with Fleur, making her toy white rabbit dance towards her on his hind legs, laughing as she giggled uproariously.

He wasn't married. She was pretty sure he didn't even have a girlfriend. But he had a way with Fleur that was a stark contrast to Tom's casual indifference.

Once, in the early days, Tom had found time for Fleur. But somehow, his affection had faded when faced with the practicalities of colic, nappies and sleepless nights. Maybe he'd never forgiven the baby for clinging to her mother and crying when Tom tried to hold her in his arms. Or maybe Fleur had become an inconvenience rather than someone to love. Did Tom lack the staying power for fatherhood? Or was it Hannah's fault? Had she hung on to Fleur too tightly because Fleur was all she had for her own? She pushed the unwelcome thought away.

'Let's go down to the sea.'

They dumped their stuff back in the car before taking the path down to the beach.

The tide was in and it was stony, but the sea was so inviting that they took off their shoes and paddled gingerly in the cool water, taking turns to dangle Fleur over the waves, lifting her high as the spray broke until she was screaming with delight. Afterwards they lay flat on their stomachs drying their legs in the sun and breathing in the sharp salt tang on the air, while Hannah's eyes scoured the stones.

'Looking for fossils, Hannah?' Martin teased.

She nodded.

'Here's one.' He handed her an ammonite, just a few circular and patterned indentations on the grey stone. 'A little piece of the past.' Their fingers touched.

Abruptly, Hannah's landscape changed. 'Thanks, Martin.' She tucked it in her pocket and grabbed Fleur. 'We'd better be getting back. Tom will be wondering where on earth we are.'

Martin nodded, rising to his feet. 'Of course.' His voice was even but there was a sadness there that she recognised. Oh, Martin, she thought. Please don't fall in love with me. I need a friend so badly. But I need a lover like a hole in the head.

When they got back to Purwood, a quick glance down the street for the car reassured her that Tom was still out. But it was time to get the house ready for his return. The misery settled in her stomach once more.

She turned to Martin with a false brightness. 'Thanks, Martin. You've been wonderful.' She hesitated. 'A real friend.'

'I had a good time, Hannah.' His voice was husky. 'Maybe we'll do it again sometime.'

She nodded. 'I hope so.'

But she wasn't sure that they could. Once was acceptable, but any more, and she might find herself thinking dangerous thoughts. Find Martin thinking dangerous thoughts. She wasn't a free agent, and that kind of pleasure – the simple pleasure of a day out by the sea – was out of bounds. Unless it was with Tom.

So what would happen when Martin came around again? Would it be for Hannah or for Tom that he came?

She went into the house, standing at the front window holding Hannah tightly to her breast as he drove away. One last, long look back. Hannah shivered. She could still smell the scent of him as he'd held her in the kitchen this morning – an earthy kind of masculinity that had somehow been so reassuring.

She was vulnerable, tucked away here in her own little hell-hole. Suffocating and alone. She had to be alone. She still loved her husband, yet she was trapped in someone else's life and someone else's body. Martin was right. If she were to survive, then something had to change . . .

Martin pulled in at the pub a mile down the main road that led to Purwood village school. Not that he wanted to drink particularly – although God knows he could murder a pint. It had been as much as he could do to stop himself telling Hannah everything – how he felt about her, what Tom was up to. As much as he could do to stop himself from taking her in his arms and kissing that lovely, trembling mouth. She was so, so beautiful. And Tom McNeil was such a bastard. He didn't deserve her.

But Martin stopped at the pub because he needed to think. It had been one hell of a strange day, after all. He really had dropped in to see Tom. It had never occurred to him that Hannah would be on her own, let alone upset and in desperate need of company. Any company, he reminded himself. He was nothing special. The poor girl would have cried on the shoulder of almost any poor bastard who had turned up on the doorstep. And run a mile if anything untoward had been suggested. She was such an innocent.

So perhaps on reflection it was a good thing it had been dependable old Martin Buckingham there when the tears started to flow, rather than someone more unscrupulous who might have given Hannah more than she'd bargained for. Martin could be relied on. That had always been half his trouble.

He climbed slowly out of the beaten-up Vauxhall Cavalier and walked towards the pub. He hadn't intended to suggest they went out together either – of course he hadn't. And even when the idea had occurred to him – because it was plain she needed to get herself out of that house – he had suggested it with a strange sense of misgiving. As if he might be starting something that one day would be beyond his control.

Martin shivered. He was reading too much into it. Being a prat. It was just a nice day out, that was all. Look at the way she'd frozen solid when he'd given her that ammonite – hardly the most romantic gesture in the world. And yet the freshness of her face when she'd relaxed and actually begun to enjoy herself had been priceless.

No, the trouble with Hannah McNeil, he thought as he entered the pub, was that she was too much in love with her husband.

He ordered his drink and looked around. There in the corner of the lounge bar he spotted the unmistakeable long legs and high heels of Jayne Stepney. And she wasn't alone.

'Well, I'll be damned,' he muttered, licking the froth of the beer from his lips.

The bastard couldn't even be bothered to take her somewhere they'd be anonymous. He was conducting his affair in full view of any of their neighbours who might pop in for a pint on the way home from work.

He walked over.

'Martin!' Briefly he enjoyed the embarrassment in her cool green eyes. Jayne Stepney was a head of department, and had perfected a way of patronising the rest of the staff.

'Tom and I were just . . .' She looked down at Tom's hand, still planted on her thigh. 'We were just . . .'

'Save your breath, Jayney. Martin knows the score.' Tom grinned.

Jayney? Martin saw her flinch. Did Tom really know what he was doing?

'Does he indeed?' Her eyes were thoughtful. Deliberately, she reached out to remove Tom's hand.

'Don't worry about Martin.' Tom spoke as if he weren't there, or was too insignificant to count. Not a trace of embarrassment, shame, anger. In fact, Tom seemed pleased that his little tryst had been witnessed. Arrogant sod.

Martin felt his hands close more tightly around the glass tankard. Maybe it would break, and give them a shampoo they'd never bloody forget.

Jayne Stepney sipped cautiously at her white wine. 'I suppose we're all civilised adults.'

Martin stared at her. That was a matter of opinion. Personally, he'd like to smash their heads together. For Hannah.

'So . . . have you had a good day, me old mate?' Tom brushed back his fair hair.

Martin blinked. Was all this matey stuff an attempt to diffuse the tension? Because even Tom must see that under her cool exterior, Jayne Stepney was positively smouldering.

'Not so bad.' Yes, he'd had a bloody, wonderful day. With your wife, he wanted to say. With your wife. What would Tom say if he knew? Would he be filled with self-righteous, hypocritical anger? Or would he simply not care?

Martin desperately wanted to find out. If it hadn't been for Hannah he would have told him right then and there. But he couldn't risk it. He wouldn't hurt Hannah for the world. It was up to her. Hadn't their outing been as innocent as a summer's day? If she wanted to tell Tom, then that was fine by him. But part of him hoped that she wouldn't. He wanted it to be their secret. The only thing they might ever share, perhaps.

'Excuse me for a minute, boys.' Jayne got to her feet and moved gracefully from the table, all five feet ten of her.

Martin watched Tom's admiring eyes sweep the length of her body. She was quite a catch, was Ms Stepney, aggressively proud of her own independence, smart and undeniably sexy. But she was experienced too. She'd been through two marriages already, to Martin's knowledge, and she was still only in her early thirties, he guessed. Martin was vaguely surprised that she'd spared Tom so much as a second glance.

'Isn't she something?' Tom couldn't seem to tear his eyes away.

Martin grunted in noncommittal fashion. Not his type. Too snooty. Too cool. Whereas Hannah . . .

'D'you know . . .' Tom leaned back in the seat, a picture of smug chauvinism. 'I never thought I'd find a woman who could match Dian in bed. So much hot, sweaty passion.' He drank some lager from his half-pint mug. 'But Jayne comes pretty close to it. She's cold as ice at first, you know?' He laughed thickly. 'And then the passion pours out of her like lava from a bloody volcano.'

Martin turned away in disgust. When he'd first met Tom McNeil there had been enough charm and easy sociability in the younger man for Martin to overlook some of his shortcomings. Like his attitude towards women, for a start. But now that he knew Hannah, now that she was a person for him, with feelings and dreams . . . well, it had changed things completely. Now he just felt sick when Tom bragged about his exploits.

'Is Dian aware of this threat to her position?' he mocked.

But the sarcasm was lost on Tom. 'She knows about Jayne. But she thinks it was a quickie in a deserted staff room one night. I wouldn't let on how much I enjoy it.'

'No, I bet you bloody wouldn't.' Martin stared at him. How could he play with their emotions like this – the women who cared for him? He was nothing but an egomaniac. And Martin had heard enough of his stories. He'd had it with Tom McNeil. He'd had a gutful.

Tom glanced at him. 'Something bothering you?'

'You don't have the time to hear about it, do you?' Martin downed the rest of his beer. There was a bad taste in his mouth and he wanted to spit it out. 'You're too busy with your drama rehearsals,' he jeered.

A light of understanding dawned in Tom's insipid blue eyes. 'You've seen Hannah.'

'I was actually looking for you.' It seemed important to make him realise that. 'She was desperate for company. The poor girl was in a right state.'

'Oh?' Tom looked him up and down, his brow darkening. 'Are you suggesting that I'm neglecting my wife?'

Martin laughed harshly. 'Are you saying that you're not?'

Tom shrugged, picked up his glass and watched Martin speculatively over the rim. 'What you can't get at home, you get somewhere else. Simple.'

The suppressed anger fired inside Martin. Carefully he placed his tankard on the table and leaned forwards until his face was close to Tom's. 'I think you should look after her better, you bastard,' he mouthed. 'That woman is lonely. She needs you.' He stared into Tom's pale eyes. They were scared. Red-rimmed and scared. 'Although God knows why.'

Tom's mouth twisted as he drew away from him. 'And what do you bloody know about it? Fancy her yourself, do you?'

He was ugly. His smooth, boyish face with the carefully preserved designer stubble on his jaw, was ugly, and Martin wanted to smash it. His fingers curled around the handle of the tankard.

But Tom was quick to react, on his feet like lightning, as if sensing the danger, his mouth working, his eyes challenging. 'Sex with Hannah is like necrophilia.' He laughed in Martin's face. 'It always has been. She's frigid as they come. She doesn't want me. She's never fucking wanted me.'

'She's your wife, man. Show some respect.' Martin's eyes clouded. He didn't want to hear this. He backed away but Tom wouldn't stop.

'She was a virgin when I met her. A virgin at nineteen. Hardly been kissed.'

And no match for a bloke like Tom McNeil. Martin could imagine it, although he didn't want to.

'I should have known then.' Tom seemed to be talking to himself. 'I should have bloody known what a woman like that could do to me.'

Martin couldn't hear any more of this. Tom's self-pity stank more than his sexual shenanigans. But he wasn't worth hitting. He wasn't worth anything. Poor Hannah. That's all Martin could think. Poor Hannah.

He stumbled out of the bar.

'You bloody well leave her alone, d'you hear?' Tom was shouting. 'Don't you ever go near her again.' He hesitated. 'Or she'll pay for it, d'you hear? Bloody do-gooders . . .'

Tom was still rambling as Martin slammed the heavy oak door of the pub behind him. He didn't need this. He felt sorry for Hannah but he had his own life to lead. She wouldn't thank him for interfering, and he couldn't bear to be responsible for what Tom might do to her.

Stay away from Hannah, Tom had said. Well, it was none of Martin's business, was it? Hannah wasn't his business. She was another man's wife. He had no right to be attracted to her. No right to ever stroke her fine blonde hair, touch her mouth as she smiled or hold her hand. Another man's wife. He had no choice. If only for his own sanity, he had to stay away.

16

It was a balmy August evening, the night before Kate's wedding.

She looked around her at the guests assembled for dinner in the spacious dining-room of Adam Horton's house on the cliff. His friends, not her friends. His world, not hers. But she had said goodbye to her world when she embraced Adam's. And tomorrow, part of it would belong to her. Tomorrow, she would be mistress of all this, no longer plain Kate Dunstan whose miserable attempts at independence had come to nothing, but Kate Horton – respected, envied, admired.

A ring at the doorbell made her spring to her feet, glancing at her watch for the umpteenth time. Nine p.m. She caught Adam's eye. He was becoming impatient. Dinner had been ready and waiting for half an hour. Some guests were on their third glass of sherry.

'That must be them.' How could her parents keep everyone standing around like this? They were coming to meet Adam and coming for their wedding. It should be important – and yet still they were late.

'Mum!' Kate felt only relief at the sight of Eileen's wonderfully familiar face, thinner and more lined than the last time she'd seen it – that was evident even in the dimming twilight. Then she realised she was alone.

'Where's Dad?'

Eileen put down her worn suitcase. She looked awfully tired. 'I tried my best,' she said.

Kate wondered why she didn't feel more disappointed. Had she been half-expecting him to let her down? But at least Eileen was here. How strange that it should still be so important, with the distance that had grown between them.

For a prolonged moment they stared at each other. It had been a long parting, but now there were only a few seconds of awkwardness, before Kate smiled, relishing just the sight of her mother, realising how much she'd missed the warmth of those green eyes that had watched over her for so long. Tired eyes. She was getting older. They had wasted too much time.

'It's so good to see you, my love . . .' Eileen's voice broke, and suddenly they were in each other's arms as if there had never been a separation.

Kate buried her face gratefully in her mother's greying dark hair, and breathed in, smelling the faint lavender in a kind of disbelief that things could be so unchanged.

'Mrs Dunstan?' Adam was beside them, his eyes cool yet welcoming, the perfect host disguising his irritation at being kept waiting for so long. 'I'm glad to meet you at last.' He held out his hand.

Eileen drew away from Kate. Her eyes were confused, yet there was a calmness about her that made Kate proud. 'And I'm glad to meet you.' She took his hand, but her expression was questioning as she glanced at her daughter.

'This is Adam,' Kate told her.

'Adam.' Eileen murmured the name. Her eyes were still curious. 'I'm sorry to be so late. I hope I haven't kept you waiting for too long.' She peered past him. 'If you can give me five minutes and show me where to put my things?' She indicated the tatty brown suitcase.

Her mother was saying all the right words, yet Kate still felt a shaft of embarrassment. She found herself remembering her weekend with Stephanie at Atherington Hall, her own worn navy case, and Julian's raised, arrogant eyebrows. How things had changed. She had a quite different role to play now.

'I'll take you up.' Kate grabbed the case and made for the stairs. 'You're in the room next to mine.'

'You look lovely, Kate.' Eileen was tidying her hair in front of the glass. She had taken off her travelling dress and was standing in her slip, pitifully thin, her skin almost hanging from her bones and breasts.

Kate could hardly bear to look at her. She felt strangely responsible for what her mother had become. A wasted figure, or so it seemed to her.

'Being with Adam must agree with me.' She tried to smile.

Eileen nodded. 'I suppose you're right.' Her voice was noncommittal.

'What do you think of him?' Kate was eager to hear her reply. 'Isn't he as charming and debonair as I told you?' She hadn't wanted to boast, but she'd been so proud in that letter she wrote to them. So proud that at last she had succeeded. She had found a man who had everything her mother had ever wanted for Kate. At last she had made something of her life. And at last, her mother would approve.

'I'm sure he is.' Eileen took out a plain blue dress and eased it over her head. Her face emerged, looking doubtful. 'Quite a man of the world, I imagine.'

'And what about the house?' Kate spun around. 'Isn't it something?'

'But you're not marrying the house.'

Kate frowned. 'What don't you like about him?'

Eileen hesitated. 'He's older than I expected, that's all.'

A wave of resentment surfaced in Kate. She couldn't rest, could she? There was always something to criticise. Nothing was ever quite good enough. 'Boys my age are boring and stupid.'

She wandered disconsolately over to the window. The spare bedroom had a wonderful view over the rock garden. She looked out towards the sea, soft and shimmering in the hazy moonlight.

'You didn't used to think that way, my dear.'

'What?' Kate swung round to meet her mother's eyes in the mirror.

Eileen was applying a dark-red lipstick that made her face look deathly pale, decorated with a streak of blood. 'You thought you loved Jason,' she pointed out in her mild voice.

'And look where it got me,' Kate snapped.

Why had she brought that up now? How could she even *think* about what had happened with Jason, on this – the night before Kate's wedding?

Eileen was silent. But there was a sadness in her eyes that seemed to reach out to her daughter.

Kate relented. 'I don't want to argue with you, Mum. Not tonight.' Her eyes were bright with unshed tears. She didn't want to think of the past. She wouldn't think of the past. This was her future, this was all that mattered now.

'Of course we won't argue. I'm sorry, my love.' In a moment, Eileen was beside her, her arms warm and comforting around Kate's shoulders. 'I only wanted to hear that you're happy.' Her whispered voice was urgent in intensity. 'I just need to know that you've found everything you want.'

Kate drew back from her embrace to stare at her. How could she ask

217

that? Wasn't all this her mother's dream as much as it had ever been Kate's dream? Wasn't this what Mum had always wanted – for Kate to escape from the shackles of Ridley and the working-class life that existed there? To have the freedom that money could buy? To be secure. To be safe. To be different?

'Look around you, Mum.' There was a harshness in her voice. 'Don't you think there's everything here? Everything a girl could ever want?'

Eileen's sigh seemed oddly dismissive. 'Yes, my dear.' She paused. 'But do you love him?'

Kate shook her head in confusion. Love? What was she talking about? It had never been love that Mum had wanted for her. Hadn't her mother stopped her from having Jason? Stopped her from keeping their baby? How could she talk of love?

'I loved Jason.' There was an old bitterness in her voice. An old, aching bitterness that had never quite gone away.

'But you were only a child.' Eileen gripped her arms. 'You were too young to be tied down like that.'

'I wanted to be tied down,' Kate wailed. Not even knowing if it were true any more.

Eileen let go of her abruptly. 'Children aren't old enough to know what they want.'

'And what did *you* want?' Kate stared at her. 'What did you want for me?'

'I wanted you to be free.' Her mother's eyes were steely and determined. She looked full blown with life again, no longer the ageing woman she had become, with the energy sapping out of her weary limbs. 'I wanted you to create your own life for yourself.'

'I tried to.' Why wouldn't she understand?

Eileen waved her protestations away. 'No, no. Not a life of drudgery like I had. An independent life. I wanted you to have a career that would give you some freedom – give you the choices that I never had.' Her head drooped at last, her shoulders sagged. 'I wanted you to be happy, that's all.'

Still Kate stared at her, mesmerised by what she was hearing after all this time. Happy? That was all?

'Well, I am happy,' she said. An uncomfortable kind of fear was nudging her in the ribs, but she wouldn't listen to whatever it was trying to tell her. 'Who wouldn't be happy, with all this?'

* * *

Downstairs, the wine and conversation flowed. Only Kate was quiet, reflecting on her mother's words, watching Adam and wondering if she was going crazy. She had been so sure that she was doing the right thing. So sure of what was important. Until her mother had taken her in her arms, she'd almost forgotten about the things that had once been so vital to her – warmth, caring, and love.

Kate sighed. She needed a friend to talk to so badly. Her mother cared, but she was bound up with her past and her old resentments. She needed Stephanie or Hannah. If only they were here, she might find the perspective to work out the truth. Without them, she seemed to have gone astray.

What did she know about the man she was about to marry? She had entered his world on the strength of a few conversations in a bar, accepted his job and money, and been drawn into the web of flattering clients, the old boy network that could achieve anything material, business lunches where contracts were agreed between dessert and Stilton, and playing hostess at Adam's infamous garden parties.

The first time he'd asked her she'd been flattered.

'What do I have to do?' It seemed so much more than a job somehow.

He smiled. 'Be yourself, be nice to the right people and wear a beautiful dress. The rest is up to you.'

Kate found it surprisingly easy. She enjoyed the sensation of being someone at last, and afterwards she knew he was pleased.

He took her arm, his fingers burning against her pale skin, his touch lingering for longer than necessary.

'You're my right-hand lady,' he laughed. 'However did I manage without you?' His eyes drummed into hers. Questioning.

'Perfectly well, I should think.' As always, she struck the right note. Challenging him, without ever flouting his authority or expecting more than he was willing to give. 'You can buy the best.'

Adam grinned. 'I'm beginning to think I've found the best.'

She shivered, conscious of the power he seemed to hold over her, effortlessly, carelessly. It wasn't just the money – it ran much deeper. Adam was drawing her out of her working-class background. He was moulding her, forming her, making his debonair lifestyle irresistible. Kate loved it and she wanted it. But she was scared. Oh God, she was scared. But still she stepped closer to whatever he was offering. Ever, ever closer.

Adam began showering her with expensive presents – jewellery of the kind she'd never dreamed of owning simply dazzled her. He took her out, for dinner and to the theatre. It was beyond her experience, still a dream world, but she was learning fast. They went to the latest London shows and patronised various galleries where Adam occasionally sponsored a promising artist. Adam was important. He had status, as well as money, and he was respected for it. And Kate was soaking it all up, absorbing everything she could.

He assumed now that she would always play hostess at his garden parties. Kate's name appeared on the invitations in gold italic lettering, as if Adam were promoting her to equal status. And why not? She was efficient at her work and good with the clients. Ravishing, and a breath of fresh air, were some of the comments made. Kate was becoming part of the Horton enterprise – an integral part, some said.

But Adam Horton never touched her. It intrigued Kate. He intrigued her. She was sure he wanted to – she recognised desire in the deep-set, grey eyes that held such dark shadows. Shadows and promises. And this was Kate's only control over the situation – over him, because he wanted her. Sex was there in the background, part of the bond that lay between them. Lying dormant but only gathering energy while it slept. Sex and power and money – irresistibly drawing her onwards.

Kate anticipated the pitfalls. So she evaded the delicate matter of sex with any of those important clients who wanted to go further than a chaste kiss on the cheek. She kept herself aloof and distant, knowing it was part of her attraction. Sensing how much might be at stake.

And in the meantime, the tension that ran tight between Kate and Adam Horton was satisfaction enough, except perhaps at night-time when she tossed and turned, gripped by old nightmares and new fantasy. Picturing his hard lips on hers. 'Oh Kate, oh Kate . . .' Pressing into her with tortured passion. At night-time she felt she was close to remembering . . . whatever it was that eluded her, whatever it was that she needed to see, to face, to deal with. And at night-time she was driven almost crazy with wanting what was so tantalisingly close. A new and intoxicating world.

The first time Adam kissed her, he avoided her mouth, his thick lips merely grazing the soft skin of her bare shoulder in the flame-coloured, backless evening dress that clashed so perfectly and outrageously with her hair.

'Kate,' he said. 'You must know how much you mean to me.' His voice was thick, and something stirred inside her.

'Must I?' She held her breath.

'I would have thought it was bloody obvious.' His eyes darkened. 'Damn it, Kate.' He took both her hands. 'I want you to be my wife.'

She stared at him. His wife? She hadn't dared to expect so much. Oh, it had been there, slinking and silent in the back of her mind, but she'd never allowed herself to acknowledge it. He was so much more than an employer. Much, much more. But marriage? What would her mother say?

A sliver of triumph slid through her. It was the perfect escape. A new world. An exciting and dangerous world with different rules and so much to play for.

She took a deep breath. 'I accept.'

Their eyes met. It was a deal. They both knew it was a deal. That was how it was – deals, contracts and compromises were taken or broken like egg shells beneath heavy feet. Money passed under the table. Clean money for dirty money. There was no room for a little word like love.

Adam, the man who got whatever he wanted, grinned in victory, and the machinery immediately whipped into action. Plans for the wedding swept Kate along on a flimsy raft made of trimmings and trappings and little else. They still didn't have sex, and he still hadn't kissed her full on the lips. She wondered why he hadn't wanted an affair, but there was too much happening for her to wonder too long. That was how he was. It only increased his air of mystery. And Kate was perfectly happy to wait.

Why me? She never asked him the question. She knew there had been women – she remembered the temp in the office on that day last autumn, with her red lips and curious eyes. There had been women. Women who had never meant very much. Who had only skimmed the surface of Adam's life, before their stilettoed footprints disappeared in the thick pile of plush, red carpeting of Adam's personal office sanctuary, never to be seen again. It was only Kate now. She had been made special. Adam Horton wanted her to be his wife.

And from that day when he'd asked her to marry him, she hardly stopped long enough to consider the consequences, hardly asked herself the right questions. She respected him. She admired him. She responded to his power and strength after the weakness of Jason, who had let her down when she needed him. This stranger-bond between them could mean anything or nothing. But it was the life he offered her that attracted her the most.

221

And as for love . . . Kate had almost forgotten about love. Until her mother had held her so close and murmured those words. 'But do you love him?'

Eileen was finding it hard to get used to all the razzmatazz. The luxury of this house on the cliff, as Kate called it. White Gates, it said on the wedding invitation.

But it was all wrong, wasn't it? Your daughter was supposed to marry from home. They should be in Ridley, shouldn't they? In the small, village church where Barbara could spare just the afternoon from the farm instead of being expected to traipse all the way to Dorset just to stay in a hotel for the night. They should be in Ridley, for all its faults. And Eileen was aware of every one.

Where all the neighbours could admire your new hat, and bring round little gifts that actually meant something. Gifts that were placed in the best front room that was hardly ever used any other time. Kept nice for weddings, funerals and the odd visit from the vicar.

Eileen felt cheated. She and Joe had not even been consulted. Not that *he* cared. But she'd saved a meagre portion of her housekeeping every week for years towards her daughter's wedding – for nothing. And here in Adam Horton's house on the cliff – in the blue room downstairs, that shrieked money as you walked into it – there was everything from expensive porcelain and delicate crystal, to food mixers and continental quilts. It made her linen tablecloth and napkins seem like nothing, yet God knows they'd cost the earth.

And now they were setting out a marquee on the lawn to the side of the house – some firm had been brought in to do it, so Kate had told her. It was all very nice. But it wasn't quite the same as enlisting the help of the whole street to make sandwiches. Eileen couldn't help thinking that this would only reinforce the opinion some of them already had – that Eileen Dunstan considered herself too good for Ridley.

She straightened her aching back. Not that she belonged in Ridley any more than Kate did. She'd had higher hopes than anyone when she was a girl, plenty of dreams that had turned to dust. And the folk of Ridley drove her mad at times with their twitching net curtains and prying faces. But they were real people at least. They had heart.

It seemed odd – the bride and her mother staying in the groom's house the night before the wedding. As if tradition was meaningless when there was money to be spent. Of course, Adam wasn't here – he'd gone to stay with the best man, so that convention was intact. But Eileen didn't feel comfortable in this house. Not comfortable at all.

Future husband . . . She sighed. She'd had a shock when she saw him. In fact if Kate hadn't written that his parents had both died when he was small, she would have taken the man for being Adam's father. Perhaps he was nice. Perhaps she was wrong. But there was something that worried her, something she couldn't quite put her finger on. And he looked so . . . worldly, standing next to her fresh and lively daughter with her glowing face and mass of red-gold hair. It just didn't seem right somehow.

She tapped lightly on the adjoining door that led to Kate's room. 'Can I come in?'

The dress was hanging in front of the wardrobe, a wonderful, frothy combination of lace and taffeta that had been designed and made to measure in record time.

'Beautiful,' Eileen murmured, hardly daring to touch the delicate fabric.

Her eyes misted as she remembered her own wedding dress, made by her mother who'd moaned good-humouredly all the while. But she'd put so much love into every stitch that the dress was priceless to Eileen. And after her wedding she'd wrapped it so carefully in tissue and cellophane before putting it away in a cupboard. Half-thinking that one day her own daughter might wear it.

Kate was sitting rigid in front of the mirror. Her eyes were red.

'You've been crying,' Eileen accused. 'What's wrong?'

'Wedding nerves.' Kate glared back at her.

'Come on now.' She'd always been a wild one. Eileen had learned over and over again that you couldn't keep one jot of control over her Kate. It was infuriating, but at the same time it made her proud.

'I've just realised that I haven't even got anyone to give me away. It's going to be a farce.' She sniffed. 'Why didn't Dad come?'

Eileen sighed. What could she say? That when they'd received the invitation, Joe had muttered, 'She'll see me bloody well dead first.'

She'd done her best to persuade him, mind. Kate was his daughter when all was said and done. But when the time came he was down the pub and already half-cut.

'I tried my best, love,' she said. She'd made an attempt to drag him out of the bar, but only got cursed for her trouble.

'She's nothing to me,' he had said, his red face bulging. 'Stop your bloody nagging and leave me be.' The drunken light in his eyes flashed a warning signal. The usual warning signal.

Eileen missed one train, but in the end she came here alone. She wasn't missing her daughter's wedding, not for anyone.

'But he wasn't interested, was he?' Kate's eyes were blank. She twisted from her own reflection. 'Why does he hate me so much, Mum?'

Eileen blinked. How long had she tried to shield this child from the truth? And where had it got either of them? What was the point? You could never hide from the past – not really. The past had tentacles with a way of reaching into your present, into your future even, and drawing you back. Perhaps after all it was better to be honest with your children – at least that way it gave them the chance to understand.

She took a deep breath. 'Me and your Dad.' She paused. 'Well, it was a bit like you and Jason, my love.'

She saw Kate's open face absorbing the information. There was a long pause. 'You got pregnant and you weren't married?' she whispered at last.

Eileen nodded. 'That's about the size of it. We'd been together six months. He was always pestering me. But I'd never, you know . . . ?' She faltered. It was hard to confide such things to your own child. 'It just happened – one summer's day.' Her expression softened. 'Up on Raddlestone Moor.'

'On the Moor?' Kate's eyes widened.

'It was a hot day. We'd got hold of some cider from the farm. We got carried away, like hundreds of other kids have probably got carried away on that moor.' She laughed bitterly. 'I learnt from my mistake, though. It was only the once.'

'What happened?' Kate took Eileen's hands in hers.

She had to go on. She had to tell it all, just like it was. Just like it had been all those years ago. 'I got fed up,' she admitted. 'I realised he wasn't for me. There wasn't enough to him. He had no ambition. No fire . . .' She tailed off. Her own mother had always given her these ideas, ideas above her station, Joe thought they were. But they were only dreams in the end. 'We broke up. Then I found I was pregnant.'

Kate squeezed her hands. 'With me?'

Eileen nodded. 'In those days things were done different. Especially in Ridley. I told Mam straight off. She went crazy but she went to see his Mam, and between the two of them they sorted it out. Women did. The men hardly realised what was going on. Women were the ones who dealt with anything important. They held it all together.'

'You had to marry him?' Kate's voice was faint.

'Listen, my lovely.' Eileen drew her closer. 'I was glad to marry him. There wasn't another choice. Anything else would have ruined my life. The shame would have finished me.'

'But you didn't love him?' Kate touched her mother's worn cheek.

Eileen felt the softness of her fingers and closed her eyes. 'No, I never did.'

'And now?'

She certainly wanted to know it all. And it was Eileen's duty to tell her. She should have told her a long time ago. Wasn't it part of your child's education – more relevant than learning Latin or Greek, some might say. It was real life, after all.

'I never have.' Eileen sighed. That was the truth. She'd never loved him and she'd never wanted him – no, not once. Not even that first time up on the Moor.

'And Dad?' Kate's eyes drifted to the window. She rose to her feet, walked over, and stared down towards the sea. 'How does Dad feel about all this?'

'He's never forgiven either of us.' Eileen held out her arms. 'I'm sorry, my lovely. But that's the way he is.' Not a bad man, she wanted to say. It's not black-and-white, is it? Maybe she had driven him into what he'd become. Every man had his needs . . .

'He drinks because he's miserable.' Kate moved towards her, holding her.

Eileen shuddered. And that's not all he does. But Kate didn't need to know about that. She was away from it now, thank the Lord. She was safe.

'And what do you do because you're miserable?' Kate's breath was warm on her cheek.

Eileen only held her tighter. She did nothing. That was her pain.

At last Kate leaned back, away from her. 'Why didn't you ever leave him?' she asked. 'Why did you stay together so long?'

'I don't know, love.' Well, what could she say? That she was scared of change? That she lacked the courage as well as the means? That those old dreams had drifted too far out of sight?

Eileen shook her head. There was no reason, not really. Yes, perhaps she should have left long ago. She had hoped he would change, and wondered what would become of them apart. It wasn't something she could imagine – they'd been together for so long. Besides, in Ridley, it just wasn't done.

'It isn't so easy,' she whispered. 'It really isn't so easy to leave.' After a while you even get to thinking that maybe, just maybe, you deserve it.

It seemed to Eileen, as they clung together, that this was a precious time. A time for the beginnings of a new closeness to grow. A closeness underlined by honesty and understanding, perhaps.

'I've always loved you, Kate.' She traced her fingers across her daughter's cheeks and realised that she was crying once more. Was it still wedding nerves? 'Never forget that. I've loved you just as much as if I'd longed for you with all my heart.' She hesitated. 'I just never wanted you to be trapped like I was.'

The words hung in the air between them. Eileen thought that she sensed a moment of indecision, before Kate's eyes hardened once more.

She took down her dress. 'Help me with this?'

Eileen held it open while Kate stepped carefully into the white flounces as if she were stepping into a different persona. A different life.

'I want you to give me away.' Her voice was firm. She looked her mother straight in the eye with an unmistakeable air of challenge.

Eileen smiled. 'Isn't it supposed to be a man?'

Kate's eyes were green liquid heat. 'I never belonged to a man. So I can't be given away by one.' She tossed her auburn hair, a crown of fire resting above the bridal regalia that wasn't Kate at all. 'You're the one who's cared for me. You're the one I belonged to. I want you to do it.'

Eileen felt so proud. Her eyes washed with tears. It was almost worth it all to hear those words.

But Kate let the veil fall over her face, and every part of her was hidden. She took her mother's arm. 'I've never belonged to a man,' she repeated. 'And I don't intend to start now.'

That night, after all the guests had gone home, Kate entered the master bedroom of the house on the cliff for the very first time. They would have only one night here before their trip to the Canary Isles – a ten-day honeymoon because Adam believed the business couldn't manage longer without them.

The room was aubergine and grey, as stylish and tasteful as the rest of the house, created by an interior decorator with no one's personality in mind. It was dominated by a huge four-poster bed.

Kate's stomach tightened as she looked at that bed. Only now did she feel nervous. Before, in the church and later, drifting butterfly-like around the guest-laden marquee in the garden in a manner she'd become accustomed to, Kate had moved as if in a trance through the afternoon and evening of the most important day of her life. Aware of Eileen's comforting presence. Aware of voices and congratulations. Assorted perfumes, freshly mown grass and champagne. Her eyes searching frantically around the crowd for Stephanie and Hannah. And Adam. She was aware of Adam. Strong, powerful and potent, by her side.

What would it be like – sex with Adam? She couldn't begin to imagine.

'This is all yours now, my dear.' Adam was behind her, loosening his tie. 'You're the mistress of the house on the cliff.' His voice was silky. His hands crept around her waist.

Kate laughed nervously. 'It's been a wonderful day.' Even though neither Stephanie nor Hannah had responded to their gilt-edged invitations. They hadn't forgiven her for what she'd done. And both had missed her moment of triumph. Her moment of empty glory. She'd been in such a trance that she'd almost missed it herself.

'Smooth as clockwork.' He released his hold on her, took off his jacket, sat down on the bed and watched her appraisingly. 'And in case I haven't mentioned it . . . you look ravishing, my dear.'

She smiled, not knowing what to say. Feeling strange and shallow. Not wanting to take the dress off, unwilling to acknowledge that she was actually married after all.

'And I have a little present for you.' He reached to pull the handle of the drawer in the bedside table, plucking out a small, soft package. 'You might like to wear it now.'

'Adam . . .' She laughed awkwardly. Silk lingerie – it must be. No one had ever given her silk underwear before. She was embarrassed.

She opened the package, aware all the time of his sunken eyes watching her, as if gauging her reactions. She hardly dared look at him. The tension remained strung between them.

'What's this?' She laughed again – less sure this time. Two scraps of black silk lay in her hands.

'A present for my little girl.' He sank to his knees in front of her. 'Put them on.'

Little girl? She picked up the bra. It was too small and had holes for the nipples to peep through. The panties were crutchless. She began to tremble. What had she done?

'Come on, baby.' His big hands crept up inside the voluminous folds of the wedding dress. Dirty hands staining pure white taffeta and lace. Not reaching her skin.

Kate pulled away. She stared at the underwear – holding it gingerly between fingers and thumb. Tossing back her head with distaste, she chucked the scraps of black silk on the floor. 'Is this some kind of joke, Adam?' Because it wasn't funny. It wasn't funny at all.

He was silent.

'You're not expecting me to wear these, are you?' Her lip curled.

'Ah, baby . . .' He buried his face in her dress. She reached out but didn't touch the dark hair, greying at the temples.

'For God's sake, Adam.' The situation was ridiculous. She felt the hysteria rising. 'I'm your wife, not one of your brainless bimbos. This is our home, not a bloody brothel.'

It was the wrong thing to say. He was on his feet in a moment, his eyes blazing, his face chalk-white. This wasn't a joke. He was deadly serious.

Before she could move, before she could even register his intention, a big hand whipped out, catching her hard across the face.

Kate staggered. Her eyes widened as she stared at him in total disbelief. Her hand moved slowly, towards the angry red fingermarks that were her husband's first touch. 'What the hell do you think you're doing?' Her voice was barely a whisper. There was fear – a new fear sprouting inside her like an old dread that had never quite left her life.

Adam was grinning. He picked up the scraps of lingerie. 'There's no need for that to ever happen again,' he said. His expression was calm.

He thrust his face into hers and she flinched. 'Just as long as you behave yourself.'

'For Christ's sake,' she muttered, backing away from him. What had she done? What the hell had she done? And how could she get out of here?

He grabbed her wrist, pulled her back. 'You're mine now.'

She struggled against his bulk. 'No . . .'

'Oh yes, my dear.' He let her go, but he was smiling, and she knew it was true.

He picked up his jacket, took a slim box from the breast pocket and handed it to her.

Wordlessly, Kate opened it. It was a necklace of emeralds. Delicate. Beautiful.

'They match your eyes.' His voice was hypnotic. She felt it closing over her, pinning her down, a new kind of trap. Her new world.

He picked up the necklace and moved behind her, his fingers grazing her skin as he fastened the clasp. 'My little Kate . . .'

She closed her eyes. She was paralysed, her strength receding until only hopelessness remained. She was unable to breathe, almost. This was a dream. Someone else's experience – but not her own, never her own.

Adam slipped the bridal gown from her shoulders, the moistness of his lips gliding over her shoulders and back. 'You're so lovely, little girl.' His voice was thick.

The dress crumpled to her feet, a mocking travesty of virginity. And still, Kate didn't move. As if this, after all, was her destiny. Deserved, requested, even longed for.

Adam undid her bra, allowing her breasts to fall free. And before she even realised it she was standing naked in front of him, wearing only the emerald necklace and for the first time aware of the power he held. He had made her. And she had almost considered it still a game.

Adam was still fully clothed. He stood, sweating heavily as he stared at her.

She felt sick. What had she done?

'Put them on.' He handed her the discarded scraps of black silk. She was both drawn and repelled by the touch of his skin.

Their eyes met. This was a contract. She'd signed the paper, done the deal. She was in his world now. He was her husband. And still, she half-needed what he was offering her. She thought of Eileen's words . . .

It isn't so easy to leave.

Slowly, she bent to fulfil his commands.

17

Hannah decided on the lemon and olive dress, the one that lit up the blonde highlights of her hair – or so Tom told her once. Once, over a year ago now. The last time she'd worn this dress. The last time she'd been out anywhere she could wear a dress like this. He rarely said such things now.

She stared resolutely into the mirror. No self-pity – not tonight, she was done with that. It was her birthday; she was twenty-three. This morning Tom had given her a beautiful silver bangle. She eased it on to her slim wrist, and admired it in the evening sunlight filtering through the small upstairs window. It was her birthday, Tom was taking her out to dinner at an Italian restaurant in Purwood, two-and-a-half-year-old Fleur was already asleep next door, the babysitter was due in twenty minutes. Everything was in place for an enjoyable evening. So she would not be miserable. Not tonight.

As she opened the dressing-table drawer, rummaging for the box in which she kept her favourite silver and jade ear rings, she saw the gilt-edged card, nestling under a piece of grey stone, along with all the other special cards she kept. Anniversaries, birthdays, even a Valentine's card this year. Tom wasn't all bad – he tried his best . . .

She felt the tears welling up again, and quickly picked up the gilt-edged card to distract herself. It was the invitation to Kate's wedding, forwarded from their old flat. And yet even this portion of formality – an invitation, but no note, no personal touch – brought a sadness to her heart. Because it had been three years since she'd seen either Stephanie or Kate, almost four years since the summer in Normandy that still meant so much to her, and nearly two years since this card had fluttered through the letter-box to create the biggest row that Hannah and Tom had ever had.

*   *   *

231

The invitation arrived with diabolical timing the morning after Hannah's outing with Martin Buckingham to Barstock. Seeming to Hannah like an intervention of fate. She wanted to see both Stephanie and Kate – she'd even discussed it with Martin – and here it was on the doormat, her opportunity to do just that. She fingered the invitation thoughtfully. It was more than an invitation to Kate's wedding. It was Kate's way of reaching out to her, an offer to renew friendship, a new start. And Hannah was determined to go.

'I don't know how you can even consider it.' Tom's expression was cold and unyielding when she told him that evening. 'After what she did to you.'

Hannah was confused. All Kate had done was suggest she had an abortion. It wasn't so very bad – now that she'd witnessed first-hand what motherhood could do, she was willing to believe at least that Kate had always had her best interests at heart.

She stared at Tom. 'She was only trying to help.' Hannah picked up Fleur and began to get her into her night things.

'Trying to run your life, more like.' Tom was sulky, she could tell. He picked up a newspaper, but behind the rustling folds she caught new glimpses of the hardness in his pale blue eyes. Tom had always hated Kate. Hated Stephanie too.

'She was a good friend to me.' Hannah felt the need to defend Kate. If Tom had his way she wouldn't have any friends. Well, look at her. She didn't have any friends, did she? She had no world outside Tom and Fleur. Martin was right, she should build up her own life again, create some sort of independence for herself. It was a safeguard if nothing else.

Tom laughed. She hated that laugh. 'She was jealous of you. They both were.'

'Why should Kate be jealous?' Hannah pulled the baby close to her and glared at her husband. 'Neither of them would want to be in my shoes, would they?' Who in their right mind would? Isolated and lonely, tired and bored. No money and no words – unable to even write about it any more.

Tom put down the paper. His eyes were like small, glittering pebbles dropped into the white pool of his face. She watched them, fascinated, realising how angry he was, and wondering why.

'That's what you think.' He smiled, thin and cruel. 'They were jealous all right.'

'What do you mean?' Her voice rose. She heard it shifting into panic, and she knew she was clutching Fleur too tightly. She mustn't scare her. She buried her face in the soft down of the baby's hair. Smelt the peaceful, baby smell. 'What do you mean?' Her words were muffled.

'Your precious Kate wanted to grab herself a bit of your man.' His voice was a sneer that slid over her.

Hannah drew back. 'Don't be ridiculous.' She hardly knew what he was talking about. She only knew that he wanted to hurt her, and if she could make it ridiculous then it might not hurt so much. But why did he want to hurt her so badly?

'Ridiculous, am I?' He got up, lounging in front of her in his tight denims and cream shirt. Tom McNeil, the perpetual student – the thought flashed through her head. Always wanting to be one of the in-crowd. That was why he was hardly with her. There would always be too many claims on his time.

'Yes,' she hissed. She got up too. She would not be cowed by him. 'You are. You're being bloody ridiculous.'

'She wanted me.' He grinned. 'Your little friend. Your little friend Kate wanted me.'

'I'm going to her wedding.' Hannah pushed past him, shielding the baby with her body. 'And you can't stop me.' She started up the stairs.

'She wanted to have sex with me,' he yelled after her. 'She begged me . . .'

'Shut up!'

Hannah escaped into the baby's room, closing the door swiftly behind them. She put Fleur down in her cot, and switched on the mobile and bedside lamp. She wouldn't even think about what Tom was telling her.

'Nighty-night, darling.' She felt like a merry-go-round of multiple personalities. Part of her wanted to scream and rage at Tom for his vicious lies. And part of her wanted to stay for ever with Fleur in this safe, darkened room, listening to Brahms' lullaby and watching little white sheep follow each other around in an ever-slowing circle.

Hannah sighed. Unfortunately, her place was beyond this room.

She left, closing the door softly, and stood at the top of the stairs, feeling strangely omnipotent. 'I'm going to her wedding,' she repeated.

'Then you're a fool.' He looked up as if only half-recognising her. 'What kind of friend tries to steal your husband?'

'Kate wouldn't do that.' She spoke with absolute confidence. Besides,

Kate had never had much time for men. She'd always seemed too bruised for love.

Tom laughed again. She wished he would stop laughing. When he laughed like that she wanted to strike out, to hurt him, to wipe the grin from that face she sometimes loved and sometimes hated.

'Ask your old friend Stephanie,' he said. 'She walked in and saw it all.'

'Saw it all . . . ?' Hannah stared down at him. God save us, it couldn't be true. Not Kate and Tom . . . 'What did she see? You and Kate . . . ?' Her voice was bleak.

It was a strange scenario. She remained at the top of the stairs. Tom at the bottom. Slowly, step by step, she came down towards him. She grabbed his shoulders. 'Did you have sex with Kate, Tom?' The hysteria passed over her, wave after wave of it. She was shaking violently.

Tom twisted away from her in distaste. 'Of course I bloody didn't. But not for want of her trying. She couldn't keep her hands off me.' He was back to being little boy sulky now.

Hannah was more used to that role. She began to relax. But Kate . . . ?

'Ask Stephanie if you don't believe me. Just go ahead and ask her.' Tom's eyes were challenging. She had to believe him. 'She saw it all . . .'

Hannah never went to Kate's wedding. And she'd regretted it ever since. It seemed strange to think of Kate married; that she too must have left college without qualifying, got involved with a man and thrown to the wind exactly what she had urged Hannah to keep. What could have made her do that? Hannah shook her head. Maybe she'd never find out now. Maybe that gilt-edged invitation had been her one chance. Her one and only. And as for the other thing . . . Hannah put it out of her mind. There was too much pain along that road. She had enough to cope with, fighting Motherhood. It was sucking her dry.

As for Stephanie – Hannah was almost scared to find out what had happened to Stephanie. So much had been said – too much perhaps, to heal.

Beside the gilt-edged invitation and the piece of grey stone was her old red address book. She flipped the pages. Someone had told her that Stephanie had moved out of hall, and that same someone had told her where she was living too – a girl from college with a sneer on her face that Hannah had never understood. But she'd rushed back home to scribble it down. Just in case . . . And maybe Stephanie was still there. Or maybe they would at least forward a letter to her.

Half-mesmerised, Hannah gazed at the words. Number 42. Basement flat. She picked up the wedding invitation. White Gates . . . She would write to them both.

Before she could change her mind she grabbed a sheet of note paper and a pen from the dressing-table, and let the words spill out. So much to say . . . Why couldn't the words pour out unfiltered like this when she perched in front of the typewriter and a sheet of blank paper, searching for the poetry that had once come so easily?

She hardly even knew what she was writing, only that she wanted – like she imagined Kate had wanted – to reach out to her friends. And she didn't want either of them to be in the slightest doubt of her intentions. 'Please get in touch,' she wrote at the end of each letter. 'Love, Hannah.'

Before she could change her mind, she shoved them both in envelopes, scribbled the addresses, ran down the stairs, and out of the front door to post them in the box outside.

Only afterwards did she panic. What had she done? She stared at the smirking pillar box. Too late now. And then she too began to smile. She should have done this years ago. Because unbelievably, she was feeling better already.

Hannah turned and went back inside, just as the phone began to ring.

She picked up the receiver. Heard the soft apologetic tones on the other end of the line.

'Tom?' There was a flutter of foreboding in her voice. Not tonight. Surely he wouldn't let her down tonight?

'So I'll have to meet you at the restaurant.' She registered the tone of his voice but hardly heard the words.

'Where are you?' she whispered.

'I told you. I'm still at school. I can't get away yet.' Irritation in his voice now. He was often irritated with her these days. When she didn't listen to him closely enough, when she was lost in her own world and failed to attend adequately to his.

There was the sound of laughter in the background. 'How long will you be, Tom?'

'Not long.' Pause. 'But I'm not leaving until I've got this bloody scene right.'

'Tom,' she wailed. 'It's my birthday . . .'

'I'll be there.'

The phone clicked. Hannah was left standing, alone in the lemon and olive dress. She'd have to get a taxi, maybe even hang around waiting for him in the restaurant until he deigned to join her. It was hardly the same as being taken out for your birthday, was it? Damn Tom and his drama teaching. It was taking over their lives. It just wasn't bloody fair.

An hour later, the door to the restaurant slowly opened and Hannah looked up, relieved. But it was Martin Buckingham who walked through the door.

'Martin?' For a moment she was filled with terror. Something had happened to Tom. An accident? She stumbled to her feet. 'Is Tom . . . ?'

'Don't worry, Hannah.' His hazel eyes were as kind and comforting as she remembered from the last time she'd seen him – almost two years ago, the day they went to Barstock. And she still had the fossil he'd given her in the drawer next to the gilt-edged invitation, the cards and the old red address book. A little piece of the past.

'Where's Tom?' She sat down again, still staring at him. What on earth was Martin doing here? 'Is he all right?'

'He's fine. He phoned me to ask . . .'

'Where is he?' Hannah didn't even let him finish. She could feel the anger rising, potent and scary inside her. 'Why the hell didn't he phone *me*? How much longer is he going to keep me waiting?' She couldn't believe that this was happening – that even Tom would do this to her. She felt such a fool. And her humiliation was made worse by Martin being the messenger.

'He's not coming.' Martin sounded so calm. There were lines that crinkled around his eyes. He must smile a lot – the thought was irrelevant, yet it seemed oddly important to Hannah.

'Not coming?' She stared at him.

He reached out and took her hand across the table. She hardly knew him and yet the gesture seemed natural. Martin had been a fairly frequent visitor. One of the precious few. Why had Martin stopped coming to their house after that day in Barstock?

'Tom said there was still a lot of work to be done. He said that he couldn't just walk out and leave the rest of them to it.' Martin's gaze was unflinching, but she thought she could see the contempt beneath it. Contempt for Tom and his values.

She looked over his shoulder. 'It's obvious where his priorities lie,' she muttered. 'It's my birthday. How could he let me down like this?'

Why didn't she feel more upset? She was angry, yes. Bloody angry. But this seemed like just another in a long line of disappointments. She stared at the hand that was holding hers. And she stared at the silver bangle Tom had given her this morning. She had thought it meant he still cared.

'I don't know, Hannah. He said he was sorry.' Martin's tone was clipped. Did he loathe passing on such messages? If so, then why had he agreed to come here? And why hadn't Tom simply phoned her here at the restaurant?

'He said you'd understand.' His eyes searched hers.

She snatched back her hand. 'Oh, sure. I always understand, don't I?'

Martin wouldn't look away. 'Do you, Hannah?'

She thought of his words on that hot July day in Barstock. Get your own friends, your own life. And some friend he'd turned out to be . . .

'Not any more.' She scraped back her chair and grabbed her bag. 'I don't understand any more. And I don't want to try. I'm going home.'

'Won't you stay and have dinner with me?' His voice was gentle.

'Was that part of Tom's message?' she scoffed.

'No.' He shook his head. 'Look, Hannah, you've got every right to be angry. I'd be bloody angry. For Christ's sake, don't imagine I agree with what he's doing.'

'And what is he doing?' She was almost in tears now. She had every suspicion in the world that Tom was being unfaithful to her. How many times had she sniffed his shirts for the faintest, most elusive perfume? How many times had she searched his pockets, rifled his papers? And yet still, even when she found something that might prove her right – a phone number scribbled on a piece of paper, a tissue smeared with lipstick – still she wouldn't listen, wouldn't see, wouldn't accept.

At last Martin looked away. 'You tell me,' he murmured. 'I'm the last person Tom would confide in these days.'

She didn't believe him. He was trying to deceive her too. If Tom no longer confided in Martin, then why had he chosen him as the man most likely to pacify his wife on her birthday? And besides, she could see the knowledge in Martin's eyes. He knew all right. And he wasn't telling. Some friend.

'I want to talk to you, Hannah.' He was pleading now. 'Stay for a while. Have something to eat.'

His hair was thick and dark, and it curled around the collar of his shirt. She looked away. 'Suddenly I'm not that hungry.'

'Don't let him spoil everything.' He seemed to be trying to tell her something. 'You look so lovely. Stay and have dinner with me.'

'There's really no need. I'm not some little child who has to be pacified, you know.' But her determination was wavering.

He smiled. 'I happen to like your company.'

She thought of his long absence from her life. 'I hadn't noticed.' But she sat down again, and was pleased to see that he looked ashamed.

'I deserved that.' Martin handed her a menu. 'But I had my reasons. And we're supposed to be celebrating tonight.'

'We are?' It was about the last thing she felt like doing.

'We are.' He grinned. 'I didn't manage a present at such short notice, but every birthday deserves champagne.' He signalled to the waiter.

Hannah blinked. No one had ever bought her champagne before. She guessed that Martin couldn't really afford it on a schoolteacher's salary, and she couldn't help being grateful that he was trying so hard. She reached out and touched his arm in thanks. He was really a very attractive man. He was easy to talk to and he was kind.

For so long she and Tom had found almost nothing to say to each other. For so long her life had been lived in an empty vista of bleak loneliness. Motherhood had taken over and there often didn't seem to be too much of Hannah left.

And so the prospect of spending the evening with Martin Buckingham was not unpleasant. Hannah took her first sip of champagne. Not unpleasant at all.

It was Hannah's birthday. Stephanie knew that it was Hannah's birthday even though she had little conception of time any more. Hours ran into more hours, some sleeping, some waking. And days ran into more days, characterised only by whether Lois was there – needing, demanding, questioning, dominating – or whether Stephanie was alone, trapped in the studio that had become her own peculiar prison. A prison devoid of joy, devoid of true creativity even while she painted on through growing despair.

She barely tried to make sense of her life any more. There seemed little point. It was hardly hers. She was only going through the motions. And as for love . . . how could she bring herself to love Lois? She asked for far too much. Besides, those that Stephanie loved were the vulnerable ones. The ones that got hurt – like Miles and Hannah. So instead, she was learning how not to feel.

When Lois was around Stephanie was plied with so many pills and so much dope that she was surprised she didn't rattle. But she wasn't complaining. She didn't care enough to complain. And it got her through the days and the nights, didn't it? Days and nights that were peopled with the hurt of her past – pictures she couldn't bear to see, pictures she could never paint although they were the ones that mattered. They were the pictures that danced in front of her eyelids until she wanted to scream . . . dig her knuckles into her eyes so that she'd see them no more.

Pictures. Kate and Tom McNeil in her studio. Half-naked and yet still hungry. Rick Allen's greasy hair framing the leer on his face as he approached her, trembling and terrified on Lois's big brass bed. Hannah's pained expression that day in Barstock – the things she'd said still made Stephanie clamp her hands to her head in shame and fury.

'You're just a slut . . . No one decent will want you . . . You haven't got love.' Perhaps Hannah had been right after all.

Stephanie groaned. And then there was the picture of Miles – the worst picture of all. Miles lying dead and alone in the summerhouse. No longer the slightest reproach in his beautiful blue eyes . . .

And so on this spring day, Hannah's birthday, Stephanie didn't take the pills Lois gave her before going to work. She shoved them in the pocket of her worn dungarees instead. And when Lois kissed her goodbye, she might have noticed that Stephanie clung to her a little longer than usual before releasing her lover to the other world of advertising, presentations and business lunches. Or if she did notice, maybe she only thought that at last Stephanie was beginning to depend on her in the way that Lois needed her dependence – for her own survival.

Stephanie would have tried to explain, but she knew Lois would stop her. So she started to write a note. But when it came to it her hands, pale and paint-stained, were shaking uncontrollably. She could hardly hold the pen.

She realised that she was withdrawing, that her body needed uppers. 'No way,' she muttered. She pursed her mouth. She wouldn't give in. Not today. She was going to be herself today – damaged though she was.

So instead she dipped her fingers in red paint. And scrawled 'sorry' across a canvas. She lit a cigarette, drawing the nicotine in gratefully.

239

Would Lois understand? Probably not. Lois loved her, but she was so screwed up in trying to balance her two separate lives into any kind of liveable sanity, that her kind of love was more than a little tinged with craziness. Lois was teetering on the brink herself. And so obviously terrified that Stephanie – like Chantal before her – would return to the world of men that Lois had so resolutely walked away from, that she would do anything to keep her. Stephanie thought of the pills and the studio and the nights of desperate, lonely love. Absolutely anything.

She grabbed the pills from her pocket and flushed them down the loo. They were too much of a temptation. It would be so easy to forget Hannah and Kate and poor Miles, and just lose herself in the kind of oblivion that was beginning to characterise her every waking moment. Because Stephanie couldn't face reality. She couldn't face the pain, and she couldn't face the guilt. The acid taste of it was eating into everything that she had ever tried to be.

But pills were always too easy. She wouldn't be using pills. She had a journey to make first. A journey back to the past that might help her find peace – because that was what she needed most of all.

Stephanie travelled to Kent by train, hardly aware of the odd looks she was getting from fellow passengers. Odd looks given to the strange creature with the mass of wild dark hair, and blue eyes burning with intensity in a gaunt but beautiful face. From the station she used the last of her money for a taxi and got the cabbie to drop her at the bottom of the drive of Atherington Hall. It was vital not to be seen. This was a solo journey. For Miles alone.

Her father would be at his office, but there would be people around – there always were. Gardeners or the woman who came in to clean.

Stephanie took a deep breath, and sprinted over the open patch of lawn that she had to cross before reaching the obscurity of the orchard.

She leaned against the rusty gate. 'Christ . . .' She was out of condition, and wheezing painfully. She wasn't used to fresh air any more, let alone exercise.

For a few minutes she stayed there, knowing she was out of sight, sniffing in the fragrance of the apple blossom she'd always loved. There had been blossom on the trees when she'd found Miles's body in the summerhouse. The bent branches had been heavy with it. Sweet, soft and pink-white.

But now she waited, scared to go further, half expecting him to still be in there, waiting for her.

She closed her eyes. Thought she heard his voice speak her name. He was calling to her. Her brother Miles, who she loved, only wanted her to be there for him – it wasn't much to ask.

She pushed open the orchard gate and walked through the long couch grass towards the summerhouse.

It looked just the same. The glass was stained with mould and lichen. The ivy clung heavy around the door, well-rooted once more since Miles had torn the tendrils from their clawing hold. She stepped inside.

The summerhouse was mostly in shade from the apple trees, and yet still the streak of sunlight lit up the place where they had first made love, the place where Miles had died. Beginnings and endings. Poor Miles had come full circle in this summerhouse.

Stephanie fingered the knife in her pocket. It was time. 'I'm coming, Miles,' she whispered, as she moved the blade closer towards her wrist. For a moment the shiny steel seemed to blind her. And then the cold, slicing touch of it eased into warm flesh. 'I'm just sorry that it took so long.'

18

Stephanie tried to move her head. Could she still be in the summer-house?

She heard movement – noises outside. She must be still here in the summerhouse because she could smell the dank, mossy smell. It was choking her. She couldn't breathe. Cautiously, she put her fingers to her wrist. She could feel the blood. Warm and sticky.

'Stephanie!'

The call shrieked into her subconscious. What was happening here? This wasn't what was supposed to be happening. This hadn't happened to Miles.

She heard more noises, background noises that were coming closer, nudging her towards reality.

'No!' That was one place she didn't want to go.

'My God.' Daddy's voice. And then his smell – understated aftershave coating panic.

But what was her father doing here? He wasn't supposed to be . . . Jesus Christ. Surely she hadn't failed again? Stephanie slipped back into the darkness.

And the she heard the ripping of cloth in the fast-moving, heavy-breathing silence. Felt a tight hold on the limpness of her arms. She was being bound. Stephanie wanted to laugh. All her life she'd been bound by something or other. So there was still no escape.

An intake of breath, then strong arms scooped her from the floor, fought their way out of the summerhouse. Ivy in her hair. Swearing softly in his voice.

She was upside down. Her limbs didn't belong to her; her matted hair hung over her face, webbing her vision from the buttercups and dandelions that squatted in the long grass like confused, tiny suns. She blinked. Oh God, let me sleep.

And the soft quilt of darkness slipped over her once more, shrouding her pain.

When she came to, she felt quite different. She was lying on a couch in a shaded room. And she knew she hadn't made it.

'I'm sorry, Miles,' she groaned, too quiet for them to hear.

Above her were voices – professional and parental voices.

'Drying-out?' Her father sounded scared. 'She's doped up to the eyeballs, isn't she, Doctor? When I got to her the only part of her that looked alive were her eyes.' His voice was trembling. He sounded angry. Was he angry with her then? Had she disappointed him yet again?

Stephanie shifted uncomfortably. Now that it was over, she was hurting. But her arm was bandaged, and she knew she had slept.

'Darling . . .' Julian was on his knees beside her. His usual immaculate, white linen shirt was ripped and bloodstained.

He took her hands in his. 'Why? Tell me why you did it.'

'Does it matter?' She felt blank of all emotion. His impotence didn't touch her. Even the bitter disappointment that she had failed to re-stage Miles's death – to join him wherever he was – had faded into insignificance. There was only an empty void before her.

'You're blaming yourself, aren't you?' Surely there couldn't be tears in his eyes? She stared at him as though he'd become a stranger. Daddy ran from emotion; he hid from it if he imagined it might threaten his plans and position. So how could he cry real tears?

She was hypnotised by the promise of those tears. Drawn to them. She had heard them before, but not been listening properly.

'You think his death was your fault, don't you?' Daddy's smooth voice wasn't smooth any longer. It was rough and urgent, demanding an answer when all she wanted was sleep.

'Maybe it was,' she whispered. He didn't know, did he? About the love she and Miles had shared. A love that was illicit – that didn't belong between a sister and brother. A love that had ruined Miles for what was to come.

'It's a cop-out, Stephanie.' She heard him as if from a distance, and yet her father's words were driving into her head. 'Guilt is a cop-out. All it does is stop you from feeling helpless. That's what we really can't stand.'

'We?' She tried to reach for the water. He helped her sit up, putting the glass gently to her parched lips.

'We all could have done things differently.' He smoothed her tangled hair from her brow as she lay back again on the couch. 'Myself more than anyone. But it's past. So we're helpless, Stephanie. Because we can't change what's past. No one can.'

'We can make amends.' She could feel the strength slowly flowing back into her, whether from the water or from the touch of his gentle hands, she couldn't tell.

'We can't.' His thumb stroked her lifeless fingers. 'That's what's so hard to face up to. We have to live with the hurting.'

As Stephanie gazed at him, she recognised the intense pain in the blue eyes so like her own. She recognised the pain because it was familiar to her. And she realised with a shock that this was where she should have come after Miles's death. She should have come to her father, because he was suffering too. She should have gone to him when she first heard his ghastly night-time crying. She should have listened to him more carefully. Maybe they could have helped one another – offered some comfort.

Daddy had loved Miles, and he loved Stephanie too. All she had done was deprive him of them both. He shared her pain – and forgiveness should only be a step away.

'I know what you're thinking,' he whispered. 'I pushed Miles too hard. I tried to make him something that he could never be. Something that I wanted. I set out to do a job and I did a bloody brilliant job. I made that boy feel a failure.' He hung his dark head, the black hair streaked with white and grey. It suited him – he was still such a good-looking man.

And he had never been so honest. Stephanie took a deep breath. Tentatively she reached out her arms to him. 'Daddy?'

He began to sob, great rasping sobs that seemed to tear his body in two. 'I only wanted Miles to have everything he could ever need. That's what I wanted for both of you.'

'She should rest now.' The doctor – her doctor from childhood – was standing by the couch. He had left them alone, but now he intervened. 'We're taking you into a clinic for a few days, my dear. To get all the muck out of your system. Is that all right with you?'

She nodded. And then? When she was empty of it all? What would happen then?

'Stephanie?' Her father bent towards her once more. 'Don't be scared any longer. I'll always be here if you need me.'

She closed her eyes.

'Rest now.' His voice sank into her senses. A healing voice. 'I love you. Never forget that. I've always loved you.'

It was Hannah's birthday. Kate still had the dates noted in her diary, though she didn't send cards any more. They'd made it clear they weren't interested in renewing their friendship – neither had replied to the wedding invitations she'd sent, if they'd even received them. And if they hadn't, then how could they ever find each other again? She might as well accept it – Stephanie and Hannah were both gone from her life. She was alone. Perhaps she'd always been alone, although she'd never felt more alone than she did now.

It was hard to get herself outside these four walls, but get outside she must. Today was also the day of their spring garden party, an event that Adam still insisted on although he hardly had to impress these little people any more, for God's sake. What was the point? He was fêted himself these days – Adam Horton, one of the most successful businessmen that Dorset had produced. And it had made him more unbearable than ever.

Inside, she had at least an illusion of safety, although the walls were closing in around her. Outside was much worse. Outside was panic. And Adam knew it. Perhaps that was why he still threw garden parties, to give Kate the chance to perform on a stage that she hated. To see if she could keep it all together just one more time.

And she could. She stepped out of the door, breezing on stage as if it were effortless. As if she hadn't just thrown up in the loo. As if she hadn't needed Valium to get her there. But once outside, she could hardly bear to watch him – the man that she'd married. The man who had taken over her life. The man who had made her what she was. He strutted from one group to another, taking the arms of the most attractive women, making them feel they were special. He had done that to Kate once. She too had glowed as they glowed. She didn't glow any longer. Now she was charred and broken.

She knew him now. She understood exactly what went on it that egocentric, perverted head of his. She'd seen his collection of pornography, she'd given him what he wanted in bed. And she'd provided what he needed the world to see and hear – her adoration and a lukewarm echo of his own politics and ideals. She'd even served on the right committees and supported the right charities in his name. And for what? For some pieces of jewellery, a daily woman to clean, and the illusion of a success that wasn't even her own. Now, she had nothing but contempt for him.

'Kate!' Adam was calling to her. At first she ignored him, the glossy, social smile still carefully pasted on her face. But then she caught a glimpse of his companion, did a double take, and wandered over to them, a warning glinting in her green eyes.

'Kate . . .' He clamped his hand around her waist. She smiled, shrinking from the clammy heat that seemed to soak through the delicate rust-coloured silk dress that she wore. The warning stayed in her eyes.

'I want you to meet one of our young hopefuls from the new branch. This one could go all the way. Bags of experience in finance. Just what we need.' He clapped his companion on the back.

Kate stretched out her hand. 'Lovely to meet you.' Noncommittal and polite. She gazed into Leon's puzzled, brown eyes. Would he recognise her, now that she seemed such a blurred echo of her former self? It had been over three years since the New Year's Eve party at Atherington Hall. Or was she the same on the outside? Couldn't anyone see what was happening to her?

Feeling herself start to tremble, she focused determinedly on Leon's sandy eyebrows. 'I'm sure you'll learn a lot working with my husband.'

Confusion in his eyes turned to shock, but Leon was clearly a quick learner. 'I'm looking forward to it, Mrs Horton.' He hardly stumbled over the name, briefly shaking the hand that she offered. Barely a touch.

Their eyes met.

Adam rubbed his hands together. 'I'll leave you with my wife, Leon, old son. She'll look after you.' With a quick glance at Kate, he strode away.

Old son. She watched him. She had given that man everything he'd asked for except children. Adam wanted a child more than anything. She supposed all this had to be for some purpose. His precious house on the cliff – his legacy. But she would deny him children. He didn't know it, but she had decided on the night of their wedding. She would never do it. Children, she would deny him for ever. He had played her so cleverly, but there was nothing left for her to give.

'Will you?' Leon was staring at her, waiting for her attention to return. 'Will you look after me, Kate?'

Reluctantly, she met his gaze, for a moment transported back to the party at Atherington Hall. It seemed like lifetimes ago. Leon's kind eyes. His lips brushing her cheek. A long embrace with Stephanie at midnight . . .

'Of course.' She took his arm. 'Come and meet some people.'

Her first instinct was to lose him in the crowd, this man who presented a threat. But Leon was still staring, as if she were a mirage, a ghost from the past. So after a quick glance around she led him away from the party, round to the rock garden at the front of the house on the cliff.

'Are you really married to Adam Horton?' Leon's eyes still showed astonishment.

'Is that really so surprising?' she mimicked. Irritated, she removed her hand from his arm. He was nice and easy to touch, but she shrank from touch these days – no matter who it was – as if through touching her, anyone could discover her darkest secrets. Her darkest shame.

He grinned. Had she suddenly become human to him again? 'Yeah, it is actually. When I met you in Kent you were pretty keen on letting everyone know you didn't belong with these kind of people. And yet here you are.' He shook his head in bewilderment. 'Married to one of them. What happened?'

'Things change.' She led the way down steps cut into the rock, following the direction of the tiny stream that gathered into a small waterfall, by the pond.

'You can say that again.' He followed her. He was as long and gangly as she remembered. Still a kid. She felt years older than him now.

'The Kate Dunstan I met would never have married a man like Adam Horton.' His voice was low.

'People change too,' she murmured, half to herself. She shouldn't have brought him here. She was in danger. Leon might get too close.

'You're certainly a hell of a lot thinner.' The words were critical.

She pulled a face. 'And that's supposed to be bad?' Listen to me, she thought. I sound so normal.

'What happened to teaching?' He was close behind her, his questions chasing her as she picked her way down the path.

'I left college.' Her eyes hardened. 'You're asking a hell of a lot of questions.' Kate didn't want to discuss this with Leon. She didn't want to think about what she had become, or see herself through his eyes. She was ashamed.

He didn't seem bothered by the rebuke. 'You ask me something then.'

She smiled. There was so much to ask, she hardly knew where to start. 'Aren't you working for Stephanie's father any more?' Stephanie. She longed to ask him about her, but she was scared to. Frightened of touching, let alone opening the shiny wrapper of the past.

'I left. Everything changed when Miles died.' His voice softened. When Miles died . . .

They were both silent, remembering their conversation at the party, just before midnight. About Miles, the boy who never grew up. And he hadn't grown up – not really. He had died before he even got the chance.

They stopped walking to sit on the boulders by the pond, side by side, resting their backs against the rocks, looking out towards the sea. They weren't like two people at a garden party. More like two kids escaping from the grown ups. And that's how Kate felt. Her agoraphobia had dwindled, as if it had never really existed at all. She knew it was temporary. But still, there was an odd sensation of release.

'The company went to pot,' Leon explained, with a frown. 'Julian didn't seem interested in making money any more. He didn't seem interested in anything much. Most of us stuck it for a while, then everyone left, in dribs and drabs.' He shrugged. 'Eventually he wound up the company.'

Kate nodded. 'Stephanie took it hard, too.' She remembered the kiss she'd witnessed in the conservatory. 'They were very close, she and Miles.'

'I reckon the old man was more cut up by what she did than what Miles had done,' Leon confided. 'She was the one he always seemed to care about the most.'

'What did she do?'

He glanced at her in surprise. 'Don't you know?'

'We lost touch.' Kate picked up a loose pebble and scratched it against the rock. Lost touch – that was one way of putting it. Lost direction. Lost friendship.

'Well, she lost touch with Julian, too.' He sighed. 'Refused to see him or speak to him, so I heard. She left college like you did. And she cut herself off from the family. Just stayed in some basement flat painting her heart out, apparently.'

Painting her heart out. Was that how it had been for Stephanie? Kate put her fingers to her lips in a nervous gesture. 'And is she still there? In this basement flat?'

'S'pose so.' Leon gazed out to sea, his expression becoming distant. 'I don't see much of the family these days.'

Kate nodded. That's how it was. Everyone drifting apart, going separate ways. She looked at Leon, so unchanged in the three and a half years since she'd seen him last, still scruffy and skinny with kind eyes and a big smile. Still a kid, and yet more real than anyone in her new world. 'You never made it to Europe, then?' she asked softly.

'No chance.' He laughed at himself, but she registered a bitterness there that Leon hadn't shown before.

'It's not too late.' Tentatively, she touched his hand. They shouldn't be here. Kate knew they shouldn't be here – that she was using the wrong script. But for a moment she'd lost sight of what she'd become; she'd slipped back into the past.

'I'm too fond of life's little luxuries these days to go travelling around Europe with a rucksack on my back.' Leon stared down at her hand, resting on his. Then he grabbed it and drew it to his lips so swiftly that she didn't have time to stop him.

'I wanted to kiss you at that party at Atherington Hall,' he murmured, his lips still brushing against her hand. 'Properly. I wanted to hold you in my arms, Kate.'

'Maybe you should have.' She watched him as if he were quite apart from her, apart from her situation, apart from the present even.

'Would it have changed anything?' His voice was urgent.

Why did Leon seem to care so much? She shrugged. Who could say? Maybe her life might have been different. Maybe she might not have lost her way. Or maybe it would have always been only a kiss.

'But you disappeared like Cinderella.' He laughed. 'Without so much as dropping a glass slipper.'

She smiled. 'I didn't feel much like Cinderella.' Over his shoulder she watched the sun dipping towards the west. It was beautiful. This house on the cliff was beautiful, yet now it scared her. Now she needed tranquillising before she could face the world. How come she had once been so brave?

'I never went to Europe either,' she confided. 'I made it up. I spent the year before college in Scotland. Having a baby.' There was no point in pretending any longer. What did it matter what Leon thought of her – what any of them thought of her? And besides, the pain that was Justine had moved at last into the background of her life. There were other pains now. New horrors to face.

Leon seemed to know that she didn't want to talk about it. 'That doesn't bother me, Kate.' He was looking at her with a strange expression. 'What bothers me the most is: why didn't you answer my letters?'

Kate turned her eyes towards his freckled face. 'I was busy.'

'Or you were scared.'

He knew too much. Of course he was right. She had been scared. She hadn't wanted a man that New Year's Eve at Atherington Hall, and she'd sensed from the start that he could never be only a friend.

Kate recognised the desire in his eyes and she shivered. She didn't want a man now, either.

She rose swiftly to her feet. 'We should be getting back. Adam will be wondering where we've got to.' Suddenly she felt nervous again. Suddenly the world was getting closer once more. She had no space.

He jumped up, grabbing her by the shoulders. 'Why didn't you tell him we'd met before?'

She stared back at him. His face was only inches away. 'Adam gets jealous. I didn't want to screw up your chances in your new job.' That was true enough, but there was more.

She didn't want a beating. Kate was Adam's property, and she was ashamed to tell Leon that. Hadn't Adam paid for her one night with a pretty emerald necklace?

'Adam gets jealous?' His mouth twisted. 'But Adam . . . Well, he . . .'

'You don't have to tell me what Adam does.' She pulled away from him, running up the rocky steps towards the bench under the arbour of yellow roses at the top of the garden where Adam had asked her to be his wife. No. Where Adam had informed her that he wanted her to be his wife.

'So you know?' Leon shouted after her. 'It was the first thing I heard about Adam Horton. Everyone talks about it . . .'

Kate turned. She could see the frustration in his eyes, in the fist he shook into the wind. She nodded.

'You know about the bars and the bimbos? The peep shows and the prostitutes?' His voice was following her although Leon stood still.

She was wrong. Leon wasn't a child. He had grown up in the last three years.

Kate fled into the wind. But she could still hear him.

'He's just a dirty old man, Kate.'

She ran on, stumbling. She could barely see where she was going. Was it the wind or tears blurring her vision? She needed more Valium.

'I thought you'd never let yourself be trapped, Kate.' His voice was fading at last. 'Remember?'

Kate remembered. And as she remembered, she ran. She was alone and she was outside, and the world was closing in around her. The plants were growing into a forest. The path was winding away from her, steepening into an incline to push her back down. The trees would wrap themselves around her at any moment.

She was panting and shaking violently. She felt sick. But she mustn't throw up all over the beautiful, rust-coloured silk dress. That wasn't the way to behave at all.

She stopped abruptly.

'Kate! What the hell's the matter?' It was Adam. She'd run right into her captor's arms.

She shuddered.

'Let's get you inside.' His voice changed. He hustled her through the front door. 'What's happened? Where's that young lad I left you with?' Suspicion in his eyes.

'Nothing. I don't know,' she managed to stammer. She mustn't get Leon into trouble. 'I was on my own. I was scared.'

'I know what you need.' He pulled her up the stairs.

'No, not now . . .' She strained and struggled against him, scratching, kicking, always forgetting how much he liked her to fight back so that she could be subdued. She had to fight to be subdued.

Adam slapped her face but the whip of his hand no longer brought any shock. It only sent her a little deeper down, made it a little harder to claw her way back.

'No, Adam . . .'

It was hopeless. With his heavy bulk, he pushed her slight figure into the room. The grin stretched his face. He was ugly, and the power was in his finger-tips. His hands reached out to rip the delicate silk from her breasts. 'You've been a naughty little girl.'

No, not that. Kate shook her head, feeling her hair – tangled and matted from the sea breeze – swinging above the torn silk. He was breaking her, sure as anything. He was breaking her will, and she was standing by.

'And naughty girls need punishing.' His eyes were wild and bloodshot.

Kate thought fast. 'Think of all the people downstairs, Adam.' She forced herself to speak calmly. While she was calm she was safe – it was her panic that inflamed him. 'They'll be wondering where we are.'

But his fingers were already on the zip of his trousers. 'Let 'em wait.'

She closed her eyes with dread. She would never know if Adam had intended their marriage to be like this. It was possible, but Kate doubted it. She believed that Adam had responded to the gauntlet of challenge she'd thrown down so carelessly. He had wanted her to play the part of his wife, but in the meantime something more had happened between them. Something dynamic, dangerous and powerful. She had brought out the worst in Adam, and she suspected that he knew it.

Success had gone to his head and made him careless. His coating of status was getting thinner. The perversions were showing through the cracks. Adam's dark side was taking over. He thought he was going up. But he was going down – all the way.

As he came towards her, her mind plunged from the present horror – she'd learned to escape it. She was dimly aware of his grunting, heaving body, the male sweat dripping on to her shivering skin, the stench of his sexuality.

And then she realised why she had felt so different in the garden with Leon. While her husband drove himself on inside her, she remembered. She hadn't been pretending. That's what it was. For the first time in ages, she had slipped back into being herself.

19

Instead of exhaustion from barely a few hours' sleep, when the alarm went off at six a.m. Hannah felt only contentment. An easy kind of contentment of bodily satisfaction that was new to her. She stretched, yawned, and raised herself up on one elbow to watch the man sleeping beside her.

Last night at the restaurant came back to memory in fits and starts – the champagne that was dizzy and bubbly and made her giggle. The wonderful food – pasta and aubergine in a rich creamy sauce, fresh tuna, and zabaglione to finish. The talking – head to head – in a way she'd never talked with Tom. The journey home in the taxi – realising that it was past midnight and the babysitter would cost a fortune. Finding everything remarkably funny. And wanting to be kissed by the man at her side.

Martin's thick, dark hair tumbled all over the pillow. His face was peaceful, his long dark lashes soft against the lined, brown skin that already seemed strangely familiar to Hannah. As if he had always been her lover . . .

As she watched him, he awoke, his hazel eyes bleary at first before snapping into awareness. His first movement was to reach out his hand and touch her face – a wondering, gentle movement that made her close her eyes in sweet recollection of the touch of last night.

His first words were, 'Any regrets, Hannah?'

She shook her head. 'I wouldn't have missed it for the world.' It was absolutely true, and yet she had surprised herself. Hannah the prude – what would Stephanie and Kate have said? She guessed they would have been proud of her, and the thought made her giggle once more, as she had giggled last night.

'Me neither.' Martin seemed relieved. He kissed her shoulder and a new, unexpected shudder of desire raced through her.

The ethics of the situation were clear to Hannah. There was no place for regrets when she was feeling so good. But it took some getting used to. Hannah had sworn to be faithful to the first man she'd ever loved – Tom McNeil – and she'd never intended to do otherwise. Her loyalty to Tom had always been so intense that she would never have thought it *possible* for her to do otherwise.

Yet here she was. In bed with another man. She traced a pattern with her fingertips into the dark forest of his chest hair, wanting to bury her face in it. She could hardly believe that she had changed so much. This much.

'No guilt?' His eyes searched hers.

She smiled, shook her head once more. 'Tom and I may be married to each other, Martin. But whatever else there was between us died a slow, painful death a long time ago.' And yet it had taken this, for her to see it that way.

The truth was that Tom had built them only a little room for Hannah to live in while he explored the world outside. And there was no space in that little room for guilt. Not even for love – any love had withered from lack of nourishment.

She hadn't accepted it; she'd fought against it, willing him to love her again so that she could regain some respect for him. But Tom had travelled too far away. And although she'd pretended not to, Hannah had read the signals – the unwritten messages that affairs are made of – and she knew how often Tom had betrayed her.

'So why do you stay with him?' Martin's voice was urgent now. Now they were getting to it.

Martin had been urgent last night too. As soon as the babysitter told them that Tom had phoned to say he'd drunk too much to drive, was staying with a male colleague from school and wouldn't be home till morning, Hannah had known that she would sleep with Martin Buckingham.

The babysitter left, she closed the front door, and he was behind her, right behind her.

'Martin . . .' She turned.

His hands framing her face. Love in his eyes. 'Hannah . . .'

His kiss – a soft brush of the lips that ignited years of frustration she'd never even recognised as such. A soft brush of the lips that made her stagger.

And then he drew her nearer; she closed her eyes and was lost, welcoming him as she'd never been able to welcome Tom. Wanting him. Loving him.

It wasn't just frustration or desire or circumstance. Or even that he was an attractive man who cared for her. It wasn't that he was good company and had bought her champagne and made her feel like a beautiful woman again instead of a drudge. Although that might have been enough . . .

No, it was the certainty that she had to change her life. With her birthday had come a turning point. It was crisis time. Sink or swim. She had written to Stephanie and Kate, made the first moves. But something else had to change. Hannah had fondly imagined that she and Tom could change together, that there was still hope despite everything. But she was being naive, desperately hanging on to something that didn't exist any longer. When Tom had let her down this time, Hannah made a decision. It would be the last time he would ever let her down.

'I'm not staying with Tom any more,' she told Martin. 'I'm leaving him.'

'Just like that?' He stared at her.

She grinned. 'How would you prefer it to be? A long-drawn-out, agonizing decision?' Hannah climbed out of bed, heedless of her own nakedness that once would have sent her into a paroxysm of self-consciousness. 'Don't worry, Martin. I've had my share of sleepless nights.'

But that was in the past. She drew a robe around her, and watched her lover drag his long dark body out of her bed – out of the bed that belonged to Hannah and Tom McNeil – and knew that she couldn't sleep there with Tom for even one more night. This man, obligingly pulling on his clothes because he would realise Hannah wouldn't want two-year-old Fleur to get up and find him there, had helped her make the decision at last.

'But what will you do, Hannah?'

'I don't know.' She wasn't even sure if this was a beginning or just an ending. She only knew that a night of love with Martin Buckingham had been as cathartic for her as she had hoped it would be. He had given Hannah the strength to leave.

'What will you tell him?' Martin tucked in his shirt and made for the bathroom.

'Nothing.' She followed him, enjoying just the look of him here. 'I'll pack our bags and we'll go.'

'Just like that?' he repeated, gazing at her as if she were a stranger.

She smiled. The wonderful thing about this morning was that she didn't feel like a stranger. She felt that this Hannah had been inside all along, just waiting for the chance to leap out and surprise the world. But she couldn't expect even Martin to understand all that.

'I know what I came with.' She remembered only too well. 'That's all I need. And Fleur, of course.'

'Fleur.' He dried himself on the blue towel, and drew her towards him, smoothing her fair hair from her face. 'What will you say to Fleur?'

She shrugged. 'I'll find the words.' Hannah was confident that without Tom holding them back, the words would come. For Fleur, and for herself too.

'It won't be easy for her.' Martin's gaze searched her face.

'Fleur won't miss him.' She guessed that Tom wouldn't press for frequent access. For Tom, Fleur had become more problem than delight. He was too selfish for fatherhood. Tom had never learned to give.

Martin tilted her chin and kissed her lips. The first of the morning. He smelt of soap. 'But he is her father.'

Abruptly, Hannah pulled away. Why did men all seem to have the same mental blockage? 'A bedtime story once a fortnight when he gets back from work on time doesn't make a man a father.'

'True enough.' Martin looked serious, worrying about practicalities that seemed irrelevant to Hannah in this frame of mind.

If she wanted to go then she could go. What was to stop her? She'd done the important bit – made the decision. The rest would fall into place. She was happy, feeling released even though she hadn't yet left this house. She was feeling strong again.

'Where will you go?' Martin pulled on his jacket. His brow remained furrowed, as if he needed the responsibility of concern.

'I don't know.' And right now she didn't care. She could stay with her parents in Sussex for a while, but the prospect wasn't a pleasant one. Her mother had never forgiven her for marrying Tom McNeil in a Register Office – and Hannah still wasn't sure which she'd objected to most, the man or the method. Jean Thompson had seen her grandchild only once, and Hannah's last phone call had been punctured with so many carping criticisms that she hadn't bothered to ring them for several months. Dad still backed her all the way. But Mother was impossible.

'You know you can always come and stay with me. I mean, you'd be welcome . . .' His voice broke into her thoughts.

She knew he was embarrassed, and that he was just being kind. 'I don't expect that, Martin,' she said softly. 'Surely you didn't think I was going to unload a family on you after one night of passion?'

His eyes clouded. 'I wouldn't mind, Hannah. You see, I've always loved . . .'

'Shush.' She put a finger to his lips. 'None of that talk, now. It was wonderful. It was one in a million. But it wasn't for ever.'

He was silent.

'Are you ready?' She held his hand as they tiptoed down the stairs like a couple of cat burglars armed only with Hannah's muffled laughter. They went through the kitchen and she opened the back door. Outside, the birds were chorusing the morning in, and the dew was clinging to the grass.

'I will see you again, Hannah?' Martin was still holding on to her hand as if he thought that any minute she might slip away and be gone.

'Do you want to?' Her eyes examined his. Once she had needed a friend, and he hadn't been there for her. He had taken her to Barstock, talked about change and never come near her again.

Martin seemed to know what she was thinking. 'I cared too much.' He rubbed at his dark unshaven jaw. 'I didn't want to be responsible for breaking up your marriage, for hurting you. And I was pretty damn sure that I couldn't see you without telling you what Tom was up to.'

Hannah nodded, but they both knew that it wasn't enough. He had been scared and she had needed courage. The betrayal hung in the fresh morning air between them.

'Friends?' She held out both hands.

He clasped them for a long moment. 'Friends.'

She knew what she was saying, and she suspected that he knew it too. Friends, not lovers. Could she keep to it? Did it even matter? 'I'll be in touch,' she promised.

Hannah became sad as she watched him go. Maybe she expected too much from everyone. Maybe she always would.

Martin's touch was still warm on her skin. Martin had loved her in a way she hadn't thought possible, brought her pleasure where she had long ago learned that pleasure could never be found. Martin had released her to begin her life again. But was he destined to remain a part of the old life that could never reach the new?

Tom had never intended to leave Hannah in the lurch on her birthday, but he'd been getting some odd signals from Jayne Stepney all day, and he wanted to have it out with her.

After school he cornered her in the staff car park, and when she refused to tell him what was going on, he found himself driving out of Purwood in the opposite direction to his own home. Driving in the direction of Jayne's Dorchester flat, following the white Peugot as if his life depended on it. Just to get things straight before he returned home to get ready for tonight, he told himself.

But it hadn't worked out that way.

'I don't want to see you any more, Tom.' She laughed her grating laugh. 'At least not in a social capacity.'

'Not in a social capacity,' he mimicked. 'What sort of talk is that? You mean you want to break things off between us?' He remained brave on the outside, but inside, his stomach was churning.

Tom didn't love Jayne Stepney – she was far too hard-bitten to be loved. But he enjoyed the taste of her power. Being a head of department with what she called a special relationship with the head, not to mention the governors, Jayne had done a lot to improve his position in the school. Small things, but things that made Tom feel good about himself. And Tom needed to feel good about himself.

Even the rest of the staff's knowledge of their long-running affair had done him no harm. The opposite. They all respected Jayne – some were even a little scared of her. And she had no idea they knew.

Her power made her exciting. She was the antithesis of Hannah. Oh, he loved Hannah in his own way. He needed her to be there for him, to be the base of security that his mother had once made her reason for existence. But it was the Jayne Stepneys of this life who made it exciting.

'That's precisely what I mean.' Her green eyes glittered. 'But now that you're here . . .' She led the way into the flat. 'Would some Earl Grey be refreshing, do you think?'

'Stuff the Earl Grey.' Tom tore his hands through his hair. He needed this woman. Because he still wanted her, and rejection was a bitter pill to swallow. He hadn't swallowed rejection since Janice, and he didn't intend to start again now.

'That doesn't sound too pleasant.' She pulled a face and put the kettle on anyway. 'Don't be nasty, Tom, darling. It doesn't suit you.'

'Why, Jayney? Why do you want to break it off?' Even to his own ears his voice sounded weak. Weak as a woman's.

'Because I'm bored with all this.' A wave of her elegantly manicured hand took in Tom and his briefcase. 'This . . . affair.' Her lip curled.

She was bored with him, then. Was she saying she was bored with him? He straightened his back. 'Why?' he asked bravely.

She sneaked a look at him under her lashes. 'Because it's going nowhere.' A frown briefly puckered the smoothness of her brow. 'And I don't believe in going nowhere.'

'Where do you want it to go?' Tom's voice was low, enticing.

Jayne drew a long, slim cigarette from a black pack, and lit it with her cold cigarette lighter. 'I'm not sure that I want it to go anywhere. I think it's time to call it a day.'

Tom was behind her in seconds, his arms encircling her narrow waist. 'But I can't leave you alone, Jayney,' he whispered in her ear. 'You're a sex-bomb. You turn me on like nothing I've ever known.'

She smiled, satisfied like a cat. 'Pour me a drink, darling. There's some wine in the fridge.'

'What about the Earl Grey?'

There was a glimmer of excitement that he recognised, coming to life within the coolness of her eyes.

'Like you said, darling – stuff the Earl Grey.'

An hour later he was lying beside her on the black satin sheets, realising that he would be late for Hannah, and feeling torn in two. Under normal circumstances, Tom was in control of his women and his affairs and could balance his life quite nicely.

But he wasn't in control with Jayney, and that's what he had to keep fighting for. His self-esteem was at stake. Jayne was demanding. Sometimes she refused to see him for days, then she'd click her fingers and expect him to come running. And Tom always did. Strong women were very dangerous. But exhilarating too.

'Stay for dinner, darling. I feel like some company.' Jayne rolled over, her breasts swaying gently, the erect nipples brushing at his chest.

Inwardly, Tom groaned. She was insatiable. 'I can't. I'm supposed to be taking Hannah out for dinner. I'm late already.' The words sank into the silence between them. Damn Hannah, Tom found himself thinking.

'Phone her.' Jayne reached for the slim white phone on the bedside table and passed it to him. The tone of command in her voice was unmistakeable.

He dialled the numbers, feeling sick.

'Hannah? I'm really sorry, honey . . .'

Her voice was soft and questioning.

'I'm pretty tied up here, so I'll have to meet you at the restaurant.'

Jayne laughed, and he put his hand over her mouth, pulling a warning face.

'Where are you?' The Hannah voice on the phone was full of questions.

Bloody hell. He became irritated. Women – they always screwed up your life. 'I told you. I'm still at school. I can't get away yet.'

Jayne took his spare hand and placed it on her breast, arching her nipple to tickle his palm. She laughed again.

Tom drew in breath quickly, feeling himself hardening once more. He had to have her again.

Hannah was asking how long he would be.

He answered her, saying any old thing, only wanting to be off the phone and inside Jayne Stepney.

But Hannah was still moaning at him, her voice a background whine he could live without. Jayne, on the other hand, here on the black satin sheets, was parting her legs for him.

'I'll be there.' He slammed down the phone, and put his fingers back where they belonged.

An hour later he phoned Martin. He didn't know what the hell else to do. He couldn't face phoning Hannah at the restaurant where she'd be sitting around waiting for him, and anyway he was half-pissed and she'd know it. Martin was the only person he could think of who would go and rescue her. And he lived near Purwood so he could get there quickly. She'd be mad but by tomorrow she would have cooled down. He knew Hannah. She could take it. She knew the score.

Tom couldn't leave this woman tonight. He just couldn't leave her. Jayne was feeding his fantasies with her fingertips. Taunting, teasing, and inviting him to plunge into her again and again. She chose every position imaginable. She was saying the wildest things to him – things he hardly dared even think to himself – and on her lips they turned him into fire. She was crazy and she was dirty, and she was pulling him into a web of sexual invitation. He was trapped. And it was bloody wonderful.

This cool lady had always turned into another creature in bed, and it was this creature that Tom could not get enough of. But never before had she been like this. This was a madness. She was drinking him dry, sucking

him into a terrifying obscurity, and he had no will to stop her. No will left
to stop her at all.

But in the morning she was a different woman. Tom had a steaming
hangover, yet she seemed fresh as rain, and a hell of a lot colder.

'I meant it last night, Tom,' she said. 'That was our farewell party.
We're finished, you and I.'

'Farewell party?' He began to laugh – how could they be finished after
the wildness of last night? But the laugh died in his throat as he looked at
her. She was painting burgundy lipstick on to thin lips. Her eyes were
narrowed in concentration, and he knew that she meant it. Last night had
been their swan-song.

'What if I left Hannah?' The thought had never occurred to him before.
Leaving Hannah had seemed impossible – she was necessary to his sanity;
she gave him what he would be lost without. And besides, there was Fleur.
He'd sworn to protect her and he hadn't forgotten that promise. It was just
that life had got in the way. But he was desperate now.

Jayne blew a kiss to herself in the mirror, dabbed her lips with a tissue,
and laughed that grating laugh. 'Don't be ridiculous, Tom.'

Ridiculous? The blood rushed to his temples, throbbing in his head in
tune with the hangover. 'What's so ridiculous about that?' He grabbed her
arm, his fingers digging into her flesh.

She stared down at his hand until he let go, his fingers wilting away
from her as she had eventually made him wilt last night.

'You've only ever been a sideline to me, Tom.' She turned away from
him. 'And don't you forget it.'

A sideline? What was she saying? 'But it could be more than that,
Jayney.' He hated to hear his voice. There was that whine in it again.
Women whined. Victims whined. And Tom McNeil wasn't a victim. 'It
could be so much more than that. Last night . . .'

'Last night was fantasy.' She twisted round to face him, her eyes
mocking. 'It wasn't real life.'

He hung his head. 'But you and I . . .'

'Don't make yourself even more of a laughing stock than you already
are, Tom.' Ignoring his despair she dabbed Chanel behind her ears,
slipped stockinged feet into high heels and shrugged on her navy blue
jacket. Once more she was Ms Stepney, head of department, cold as
bloody ice.

'You and I are not an item, Tom,' she said. 'You were a release for me, that's all.'

A release? He stared at her.

'To be brutal, if I were looking for a partner . . .' She laughed. 'Although God knows I'm not – I've been down that road twice too often already.' She hesitated. 'But if I were – you'd be a long way down the list.'

She was unbelievable. Tom couldn't stop staring at her.

'Sorry, darling. But you don't have what it takes.' She picked up his briefcase and tossed it towards him. 'You're good in bed but even sex palls eventually. And now I suggest that you get a move on.' Her face was an emotionless mask. 'You don't want to be late for school.'

Tom's sense of failure stayed by his side all day. A brisk nod was all he got out of Jayne Stepney in the staff room, and he didn't have the courage to press for more. His courage – something he'd never questioned – had disappeared. That stuck-up bitch had snatched it from him. He couldn't face any more of her barbed remarks. No holds barred. No feelings spared. She *had* no bloody feelings.

You're a laughing stock, she'd said. But it wasn't true, was it? Lots of women still wanted him. Lots of women would always want him. He had Hannah and he still had Dian. His eyes softened. He would always have Dian and Hannah. Neither of those two would ever leave him.

The girls he taught all looked up to him – good God, most of them probably had a crush on him too. Girls of that age did. Oh no, Tom McNeil wasn't finished yet. He wouldn't let a cold bitch like Jayne Stepney finish him off. There was plenty of life left in him. After all, it wasn't Janice all over again. Who the hell cared about Jayne Stepney? It wasn't as if he loved her . . .

The last period of the day was drama with his own form, and gradually he felt himself relax. This bunch of fourteen year-olds were all right. He would be all right. Bugger Jayne Stepney.

But still, he was relieved when the bell signalled the end of the school day. He would cut off school early tonight, and make it up to Hannah. He'd always been able to make it up to Hannah.

'Shall I help you carry these scripts back to the classroom, Sir?' Becky Travis was standing in front of him. A nice kid. They were all nice kids. He liked being called Sir.

'Thanks, Becky.' Tom followed her down the corridor.

On the way there, they passed Jayne Stepney. She nodded curtly, her eyes blank of emotion. Could it be possible that this was the same woman he'd fucked into oblivion last night?

'Do they go in here?' Becky entered the empty classroom and went into the dark storeroom. 'On the shelf in front?'

'Yeah.'

He waited for her to come out so that he could lock up, but she didn't appear.

'This stockroom is a mess, Sir.' Her eager voice rang out. 'I could help you clear it out some time, if you like.'

The stockroom was a mess. Who was she trying to kid? He wanted to laugh. What about his life? His life was a bloody mess. He was a failure, wasn't he?

'Oh, it's not so bad.' He peered inside.

In the dim light coming from the classroom, Becky Travis was standing watching him. She had undone her ponytail, and her long hair was cascading in a golden curtain over her shoulders. She seemed different, older somehow.

'What are you up to?' He grinned, leaning on the door frame.

'I've been watching you, Sir.' She took a step closer. She had put on some perfume too, something sharp and potent that made him catch his breath.

'And what did you see?' Tom was fascinated. He'd always been aware that Becky Travis paid more attention to him than most. And he couldn't say in all honesty that he hadn't noticed a certain look in her baby-blue eyes which were going to do a lot of damage to some boy one of these days.

'I thought you looked depressed, Sir.' She hung her head. 'I thought maybe I could cheer you up.'

Depressed? Hadn't he been told he was a laughing stock? Oh yes, Jayne's words still stung.

With a start, Tom realised that the girl in front of him was undoing the buttons of her blouse. 'For Christ's sake, Becky,' he said.

She slipped off the schoolgirl's blouse to reveal beautifully rounded breasts tightly encased in white lace. And she took a step closer.

'I'm not a child, Sir . . .' she whispered.

20

Dian swung herself off her bike, locked it up, and strolled into Purwood school. It had taken only twenty minutes to cycle from the school she now taught at, to Purwood – where she'd done her final teaching practice.

'Hi.' Just her luck that the first person she ran into was Ms snooty Stepney. Had Tommo really managed a quickie with her? It seemed incredible. And it was also incredible that Tom had no idea what it did to Dian. How she seethed with jealousy whenever he so much as mentioned another woman's name. And yet he always wanted to share them with her – his precious sexual conquests. It turned him on in bed.

'Dian, isn't it?' The elegant woman stopped, her cold eyes becoming thoughtful. 'How can I help you?'

Dian pulled herself up to her full five feet six – in heels. This woman had a way of making her feel small and inferior. She'd been perilously close to failing that final teaching practice because of Jayne Stepney's attitude. Well, stuff her. Dian had no reason to be scared of her now.

'I'm looking for Tom McNeil.' Her voice was casual. 'Any idea where I might find him?'

That made her sit up and take notice all right. Dian smiled to herself. Jayne was immediately on guard, her eyes becoming shuttered and more distant than ever. Seemed like Tom hadn't been making it up then. Dian's heart sank. He really had made a play for Jayne Stepney and he'd succeeded. Would he ever change? Was she wasting her time waiting for him to change? To be hers and hers alone?

'Is he a friend of yours?' Jayne paused over the word friend.

Dian laughed. 'You could say that. We were at college together. And we haven't lost touch.' She looked the other woman up and down. So what if she realised that Dian was Tom's mistress – Dian didn't give a shit who knew. And so what if she sussed out that Dian knew the score about Tom and Ms hoity-toity Stepney. It would serve her right. Serve Tom right too.

Jayne's expression changed once more. 'This is a school, not a general meeting-place,' she snapped. 'Can't you contact him at home? Do you have to follow him around at work?'

She was really pushing it, the snooty old cow. 'I'm sure you know the answer to that one, Jayne,' she retorted, with a sweet smile. 'His *wife* is at home.' Let her sweat.

'His classroom is down there, first right, second left. His name's written on the door. And if he's still there, perhaps you could be so good as to tell him to meet his friends elsewhere in future.' She spun on her high heels and strode off in the other direction towards the staff room. She was fuming.

'Touchy . . .' Dian's voice was soft.

Tom might be cross with her, but she'd always been able to get round Tom, so she wasn't too bothered about that. And she hadn't come here to cause trouble, only to surprise him, and find out if they were still on for next week-end in Amsterdam. She'd been looking forward to it for so long – having him to herself for two whole days in a relaxed city like Amsterdam where you could get stoned in peace without anyone bothering you. She sighed. A taste of paradise.

Dian had kept away from Tom for a while after he'd married Hannah. She had some pride. And all she could think was – it should have been me. Hannah Thompson had tricked him; Hannah Thompson had got herself pregnant. But it was Dian who knew Tommo better than she even knew herself. It was Dian who had always been there for him when it mattered. There was no doubt in her mind – it should have been her.

And maybe he agreed with her, because Tom wouldn't take no for an answer. He wouldn't leave her alone. He was miserable and sad and lonely without her, he said.

She laughed at first. But she saw him get bored with Hannah Thompson and she knew that soon he would find another woman – if he hadn't already. He begged, pleaded, and drove her crazy with wanting him again, until at last Dian caved in and welcomed him back to her bed. Pretty soon it seemed like he'd never been away.

Tom was too hard to resist – they were too good together – he knew it and she knew it too. She needed to be the woman he wanted, and if that meant she couldn't live with him, then that was how it would be. If that was all she could have of him, then she would take it. And wait until there was more on offer.

And as time went by, she was convinced there would be more. She knew he hardly slept with Hannah, that Hannah was frigid, giving herself in sex only as a sacrifice, until poor Tommo could hardly get it up. Oh yes, she knew all Tom's sexual secrets. Hadn't she always known them?

So she bided her time and waited. The more available she made herself the more likely he was to look elsewhere. So she maintained a pretence of a life. A life where she had other men, other friends, other excitements. But in reality, there was only Tom.

Dian found the classroom – the door was shut but not locked – and walked in. Tom's writing, large and scrawling, was on the blackboard, his briefcase still on the desk. She looked around her in surprise. Where was he, then?

There was only one other door – the door to the stockroom. It was closed, but . . . A faint shimmer of foreboding ran over Dian as she crossed the room. She took a deep breath and turned the handle.

Illuminated by a naked light bulb, she saw two figures, both frozen in horror for a fatal second as she opened the door.

One was Tom, on his knees in front of a girl – a schoolgirl, for Christ's sake! She was in school uniform, or at least a school skirt. Her breasts were bare. Tom was fondling one breast and suckling on the other. His other hand was under the grey schoolgirl skirt.

Dian put her hand to her mouth. She felt sick. As the girl's jaw sagged and her eyes bulged, Tom staggered to his feet. Dian registered his expression. He was scared out of his mind.

'Jesus Christ, Tom. You're a fucking pervert.' Dian stumbled out of the stockroom, out of the classroom, into the corridor.

'Dian!' He shouted. 'Come back . . .'

She ran. Heard him following and ran on, almost colliding with Jayne Stepney, dimly aware of the cool, inquisitive eyes and voice. Ran on and out of the building into the fresh air.

Her mouth twisted with distaste. He was despicable.

She leaned against the door, caught her breath, and then made for her bike, fumbling with the padlock, up on to it and away. Away from this place. Away from Tom McNeil with his sordid secrets.

How could she have been so wrong about him? He was pathetic. He disgusted her. She hadn't known all his sexual secrets at all. Tom McNeil – the man she'd loved for so long – was nothing but a piece of filth who abused young girls. Worse, because he was in a position of trust.

Dian's head was reeling. But one thing she knew for sure – if she never saw Tom McNeil again, she would be glad. It was over between them. She wanted no part of his squalid little world.

Kate swallowed some Valium and read Hannah's letter once more. She must have read it twenty times already. Soon she would know it by heart. And Hannah had certainly poured her heart into this letter. Typical Hannah – she had always been so good with words.

Kate felt the tears pushing their way forwards again. Always so close to the surface, and yet once it had been hard to cry.

Hannah said little about her own life and nothing about Tom. She wrote briefly about her daughter, Fleur. But most of what she wrote belonged to the past, to her own past, her childhood pains and pressures not to disappoint a mother who could never be satisfied. And to their past – the past of Normandy and the early college days when they'd met, become friends and sworn mutual support in times of trouble. What Hannah had hoped for in those first months of their friendship, the dreams she had clung to.

'It's too easy to lose touch,' she said. 'But I don't want it to be that way. I want to see both of you. I need to see you. Can we get together again? Please?'

Darling Hannah, always a bridge between them.

There was a phone number at the top of the letter. Kate fumbled in her bag for tissues. Would she dare to contact her? Could she bear to let even Hannah see what she'd become?

She walked down the stairs, remembering yesterday's garden party. Leon's kind, freckled face. His voice shouting after her as she ran towards the house . . .

'You know about the bars and the bimbos?'

Oh yes, she knew all right. That's what she was so ashamed of. That she knew and did nothing. That she allowed it to go on. That she stayed here and merely closed her eyes when it all got too close.

Kate knew everything there was to know about the man she'd married. And still she couldn't leave him.

She thought of her mother's voice. 'It isn't so easy to leave.'

So many voices harmonising in her head. Joining with Hannah's letter in a bitter melody that re-lived the past, re-created what could never happen again for Kate. She'd sunk too low, couldn't they see that?

Leon had thought she would never be trapped.

He was wrong. She was trapped by this world that had never been her dream and turned out never to have been her mother's dream either. Such a cruel irony that it had only ever been a farce.

Kate wandered into the pristine kitchen. She was hungry. How strange that she could still be hungry.

She found the chip pan that was hardly ever used, since Adam required something a little more refined to come out of his kitchen, and poured in some oil. It glugged and slurped its way into the pan. Kate wanted to laugh.

She lit the gas and watched the pan of oil couched in the blue flame as it heated. She forgot about potatoes. It mesmerised her, the thick amber oil glistening and thinning in the pan, bubbling and creeping up the sides as if wanting to escape, the thick blue vapours clouding in front of her eyes.

A muscle twitched – a moment when she might have reached out to turn off the gas. But the spark of suppressed rebellion was stronger. No more.

Instead, she fingered Hannah's letter, still clutched in her sweating palm.

The Valium was in her bag. Kate took it out. She could end this. She could really end this.

She squinted at the number written at the top of the letter. She could do it. She could really speak to Hannah. Slowly she moved towards the phone . . .

When she left the house, Kate was humming softly as she stepped into the surreal brightness of the afternoon outside. It was Strauss's 'Blue Danube'. The disc she would take with her to a desert island – *If you could take only one, which would it be . . . ?* If you were going nowhere . . . She took nothing else – not even the pills. Where she was going she had no need of them.

She stopped when she was still quite close, to look back at the house – to watch it burn. She wouldn't feel that she had really escaped from that house, until she saw it burn.

The house on the cliff seemed to rest within the smouldering bosom of the fire, as if not sure whether such warmth could really mean destruction. And then slowly, they crept into view – snaky flames fingering the air. Licking and exploring, carnal and hungry. Wanting to consume, wanting it all.

Kate had wasted two precious years in this house. Resentfully, she pushed the tangled auburn hair away from her pale face. Two years of humiliation spiralling into despair. That's what Adam and his precious house on the cliff had done to her.

No wonder then, that the fire seemed like a friend to Kate. She stood still, savouring the very heat that tore at her half-closed eyes. Tasting the parched ashes with every breath she took. And smiling as she saw the sprawling carpet of the flame sweep in one brilliant and majestic rush across the elegantly tiled kitchen floor.

That was just the beginning. She jumped, as a sharp explosion lacerated the air. In wild response, flames writhed and twisted like a legion of mad genies. Battering smoky windows, searching for the kind of escape that had always eluded Kate.

She giggled. It should be obscene – laughing at devastation. But it felt good. The fire was grinning too. Inside the web of bloody tentacles, she could see charcoal teeth and a gaping black hole.

The fire was devouring one of Adam's infamous five-course dinners. Kate narrowed her bitter-green eyes. No one prepared five-course dinners like Adam. Only this time the menu was a little unexpected. Because the fire was snatching and swallowing the roles she'd been forced to play with him, so that she'd never have to live them again. Swallowing them, and spitting them out like some dissatisfied casting director. That's what she should have done, long ago.

First course? The kitchen – where Kate had been given the role of creative cook.

To follow? The sitting-room – where as perfect hostess she'd entertained anyone who might ever be important to Adam.

Next? The bathroom – where every day she carefully painted on the mask of respectable, high-status wife.

Not full up yet? Oh no. Then how about the spare bedroom – intended for Adam's future offspring – where Kate would play the ideal mother?

And finally? The master bedroom. She shuddered. Appropriately named. Where Adam required her to be his student slave girl.

Kate stared in horrified fascination as the first flames stroked the master bedroom with their particular brand of passion.

The fire raged on. Pretty soon it was hard to make out the shape of the house at all. The heat scorched Kate's face red-raw, until she was forced farther back down the drive.

Her mother had been right. It wasn't easy to leave. But it was remarkably easy to destroy. And sometimes destruction was the only way forward.

The taste of destruction was a taste of freedom for Kate. She was laying them to rest – these parts she'd played all her life. Roles that others had given her, not roles of her own choosing.

It was too easy to slot into a role. Too easy to lose the individual identity that made you a separate being – with a separate life. Kate clenched her fists. And it was bloody difficult to claw your way out – to find your own destiny.

By the time the gleaming BMW screeched into the drive beside her, Kate was feeling as if she and the fire were joined in one purpose.

Adam slammed on the brakes. His heavy jaw sagged. He lurched out of the car.

'Jesus Christ.' He stared at the molten mass of flames that had been his house on the cliff. 'What the bloody hell's going on?' His face was white – chalk-white with curious spots of red, growing larger by the second.

She felt perfectly detached. 'The house is on fire.'

'I can see that, you stupid bitch.' He grabbed her arm, his fat fingers digging into her flesh as if he wanted to gouge it from the bone.

'Have you phoned the fire brigade?'

'I only phoned Hannah.' A prisoner allowed just one call. Trapped in her kitchen while the smoke and the dust began swirling into a gritty heat around her, Hannah had seemed the obvious choice.

'Hannah?' His voice rose into a hysterical screech.

She nodded. He wouldn't understand about Hannah. There was no point in trying to tell him.

'Jesus Christ . . .' Adam tugged at the car door. He grabbed the phone and called the emergency number.

It's too late, she thought. Much too late for the house on the cliff.

He gave the address, his thick lips moving as if he could hardly mouth the words. Then he lumbered towards the burning inferno, his bulky form in its black suit becoming insect-like and ineffectual against the vast backdrop of flame.

After a few moments he was beaten back by the heat. Gagging on the smoke, he returned to her. Grabbed her by the shoulders.

'Kate? How the hell did this happen?' He was shaking her as if the truth would spill out.

She wondered briefly whether to lie. An 'I don't know, I'm lucky to be alive' might keep her going until some fire expert proved negligence. And by then she would be free of Adam.

She looked into the surface tension of his eyes. 'Cooking oil,' she said. 'I wanted some chips.'

'Chips!' He stared at her, this alien-wife.

And then she realised that the red spots had suffused his entire face, and that the deep-set, grey eyes were serial-killer cold.

His big, bloated hands closed around her throat.

In an instant, part of Kate's mind went black and another part, long-forgotten, lit up, as the years were stripped away. Big bloated hands on her throat. Her mother pulling them off . . .

'What d'you think you're doing?'

The sound of thick male panting, and the feeling of release.

'Don't you ever touch her again. Do you hear me?' Her mother's voice was firm but gentle, not yet aged into bitterness.

She couldn't feel Adam's hands. All she could feel were those other hands on her throat, all those years ago in Ridley. Her father's hands.

Kate's head was reeling, she thought she was dying. This was it then. This man, Adam Horton, was the replacement she'd chosen – for the other man whose resentment had turned to bitter hatred for his own daughter. Her father – she could still smell the stale beer clinging to his breath. Her father – who had tried to kill her.

And now like some diabolical destiny, it was happening once more. The inescapable . . .

He had beaten her often. Now she could recall the look in his sunken eyes – crazy like Adam was now crazy, wanting to possess like Adam wanted to possess. Crazy with beer and frustration and hatred. That was her father, and that had been her life. Her husband had unlocked the memories of her past.

'What the hell are you doing?' A different voice broke into the images dancing in the darkness.

Strong female hands tearing at Adam's fat fingers. Hannah's blonde head bending. She bit his hand.

Adam yelped like a dog, but let go. Some sanity returned to his face. He was waving his hand around, and Kate had to concentrate hard to see the tooth-marks. Clever Hannah.

'Bitch! Bitches, both of you! Look what she's done to my house!'

He was almost crying. Kate felt nothing. But then, *her* tears had never moved *him* to compassion.

The expression in Hannah's calm brown eyes reduced the importance of the house on the cliff to nothing. 'If you ever come near her again, you're finished,' she said. 'Believe me.'

Kate stared at her. This self-assured young woman didn't seem much like Hannah at all.

Only the low, insistent crackling of the fire fractured the silence between them. All that was left of the house on the cliff was a broken shell – and ashes, drifting like tiny grey paragliders on the sea breeze. And what about Kate? Did she have anything more?

She shook her head in confusion. The pills were making her woozy. She could hardly stand.

Hannah took one look and grasped her arm firmly. 'Come on, Kate. You're coming with me.'

It would be okay then. She'd been right to phone Hannah. Perhaps everything that had come between them hadn't destroyed their friendship after all. If she groped long enough in the darkness – this darkness that came and went as Kate slipped in and out of semi-consciousness – maybe she could even find it once more.

The new, strong Hannah led her to a beaten-up Vauxhall Cavalier parked at the end of the drive. There was a man in the driving seat. Kate hesitated, but Hannah pulled her forwards. 'It's all right, Kate,' she whispered. 'This is Martin.'

And then she saw the little girl sitting in a car seat inside. Hannah's daughter. Kate smiled. She climbed into the car.

Tom stopped running after Dian when he saw her collide with Jayne Stepney. Dian . . . he would have to talk to her later.

What she had witnessed hadn't meant a thing. How could it? It had been perfectly harmless – he'd been feeling a bit low, and had just given in to temptation for a minute. Couldn't Dian see he was only messing about? Tom would have thought it was obvious.

He ducked into the men's loo to avoid Jayne, stayed there for five minutes until his breathing returned to normal, and then walked slowly back to the classroom, feeling calmer and in control.

Becky would have gone home by now. Okay, it was a pretty stupid thing to have done. He would see Becky tomorrow, make sure she realised it must never happen again.

And yet there was no denying that he'd been flattered. And it had been one hell of a temptation, seeing her standing there with blonde hair hanging over her shoulders, and big baby-blue eyes gazing at him in adoration. And when she'd undone her blouse and unclasped her bra to reveal herself in her full glory – well, she hadn't seemed much like a schoolgirl at all. Fourteen going on twenty, more like. Only fourteen . . . Perhaps it was a good thing that Dian had turned up when she did. Who knows what might have happened?

Tom strode into the classroom, then stopped dead as he saw them on the far side of the room. A scared-looking Becky, doing up the buttons of her blouse. Jayne Stepney's arms around her shoulders.

He stared at them. Jesus Christ! His stomach somersaulted into panic. What was going on here? What had she said?

Jayne looked up at him and he would swear he saw a glimmer of a smile flickering amidst surface disgust.

'He made me, Miss,' Becky wailed. 'He made me.'

An hour later Tom arrived home. He didn't notice the Vauxhall Cavalier parked outside. He was knackered and he was furious as hell. Jayne Stepney, that cold bitch, had as good as persuaded young Becky Travis to make a complaint against him. Sexual assault.

Becky was saying that Tom had instigated the whole situation. And he wasn't exactly in a position to deny it. Even if he hadn't instigated it, he was still at fault. He was done for.

Jayne Stepney's harsh voice rang in his ears. 'You're finished, Tom.' And she was right. Tom could see no way out.

'Hannah!' he yelled.

Voices from upstairs. Voices?

'Hannah!' He took the stairs two at a time.

In the bedroom, Fleur was playing with her toy farmyard on the floor, Hannah was putting clothes into a suitcase, and Kate Dunstan was sitting on the bed watching her. All three looked up as he charged in. He waited, hovering in the doorway, suddenly unsure.

'What's she doing here?' He glared at Kate. This woman was the last person he wanted around. She could only be here for true confessions that were better off staying in the past. And Tom needed Hannah's support more than ever before. For the present.

Nobody answered him. Kate gazed at him with a strange vacant expression that made him more uncomfortable than ever.

'If you've come here to cause trouble then you can leave my house right now.'

Kate seemed confused, as if she hardly knew him. Maybe he was wrong. She looked different, very different from the last time he'd seen her. Thinner, expensively dressed, and a hell of a lot less lively. Even her bright auburn hair, which had once been her crowning glory, was lank and dull, pulled into a tight knot at the back of her head.

Hannah stepped protectively in front of her. 'She's not going anywhere.'

Tom blinked. There was something different about Hannah too. Suddenly he realised what she was doing. She was packing, for Christ's sake. 'What's she been saying?' He shook his fist threateningly, but at the sight of Hannah's calm expression, found his hand flailing, useless at his side.

'Nothing.' Hannah turned to fold more T-shirts. 'She hasn't so much as mentioned your name.' Her hand brushed against Kate's shoulder. 'Can't you see she's not well? Leave her alone, for heaven's sake.'

'But what are you doing? Where are you going?' Tom felt lost. He looked at Hannah, and he felt utterly lost.

'I'm leaving you.' Hannah snapped the case shut as if she were snapping the folds of their life together – snapping them away, like a photo album whose contents belonged only to the past.

'We've found a place to stay for a couple of weeks. I've left a forwarding address downstairs.'

She was so matter of fact. Tom's jaw and shoulders sagged. His eyes strayed to the child on the floor. 'Fleur . . .' Even his voice was broken.

'Don't bring her into this,' Hannah warned. 'You've never lifted a finger to help me with her, so don't dare to lay some twisted sort of claim to her now.' Her breath was coming fast. 'She's my daughter.'

'Oh, yeah.' Tom glared at her. 'You've always made damn sure of that.'

She spun away from him. 'C'mon, Kate.'

'But why, Hannah?'

Her eyes blazed. 'How can you ask me that, Tom, after what you've done?'

What had he done? Tom tried to focus his mind. 'Dian's been here,' he said miserably. He knew it must be true. What other explanation could there be? The events of last night and Hannah's birthday had been altogether wiped from his mind by the more urgent events of today. Too much was happening to him. Tom could only concentrate on one thing at a time.

Hannah's lip curled, but she was silent, getting the bags together.

'I was only messing about with that girl in the stockroom,' Tom moaned. 'I don't know why everyone's making such a big thing about it. I could lose my job over this, but none of you seem to give a damn about that. The girl got her tits out, for God's sake. What was I supposed to do?'

Hannah and Kate stared at him.

With a grimace of distaste, Hannah passed the bags to Kate, and grabbed Fleur. 'Let's go.'

'But, Hannah . . .' He watched her as she practically ran down the stairs. She couldn't wait to be out of here, away from him. He had broken the sense of stillness in her that he had once loved, once needed.

Where had he gone wrong? Tom put his head in his hands. He heard the door slam shut behind them. Heard a car start. Whose car? He hadn't even seen a car.

His mother would never have left the family home voluntarily, no matter what his father did to her. There were always more important things than infidelity – and she would have seen that. Like loyalty to your husband, for a start.

Tom went over to lie on the bed. This house was full of Hannah. Crammed to the brim with Hannah. This room smelled of Hannah. How could he get her back?

But he was exhausted after the night before, and soon he began to doze. The two of them had both loved him – Hannah, and his mother Mary, who had left him only through death. As he dozed, the two women seemed to switch rôles – it was his mother who suffered his infidelity and neglect, and Hannah who stayed with him till death. Because she was his perfect, virgin wife. Unlike his mother, she had been possessed by no other man. Hannah was his and only his, to do with as he willed.

She was his mother, but in the end, Mary had given no legacy to Tom.

She had not taught him to love selflessly or to be loyal to the end. She had not given him kindness or the ability to care. Because ultimately, Tom had only done what his father too had done. No matter how much he despised him, it was his father he had emulated and his mother he had abused.

Stephanie Lewis-Smythe was brushing her thick dark hair in her bedroom at Atherington Hall, when her father knocked on the door. She recognised even his knock.

'Come in, Dad.'

He entered the room, more tentatively than usual. She'd noticed, in the few days that she'd been back from her week in the clinic, just how much he'd been affected by the events of the past few years – by her own rejection as much as by the death of his son. He had changed in physical appearance – his shoulders were slightly stooped, his dark hair was streaked with so much more white and grey, and his good-looking face seemed worn at last. But his character too had mellowed. As if he had lost his arrogant belief that Julian – and Julian only – always knew which direction was the right one to take.

'You've made up your mind then?' He pointed to her half-empty case lying on the bed.

She nodded, suddenly reminded of the night before she first went away to college in Dorset. When he'd walked into her room while she was packing.

So much had happened since then – it was hard for Stephanie to believe she could be the same person, that her father could be the same man who had tried to persuade her not to go. Who had offered her pocket money and urged her to get a flat somewhere and 'dabble'.

Stephanie smiled. Maybe she wasn't that person any more. Maybe that girl had gone for ever.

'I'll miss you.' He looked so sad – as if he'd found her again, only to lose her immediately – that she rose, to hug him close. She could smell the familiar smell of him – even now, the understated aftershave and sandalwood soap.

'It's not so very far away,' she whispered. 'You must come and visit. I really want you to. And I'll be back. Often.'

He nodded, understanding in the deep blue eyes so like her own. 'If you think it's the right thing to do . . .'

'I'm not running away.' She needed to reassure him.

Stephanie hadn't wanted to accept the money from the insurance policy at first. Her mother's parents – who had died some years ago – had taken it out when she was a baby, as a christening present.

'It's yours by right,' Daddy told her. 'Yours to do whatever you like with. It matured on your twenty-first birthday.'

And she couldn't help but see the possibilities. After all these years, the payout amounted to a considerable sum of money. Her mind flew ahead to what she could do with it. How she could get strong again, how she could give something back.

Her father smiled. 'I know you're not running away.'

Did he really? He seemed to know exactly how she felt. But could she expect him to see that no matter how much she loved him, no matter how much she had always loved him, this place of her childhood was too bound up with pain for her to stay here? Because that childhood had belonged to Miles, and now that Miles was gone, it was too hard for Stephanie to heal, forever here in his shadow. She needed her father – although she had never admitted to needing him before. But she also needed to be free, to grow unfettered, away from everything that others had wanted her to be.

'I almost forgot.' Julian was watching her. 'I came up to tell you that you've got a visitor. A woman. She's downstairs.'

Stephanie's heart missed a beat. Could it possibly be Hannah or Kate, after all this time?

But as she descended the stairs, she was surprised to see Lois standing alone in the hall. It was funny, but she'd never dreamed Lois would come here.

It was Lois, and yet it was the Lois that she'd seen so rarely. The well-dressed, elegant woman who went out to work, presenting herself in her almost perfect disguise, as someone she could never be – not completely. And Stephanie recognised why she had come here in this way. Passing on a message that she hadn't come as a lover.

'I was worried you might have done something silly.' Lois held out her hand in greeting. 'I'm glad you're okay.'

Stephanie nodded. 'I'll be fine. And you . . . ?'

'I'll manage.' Her voice was brisk. 'I knew you'd come back here.' She tried to smile but there was a sadness in the light green eyes that tugged at Stephanie's heart.

'I had nowhere else to go, Lois.'

'I haven't come to try and persuade you to come back,' she said quickly, and Stephanie saw the pain, only half-hidden on her face. Poor Lois. If only things could have been different.

'It was just that this arrived the day after you left.' She handed her a letter. 'And I thought it might be important.'

Stephanie took the envelope, recognised Hannah's handwriting immediately and smiled. 'It could be. Thanks, Lois.' She felt awkward, talking to her like this, here at Atherington. But she sensed that Lois had needed to see her for one last time. And she couldn't deny her that.

'I'm sorry I couldn't live that way,' Stephanie whispered. She had done her best to. Oh God, she had even wanted to.

Lois nodded. 'I should never have tried to keep you there. To make you . . .' She seemed about to say more, and then her eyes filled, and quickly she turned around. 'Goodbye, Steph.'

'Goodbye.' Stephanie opened the door and watched her go, towards the black Renault parked outside, back to whichever life drew her the most strongly. Who could tell? Lois, despite the time they'd spent together, remained a closed book.

Stephanie was sad, but she couldn't go after her. She had learned a lot from Lois, despite the pain. About women and sex and slavery. She smiled slowly. But they both knew it was finished, that it would always be finished. There was no other option.

And as the car pulled away, already Stephanie was ripping open the envelope. Reading Hannah's letter.

She went back inside, ran up to her room and grabbed a pen and paper.

'Darling Hannah,' she wrote. 'I was so glad to get your letter. I'm writing back quick, because I've had this wonderful idea. You see, I too can't help thinking of the past . . .'

21

It was a perfect, late afternoon slowly dimming into dusk, in Normandy, France, as Kate sat sipping Calvados on the terrace. The sun was still warm on her face, and memories of a summer five years ago were all too near. Stacked so close to the here and now, that past and present intertwined in her head, making her unsure that she had recovered from her experiences with Adam quite as thoroughly as she had believed.

Behind her, the tiny Chateau des Marettes – the chateau that Stephanie had bought from her Aunt Rae with the insurance money she inherited a year ago – threw its eccentric shadow onto the lawn. It was still damp, spooky and inconsistent in its provision of hot water and electricity, but in other ways this place had changed dramatically.

The money left over had helped convert the derelict barn into a light and airy studio where Stephanie now worked. She had bought a second-hand potter's wheel and rusty kiln, and could be seen most mornings throwing earthenware pots coloured with the natural pigments found in the earth of the region. Her pots were practical – with bold designs, shaped from a past that only Stephanie seemed to know about, and with a simplicity that echoed this honest peasant landscape.

But of course Stephanie didn't only create pots. Kate smiled. She also painted. How could you stop Stephanie painting? The studio was crammed full of canvases, oils, turpentines, and brushes. Stephanie was in her element, growing in stature as if finding her own way forward as she painted Normandy – its people, its land, its history. And there was so much to paint – mediaeval, timbered buildings, decorated with window boxes of wild colour, that lined narrow streets. Sloping vineyards and fields of sunflowers, backed by church spires that spiked the skyline. Her work was fast becoming popular in Rouen and the galleries of Honfleur.

Stephanie visited the old fishing port of Honfleur regularly, becoming one of the artists who painted by the harbour cafes on the waterfront. Impressionist painters had trod the same cobbled paths in Honfleur, inspired by the city of art and history that drew artists with a magnetism hard to resist.

As Kate watched, Stephanie emerged from the studio, deep in conversation with a French boy of about ten – one of her students. Stephanie was doing what she'd always wanted – giving back to the art world some of the uncluttered talent of youth, as she called it. Kate smiled again. Uncluttered by adult demands. A child-like view of the world was encouraged in Stephanie's studio. Children could develop in their own directions rather than be squeezed into a shape dictated by others. And no-one was excluded. Enthusiasm came first, and the question of fees came a flexible second.

Stephanie was slowly getting well again.

'Okay, darling?' She came over to the table, poured herself some Calvados, and ground her Gauloise out in the ashtray. She glanced towards the leafy pool, her eyes as intense and beautiful as they had ever been, her body becoming more healthy as every day passed, her face less etched with pain.

'I was just thinking.' Kate smiled. 'When you're about to leave a place, it's a good time for thinking. Helps you to remember it when you're far away.'

Stephanie's expression grew sad. 'It's also time for a swim.' She pulled off her paint-stained waistcoat and baggy jeans with easy grace, and ran sure-footed towards the pool.

Kate watched her. She had been shocked when she saw Stephanie again last year, after their long separation. By the time she and Hannah had received Stephanie's letter, Kate herself was taking the first uneasy steps of recovery away from the trauma of her own failed marriage.

'I can't believe it.' Hannah had waved the letter in the air. 'Stephanie wants us all to go to Normandy again.'

'For a holiday?' Kate was confused.

'Maybe . . .' Hannah looked mysterious. 'Of course she doesn't know yet that you and I are single again . . .' She laughed triumphantly as if this had been their greatest achievement to date. 'But reading between the lines, I'd say she's planning to live there for a while.'

'Live there . . .' Hannah and Kate stared at each other, both knowing what the other was thinking.

'There's no going back . . .' Kate knew there was no going back. They were three very different people from the three naive college girls who had taken a summer break working for Stephanie's Aunt Rae in Normandy. Girls who had pledged a mutual support that had become buried beneath the layers and circumstances of real life. Normandy had only been a dream – a short glimpse of another world. Once you'd woken up, you could never return to a dream. It was impossible to go back.

'We wouldn't be going back.' Hannah's brown eyes were eager. She seemed strangely insistent, and very different from the Hannah who had always been a bit scared of life.

'No?' Kate wasn't so sure.

'The first time we went to Normandy we were just finding our feet.' Hannah elaborated. 'We thought we'd managed to escape our backgrounds. We thought it would be easy to lead our own lives.'

'And we only got drawn into other kinds of domination.' Kate was thoughtful. 'But what makes it so different this time?'

'There's more to leading your own life than rejecting the past,' Hannah told her. 'You have to fight for independence, and you have to learn to step out of the circle everyone else weaves around you.' She smiled. 'That's what the three of us have done. But we can still reach far enough to hold hands with the people we love. Can't we? No matter how far apart we are?'

Kate nodded. She felt unable to speak.

'It's not going back.' Hannah put an arm around her shoulders. 'We'll be seeing it through different eyes. Don't you understand?'

Maybe she was right. Maybe it wasn't going back. But there was an undeniable sense of history repeating itself in the very air of Normandy. She felt it herself most keenly, but the others too had lived out a kind of legacy from their ancestors. Way back, they might have given the younger generation its freedom . . . Kate thought of the war graves she'd visited and the landing beaches of Arromanches and Omaha that never failed to bring a lump to her throat. But their own parents had withheld that freedom. The younger generations had to fight too – in their own ways.

She thought of herself and Eileen, of Hannah echoing her own mother's fears, of Stephanie's intense kind of loving – so like the demands of her own father. History repeating itself in a never-ending pattern over the generations. And she wondered about going back to Normandy. Whatever Hannah said, Normandy was the past. How could it ever be her future?

But when they met up with her a few days later, Stephanie seemed to share Hannah's confidence.

'You're welcome to stay for as long as you like,' she said. 'No pressure. But for me, it's a new start.'

And she looked as if she needed it. Kate could hardly recognise the thin and ravaged creature that was Stephanie. She looked old before her time, gaunt and ill. Only the intensity of her deep blue eyes was the same as ever.

She drew Kate aside. 'I know someone who's been trying to get in touch with you,' she whispered. 'He's given me a letter . . .'

Kate took it, recognising the large, scrawling handwriting immediately. Would she ever be able to reply to one of Leon's letters?

That was a year ago. And now, here they were. Kate could never resist the enthusiasm of the other two. She had come and she had stayed – always meaning to leave, but finding herself irresistibly drawn to the magic that was Normandy. And maybe even too scared to return.

She lifted the glass of sharp apple liqueur to her mouth, savouring the smoothness as it kissed her lips and coated her tongue. A taste of heaven.

She had known from the start that Hannah would stay here in Normandy with Stephanie. The two of them had always shared a special bond, and it was natural that they would want to help each other, now that they were re-united – bruised and tender but even closer than they'd been before.

Like Kate, Stephanie had loved Hannah's daughter on sight. She scooped her to her breast and held her close, the dark head bent next to Fleur's blonde curls, like knowledge next to hope.

'But I'll have to do something,' Hannah wailed, after the first euphoria of reunion had died down, and they'd agreed to go back to France with Stephanie – at least for a while.

Stephanie seemed to understand this immediately. 'English lessons, darling,' she suggested. 'Your French is good enough to give English conversation lessons – all French kids learn English at school – but you can go private. It'll be a doddle, and well-paid too.'

'I'm not qualified . . .' Hannah was doubtful.

'Rubbish.' Stephanie squeezed her arm. 'You're the best qualified person I know.' She paused. 'And in your spare time, you can write. Normandy was always such a fantastic inspiration for you.'

Hannah was silent.

'Poetry – or even travel articles.' Stephanie's voice was husky and persuasive. 'Aunt Rae could give you masses of material to work from.'

Hannah's mild, brown eyes clouded. 'I don't write any more.'

They both stared at her. Hannah without poetry was like French bread without cheese.

'But why ever not?' Kate said what they both must have been thinking.

Hannah shrugged. 'I can't do it. I thought it was all the problems I had with Tom . . .' She paused.

Hannah had confided little about her life with Tom, but Kate at least had guessed enough from their conversation back at the house. Tom McNeil obviously hadn't changed, and Kate was only bitterly sorry that she herself had been one of the women who fed his egocentric fantasies.

'But it wasn't because of the problems with Tom?' Stephanie's voice was soft.

Hannah shook her head. 'After we left, I still couldn't get any of it down on paper. All the things I was feeling. There seemed to be too much, all jumbled in my head, but it couldn't get through the barriers. It just couldn't get through.' Her eyes began filling with tears.

'It'll come.' Stephanie took her hand. 'Believe me, Hannah. It'll come back. And when it does, there'll be no stopping you.'

Kate sighed deeply, and sniffed in the delicate scent of trailing white summer jasmine that surrounded the terrace. Memories. Stephanie had been right, of course. Hannah's poetry had returned to her.

She started tentatively enough, with a couple of small pieces for Aunt Rae's brochures. But pretty soon there was no stopping her – and her work was better. Instead of the outpourings of an emotional child, she wrote with the experience of a woman behind her.

And once more Kate was conscious of a twinge of envy. It seemed that whatever happened to these two women, their creativity would always be on hand to get them over the worst, to give them a reason for existence that sometimes Kate herself found lacking. And yet there were the letters in her bag . . .

A new start?

'Aren't you coming in, Kate?' Hannah was still swimming in the pool, her golden skin gleaming as she lifted Fleur high in the air.

Fleur screamed with delight. She could already swim like a fish, and here in France she had blossomed into a mischievous little girl, the image of Hannah but with none of her old timidity. Fleur was already speaking

French, and would soon be attending a nursery school in Pont Audemer. It seemed unbelievable sometimes.

'In a minute.' Kate just wanted to sit here awhile, absorbing the atmosphere of the small chateau and the women who had made it their own. Breathing in that sense of finality that was never far away for her.

Before they had returned to Normandy last year, Kate had tried to persuade her mother to come too. But it was no use.

'Why not?' she demanded.

'Because it's too late for me, my love.' Eileen smiled, her eyes weary with fighting, her face lined with pain.

'It's not too late.' Kate wanted to fight for her. She was strong enough now. 'I left Adam. It's possible to leave any situation if it's bad enough. It has to be.'

Eileen reached out to smooth Kate's hair from her face. 'For you, maybe.' She sighed. 'You're young. I've been there for too long. It's habit.'

Kate's eyes became angry. She tugged her mother's blouse gently from her shoulder to reveal a plum-coloured bruise, yellowing at the edges with time passing. 'And what about this?' she murmured. 'Is this a habit?'

Kate had known for a long time. Known and yet hidden it from herself. But when Adam unlocked that door of the past for her – showed her father's violence through his own violence – her eyes had been opened at last. It all fell into place like a jigsaw where you hadn't been able to find that missing piece for years. Or hadn't been looking.

Her mother's pregnancy. Her marriage to a man she couldn't love and didn't want. His jolly face and vile temper. His drinking. His aggression. His child Kate, was his property. His wife Eileen, was his property. Both should have been his to use and abuse – and only one had been denied him.

Kate understood all her mother's reasons for wanting a different life for her own daughter. For wanting Kate to be safely out of it – not forced to witness it, and not in danger herself.

And yet Kate had repeated her mother's mistakes. She too had become pregnant at seventeen, blamed her mother for trying to rescue her in all the wrong ways, and finally married a man who would destroy if he couldn't dominate her.

All she'd been searching for was her mother's own dream. A dream that she had never understood. Perhaps she had blocked out the memories of her father's violence too effectively. Perhaps it would have been better not to forget . . .

'You get used to it.' Eileen pulled back her blouse, refusing to meet her daughter's eyes. 'I'm too old for rebellion.'

'And?' Kate had known even then that there was more.

Eileen shook her greying head. Dry as dust she was. Her skin, her hair, her lips. All seemed grey and colourless now. 'And nothing, my girl,' she said with a spark of her old fire. 'It's time you went your own way. I'll be just fine.'

But Eileen wasn't just fine. Since being in Normandy, Kate had kept tabs on her by frequent phone calls to Aunt Barbara. And she listened to her mother's voice. When she heard what she had been half-waiting for, she knew that the time had come for her to leave.

Now, she got up slowly, and walked across to the pool, stripping down to her plain black costume that contrasted with the paleness of her skin. She executed a perfect swallow dive into the shimmering blue. The water – hardly warmed by the summer sun – was like an icy hand on heated flesh.

'What will you do, when you get back?' Stephanie's languid form floated towards her, her dark hair streaming through the water, her eyes wide open, but without that hunted expression that they'd had five years ago. She'd found her way out, Kate realised.

'Look after Mum.' Her words fell into the rippling silence of the pool.

Eileen was sick. She had cancer. She had been holding it to herself for years, but now her remission was over. She knew she was going, and Kate belonged by her side.

'Poor darling.' Stephanie reached out to take Kate's hand, and squeezed. 'And after that? Will you stay in Ridley?'

At times Stephanie seemed to know something that Kate hadn't quite got hold of yet. At college she had been the same – as if sensing what was ahead.

'I might.' She had thought she never would. And now? Kate didn't know where she was heading, that was the truth. There were the letters in her bag, but she didn't want to think about them yet. Leon said that he was still waiting – that she should take as long as she needed, and that he understood. But Kate still didn't know for sure.

The immediate future was looking after her mother, and that was as far ahead as she could think right now. Her future was a tunnel, and she hadn't yet spotted much light. There was a glimmer that held some promise. But it was still only a glimmer.

'You could always come back here.' Hannah was squatting on the edge of the pool, wrapping a huge towel around Fleur. 'We'd love that, wouldn't we, Steph?'

'Of course. It would be perfect.' Stephanie swam away with a long, sweeping breaststroke, the water parting before her. She knew.

'No.' This was one place that Kate wouldn't be living. She didn't belong here with these two – she never had. She'd always been conscious of exclusion, and however hard they tried, she was conscious of it still.

She had done her share – working with Aunt Rae in her tourist business, helping to grow the vines, fruit and vegetables that supplemented their income, looking after Fleur when the other two were busy. It had been fun, but it still wasn't quite real. It wasn't the right direction for her at all.

'I'll be coming back for holidays though.' She smiled to soften her previous harsh word of denial. 'You can count on that.'

And she wasn't the only one who would come here – in the past year Julian had stayed for six weeks, and even Hannah had welcomed a visitor who brought a flush to her cheeks and seemed to hold a special place in her heart. Perhaps Martin Buckingham would only be a visitor, perhaps Stephanie and Hannah were too close to be prised apart. Or perhaps one day Hannah might let him in to stay – who could be sure?

Her last night here, Kate looked back towards the chateau, to the rustic wooden table and three glasses of Calvados side by side. A notebook of Hannah's, a sketch pad of Stephanie's. What did Kate have to call her own?

Fleur disappeared into the chateau to get her orange juice, while Hannah exchanged a glance with Stephanie, ran to fetch the glasses of Calvados, put them on the side, and slipped into the pool. The two of them were on either side of Kate, treading water, wet hair hanging in seaweed tails, framing their glistening, child-like faces. Kate thought of Hannah's words . . .

'We can still reach far enough to hold hands. No matter how far apart we are.'

Solemnly Stephanie grasped the glasses of apple liqueur, one by one, passing them around.

'To the future.' She raised her glass. 'To walking away from pain.'

290

Hannah smiled. 'To new beginnings and the end of old limitations.'

Kate thought of Leon – tall, gangly and sandy-haired. Maybe she did have something after all – she had the promise of love, and that was a starting-point, wasn't it? The right kind of love . . . the kind that didn't hold you back. The kind that left you free to find your own direction, your own identity.

She tossed her head back, defiance in the bitter-green eyes. 'To hell with playing a part someone else chooses for you. Here's to friendship . . .' A smile touched the corners of her mouth. 'And to leading separate lives.'